Legions of the Forest

MARK L. RICHARDS

ISBN: 0692289194
ISBN 13: 9780692289198
Library of Congress Control Number: 2014916090
Mark L. Richards, West Chester, PA

Dedication

In fond remembrance, this book is dedicated to my late parents, Mathew and Helen Richards.

Preface

The year is 9 AD, the golden age of Rome. She basks in her glory under the rule of the aging Caesar Augustus, arguably one of the greatest leaders of antiquity. He has transformed Rome from a city of bricks to one of marble. The *Pax Romana* governs the western civilized world behind the might of the twenty-eight standing legions of the seemingly invincible Roman Imperial Army. Expansion of the Roman domain appears unlimited. Indeed there are plans to extend the borders to the Ukraine. After years of civil war and barbarian revolts, there is an enduring peace.

Augustus Caesar appoints Publius Quinctilius Varus, former governor of Syria and related to the imperial family by way of marriage, to rule over the Germanic tribes in the north. Varus believes the Germanic peoples to be subjugated and the lands ready for annexation as a Roman province. He was wrong!

Organization of a Roman Legion

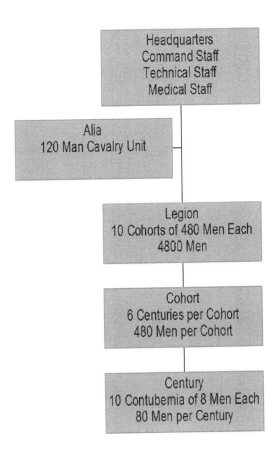

I

Shivering, Lucius pulled the rough woolen cloak tighter around his tall form. As he exhaled, frosty plumes of vapor appeared against the winter darkness. He stamped his feet, and then took a large gulp from his wine goblet. He couldn't remember ever being this cold, not even when making deliveries for his father, driving the cart through the frigid air. He wished he were inside his father's house, sitting by the hearth, sipping his mother's hot soup. But no—after a full day of transporting amphorae in the frigid air and gusting winds, here he stood under the bright stars on a January night, waiting his turn.

Earlier, well after dusk, Lucius had returned to his family dwelling. He'd made a delivery to a distant villa some ten miles away. He unhitched the oxen from the cart, coaxed the animals into their pen, and then fed them. Having ensured they were secured for the night, he hurried to the house, barged through the door, and headed directly to the hearth to warm his hands. He observed a smile of relief from his mother, Aquilonia, for he was usually home long before this time.

Lucius rubbed his hands vigorously in front of the dying embers, muttering a curse under his breath about the cold.

"What did you say, Lucius?"

"Nothing, Mother."

She gave him a warning look. "Your dinner is on the table, Lucius."

Lucius grunted a reply, walked over, and sat. Only his mother and father were present. His younger brother and sister must have already retired for the night. Aquilonia placed a large, steaming bowl of stew plus a huge hunk of bread in front of him. Lucius ripped chunks of bread from the loaf and dipped them into the stew.

His father, Petronius, looked up from a chair at the end of the room. He was an imposing figure, tall and broad. Although the years had worn his countenance, his face was still handsome, especially the broad forehead and high cheekbones.

"Any trouble with the load?"

Lucius continued chewing his food before he spoke, aware that the delay in his response would irk his father. He also knew that his father would inquire about the transport. "I had to wait two bloody hours for those fools to decide where they wanted to put the amphorae, and me with a three-hour return journey in this cold. I had to relocate the vessels four different times until they found a suitable spot. I mean, how difficult can it be?"

"You didn't say anything, did you? He's a good customer."

"Of course not, Father. But I wanted to."

His father offered a relieved smile. Lucius gobbled some more food, wiped his arm across his mouth, brushed the crumbs off his already-soiled heavy tunic, and stood. "I'm going out."

Aquilonia looked at him in alarm. "Lucius, how can you? You are practically blue from the cold. Stay home with us. Keep warm."

"Can't, Mother. I promised my friends I'd meet them at the festival, and I'm already late, thanks to our good customer."

His father frowned in disapproval at the sarcastic remark about the good customer but remained silent. Lucius hid his smug grin. He had gotten just the reaction he was looking for, and why not? Lucius was the one who had the most interaction with the clients. While most were a fairly decent lot, some were a real pain in the ass.

His mother continued to fret. "Lucius, you'll become ill from the cold." She looked beseechingly to Petronius for assistance.

"Let the boy go, Aquilonia. He'll be fine. It is a festival, you know, and many have celebrated most of the day." He turned toward his son. "But, Lucius, I expect a full day tomorrow. Not too much wine. Understood?" His father stared at him, letting Lucius know he was serious in what he said.

"Sure, Father. I'll be up with you." He quickly kissed his mother's sallow cheek good-bye, avoiding her worried blue eyes. He went out, slamming the heavy wooden door behind him. Smirking triumphantly, he prepared to venture into the cold night to join his friends. His father would not oppose his going out after the guilt he'd laid upon him. Setting off toward the distant torchlights, Lucius stopped abruptly when his father appeared in the doorway. He beckoned toward him. Lucius returned to the house.

"Lucius, I meant what I said about drinking too much wine. You be prepared in the morning for a full day. You hear me?"

"Sure, Father. I told you I'll be ready to work in the morning." Lucius turned to leave, but his father reached out again, halting his progress.

"And, Lucius, I know there will be ladies of the evening who have set up their tents out there tonight. You stay away from them."

"What?"

"Don't 'what' me. You know what I'm talking about."

Lucius now understood why his father had stepped outside. He didn't want his mother to hear what he had to say. "Dad, I'll be with my friends."

"I know. That's why I'm talking to you now. Stay away from them—I mean the ladies of the evening."

"I promise not to visit the ladies tonight or drink too much. Can I leave now?"

His father nodded brusquely, then quickly slammed the door against the bitter cold.

Lucius and his friends were celebrating the festival of Janus. The town was holding a gala that would stretch into late evening. Oil lamps and torches burned everywhere around the festival grounds, illuminating the various booths and tents that featured food, wine, and other assorted pleasures. Laughter echoed into the night. The populace of the town paraded around, some staggering, reveling in the party atmosphere.

Petronius had spoken at length to his children about the festival of Janus. He told them it was a huge social event in Rome. All the proper sacrifices to the gods were made to honor the new beginnings of the year. Then the celebrating began. He had noted with pride how the influx of Romans into Gaul had introduced the native people to this holiday. This was most likely another reason he had permitted Lucius to attend the celebration. On the other hand, Lucius's mother was a native of Gaul and had little fondness for the gala. She believed it was a festival of false gods and certainly not of the deities she had worshiped.

Lucius found his three friends, Donatus, Crispus, and Valtus, quickly enough. The crowd had dissipated as a result of the lateness of the hour and the harsh conditions.

"Lucius, where have you been?" asked Donatus.

"Had to work late."

"We didn't think you were going to make it. Here, take this goblet. It's almost full. We're way ahead of you."

"Thanks." He chugged the entire contents, then wiped his mouth on his sleeve.

The group wandered around the festival grounds. They stopped at another wine booth. Donatus, Lucius's best friend, spoke, slurring his words. "I heard that there is a sibyl at the festival who has set up a tent."

There was a silence among the four young men.

"So what?" said Valtus. "They have been here before."

Donatus took another deep drink from his goblet, then wiped his mouth on his sleeve. He continued. "I heard there was this guy; don't remember his name. He lived in our neighboring town, Baltius. He went to see a sibyl." He paused to gather the words from his fogged brain. The three others, including Lucius, waited in anticipation for him to continue.

"And afterward, he cried for days, saying that he was doomed. Then he disappeared, never to be heard from again."

Lucius knew crap when he heard it, and he wasn't going to let Donatus get away with this tale. "Oh, come on, Donatus. By Jupiter's gray beard, where did you hear this? And, of course, the man's name was conveniently forgotten?"

Donatus, now on the defensive, was indignant. "It's the truth, Lucius."

"Then how come none of us have heard this?" He looked to Valtus and his other friend Crispus for agreement, but both just shrugged.

Donatus continued. "Lucius, if you don't believe me, why don't you visit the sibyl?"

"For what purpose?"

Crispus, now siding with Donatus, flashed a grin, then flipped Lucius a small coin. "Here, Lucius. I'll even pay."

Lucius looked toward Valtus for support. He seemed to be in his camp on this one, but Valtus remained silent, nodding in agreement with the others. Lucius was trapped.

Janus was a festival of beginnings, and, unknown to Lucius, this was to be a launching of his new life. A different portal was opening for him, drawing him into a new reality that would make men shudder and emperors weep. As for the present, Lucius was trying to stay warm while he waited his turn. At least the wind had abated. Instead of being cold and windy, it was just plain cold. For lack of anything better to do, he tilted his head back and stared at the heavens above. The air was crisp, the night sky crystal clear. Funny, he thought; the stars appeared to blaze brighter tonight than he'd ever observed before. He swore he could see the gleaming objects in the night sky slowly rotate. Maybe too much wine, he said to himself. Perplexed, he surveyed the heavens once more. He swayed slightly off balance, almost falling.

"Definitely the wine," he muttered. His so-called friends stood behind him, urging him forward. Lucius shuddered once again. He wasn't exactly sure whether his chills were from the glacial winter evening or what lay before him. With his head buzzing from the grape, he edged ever closer to the tent opening.

"Go on, Lucius; it's nothing. You can do it," yelled a voice from behind him.

"You're welcome to join me, you know," replied Lucius laconically over his shoulder. He turned to face his supporters and was greeted by a few smirks.

"That's what I thought. You guys are all sniveling cowards, and you know it."

His remarks were greeted with some more hoots from the pack. He turned back from his friends to face the tent entrance.

"Some friends I have," he muttered.

Minding his father's advice about avoiding the whores, here he was entering into the mystical world of fortune-telling. The physical talents of an alluring female seemed to be a better alternative. A group of young women passed by him, offering warm smiles. One of them cooed at Lucius, then hurried away, giggling with the others. Was that an invitation? It sure seemed like it, yet here he was, stuck waiting. Under different circumstances, he would have pursued the young lady to see how much interest she really had in him. With an angular jaw line and prominent cheekbones, he might be considered handsome but for his nose. It had been broken in a fight with the town ruffian some two months previous. It was now slightly crooked. In a strange way, it contrasted with his bright-blue eyes and his short brown hair, perhaps adding a touch of charm.

Sibyls were a combination of witch and seer. This particular one for whom he was waiting had arrived in town for the festival. Sibyls were uncommon in the more rural areas of Gaul, and many people feared contact with these so-called prophetesses. In Rome, citizens accepted these seers, but out here, some five hundred miles from the great city, things were different. The Romans were a superstitious people. They often viewed natural events such as storms or the appearance of birds or animals as a portent of things to come. The Gauls were a bit leery of oracles and prophecies, or perhaps they didn't understand, preferring to just let life's events unfold.

So here he was, with no chance to escape his quandary. He took another swallow from his goblet to bolster his courage. The admonishment of his father about drinking too much wine was long forgotten. Should have kept my mouth shut, he thought. Better yet, he should have listened to his mother and stayed home. He thought briefly of the warm hearth and shivered once more.

At last, an old man exited the tent. He looked about to get his bearings, then hurried out into the night. It was Lucius's turn. Why was that man running away? Lucius was ready to bolt, but before he could act, the tent flap opened and a hooded figure appeared. Her face obscured in shadows, she pointed at him, beckoning him forward. Too late now. He took a large gulp of cold air to clear his head. I'll show them. He turned around and, in a show of bravado, casually tossed his now-empty wine goblet to his friends, who remained cautiously away from Lucius. He proceeded forward, briefly feeling the flare of heat from the guttering torch at the entrance. He paused slightly before the opening, then boldly entered. The folds of the tent flaps closed quickly behind him, shutting out the sounds of night revelry. All was eerily silent.

Lucius adjusted his vision to the dimness of the tent. Faint tendrils of smoke drifted about. A variety of tiny oil lamps cast a strange glow. They flickered on the small wooden table in front of the sibyl. Several bronze braziers burned, providing a degree of warmth in the enclosed space. Lucius wrinkled his nose and drew his head back as the aroma from the incense, a pungent combination both sweet and acrid, permeated his senses.

The sibyl threw back the hood from her cloak, revealing her features. The woman sitting in front of the small wooden table appeared to be about thirty. Her dark hair cascaded over a long white linen robe. Her garment bulged in all the right places. He decided the woman was moderately attractive. He'd always pictured these seers to be old, wizened crones, but this was hardly the case.

Lucius, feeling somewhat relieved based upon the physical attributes of the woman, sat on a small campstool opposite the sibyl and offered a vacuous smile. "Hello," he muttered.

The woman smiled at him but said nothing. She stared into his eyes. Lucius tried to remain calm, but his nervousness betrayed him.

He fidgeted with his hands and averted his eyes from the penetrating gaze of the woman. After a brief pause, she spoke in a low, throaty tone.

"What is your name, young man?"

"Lucius," he replied.

"How old are you, Lucius?"

"I was twenty in November."

"Do you know the day in November you were born?"

"I was born two days after the ides."

"Is it possible that you know the approximate time of day or night you were born?"

"I was told I was born a little after midday."

"I see," she said, smiling back at him reassuringly. The woman consulted several scrolls lying in a basket next to her. She examined one that appeared to chart the heavens. Lucius could make out representations that he guessed were the sun and the moon. Staring intently at the markings, the sibyl remained silent. Lucius craned his neck to examine the scroll more closely but could see little in the dim light. She glanced up at his face several times, gazing into his eyes as if she were searching for something. Lucius just sat with a fatuous expression. The silence was unnerving, but he couldn't think of anything relevant to say.

She dropped a pinch of powder into the incense burner. The unusual aroma returned, but sharper. Lucius was uncertain whether he liked the smell or not. It was damn peculiar. His senses reeled, and his head began to spin. Was it the wine or the powder? He had no idea, but something sure was odd. The sibyl picked up a glazed bowl with strange designs on it, then slowly shook it around in a circle. She used both hands, holding the bowl directly in front of her. Lucius couldn't see in the basin, but he could hear objects moving within. She emptied the contents with a flourish onto the table. Out clattered onto the wooden tabletop some small bones, a handful of smooth colored stones, and a few wooden cubes covered in lacquer. She stared intently at the configuration of the strange objects.

Again she consulted the scroll, then spoke in a husky tone. "I see you going on a journey away from your home, Lucius. The passage will be soon. The stars and the date of your birth foretell this. This journey will be far. You'll be among strangers." She paused for a moment and studied the scroll again. "You'll meet a young woman who will capture your heart." She looked up, offering a warm smile at Lucius.

Lucius was starting to like this very much—and to think he had been nervous about this session with the sibyl. Lucius was about to say how much he admired her prophetic skills when the sibyl continued.

"You'll find a new life like none you've ever known. I see rivers and great forests." She examined the array of objects on the table before her and glanced at the chart again.

"What time did you say you were born?"

"A little after midday."

The sibyl frowned slightly, then rummaged through the basket at her side and produced yet another scroll with odd markings on it. She squinted at the strange symbols on the parchment in the semi-darkness. He witnessed a look of panic cross the sibyl's features. The woman gasped and brought her hand to her mouth. Lucius could see the whites of her eyes. The sibyl avoided his gaze, her lips tightly pursed. Lucius wasn't fooled. He was suddenly sober.

"What do you see, sibyl?"

"I am unable to foretell beyond what I have just let you know." She averted her eyes when she spoke.

Lucius attempted to peer over the table at the scrolls. In response, the sibyl covered them with both hands, then hastily scooped them up and put them in the basket.

"What else do you see, sibyl? What of my future?" he demanded.

"Our session is over," blurted the woman.

"Are you sure? Tell me."

"I've told you all I know."

Lucius had lost all trepidation regarding the sibyl. He bolted clumsily off of the stool, knocking over the table with all of its contents.

"Tell me what you saw, sibyl," he commanded.

9

The woman cowered in fear at the outburst. "Please don't hurt me," she said.

Lucius was ashamed of his outburst. He had not meant to scare the mysterious woman. Disappointed and knowing she was untruthful to him, he slipped her a small coin, a copper *as*, mumbled thanks, and then hastily began to exit the tent. He glanced back one more time. The sibyl remained seated, staring at him, eyes wide and her mouth in a grimace, no doubt relieved to see him leave. Lucius pushed aside the tent flap and inhaled deeply of the cool night air. He stopped and took a second deep breath.

His friends were all there in a pack waiting for him. They all looked at him curiously. Lucius gazed back, saying nothing.

"Well, c'mon," said Donatus. "What did she say?"

"Oh, you know, the usual nonsense. I'll find a nice girl and have a family someday. It was nothing."

"Is that all?" said Valtus. "Nothing mysterious? Anything about your death?"

"No, it was a waste of a coin. One of you should try it. She's pretty good looking, too. Really, it's not too bad."

Lucius's remarks were met with silence. There were no takers. The group wandered off in search of another wine stall. The young men had had way too much wine to notice that a now-subdued Lucius had little to say the rest of the evening.

Far from Lucius's home in Gaul, hundreds of miles beyond the Rhine, a solitary figure, wrapped in a heavy deerskin cape draped over rough woolen trousers, stared down the length of the river valley. From his perch on a high bluff, he overlooked the forested terrain below. His future would be a part of Lucius's, although the two men certainly knew nothing of each other. Stinging sleet pelted the man's exposed face as the wind whipped about, changing directions in the beat of a heart.

Overhead, storm clouds raced across the winter sky, obscuring any traces of the midday sun. Most men would have quit this isolated perch or at least covered their faces from the buffeting elements, but the powerfully built man paid it no heed. If anything, his gaze intensified. A falcon circled above the escarpment, soaring back and forth in the wind currents searching for prey. The man shifted his gaze, staring at the raptor. The warrior spoke out loud, although no one was around to hear his words. "Good hunting, brother."

Soon the soldiers would arrive again. They would come directly down this river valley. When the weather broke in the spring, the Roman legions would march out of their heavily fortified bases on the Rhine, led by their silver eagle standards, to enter the deep interior of his country. There would be a great number of them, perhaps as many as twenty thousand. They would build their massive encampment close to the river and from there venture forth to tax his people. He quashed the rage that momentarily welled up inside him, for anger, no matter how intense, wouldn't defeat these invaders.

No, he reasoned, he'd need a plan to catch the Roman soldiers off guard and out of their element. Then could he kill them. He knew quite a lot about killing. He'd served with the Roman soldiers as an auxiliary officer in the province of Pannonia. The people of that ill-fated province had rebelled at the yoke of Roman rule and heavy taxation. The defiant warriors had fought fiercely; they knew their craft. But in the end, the Romans slaughtered them. Those combatants who weren't killed outright in battle were either executed or sold into slavery.

He grimly recalled how the bodies of the insurgents had formed a pile in front of the Roman lines, yet they continued to come on, shouting their war cries, brandishing their weapons. The Romans, in their suits of iron, with their heavy shields and short stabbing swords, methodically disposed of the rebel foe. The legions seemed invincible. Were they? He pondered this question as the sleet sliced the winter air. Could he come up with a plan to drive the Romans out of Germania? If he didn't do something this year, the Romans would put a permanent stranglehold on his country, as they had done to so many others.

But he had an advantage that others who had opposed Rome did not, for he knew his enemy much better than most. He'd spent his

Mark L. Richards

formative years in Rome as a hostage due to his father's rebellious actions against Rome in the Cheruscan revolt years ago. The young boy had been carted off to Rome to ensure that his father, Sigimer, and the Cheruscans behaved themselves, staying friendly to Rome. He wasn't treated as a captive but was schooled as a young noble in the hope that he would prove to be a strong ally in the next generation of Germans. His hostage period over, he'd dutifully continued to serve with distinction in the Roman army.

Yes, he knew their language, their customs, and most of all, their battle tactics. He had in-depth knowledge and firsthand experience about how they fought. When the Roman army had entered the German interior last spring, they sought friends to help them pacify and win over the native tribes. They had quickly identified him as an ally of Rome, one who could be trusted. The fools! Did they really think he had forgotten who he was, that he was enamored with their pampered life, that he had lost his German pride and love of his land?

The man's Latin name was Arminius. It was one the Romans would come to dread. His name would echo through the rolls of history for millennia to come.

The goddess Fortuna abruptly entered Lucius's life a few weeks later. Lucius's mother, Aquilonia, was startled by the arrival of three official visitors to her door at midday. The three men stood politely outside the entrance of Lucius's home. She peered at them hesitantly through the partly opened door.

"May I be of assistance?" she inquired. Aquilonia, a fairly shrewd woman when it came to human character, didn't like the looks of them. A sense of dread enveloped her. She recognized one as the local constable. The unpopular man had the reputation of a public official who used poor judgment and sometimes more force than necessary. He looked like a weasel, with his beady eyes and pointed nose. How could their town magistrate, Cornelius Piso, tolerate this man? She knew many in the village had complained to Piso about the constable, but the scoundrel remained in office.

She had never laid eyes upon the other two men, but they were obviously soldiers. There was something brutish about them. Both were large men in the familiar trappings that marked them as legionnaires, replete with armor and weapons. Heavy woolen cloaks were draped across their shoulders, fastened at the neck. Against her better judgment, she opened the door, motioning for the men to enter. She could see their swords hanging from their belts. Aquilonia frowned in disapproval at the presence of armed men in her home. What? They were afraid she was going to attack them? The two legionnaires fidgeted in front of her as if they didn't know how to conduct themselves in this setting.

"We're here to see your oldest son," grinned the constable. He spoke as if he knew something she didn't. Aquilonia attempted to hide her loathing. She could feel her heart beating faster, alarmed at his request to see her son.

"He's not in trouble, is he?" said Aquilonia. "My son is a good boy."

"No, it's nothing like that," said the constable. "These men are here to see your son about the legions."

She was relieved that he wasn't in difficulty with the law, but she still did not understand the purpose of these men.

"Oh, I don't believe he's interested in the legions. He works for his father in the family business."

The constable let out a guffaw, annoying Lucius's mother even more. The two military men both looked away.

"You don't seem to understand," he said with a certain glee. "This is not about choice. The emperor needs good men, and your son's name came up. It's Lucius, correct?"

Aquilonia had a sinking feeling in her stomach. "There must be some mistake. My son is only twenty. He belongs here with his family."

One of the military men spoke gruffly. "No mistake, lady. We've been ordered to recruit men for the legions by order of the emperor Caesar Augustus. Your son's name was picked." The constable handed Aquilonia an official-looking document. She hesitantly unrolled the paper and read in silence.

The awkward quiet was suddenly broken as Lucius barged into the house. He discarded his heavy cloak, revealing a sweat-soaked tunic that clung to his torso, highlighting sinewy muscles that stood out like ropes on his frame.

"Mother, I'm absolutely famished. What do we have to eat?"

He stopped dead in his tracks at the appearance of the three strangers in his house, then fixed them with a tremulous smile. The two legionnaires stared at him up and down as if he were some farm animal. He saw the two soldiers turn toward each other and exchange knowing grins.

"Lucius," his mother said, "these men have come to see you about the legions."

Lucius gaped at the strangers, still not quite understanding the purpose of their visit. He would always remember those chilling words from his mother.

The constable looked at the two soldiers, who nodded in confirmation. He turned to address Aquilonia and Lucius. "You will be receiving official correspondence as to when Lucius will be required to report for duty. I have not received word yet as to the date."

"How soon?" inquired Aquilonia.

"As I just stated, I don't know. It could be weeks or months." With that, the constable and soldiers abruptly departed

When his father, Petronius, came home that evening, Aquilonia told him the news. Before the entire family, he vowed to visit Piso, the local magistrate, the next day to see if additional light could be shed on the subject. Petronius assured his wife that all was not lost. He would get the matter straightened out.

Petronius pondered his son's plight. Throughout the empire, the Roman colonies were under the jurisdiction of Rome, and that meant Roman laws. An integral part of this legal system was the local magistrate, who exercised enormous power. Fortunately for Lucius and his family, the man appointed as the magistrate for their town was a competent official who took his job seriously. Piso was a rational man who judiciously governed this community, but in addition, he was part of the fabric of the village. The magistrate didn't see himself as a mighty appointee of Rome, but rather as a man who had adopted the town as his own. Overall, he performed his duties astutely, with perhaps the exception of his choice for a constable.

Petronius knew that the legions were for the most part filled with volunteers from throughout the empire. In the early days of the republic, one had to be a citizen and landowner to serve. The commanding legates and prefects used to have the *dilectus*, the call for enlistment to form a legion. Those times were long past. The legions had been able to fill their ranks with willing volunteers, eager to fight for the glory of Rome and for the ample booty that they might share. He reasoned that there must be some serious holes in the ranks of the legions for the emperor to resort to conscription.

While he offered calming words to his wife, he was filled with a sense of foreboding, which he masterfully hid from her. Petronius was a Roman citizen raised not far from the gates of Rome. He knew something of how the empire was administered and of the workings of the Roman government. The conscription of his son wasn't a matter to take lightly. In this respect, Rome could be heavy handed in how it enforced military enrollment. Perhaps, he hoped, Piso would make it all go away.

Early the next morning, Petronius ventured toward the center of the town. There was a small crowd of patrons gathered outside Piso's office to see him. Much to his delight, he was received immediately. He was swiftly ushered in ahead of the others. He was given some dirty looks by those who had been there before him. He proffered a smirk at the waiting patrons, then walked past them through the foyer and into Piso's chambers. Buoyed in spirit by quick admission, Petronius entered the space of Piso's inner sanctum.

"Cornelius Marius Piso, how are you? I trust you and your family are well?"

Piso stood up from behind a polished wooden table upon which several documents lay in a pile. He was a short man with thinning hair. A small, oiled beard adorned his chin. The magistrate was attired in a heavy white toga with beautiful folds that fit him perfectly.

Petronius looked down at his own rough woolen tunic and muddy sandals, silently cursing himself for not being dressed more appropriately. No wonder Aquilonia had frowned at him as he departed the house this morning.

"Ah, Petronius, my friend, how are you? It's been some time since we've seen each other." For the first time, he noticed a scribe seated in the corner with his wax recording tablet. Lucius's father frowned. He'd hoped to talk to Piso alone, but it would be impolite to ask the other man to leave. Petronius gazed directly at the scribe, hoping Piso would get the message. He trusted Piso would act on his not-so-subtle hint, but the intimation was ignored. Petronius knew at that moment something was wrong.

"Come sit down, and we can talk." Piso gestured toward a single chair placed directly in front of the long wooden table. "How about some refreshments? I have some excellent cheese that my wife purchased yesterday. Marvelous flavor. What do you say?"

Petronius struggled to keep his voice neutral. He did not want to convey his trepidation. "Thank you, Piso, but I already ate this morning."

"Very well."

Both sat down facing each other. There was a brief silence. Piso picked up a small decorative dagger from the table. He fiddled with it. "Let me guess. You are here to see me about Lucius."

"You are correct, Piso." He produced the rolled document with an official wax seal that the constable had given to Aquilonia, formally notifying Lucius of his conscription. He slid the papyrus across the table to Piso.

"His mother is frantic about this situation. I desperately need Lucius to help with the family business. Is there anything you can do to help us?"

Piso gave the document a cursory glance, leaving it untouched on the table. He frowned, then toyed with the dagger some more, as if this would dispel his discomfort. He looked up at Lucius's father.

"You and I go back a ways, Petronius. You know I would do anything to help you. Remember that tax matter last year that we straightened out?"

Petronius was dismayed by those opening words. He had a sinking feeling in his stomach.

"You know how much I appreciated that help. That's precisely why I came to see you. You can fix any problem."

"I'm afraid I'm unable to help with Lucius."

"I don't understand—"

Piso abruptly cut him off with a wave of his hand. "The word has come down from the emperor, Augustus Caesar. He wants conscripts for the army. Apparently the revolt in Pannonia has weakened the troop strength of the legions. Entire cohorts were shifted from Germania, leaving those garrisons on the Rhine considerably under strength. The emperor approved the mobilization several months ago on the advice of his advisors and military commanders." He paused briefly, then continued.

"Unfortunately, the conscription didn't go as planned in the Italian provinces. There was word that a good number of citizens made all sorts of evasive maneuvers, employing whatever trickery was at their disposal to avoid military service. When the emperor was informed about those attempting to dodge their duty to Rome, he became enraged. The rumor is that he has made examples of some of those caught evading military service. Some were quickly sentenced by a military tribunal, then executed. Others had their hands chopped off. So the edict is that those selected must serve. No exceptions."

"I need my son at home to help me with my business. Surely there's something you can do?"

Piso placed the dagger firmly on the right-hand corner of the table, then looked directly into Petronius's eyes. His tone changed, closer to an authoritative voice.

"You aren't listening to me, Petronius. There's nothing I can do. Even as magistrate, I have no authority on military matters, especially ones that emanate from Rome. I'm sorry, but I can't be of assistance."

Petronius wasn't finished yet. A wave of anger engulfed him at the unfairness of it all. His voice turned raw with emotion. "I'm sure none of the dandies in Rome are being conscripted. Just working citizens, like my son."

Piso stared back, his face reddening in ire. Petronius knew he'd crossed over the line of civility. His comment about the dandies was a thinly veiled reference to Piso's son, who was studying in Rome.

"I think our business here is concluded, Petronius. I have other appointments." He gestured toward the waiting area for emphasis.

Petronius stared back. There was nothing more he could say. The matter was done. His wrath faded to numbness and dejection. His voice was now barely above a whisper. "And when will Lucius have to leave us?"

"I'm told they want the troops in training as soon as possible. I don't have a date, but I'd guess as early as a few weeks, by early spring at the latest."

Petronius, his eyes downcast, nodded slowly in defeat, and then he departed without saying good-bye. He was aware of Piso's eyes upon his back as he exited, probably greatly relieved the encounter was over.

Petronius returned to his house a short while later, tight lipped and grim. Lucius, his younger brother Paetus, his sister Drusilla, and his mother were gathered in the dining area waiting. They all looked at him expectantly.

"I spoke to Piso this morning. He was gracious to see me on such short notice." His father stopped for a moment to collect his thoughts.

"There's no way for Lucius to avoid his conscription," he blurted.

"No, that can't be," cried Aquilonia. "There must be some mistake."

Lucius gasped. "This can't be true. I don't understand this."

Petronius held up his hand to silence his wife. "I said the same things. Piso was as polite as possible. He said this conscription order comes from the Emperor Augustus. And it's final. Apparently the recent revolt in Pannonia resulted in significant troop losses. The troops who fought there had been shifted from the Rhine garrisons. The legions occupying Germania are weak and under strength and need to be replenished."

"Where's Pannonia?" interrupted Paetus, the youngest son.

"A long way from here to the east," said his father. He jerked his thumb in the general direction.

His mother was now wringing her hands. "Is there nothing we can do?"

"I'm afraid not. Piso was firm in his pronouncement."

"When will Lucius have to leave us?"

"Soon, although he couldn't give an exact date. They're desperate for men. I would guess by early spring at the latest."

With that, Aquilonia stormed out of the house. Petronius looked after her in annoyance.

"Come on, Lucius. We have work to do. You need to haul that load to Vestula today. We can worry about this legion business afterward."

That afternoon, Lucius drove the family wagon with the two oxen. He was lost in thought, contemplating his fate in the legions. He had ambivalent feelings about his new direction in life. He guessed the military training would be arduous, but in truth, he didn't look forward to a life in his father's trade. The physical labor was hard and his prospects boring. His family got by with the earnings from the small business, but there was little money left over after caring for their basic needs. Like many young men, he yearned for some adventure and excitement. He wanted to experience life beyond the locality of his village. Lucius had never traveled more than forty miles from his home. Of course, the legions wouldn't have been his first choice to explore the Roman world, but fate, it appeared, had already decided for him. Maybe this was his chance. The problem, as he saw it, was that he knew nothing about soldiering.

To shed some light on his soon-to-be profession, he decided to make a detour from his deliveries that day to visit the one former legionnaire he knew of who lived in the vicinity. The man's name was Gallus. It was rumored that he had served many years in the legions before retiring to the quiet town where Lucius resided. He was a stranger to Lucius. Gallus was a fairly recent arrival and pretty much a loner. Lucius figured there was no harm in asking about his military service in the legions.

He secured the oxen to a wooden railing in front of the conclave of houses. He asked an old woman who was leading a donkey on a tether where the dwelling of Gallus was located. She silently pointed two houses down. He nodded his thanks and approached the house. Out of habit, he glanced back to ensure the oxen were standing peacefully and not attempting to break free. They were fine. The beasts stood motionless, looking placid.

Inhaling deeply, he boldly knocked on the man's front door, although he was not sure of exactly what to say. He was silently composing his words when a rather large figure abruptly filled the doorway. The man had craggy features, his face a weathered appearance. His skin had the texture of toughened leather. His hair was cut short in the legionnaire's style.

Lucius, startled by the appearance of Gallus at the door, stood silent. Finally he uttered, "Sir, I've been told that you were a legionnaire. I could use some advice, as I've been conscripted."

Gallus stared him up and down and then gave a knowing smile. Lucius wasn't sure what that was all about.

"Come in, come in."

Gallus ushered him into his small abode. Shafts of late-afternoon sunlight slanted through the one window of the tiny dwelling. Lucius followed him into an alcove. Gallus gestured to a stool opposite him.

"So you're going to serve under the eagles?"

Lucius stared back at him, not sure what he meant. Gallus waited for a reply, and hearing none, spoke. "You really don't know much about soldiering? You know, the Roman eagle standard of the legions. Under the eagles."

"Oh, I wasn't sure what you were referring to. Now I understand. Yes, I was conscripted just the other day. I'm to leave sometime soon, but I don't know much about the legions."

"Yes, that's obvious. Listen to me, Lucius. That's your name; am I correct?"

"Yes, it's Lucius." He was embarrassed. He realized he'd not even introduced himself. He wasn't sure how Gallus knew his name, but he did.

"Lucius, a soldier's life can be hard, make no mistake about it. But it can also be rewarding. You'll make lifelong friends. It's about loyalty to your comrades and your friends. I know you find it difficult to understand these things now, but you will."

Lucius pondered these thoughts for a moment before asking another question. "What if I don't like the legions? Can I get out?"

Gallus looked at him with pity. "You're in for twenty years, boy, like it or not."

"Twenty years? But that's a lifetime."

"Nobody told you?"

"Not really."

"Calm yourself. It's better than you think. Listen, the pay is good. You start out at 225 denarii. They deduct for your uniforms and whatnot, but you always have spending money. The best part is you have a great retirement. Look at me. I don't have a care in the world."

"What if I don't make it that far?"

"The legions pay for a proper funeral." Gallus laughed. "Lucius, there are few jobs that pay as much; plus, they feed you good food. Also, you get to see the world. You want to stay here the rest of your life? I mean, this is a nice place to live, and I for one chose to retire here, but Lucius, my friend, is this really where you want to spend all of your days?"

Lucius was silent.

"Well?"

"No, I guess not. I've always dreamed of seeing other lands of the empire."

"See? Things are starting to look better. Come on, Lucius, agree with me. Admit it now." Gallus gave him a knowing grin.

"I guess so, but I'm not sure of what to expect, if you know what I mean. How should I act?"

Gallus paused in thought before speaking.

"That, I cannot explain to you or teach you. You'll have to experience it firsthand. It can be an intimidating time. If there's one thing I would say to you, it is to be obedient but show no fear."

"I'm not sure I understand all of this, but I'll try to remember."

"Good." Gallus laughed and clamped his massive hand on Lucius's shoulder.

"Now let's have some wine. I'll tell you all about life in the legions. Don't look so glum, boy. You'll make a good soldier. Look at the size of you, tall and strong. You're going to make some centurion proud somewhere."

Gallus guided Lucius over to a small wooden table with two chairs, then retrieved an earthen jug from the kitchen area. He poured two huge goblets full of wine and handed one to Lucius. "To the legions," he said.

Both men raised their cups of wine.

The ex-legionnaire loved an audience. He told Lucius stories of strange places he'd been stationed, such as Thracia, Dalmatia, Hispania, and Germania. He spoke of the people and their customs. He talked of legates under whom he had served, the heroics of legionnaires, and the women, and then he complained bitterly about a certain centurion in Hispania. Lucius departed with his head spinning from all of the wine he'd consumed and no more the wiser of what he might expect when he entered the legions.

The short winter days had come and gone, and it was now early spring. If the legions were in dire need of new men, they sure took their sweet time about it. Lucius had been waiting almost three months. But his orders finally arrived. He was to journey to a legion training base in Lugdunensis, some fifty miles from his home. He stood on the outskirts of his town at the crossroads with his family, waiting for his authorized transportation to appear. Oddly, Lucius was the only man from his village who had been selected. This didn't make him feel any better, and it pointed to the unfairness of it all. He had heard that there were others whose names had been on the list, but they had been rejected. He was to learn later that the legions liked their men big and strong. Also, the conscript had to have no physical deformities. More important, the conscript had to be a Roman citizen.

Lucius carried a cloth satchel with a few possessions, including some extra clothes and his personal kit. His mother had packed him a loaf of bread and a jug of wine for the journey. He wore a long woolen tunic with trousers to ward off the chill in the air. On his feet he wore leather sandals. An open wagon with a single driver pulled up on the side of the road with a lone occupant seated in the back, most likely another of the legion's new entrants.

Lucius's family gathered around him. His mother and sister had tears running down their faces. His younger brother, Paetus, and his father stood by stoically with their arms folded against their chests, staring off into the distance. They sure are a big help. He inhaled deeply, hoping the crisp morning air would dispel the large lump suddenly lodged in his throat. At a loss as to what to do, he just stood there helplessly, longing to board the wagon. He needed to get away from the scene unfolding before him. Lucius didn't know when he would get to see his family again, but he guessed it might not be for a long time.

The driver of the wagon, a rotund figure attired in filthy garb, gruffly bellowed out, "Time to go. We've several more towns to stop by today. Hurry. Say your good-byes. We've got to roll."

Lucius quickly hugged his mother, then Drusilla. Paetus just kind of waved good-bye and walked away. His father stood before him, tall and erect. Lucius caught his father's eyes glistening.

"Good-bye, Father," he said in a half whisper. "Take care of everyone."

His father clasped his forearm. "I shall, my son. May the gods be with you."

"And with you, Father."

Lucius threw his satchel into the wagon, then quickly hopped onto the back, ignoring the other passenger. The driver glanced over his shoulder to see that his human cargo was aboard. The man flicked his whip at the two oxen pulling the wagon.

"Ha! Go now," he bellowed.

The wheels of the vehicle turned one slow revolution, perhaps taking Lucius forever from his family. He sat on the edge of the cart with his feet hanging off the back. He gave a desultory wave of his arm. He watched his family slowly recede in the distance, and then they were gone. He wiped his eyes with his sleeve, his mind churning at his unanticipated fate.

"If you don't mind my saying so, you're the most miserable-looking person I've seen in a long while."

Lucius turned toward the other passenger, not quite knowing how to respond. He studied his fellow recruit. The young man was favorably proportioned and heavily muscled but shorter than Lucius. He had dark hair above dark eyes that sparkled with life.

"Are you going to say something or sit there moping all day?" His fellow occupant leaned closer, waiting for a response.

"Sorry, I'm a bit out of sorts. I don't know if I'll ever see my mother and father again."

"Thank the gods you can talk. Cassius is my name, oh silent one."

"Name is Lucius. Glad to meet you. Didn't mean to be rude."

"You were. Listen, Lucius, life is short. There's no time to be melancholy. If truth be told, I miss my family, but I figure what the Hades. I look at this as an opportunity to see the empire, something I'd probably never do if I hadn't been conscripted."

"That's what Gallus told me."

"Who's he?"

"A retired legionnaire I spoke with before I departed."

"See, Lucius? Great minds think alike. What else did this Gallus say?"

"He said that one should be obedient but show no fear."

"And what exactly does that mean?"

"I have no idea. He told me stories while we drank a lot of wine. I don't have the foggiest notion what the Hades he was talking about." They chuckled in unison.

"This Gallus fellow sounds like someone I'd like to meet. But not to worry, Lucius. We'll get through this. How bad can it be? Many others have done it."

"Right you are, Cassius. As you said, maybe we can tour some of the empire. You know, get to see places and things away from here."

"Where would you like to go, Lucius?"

"Don't know. Maybe to the east, or perhaps Hispania. I guess we'll find out soon. Enough of the legions for now. Where're you from, Cassius?"

"About ten miles or so from here. A village called Eridarcus."

Lucius shook his hand. "Cassius, I've been at your village before. I delivered some amphorae there for my father. Maybe it was at your villa I stopped."

"Not bloody likely. My father is a stonemason. It wasn't my villa." They both laughed.

The two men talked easily long into the day about everything and nothing. They shared the loaf of bread and jug of wine that Lucius's mother had packed. There were no awkward silences or pauses. It was as if the two had been friends for years. They spoke about their families, their work, women, and food. Later that day, in the early afternoon, the wagon stopped to pick up two more men. Lucius and Cassius introduced themselves.

"Welcome aboard our chariot," said Cassius. "That man over there is my friend Lucius, and my name is Cassius."

Both men grinned back.

"Domitius," said the thin one with delicate features. "Flavius," said the other. Flavius had a muscular build and a certain lithe grace in his movements. He flashed a warm smile at Cassius and Lucius.

The two new arrivals reached into the folds of their cloaks and produced wineskins. They passed the wine around. The conversation became increasingly boisterous with each passing mile.

"Are we all ready to defend Rome from the barbarian hoards?"

The men laughed in unison.

"I was born to be a soldier," said Cassius. "Once they realize how good I am, they'll make me a prefect."

Lucius retorted, "Can we be your legion commanders, oh noble one?"

"Why, of course. I'll be in need of able-bodied assistants. I couldn't possibly command the legions alone."

They laughed jokingly. The fat driver of the wagon turned around from his perch in front. "You laugh now. Wait until that centurion at the fort gets a hold of you. You'll sing a different song. He knows how to take care of the likes of you. Yes, indeed." He chortled in derision at the young men.

The men stared back in silence. Flavius snorted. "To Hades with this centurion, and with you, too. Just drive and let us be."

The driver glared in anger, prepared to issue a nasty retort, but Flavius gave him a hard stare. There was a hostile silence, tension in the air. The three others joined Flavius, defiantly glowering at the driver. He finally turned back in resignation, muttering a curse.

The conscripts fell back into hilarity and jokes about their plight, carefree as only young men can be. After stopping for the night at a rather filthy way station, followed by another long-distance journey the next day, they arrived at the Roman fort. The driver was indeed correct. It would be some time before they laughed again.

II

SPRING, 9 AD
PROVINCE OF LUGDUNENSIS

*T*he parade ground was like that of most garrisons of the Roman imperial legions. It was a grim affair with bare earth packed hard, worn from the constant pounding of many *caliga,* the iron-shod marching boot of the Roman army. Small, isolated tufts of spring grass that had somehow escaped the trampling appeared here and there, but for the most part, the assembly area was brown compacted earth, prone to billowing dust or dark, syrupy mud when the rains came. A slight breeze rustled through the air. It was but a whisper on this particularly warm day, but all of the eighty recruits strained to catch the cooling air on their exposed arms and faces as they stood silent, baking in the hot Gallic sun. Few would have noticed the slight change in the wisp of air, but to those men clad in their heavy iron armor, it was a sweet gift from the gods not to be ignored.

The lives of these unfortunate souls over the next nine weeks as conscripts under the Roman imperial eagles would be no better than those of slaves. Perhaps their daily being might be better than those who toiled in the salt mines of Numidia, but not by much. The Roman army was built on the foundation of iron discipline plus physical toughness. It all started here.

The new home of the recruits was this small training garrison in Gaul. To the immediate left of the motionless recruits was an exercise area with a number of large wooden posts firmly embedded in the earth. The recruits could but guess the purpose of these stark wooden sentries. They would find out soon enough. Beyond the area of the posts were a series of log obstacles about six feet tall and a tall wooden scaffold with hanging ropes. Directly to their front was the open parade ground. Beyond that was a series of buildings comprised of a crude wooden barracks constructed of rough-cut logs to house the recruits, an armory for weapons, several miscellaneous structures to house the training staff, and a bathhouse.

Absent from this garrison were the customary walled fortifications with which the Roman legions surrounded almost every base and camp. Either the legions considered this site not worth defending, or they believed the province stable enough that the thought of any uprising was out of the question. It was probably a combination of the two. This humble place was where Lucius and his fellow conscripts would be indoctrinated and schooled in the ways of the legions.

Lucius, now officially a raw recruit in the Roman Imperial Army, stood motionless at attention in the center of the dusty parade field, sweating under the weight of his recently issued iron helmet and heavy chain-mail coat. He was accompanied by seventy-nine similarly clad, ill-fated individuals. In time, they would form a tight bond and become brothers-in-arms. But for the moment, they were strangers in suits of iron.

Lucius experienced a burning sensation in his eyes as rivulets of sweat rolled down his forehead. His nose started to itch as more perspiration streaked down his face. He resisted the urge to wipe his face with his hand. The training cadre had admonished the recruits in no uncertain terms that they were to remain at the position of attention and not to look about, scratch their ass, or anything else.

He was set in a rigid posture with his feet together, legs straight, his arms against his side, and his shoulders square. He knew he was being observed by the soldier cadre, so he dare not break his position.

As unobtrusively as possible, Lucius shifted the weight from his right leg to the left to relieve the strain. He did it slowly, so no one could detect his movement. Lucius was pleased with his minor triumph and experienced a brief flash of joy, relieved that no one took notice of his transgression.

The silence of the formation was punctuated by the drone of small insects that darted in and about, tormenting the young men. It was as if the creatures knew they wouldn't be swatted down. Lucius ignored the pesky insects, staring straight ahead.

Earlier in the morning, the cadre had patiently demonstrated to Lucius and the other bewildered conscripts the correct way of standing at attention and where their assigned places were in the formation. They had made sure each man got it right. It had taken a while, but eventually, even the most dim-witted of the eighty men knew how to stand correctly and where. The cadre were demanding, spotting the slightest infraction. Lucius stood straight and tall for the Roman soldiers, attempting to mirror the way they had instructed him. How difficult could this be? Surely they would be pleased with his efforts. That was hardly the case.

The two soldiers had swarmed around him. They were almost touching his face with theirs, peering at him up and down.

"Tuck that chin in and put your heels together. Those arms go straight down, boy. They're not wings. What, do you think you're some kind of bird?"

Lucius said nothing, dismayed that he was doing so poorly.

"Speak up. Are you some kind of bird?"

"No, I don't think so."

"Then start looking like a Roman soldier and not some fucking bird."

The two training cadre continued their mockery.

"Allius, where in the Hades did they get this one from?"

The other soldier, who was equally as malicious, replied, "Don't know, Terrentius, but they sure weren't real selective when they got this bunch. We have a bird here. Let's see what the next one looks like."

Both laughed in scorn, then moved on to the next unfortunate recruit.

As with all things in the legions, there was an intention behind making the recruits stand in their rigid postures under the heat of the day. Lucius and the other men were awaiting the appearance of their training centurion. They had not yet had the pleasure of his company. He had been away on leave when the recruits arrived yesterday. Each of the bewildered eighty men, including Lucius, was mentally preparing himself, but no one quite knew for what. To a man, they were also wondering why they couldn't wait in the shade instead of out here in the full sun. The recruits would find out soon enough.

Lucius was in the front rank of the formation, which was ten across and eight men deep. The eighty men comprised the newly conscripted training century. The century was the basic fighting unit of the Roman legions. In earlier days, the century had contained one hundred men, thus the namesake. But over time, the unit had been streamlined to its present number of eighty. The eighty-man century was subdivided into ten squads of eight men, known as *contubernia*. Lucius was in the front row of the third *contubernium*. The other seven men of his squad were directly behind him. Like it or not, this was to be his new place in the world for the foreseeable future.

He would much prefer the anonymity of the back ranks. He was exposed to observation in the front of the formation much more than if he were buried somewhere in the rear. Just his luck, he guessed. His prominent location in the ranks further discouraged him from any attempt to wipe the rivulets of sweat that trickled down his face. The men to his immediate left and right, each precisely one arm length away, were in a similar position. They hadn't moved, so neither would he.

While not yet familiar with the ways of a soldier, the conscripts understood intuitively that it would be unwise to move or make a sound. It didn't matter that it appeared senseless to stand in the sun for such a long time. They had been ordered to stand and wait, so they waited.

The silence was shattered by someone loudly breaking wind. My sentiments too, thought Lucius. He clenched his teeth to stop from laughing; his face turned red. He could hear the strained efforts of the others to stifle their laughter. Their fatuous grins disappeared in an instant.

Suddenly a huge bear of a man rapidly strode onto the parade ground, accompanied at the rear by the two training cadre, one on each side and slightly behind him. The recruits were all large men, but the figure approaching them was physically imposing. He was not only tall, but he had a large girth about him, none of which appeared to be fat. He exuded raw power and brute strength. This had to be their training centurion.

His tunic was red, and he wore a wide belt with silver inlay. In his right hand, he gripped a sturdy wooden staff known as a *vitis*. His face appeared to be chiseled from granite. On his head, he wore a helmet with a bright-red plume that made him look even larger. The red plume was side to side across the top of his helmet. This distinguished him from the common soldiers, whose plumes were in a front to back direction to the helmets. On his torso, he wore a leather muscle cuirass. His armor, helmet, and tunic fit him perfectly, the quintessential image of what a centurion in the Roman legions should look like.

The centurion stood before them, glaring, not saying a word. He scrutinized the faces before him with an intimidating scowl. A sense of fear hung in the air around the dazed recruits.

Centurion Rufus Longinius of the Lugdunum training center knew the recruits were uncomfortable. He'd been around soldiers long enough to know exactly how they felt with the weight of the unfamiliar armor and the heat. He'd deliberately delayed his appearance. He wanted them to experience suffering. His responsibility was to train these conscripts and make them soldiers. He excelled at it. For the past eight years, he'd trained legionnaires. In truth, he rather enjoyed molding raw recruits such as those before him into Roman soldiers. He knew that this was not the most desirable path for promotion to the slot of *primus pilus*, the first centurion of a cohort, but he figured the odds of ever getting to such a rank weren't that good anyway, so he might as well do something he relished.

The centurion was pleased thus far. The men in the ranks had held their positions, not moving despite the warmth. This was a good start, but there was much more to be done; oh, yes, a great deal more. He grinned wolfishly in anticipation of the days ahead. Nothing worse than a bad bunch of conscripts. It made his life that much more difficult. It wasn't that he ever failed to properly train legionnaires. Once the men were in his garrison, their asses were his. In the past, he had had stupid men, those who were timid, and others insolent. By the end of the training regimen, he had shaped them all into Roman soldiers. He had instilled them with absolute discipline. This was what the legions were all about. He would forge these men into tough and fearless legionnaires; of this he was certain. His methods were harsh but effective.

It was time to begin. The centurion motioned for the two cadres to follow him, then he strode forward. The two men dutifully fell in behind the centurion. The recruits were about to meet their first centurion of the Roman army. It was an experience they would long remember.

The centurion began his inspection in the back ranks. He stopped before each man, taking the measure of him. Except for an occasional grunt or scowl, he said not a word. Lucius, in the front ranks, nervously awaited the centurion's appearance. They advanced ever so slowly. It seemed to take forever. He could hear the shuffling of the centurion's entourage. Where were they? Lucius tried to guess the place they were within the ranks but gave up. He even attempted to sing songs to himself to pass the time, but he couldn't concentrate or remember the words.

He shifted his weight once more to relieve the strain on his aching legs. At last the centurion and his two accomplices reached the front row of men. The trio approached closer to Lucius, stopping in front of the man next to him. The centurion gave the recruit to Lucius's right a cursory glance, then proceeded on squarely in front of Lucius.

He stiffened even more and held his breath, staring straight ahead. Lucius was petrified.

Lucius congratulated himself for having the wisdom not to move while in formation. This was a man he did not want to piss off. He could feel the centurion's eyes bore into him. Lucius met the intense glare, continuing to stare straight ahead. It took all his willpower not to look away from the penetrating gaze of the centurion. The man's eyes were locked onto him, waiting for him to flinch, but Lucius's face was impassive. The centurion brought his wooden staff up and under Lucius's chin. He turned Lucius's head to the left and right, slowly examining his face like some farm animal.

"Your nose, conscript—it was recently broken?"

Lucius hesitated. For the moment, he was paralyzed, unsure of how to answer.

"Answer me, conscript. The question wasn't that difficult."

"Yes, it was broken a number of months ago."

"In a fight?" demanded the centurion.

"Yes," replied Lucius.

"Did you win this fight?"

Lucius blurted out, "No, I lost."

"Bah, what kind of conscripts are they sending me? They can't even win a little fistfight, and I have to train them to face Germans." The two training cadre accompanying the centurion snorted in derision.

The centurion turned away from the bewildered Lucius and went to the next man in formation. Lucius wondered how he should have answered the man. He could feel his face flushing. Why me? Why was I the single person he spoke to in the entire century? Lucius's thoughts of his humiliation were suddenly interrupted.

The centurion, now two men away from Lucius, abruptly whirled back to the first man in Lucius's row to his immediate right and leveled the man with a savage backhand punch to the face. The unfortunate recruit fell to his knees, blood pouring from his mouth. The conscript, believing he was out of the range of vision of the centurion, had wiped his brow.

"You were told not to move." The centurion calmly returned to his inspection of the last of the men. The recruit shakily picked himself up off the ground, quickly wiped his bloody lips with the back of his hand, and returned to the position of attention.

Centurion Longinius was pleased someone had taken the liberty to reposition himself. An example had been made for all to witness, and, much to his delight, in the front ranks. It sent a message to the recruits. It was one of fear, and as far as he was concerned, fear was good. He would cast this bunch into fighting men as he had all of the others. He had his methods, yes indeed. The life of a soldier involved hardship, and it was time these conscripts began learning this lesson. Finished with his inspection, he strode rapidly to the front of the formation and stood before them.

He didn't speak to the assembly. Instead, his words were more of a bellow in a deep bass voice.

"WELCOME TO THE LEGION, CONSCRIPTS. THERE'S ONE THING EACH AND EVERY ONE OF YOU NEEDS TO UNDERSTAND. THE UMBILICAL CORD HAS BEEN CUT. YOUR MOTHERS ARE NO LONGER HERE TO TAKE CARE OF YOU. THE LEGION IS YOUR NEW MOTHER AND FATHER. THIS IS YOUR NEW HOME FOR THE NEXT TWENTY YEARS, ASSUMING YOU SURVIVE."

The training cadre posted behind the centurion smirked at the last remark. This earned them a withering backward glance from the centurion. Both quickly adopted a blank expression and stood at attention like the recruits.

"MY NAME IS CENTURION RUFUS LONGINIUS. YOU'LL ADDRESS ME AT ALL TIMES AS CENTURION. YOU'LL LISTEN TO AND OBEY EVERYTHING I SAY. IF YOU DON'T, BY JUPITER AND MARS, HEAVEN HELP YOU." With that, the centurion smacked with his vinewood staff a wooden post struck in the ground in front of the formation, resulting in a loud thwack. The entire formation of recruits flinched in unison at the sound.

"IS THAT UNDERSTOOD?"

There was no response.

"I DIDN'T HEAR YOU. SPEAK UP."

"Yes, Centurion," the group answered.

"GOOD. THEN WE UNDERSTAND ONE ANOTHER. YOU HAVE ALREADY HAD THE PLEASURE OF MEETING MY TWO ASSISTANTS. TO MY LEFT IS LEGIONNAIRE ALLIUS MAESA, AND TO MY RIGHT IS LEGIONNAIRE TERRENTIUS NORBANUS. YOU'LL GIVE THEM THE SAME RESPECT YOU GIVE ME AND OBEY THEIR COMMANDS WITHOUT QUESTION. BOTH ARE EXPERIENCED SOLDIERS AND COMBAT VETERANS. YOU CAN LEARN FROM THEM.

"YOU'LL BE HERE UNDER MY DIRECTION FOR THE NEXT TWO MONTHS. DURING THAT TIME, YOU'LL LEARN TO MARCH LIKE A LEGIONNAIRE. WE'LL TEACH YOU HOW TO USE YOUR WEAPONS AND TO FIGHT LIKE A LEGIONNAIRE.

"WE WILL TOUGHEN YOU UP SO YOU CAN ENDURE THE RIGORS OF BEING A LEGIONNAIRE. YOUR TRAINING WILL INCLUDE FORCED MARCHES OF TWENTY MILES AND OBSTACLE COURSES. LATER WE'LL TEACH YOU BATTLE DRILL.

"AT THE END OF YOUR TRAINING, YOU'LL BE JUDGED ON YOUR NEW SKILLS, AND IF WE FIND YOU ACCEPTABLE, YOU'LL BE ALLOWED INTO THE LEGION. AT THAT TIME, YOU'LL TAKE THE OATH TO THE EMPEROR, THE *SACRAMENTUM*.

"THOSE OF YOU WHO THINK YOU'LL BE STATIONED AT SOME CUSHY POST IN THE EASTERN EMPIRE WHERE YOU CAN VISIT THE LOCAL FLESHPOTS EVERY NIGHT, FORGET IT. THIS ENTIRE TRAINING CENTURY HAS ALREADY BEEN ASSIGNED AS REPLACEMENTS TO THE LEGIONS IN RHINE, GERMANY. SO PAY ATTENTION TO WHAT WE TEACH YOU, AND MAYBE YOU'LL LIVE.

"LEGIONNAIRE ALLIUS AND TERRENTIUS, GET THIS RABBLE OUT OF MY SIGHT. TAKE THEM TO THE ARMORY TO DRAW THEIR WEAPONS."

With that, Centurion Rufus Longinius smartly did an about-face and strode off to the administrative building. Lucius grimaced and thought, Welcome to the legion.

Lucius sat pensively on his cot in the barracks. He was clad in his gray woolen tunic and iron-shod sandals. He stared straight ahead at nothing, too numb to feel sorry for himself. Several other figures in the small room reclined on their cots, one arm folded over their eyes, perhaps hoping they would wake up someplace else.

The fading sun's rays barely penetrated the small window openings of the enclosed room, most of which was now in deep shadow, a perfect match for the apparent gloom of those inside. From outside, he heard the late call of a nesting bird. He ruminated briefly on the freedom of the creature. Oh, he could attempt to escape, but to where? One couldn't go home, for that was the first place the authorities would look. He'd be hunted down like a wild dog and disciplined severely. The cadre had informed the recruits with great relish the possible punishments for attempting to flee, and they emphasized the word *attempting*, for no recruit had ever been successful in that endeavor. The penalties ranged from severe beatings and confinement to crucifixion. At least that was what the cadre had told them. Lucius wasn't sure whether or not to believe them, but he had no reason to doubt them.

He gazed about his humble surroundings. His quarters were spotless, without a dust particle to be found, and smelled of raw, fresh-cut wood with a hint of vinegar. Lucius was in his section of the wooden barracks with seven other men who comprised his contubernium. Their sleeping billets were small, about twenty by twenty paces square, and packed with eight cots.

Outside this room was a smaller chamber that served to store all of their equipment and weapons. This storage area was perhaps ten by fifteen paces. Everything was arranged just so in a precise location, as dictated by legion standards. There were special hooks and racks to accommodate all of their gear in an orderly fashion. After what seemed like hours of fumbling around, each man had finally placed his kit in its exact location to the satisfaction of the training cadre. When not in use, their equipment and weapons, free of any dirt or grime, were to be placed and hung in these precise locations, no exceptions.

At the armory earlier in the day, they had each drawn a short sword known as a *gladius*, a scabbard for the sword, and a wooden training sword. In addition, each man received a throwing javelin known as a *pilum*, a wooden training javelin, a shield known as a *scutum*, and a dagger, *puggio*, with a scabbard. They had their first bit of instruction at the armory on how to care for their weapons. Each was given a scouring stone to keep all of his weapons sharp and free of rust. Accompanying the shield and weapons was a bewildering assortment of belts and straps used to secure and support their equipment.

As a final blow to individuality, each legionnaire had been given a number, one through eighty, based upon which of the ten squads of eight men he had been assigned. Thus, the first man in the first squad was number one, the second number two, and so on. The ninth man would be the first man in the second squad, the seventeenth man the first in the third squad, and so on.

Each day they were to line up in this precise order. Each man's number was painted on two pieces of cloth connected by two leather thongs that the recruit put his head through, draping the two cloths on both the chest and back. Each recruit was recognized by the number on his cloths. They were to wear it all of the time with the exception of sleeping. Lucius was the first man in the third squad and thus assigned the number XVII.

Cassius, Flavius, and Domitius, his travel companions, were assigned the same squad as Lucius. It was as if the gods had intervened, placing the comrades together. Lucius was comforted that he'd already made several friends who were going to be next to him during their course of training.

The eight men in his squad congregated in the fading light in an attempt to draw some solace from one another. Like it or not, they were all in this misfortune together. Each of the eight men took a turn speaking about himself and his background. The seven men of Lucius's squad, besides Cassius, Domitius, and Flavius, included Severius, Cornelius, Antonius, and Julius. To a man, they were all from Gaul, within a hundred miles of this training garrison. All spoke Latin, though some more fluently than others.

Flavius had just finished his introduction. He was athletic looking and sculpted like a god. He was lean, with a crop of short brown hair. Flavius had relayed that he was the son of a metal worker, but he had no desire to follow in his father's footsteps. He lived a rather comfortable life but wasn't particularly disturbed when he was informed of his conscription. He was always cheerful, with an infectious grin. Flavius could be happy anywhere.

Lucius's friend Cassius now had the floor. "My name is Cassius Malventis—or, rather, it used to be. You can all call me Number Eighteen." Everyone got a chuckle out of that. He continued. "My father is a stonemason. He builds and sculpts all kinds of stone. He wanted me to follow in his footsteps. Frankly, I hated it."

Antonius shouted from the back of the small gathering, "What do you want to do, Eighteen?"

"Drink wine and make love," he shouted back.

Everyone agreed that Cassius had the right idea. They looked about to see if anyone had not yet addressed the group.

"Who hasn't spoken yet?"

Lucius stood before the group. He was the last to speak.

"My name is Lucius Palonius. I lived about fifty or so miles to the east of here, not that far from Cassius. My father transported amphorae. I have a younger brother and sister."

"Can we meet your sister?" shouted a voice from the back.

"Not a chance. Do you think I would introduce my baby sister to this bunch?"

There were several protesting retorts as to the nobility of their character. Lucius continued. "I don't know much about soldiering except maybe which end of a sword to hold. Like it or not, here I am. I don't think the next two months are going to be a lot of fun."

Severius, a strapping farmer's son from southern Gaul, interrupted. "I don't get it. Nobody *asks* you to do anything here. They order you to do it with an attitude. It would seem that if they just asked you to do something nicely, everyone would get along just fine. I've never been treated like this before. It's like you're a lump of cow dung." There was a muttered chorus of approval from the others.

Flavius continued the discussion on a more serious note. "If we are all going to Germania as the centurion stated, does anyone know what it's like there?"

There was an uncomfortable silence, and everyone looked around to see who might know something. The men had little reason to know much about the Germans. The raids across the Rhine by marauding German tribes were a thing of the past, and besides, they were far west of the German border.

Antonius stood and spoke. "I don't know anything firsthand, and I certainly have never been to Germania. We did have some of the legion stationed in our town as a stopping point for the supply trains going north. What I heard wasn't good." Everyone leaned closer to Antonius who paused in his description.

Flavius, with a hint of mock irritation, spoke. "Go on. Don't leave us hanging"

Antonius continued. "The soldiers complained of the cold there, much colder than here. I heard deep snowfalls are common in the winter season, even in the lowlands. The land is heavily forested, with many broad, swift, flowing rivers."

He paused. The several voices urged him on. "What else have you heard?"

"The soldiers said the people are fierce. They're large men with blue eyes and long blond or sometimes rufous hair and beards. The various tribes compete with one another for the land and are frequently at war with neighboring clans. Their diet is mostly meat. They dress themselves in the furs of animals. They especially don't like Roman soldiers occupying their territory. Their most prized possessions are their cattle. I remember the legionnaires mentioning the names of tribes. They're kind of weird names. Let me think...there are the Suebi, Cherusci, Cimbri, Usipetes, and Tencteri. There are others, but I can't remember them. Definitely strange names."

There was a lull as everyone pondered the ominous remarks.

Cassius cursed. "*Stercus.* Of all the places in the empire, why do they have to send us to Germania?"

39

Julius, perhaps the most handsome of the bunch, asked the inevitable question. "What about the women in Germania?"

"The legionnaires said the people hate us, and I guess that includes the women," said Antonius.

"I'm sure that when they see me, they'll quickly forget their hate and think of passion."

This remark brought a collective chorus of groans from the group while Julius beamed at his comrades.

"Is there anything good about this place called Germania?" asked Flavius.

Antonius paused in thoughtful silence for a moment. He replied, "I did hear the soldiers say that the people prefer a wonderful beer from fermented grains. They say it can take your head off."

The group all agreed that perhaps this was one thing they might look forward to experiencing at their future posting.

Lucius decided to ask a question that had been troubling him. "Does anyone have any idea what they plan for us tomorrow? They said that we would begin our training. What does that mean?"

His question was greeted by an uncomfortable silence.

Servius answered. "I guess they'll teach us to march. All soldiers must learn to march."

Everyone nodded sagely in agreement.

Julius responded. "They said physical training and toughening us up. I don't like the sound of that shit."

Everyone laughed. "Me either," chorused several other voices.

"What are they going to make us do to toughen us up? Anybody know?"

Flavius answered. "I guess we'll find out soon enough."

Cassius hopped up on a wooden stool with his hands on his hips and began to imitate the welcoming speech of Centurion Longinius in a false baritone. "Recruits, there's one thing you need to understand. The umbilical cord has been cut." He puffed out his chest in mock bravado and continued. "Your mothers and fathers are not here to take care of you anymore."

He was about to continue when, as if perfectly timed, Centurion Longinius strolled into the room with a bemused expression. No one had seen him lurking in the adjacent room for storing weapons.

"It appears I have a double. Not a bad job of imitation at all. What's your number, recruit?" Cassius wasn't wearing his number in the barracks. He, like everyone else in the room, was speechless.

Cassius managed to squeak, "Eighteen, Centurion."

"I didn't hear you, recruit. You were speaking loud enough a moment ago. Now, what's your number?"

A mortified Cassius managed to blurt out, "Eighteen, Centurion."

"Number Eighteen and the third contubernium. I'll make sure to pay special attention to this group in your training tomorrow. Since you have so much energy, we'll see what you're made out of this week. Sleep well, recruits. You are going to need all of your strength tomorrow." With a bellowed laugh, he turned and exited their room.

There was a stunned silence in the room. Finally, Julius spoke. "Way to go, arsehole! As if this training won't be difficult enough, we're on his stercus list already, and we haven't even started yet." Others mumbled their agreement with Julius, with comments about the dubious nature of Cassius's character and parentage.

The conversation for the night ended abruptly. The men shuffled toward their cots, grumbling about what a dumb shit Cassius was. The last oil lamp was extinguished. Lucius lay on his cot in the darkness, staring at the wooden rafters of the roof. He leaned over to the cot next to him where Cassius lay.

"Hey, Cassius, you still awake?"

"Yeah, Lucius. I'm awake."

"You sure know how to make friends." Lucius attempted to stifle a laugh at his own barbed humor.

"Fuck you, Lucius."

Like the others, Lucius was apprehensive about the next day. What should he expect in the morning? How bad would it be? His exhaustion soon overcame his uneasiness. He slowly drifted off.

III

*L*ucius stared into the captivating green eyes of the long-haired beauty. They were seated alone by a small brook. He bent and softly kissed her neck once again. She smiled shyly back at him. Lucius reached forward and slowly slid her stola from her shoulder, revealing the perfect white mound beneath. Lucius gasped in delight, blood pounding through his veins.

What was that? Shouts interrupted his reverie. He abruptly bolted upright to a sitting position. By the gods, where in the Hades was he? The image of the beautiful woman faded in an instant. Lucius groggily viewed his surroundings. The memory of where he was returned to Lucius in a flash. Had these people taken leave of their senses? It was still dark outside. One of the cadre materialized, holding a large burning oil lamp.

"Out of bed, conscripts. Centurion Longinius awaits you, and he's definitely not in a good mood," shouted Allius. "Only tunics and mail armor. Don't forget your identification numbers. No helmets or weapons today."

Some didn't react quickly enough to his urgings.

"I said out of your racks, and that means now. OUT." This was followed by the sound of running feet.

Shivering in the morning chill, Lucius, like the other recruits, fumbled about, attempting to get dressed in the half-light of early dawn. He quickly shrugged himself into his woolen tunic, then retrieved his heavy iron-mail shirt from its designated peg. He groped with the leather straps on his iron-clad sandals. His nervousness was compounded by the fact that he could barely see what he was doing. All the while, the cadre were shouting at the recruits. "MOVE, MOVE. GET A MOVE ON IT, PEOPLE. WE DON'T HAVE ALL DAY."

Lucius hurried out of the barracks with the other recruits. The first violet streaks of dawn appeared on the horizon. He rushed to his assigned spot, first man in the third contubernium. Each row was separated by an arm's length in the eight-man-deep column. Each recruit was directly behind the man in front of him—not slightly to the left or right, but precisely behind the man.

The scowling centurion paced back and forth, rhythmically whacking his leg with his vitis, the wooden staff and, as they would soon learn, his instrument of pain. Lucius wished again that he could be in the back of the formation and out of sight of the menacing figure before him. The centurion fixed each man with a passing glare. He stiffened as the centurion passed in front of him, eradicating the last vestiges of sleep from his addled brain. He tried to ignore the rumbling in his stomach. Suddenly he longed for his home and the delicious warm bread his mother and sister served in the morning.

The centurion stood to their immediate front with the two cadre at his side.

"It's about time. Each and every one of you needs to understand that you never keep me waiting. When I step out here in the morning, I expect all of you to be standing in your assigned spots waiting for me. UNDERSTOOD?"

"Yes, Centurion," the group replied.

"Furthermore, my cadre tell me that you people didn't get up when ordered this morning. Let me explain this to you one more time. When you're told to do something, by Jove you'll do it, and right away. No hesitation. UNDERSTOOD?"

"Yes, Centurion."

"All right, then. The first thing we're going to do this morning is to teach you the basics of marching." The centurion used his two assistants as demonstrators and went through the basics of stopping, starting, and turning.

"Recruits, this is not difficult. The day is wasting away, and we have much to do. Let's get started. READY."

There was no response.

"LET'S TRY THIS AGAIN. READY."

"YES, CENTURION."

Their shouts broke the early morning stillness. Several startled birds took wing from one of the few trees surrounding the compound. The centurion gave the command, "FORWARD MARCH."

The century marched out in unison—actually not too bad for beginners. Lucius marched, moving his feet with the cadence. His arms swung freely, with his hands in loose fists. The men were tense. They didn't wish to incur the wrath of the centurion by making a mistake.

The centurion bellowed, "STAY IN LINE WITH THE MAN TO YOUR RIGHT AND COVER DOWN TO THE MAN DIRECTLY IN FRONT OF YOU. THIS IS A MILITARY FORMATION, NOT A PARADE OF THE VESTAL VIRGINS. LEGIONNAIRE NORBANUS, DRESS THOSE LINES FOR ME."

The men continued marching. After about a hundred yards, the first command was given: "CENTURY." Then a distinct pause, and "HALT."

It was a disaster. Some men stopped abruptly before the command was fully issued, and others one step after, colliding with the man in front.

The centurion screamed, waving his staff in animation. "What kind of recruits have they given me this time? I've seen chained slaves do a better job than that. You'll stop when I give the command HALT. Not one step before or one step after. Let's try this again, recruits. Do it correctly this time. DO YOU UNDERSTAND ME?"

"YES, CENTURION."

They started again and ended with similar results. The centurion lamented with the cadre.

"Terrentius, Allius, where did they dredge this bunch from? If these men are indeed to be Roman soldiers, then the empire is in trouble. All right, one more time. Here we go."

They went through more drills. After several clumsy attempts, the century managed to stop as a unit.

"THANK JUPITER FOR SMALL FAVORS. HOLY STERCUS, ALLIUS, DID YOU SEE THAT? THEY ALL STOPPED AT THE SAME TIME."

In return, Allius offered a sarcastic smile. "Miracles never cease, Centurion. Perhaps there's hope after all for this bunch."

It was time to advance to the next plateau. They were now marching forward again when the centurion issued the command "COLUMN LEFT MARCH." About seventy recruits did it correctly. The others turned right.

"FREEZE," shrieked the centurion.

"What's so fucking hard about turning to your left?" The centurion waded into the ranks to confront the offenders, who were noticeably out of position. He went right up to their faces screaming at them, spittle flying from his lips. To get his point across, the centurion slashed at the unfortunate souls with his vitis, beating them about the arms and head.

Lucius stood still, eyes straight ahead, cringing. He heard the distinctive crack of wood striking flesh. He dare not look, or he'd suffer the same fate. They continued their marching drill with dubious success for another hour. Lucius remained at the front of the column, so none of his gaffes could be masked or hidden by the other recruits.

The centurion screamed at him, "Number Seventeen, are you the only one in step in this entire century?"

Lucius turned his head in the direction of the centurion to be sure the man was speaking to him. It was a mistake. He was rewarded with a stinging blow from the centurion's staff across his arm.

"Your eyes are to the front at all times. Did I tell you to turn around, Seventeen?"

"No, Centurion."

Lucius quickly adjusted his step with a slight skip to march in step with the rest. He desperately wanted to rub his arm, which now had a large welt forming, but he knew better.

The recruits managed to march in step for about two hundred yards without too much tripping over one another or some fool turning the opposite direction of the column. They were now at a new destination. Immediately to their front were ten huge logs lying in the grass, with a wide-open field beyond that. Each of the ten contubernia was assigned a log, and they dutifully lined up behind them. The logs were about five yards apart. The wooden objects were big, rough-looking things with coarse bark. They were at least ten feet long and wide around.

The centurion addressed the recruits. "The object of today's training is to carry these puny logs from where you stand to the place where you see legionnaire Terrentius." He gestured with his vitis in the direction of Terrentius, who stood some fifty yards away. The centurion paused as if in thought.

"Oh, by the way, you'll not just carry the logs on your shoulders; you'll be in competition with the other contubernia. The squad that finishes last will be required to do twenty-five log lifts in the air above their shoulders, with full extension of the arms. All right, then, let's get started. I want four men on each side of each log. They all are the same length and weigh about the same, so no one squad is advantaged. Come on, be quick about it."

The men positioned themselves next to the logs. Lucius lined up on the right side behind Cassius. He glanced around and saw all of the squads were now in position.

"LOGS UP."

Lucius squatted and grasped the rough underside of the log. They raised the cumbersome object in unison. He exhaled loudly as he lifted. Lucius was surprised by the weight of the object. The muscles in his shoulder protested under the burden. He could feel the weight pushing down to his ankles and knees. What were these things made out of, wood or stone? Lucius's musings as to the physical properties of the logs were interrupted by the centurion's sudden command.

"GO."

His squad was caught off guard by the quick command, as were the others. They recovered quickly and surged forward as the race began. Each team attempted to find a rhythm as they raced toward Terrentius off in the distance. It wasn't a quick pace, more of a walk-ing run. Lucius and friends strained and grunted, running as nimbly as possible. They passed two of the slower squads near the end point, finishing third from last, then immediately dumped the log from their shoulders. They gasped for air, the count of the log lifts for the unfortunate eighth squad echoing in the morning air.

"LOGS UP." With a collective groan, ten logs were hoisted in uni-son on to eighty shoulders. Immediately thereafter, the men shifted the weight to balance the dreaded object comfortably and evenly. Lucius stared blankly at the back of Cassius. This was his entire fo-cus. With sweat stinging his eyes, he gazed straight ahead, waiting for the inevitable command.

"GO!"

They were off again. The grunts of exertion and the pounding of their boots over the hard ground filled the air. With a burst of energy at the finish line, they completed the race ahead of most of the other squads. They dropped the log, careful not to let it land on their feet. The men stood bent over, hands on their hips, panting. Julius and Domitius retched. Lucius could feel the bile in his throat but man-aged to hold it down.

Flavius wheezed, "Any objections to switching sides? My right shoulder is killing me."

Lucius and company nodded in affirmation. The eight men switched sides. Now both shoulders could hurt equally.

The dreaded command came once more. "LOGS UP. GO."

Lucius exhaled in a ragged rhythm to the pace of the squad. The rough bark of the log cut cruelly into his cheek. The eight men stum-bled slightly, almost falling, but managed to right themselves. They finished the race, barely avoiding the infamous honor of last place. The eight men stood gasping. The centurion paced back and forth, counting the log lifts for the unfortunate losers.

Cassius decided to exhort the squad. "C'mon, guys. We almost lost that one."

The rest of the men stared at him in numb fatigue.

Finally Severius found enough energy to speak. "Are you shitting me, Cassius? You think we're not trying?"

Cassius responded, "I was just pointing out how close we came in that last race."

Julius replied, "Hey, save your breath, asshole. You've done enough damage already."

Lucius stared at the ground in silence. He felt bad for Cassius. The men were on edge. Cassius had become the focal point of their ire and deserved better. There was no need to rub salt in the open wound, but now was probably not the best of moments to get in a debate with the others about Cassius's unfortunate blunder. Actually, his impression of the centurion wasn't half bad. He smiled in spite of his current misery. Perhaps later, after this torture was over, they could forgive Cassius.

The recruits ran six more races. Lucius and friends had thus far defied the odds, not finishing last. They had come close several times, but on each occasion, one of the other squads would totally bungle their race and fall down. All were exhausted, and their stamina was gone. Sweat was pouring off every recruit, and their legs were so wobbly that some men could barely stand. With each succeeding race, the tempo of the men had become more ragged, almost as if they were drunk. More of the men were retching.

"I DON'T WANT TO SEE ANYONE ON THE GROUND. YOU'LL BE ON YOUR FEET AT ALL TIMES."

The best they could do was to bend over from the waist, suck in as much air as possible, and ignore the terrible cramping in their extremities. The centurion showed little compassion for their plight. He paced back and forth like some caged animal, always tapping his vitis rhythmically against the side of his leg.

"AM I TRAINING LEGIONAIRES OR NOVICES FOR THE VESTAL VIRGINS? WHAT'S THE MATTER WITH YOU PEOPLE? WHEN I TRAINED, WE DID TWENTY OF THESE RACES WITH NO PROBLEM! LOGS UP."

With a groan from every man, the logs were lifted to their bruised and sore shoulders.

"GO."

Lucius and his fellow squad members raced out and had managed to rumble about halfway to the finish when disaster struck. Cassius, the lead man on the right side directly in front of Lucius, was unable to compensate his pace to a slight depression in the ground. Ordinarily, he would have been able to recover from his slight stumble on the uneven terrain, but his strength and reserves were depleted. He crumbled in a heap. Lucius, directly behind him, couldn't stop and tripped over his fallen comrade. The entire right side of the squad, all four men, collapsed, with the heavy log rolling on top of them. Luckily for Cassius, no one realized he had been the first to fall, or he would have gotten more blame. The group's collapse had almost been instantaneous.

Lucius lay there stunned, unable to get up, too exhausted to get up. He just wanted to lie there and rest for the remainder of the day. This was not to be. The centurion charged in, striking the fallen men with his staff. Lucius felt a stinging blow to his back, creating a jolt of pain to his already-burdened nerves.

"GET UP AND GET MOVING. NO ONE ELSE IS RESTING, AND YOU WILL FINISH THIS RACE."

They managed to get the log back on their shoulders and wobbled to the finish line. His squad dutifully performed the obligatory twenty-five log lifts. With that, the centurion gave the command for all to rest. The eighty men appeared to collapse as one upon the earth. Lucius curled up in a ball on the grass and closed his eyes to the pain.

Centurion Longinius surveyed the pitiful scene before him. He smiled. This was good training. He looked at his two cadre, Terrentius and Allius, catching their eyes. They smiled in smug satisfaction.

The next stop in this day of Hades was a towerlike scaffold about twenty-five feet high, with three ropes about five feet apart hanging down to the ground. Battered and bruised, they had somewhat recovered from their previous exertions with the logs. The century gathered around the scaffold, listening to the centurion.

"In your service to the legion, you may be required to assault a fortress or build a bridge, a wall, or some other structure. You'll need to know how to climb a rope. Legionnaire Allius, please demonstrate to our recruits how easy this task can be."

Legionnaire Allius stepped up to the rope and nimbly shimmied up with apparent ease. He touched the top of the scaffold, then descended hand by hand to the bottom. It looked almost effortless.

Lucius had never climbed a rope, so he paid close attention to the technique of Allius. It didn't look hard, but still, he'd never done this before. Why would he possibly have a reason to climb a rope?

The centurion looked over the group to choose the first climber. Lucius was visualizing exactly how he would proceed with this endeavor. He was startled out of his imaginary climb when he realized the centurion was calling him.

"Number Seventeen, get up here and show these men of the logs how to climb this rope. Have you ever climbed before? I know you've never marched before." The sarcasm was lost on Lucius.

"No, Centurion, I haven't climbed."

"Even better. Show these recruits how easy it is. Go now."

"Yes, Centurion."

Lucius reached up and grabbed the rope tightly. He glanced toward the top, where the rope was fastened to the wooden beam. It looked high. He started up but progressed slowly. His effort was all in his arms, pulling his dead weight up the length of the rope.

"Use your feet and arms together, Seventeen. We'll be here all day at this pace."

Lucius appeared to be struck by some divine intervention of the gods, or perhaps it was the sound of the centurion tapping his wooden staff. Suddenly he figured exactly how he was supposed to climb. In no time, he touched the top and managed to come down without falling off the rope. He touched the ground with a big grin.

"Now, recruits, see how easy this is? I want you lined up in numerical order to climb. Numbers one, two, and three, I want you on that rope now."

"Yes, Centurion," replied the recruits. For the most part, the century did decently on the rope exercise, but there were a few who just didn't get it no matter how much they were threatened. Centurion Longinius, never at a loss for words, bemoaned the lack of prowess from the unfortunate nonclimbers.

"The legate is going to have my balls on a platter if I deliver to him legionnaires who can't climb a little old rope. Legionnaires Allius and Terrentius, get the numbers of the idiots who can't climb, and we'll be back here with them at a later time."

Lucius, somewhat proud of his rope accomplishments and his spirits buoyed, marched with the others toward their next destination. This isn't so bad, he thought. The log races are behind us, and the worst is over. He was wrong.

The remainder of the day consisted of activities such as scaling twenty-foot log walls and running. After a quick break for a midday meal, they learned through hands-on experience the use of the pickaxe and entrenching tool. The Roman legionnaire was skilled in the use of the javelin and sword, but he spent far more time using the sickle and pickaxe. The engineering feat of moving the earth around wasn't just for exercise purposes. It was based on one of the basic tenets of the legion—building a fortified camp wherever they went. This was to be a common theme in their training. They dug six-foot-deep trenches, then filled them in.

After what seemed like an endless day of physical and mental abuse, the conscripts were marched back to the barracks. The formation of men was a ragged affair, devoid of straight ranks and order. One could clearly see these men were drained. Not just tired, but bone weary to their core. They dragged their feet. Their backs were bent, heads drooped forward. They all had this hangdog look as if they couldn't care less if they were executed on the spot. The century was halted about one hundred yards from their quarters. The centurion stood in front of the group.

"I hope you all enjoyed your first day of training. Get used to it, because there'll be many more like it. Everyone is dismissed except the third contubernium. Since they had so much vigor last night, they're going back to become better acquainted with their log."

Lucius couldn't believe it. After what they had been through on this day, one would think the centurion would show a little compassion. He wondered if he had any reserves remaining. The squad proceeded to the logs under the baleful stare of the centurion. Cassius wasn't a popular guy at the moment.

Lucius and friends were put through their paces again with the log. After five trips with the log, everyone was retching again. The centurion just stood by with his hands on his hips observing each carry.

"ALL RIGHT, ONE MORE TRIP SHOULD DO IT FOR TODAY. THEN YOU CAN GET SOME FOOD IN YOUR BELLIES. YOU SEE, I'M A COMPASSIONATE MAN AFTER ALL." The centurion laughed and walked away.

Lucius walked with the seven others of his squad. He took stock of his various aches and pains. He couldn't decide which hurt the most. Both shoulders were sore from the weight of the logs bouncing on them. His hands were blistered and sore. The rope climb and the digging in the earth had rubbed them raw. His legs were aching in the calf and thigh. There wasn't much that didn't hurt. Mud and dirt were ground into every exposed part of his flesh. They returned and rinsed their gear and themselves off as best they could and entered the barracks.

They stripped off their soiled clothing and donned fresh tunics, and then it was on to the mess hall. They were the last to arrive. Everyone was already eating. The men were shoveling food into their mouths with abandon. Some would pause to occasionally wipe their mouths with their arms, then continue eating. A few curiously looked up as Lucius and friends walked into the mess area. Others smirked, aware of the reason for their punishment. Word had spread quickly among the ranks about Cassius's transgression.

There were long wooden tables with wooden benches. At the front of the rather large room was a serving area. Slaves ladled the food from huge, steaming pots. The meal consisted of bread and boiled vegetables with some scraps of unidentifiable meat. The food was bland, but there was plenty of it. There was no talking allowed during meals. Silence was to be observed at all times. Legionnaire Allius was on duty to ensure there were no infractions of this rule.

After the dinner, the conscripts were free to visit the bathhouse. This wasn't a privilege granted to the conscripts every day, but given their current filthy condition, it was a necessity. The bath wasn't an elaborate facility like those one might find in the larger cities or even in the more luxurious homes and villas, but it served its purpose. Lucius and his comrades of his contubernium gathered around a stone bench at the edge of the warm bathing pool. They all looked as if they'd just fought in a major campaign. Everyone had abrasions, scratches, and assorted raw patches of flesh.

"By the gods, even my hair hurts," intoned Cassius.

Everyone moaned in agreement.

"What could they possibly do to us tomorrow that could be worse than today?" said Domitius.

Lucius replied, "I don't know, but would you please pour another bucket of water over me?"

That night, Lucius reclined on his cot in the dark. There was a roaring thunderstorm with brilliant flashes of lightning. Rain beat a steady rhythm on the roof of the barracks. At least I am not outside in that mess, thought Lucius. Despite his physical exhaustion and many aches, he couldn't sleep. How had he gotten there and had his tranquil life so completely changed? How was it that Gallus, the ex-legionnaire, had not told him of these physical horrors that he faced? He hadn't been thrilled with his future in his father's business, but those prospects now appeared idyllic given his current state.

He attempted to make some sense of his fate. His foreseeable future was bleak. To Hades with this adventure stuff. I want to go back home. Lucius reflected about his family and the simple joys they shared—their evening meals together, the sense of accomplishment with the business, teasing his little sister, his mock battles with his brother, the family celebrations of the festivals, and the love of his parents. Lucius stifled a sob and stared at the wooden eaves of the barracks. Tears dampened his eyes. Some legionnaire I am, he thought. It had to get better, didn't it?

IV

ROME
THE FIELD OF MARS

*V*alerius adjusted the heavy bronze helmet so that it fit snugly. He was already sweating, and the mock combat had not yet begun. He didn't really mind. It had been a long winter, and the early spring warmth was a welcome relief. He tugged the weighty chainmail armor down to ensure it covered the vulnerable area below the waistline.

Glancing up from his preparations, he saw his opponent across the makeshift arena performing similar tasks. The circular arena was a small piece of ground covered in sand and cordoned off with rope. Fellow tribunes in training surrounded the arena, waiting for the contest to begin.

The two combatants were outfitted in the armor and weapons on the common legionnaire except that they had the heavier wicker shields and wooden training swords instead of the steel blades. Their training officer, Centurion Mauritinius, had informed them of how tiring it was to fight in the heavy armor of the legionnaire and that they needed to experience this. The men were expected to give their full measure lest they be embarrassed in front of their peers. The mock combat required full devotion, for the lead-filled wooden training swords and wicker shields were capable of inflicting serious injuries. This was no game.

Valerius looked across the at his opponent, whose name was Castor. Valerius didn't especially care for Castor, a sentiment shared by most of his fellow tribunes in training. They considered him to be haughty and of a mean disposition. Castor was of the senatorial ranks, while Valerius and his colleagues were of the equestrians. The senatorial tribunes were distinguished by a broad purple stripe that ran down the front of their togas. It was from these individuals that the top leadership positions in the Roman government would be selected. To many, there was little distinction between the two ranks, but others, such as Castor, perceived a wide chasm. In short, like many of the patrician class, he was a snob..

Valerius had decided how to engage his adversary. Castor's advantage was bulk, but he lacked speed and finesse. These were the strong suits of Valerius. He assumed Castor would attempt a straight-ahead rush to knock him off balance, then attempt to finish him. Valerius would exercise caution and not let the initial charge overwhelm him, then he would dart in and thrust.

The protocol for these fights was well established. Centurion Mauritinius stood in the middle of the ring with a wooden staff. When both opponents were ready, he would raise the staff, then drop it to signal the beginning of the combat. Valerius hefted his wicker shield and fit the grip snugly on left arm. He was in the process of picking up his wooden training sword when he heard a gasp from his fellow trainees. Looking up, he saw Castor bearing down on him. Valerius barely had time to dodge a wicked blow aimed at his head. Nevertheless, he received a glancing whack that made his ears ring, pushing his helmet forward toward his nose. If the strike had fully connected, it would have caused some significant damage, even with the protection of the bronze helmet. As it was, a small trickle of blood was seeping from the bridge of Valerius's nose from the force of the helmet jammed against his face. Valerius, dazed and with one knee on the ground, barely scurried away from the next onslaught by Castor. He quickly dashed to the opposite side of the ring to clear his head.

He had no time to recuperate. Again Castor bull-rushed him, then aimed another swipe at his head. Valerius recovered enough to readjust his helmet and meet the charge in a ready position. His vision lacked focus; objects were blurred. He managed to deflect Castor's sword again. Valerius retreated and regained his equilibrium. Enraged at the treachery of Castor, he was going to get some retribution. Castor lunged, but Valerius deftly stepped aside, then pivoted. He whacked Castor hard on his butt as he moved past him. Castor yelped in pain. This drew laughs from the other tribunes-to-be.

Valerius rather enjoyed the attention, making a mockery of the battle, for Castor was no match for him. Valerius was by far the best swordsman of the group. He possessed a combination of speed and agility that none could match, plus, he had the strength to parry the heaviest of sword strikes. He whacked Castor again on the butt. He toyed with Castor mercilessly, hitting him hard many times with the heavy wooden sword. Perhaps he did overdo it a bit. He was showing off at the expense of Castor, humiliating the man for his deceitful conduct, but in Valerius's mind, he deserved everything he was receiving and more.

Centurion Mauritinius let the combat continue longer than needed, no doubt as punishment to Castor for his ungentlemanly behavior. At the end, Castor stalked off alone while the others congregated around Valerius, congratulating him on his victory. Valerius basked in the praise of his fellow trainees. The soon-to-be tribunes shared several goblets of wine in celebration, for their days of arduous training were almost complete.

Unfortunately for Valerius, his elation was short lived. Trouble followed him home. Valerius was seated alone in the atrium of his home when his father, Sentius, approached. "What happened to your face?"

"Nothing much. A little training accident this afternoon on the drill field."

His father sat down next to him. A feeling of dread came over Valerius. He knew what subject was about to be broached. Of late, Valerius had been at odds with his father and mother, and it wasn't just a minor disagreement. It was more like all-out warfare. His refusal to marry into what his mother and father considered a proper Roman family had created intense friction that had thoroughly disrupted the household of Maximus.

Valerius was enamored with a young woman, Calpurnia, who didn't fit his parents' criteria, especially that of his father, of a proper match for their son. Calpurnia was the daughter of a tradesman, certainly not the pairing his parents intended. In Rome, marrying and association with the proper family was everything. Valerius was acutely aware of his father's ambition to have him eventually serve in the Roman Senate. Finding the appropriate match for a spouse was an important step in that direction.

His mother and father had attempted many ways of discouraging the union. They were constantly introducing him to women from what they considered proper families. It was almost comical. Their efforts were so transparent. Did they not think he could not see right through their guise? Valerius had stubbornly resisted their plans. He had no intention of breaking off with Calpurnia. She was a raven-haired beauty of exquisite proportions. Valerius had found it so easy to talk with this woman of the light laugh and sparkling eyes. The two had formed an uncommon bond in their understanding of each other. They were happy together. The other women of high Roman society whom his parents had been so eager for him to meet had seemed so shallow. All they cared about was the latest fashion and gossip in Rome. Of course, Valerius gave them no chance to begin with, for all he wanted in his life was Calpurnia.

He knew his parents could force him to marry into another family. Valerius had avoided that pitfall by stating that he couldn't possibly wed, as he would be away on the German frontier for the next several years. His position was quite logical, and, in the end, his reasoning had served to mollify his parents' ire. Though the marriage question was temporarily diffused, it was by no stretch of the imagination resolved.

In a serious tone, his father said, "Son, your mother and I are extremely proud of you, Valerius Maximus, a tribune in the legions. That makes a statement now, doesn't it?" Not waiting for an answer, he continued.

"There are defining moments in a man's life, whether they're large or small. I believe this is clearly one of them for you. Your very future will be cast by events in your service as a military tribune. You'll recognize these moments when they come. Mark my words, Valerius, and remember them."

Valerius knew he needed to respond to his father's words. To remain silent would be impolite. His father was attempting to have a serious discussion with him. The trouble was that Valerius didn't want to talk. He knew exactly where this conversation was heading. It wasn't that he didn't find some wisdom in his father's words. They made sense, but Valerius was certain the next statement by his father would be about duty and family. From there, it was but a short step to his future marriage. This wasn't a dialogue he wanted to have with his parents before leaving to his first duty posting, only weeks away.

He gazed up at his father, who looked back at him expectantly. His father was adorned in his usual white toga. The wisps of short gray hair around his balding pate and his soft features made him appear scholarly and wise, a fitting appearance for a magistrate. He appeared calm and collected, certainly not confrontational. Sentius was rarely quarrelsome. He was so damn logical, which made it all that more difficult to argue with him.

Valerius searched for the right words, ones that wouldn't provide an opening for Sentius to plow ahead about one's obligations concerning family and marriage. Finally, after a lengthy pause, Valerius spoke. "You're correct, Father. After all of this time, my duty calls. I must remember all of the things that have been drilled into me during my training."

"I'm sure you'll perform your duties in an extraordinary manner, Valerius," his father said reassuringly. "Now let's be frank with each other, shall we?"

Valerius knew the dreaded moment had arrived.

"You know all the good Roman families find the proper marriages for their children. It paves the way to advancement in one's career. Just look around at most of your friends and their relationships. They all married into the proper families; it's the way of Rome."

Valerius interrupted. "Father, I thought we'd agreed that any thoughts of my marriage wouldn't be discussed until my return three years hence."

"I know. I know." His father held up his hands in a placating gesture. "But I thought it important to clear the air, so to speak. We must all understand what's expected of you upon your return from military service. Now, as I was saying, it's the Roman way to marry into a good family. There are lots of good women from the right families who would make a good match for you."

Sentius looked at Valerius inquiringly, but Valerius stared back, his face a mask of stone.

"Come now, Valerius, you can't keep up this charade. It just won't do."

"Father, you and Mother want what's best for me, don't you?"

"Of course, Valerius. You know that. Your mother and I care very much about you."

"Then you'll let me marry Calpurnia, because that's what I want. That's what would make me happy, not the trappings of some political career."

Valerius could feel his anger bloom. He knew his father was taken aback by the sharp response.

Sentius paused a moment before responding. Valerius stared back at his father, challenging him to counter his words.

"Valerius, I know you love the girl, but she'll just hinder your future. Listen, you could marry a proper Roman matron, and if you wanted to get a little something on the side, who would know about it?"

"Father, that will definitely not do. To even think of such a thing as treating Calpurnia like a common harlot is out of the question. Maybe you're concerned in what light it will cast you and Mother if I marry a commoner."

"Calm down, Valerius. That's not what I meant to say."

Before his father could continue, his mother appeared.

"Sentius, I need your assistance with the dinner invitations for next week."

His father frowned in annoyance at the interruption but stood to follow her. Valerius said a silent prayer to the gods for his rescue from the situation. He stared at the retreating form of his mother, wondering if she'd heard the entire exchange. It certainly had gotten loud enough at the end. Perhaps she'd stepped in to avoid a major confrontation.

Two weeks later, M. Valerius Maximus—correction; make that Tribune Valerius Maximus, for he was now officially a tribune in the Roman Imperial Army—gazed at the image reflected in the burnished metal mirror. He straightened his stance, then turned slightly to the left, presenting an even more striking profile. Valerius had to admit that he did look impressive in his military uniform. The great Augustus Caesar himself, ruler of the Western civilized world, had signed his appointment to tribune in the imperial legions. Not that Valerius knew the great man or had even met him, for Valerius was just an eager tribune off to perform his duty for the empire.

The full-length mirror revealed an imposing figure in full military uniform. At the age of twenty-one, Valerius was somewhat taller than medium height, with delicate features hinting at his aristocratic origins. His general physique was sleek. He had brown hair cut short in the legionary style. The uniform, particularly the brightly polished cuirass, added bulk to his otherwise narrow frame. This was not to imply that young Valerius was physically weak. On the contrary, his body was laced with sinewy muscle of surprising strength.

His shining breastplate was befitting of a tribune. It looked ready for a dress parade, but it was not just for show. The armor was strong and resilient, capable of withstanding the fiercest javelin thrust or sword cut. In his right arm he held his helmet, complete with horsehair plume. Like his armor, the helmet was a work of art. The exterior of the headpiece was covered in intricate designs. Like the breastplate, it would provide ample protection in armed conflict.

Like all legionnaires, his uniform included the ubiquitous gray woolen tunic that reached to just above his knees and the iron-shod sandals or caliga. Completing his wardrobe was a magnificent belt around his midsection, inlaid with gold and silver. Attached to the belt on the right side was a scabbard that contained a steel sword of considerable length. This wasn't the standard short stabbing sword or gladius issued to common soldiers; rather, it was a longer, thinner version forged in Spain with a special carbon-rich iron. The hilt was plated in gold with fancy scrollwork. It was a formidable weapon of superior strength and suppleness that would hold a razor edge.

It had cost his father a small fortune, taking months to be completed. The iron had been shaped and folded over upon itself many times by the most skillful of craftsmen. Valerius had fretted that the sword wouldn't be ready before his posting, but it had arrived by courier a few days ago, just in time for his upcoming departure. Upon receiving the sword, he went immediately to his room to test the blade. He held the weapon before him, the burnished steel glinting in the afternoon sunlight. The sword grip molded to his hand. His arm and the blade were like one. It was beautifully balanced, but with enough heft to create havoc. He slashed at an invisible foe. The blade whistled through the air, making a menacing hissing sound. He whirled around to engage an imagined foe to his rear. Unfortunately, he made contact with a linen drape, severing it in two. He couldn't believe the sword was that sharp. He stared in horror at what he'd done.

His mother, Vispania, would be furious when she discovered the destruction. He knew she had paid dearly for this fine linen that had come all the way from Damascus. He quickly hid the incriminating evidence with the rest of the soiled laundry. By the time she uncovered his foul deed—and she would find out eventually, for there was little that escaped his mother's careful scrutiny of the household affairs—he would be long gone.

He gazed again at the figure in the mirror, not quite believing the striking image before him. Was this really he? Valerius couldn't fully comprehend that he was actually a tribune in the Roman Army. In a mock salute, the tribune drew his sword out of the scabbard with a flourish. Raising the sword, he echoed the standard cry of the gladiator: *"Morituri te saluamus."* "We who are about to die salute you."

A wave of nervous nausea gripped Valerius's stomach. To say that he was apprehensive about his imminent posting was an understatement. True, he'd trained and studied for years to take on the leadership mantle of a tribune, but this was a big step for a young man. For the first time in his life, he would be on his own. Valerius attempted to dispel his trepidation. He reasoned that he was the product of a superb education and training. By the gods, he'd been drilled, schooled, and coached almost every day of his young life. He was skilled in the classics and could speak Greek fluently. He'd been tutored in the law and oratory. His military instruction had begun years ago. He'd toiled for hours on the Field of Mars, training in the art of warfare. But no matter how much he rationalized, there was always that element of doubt that fueled his nervous anticipation of events to come.

What if he failed in his duties? What kind of situations would he encounter? What would the ordinary soldiers think of him? Perhaps it was the strong sense of duty that invoked such worry. He mustn't falter. There could be no greater shame for his family than for him to fall short in his obligations as a tribune. The Roman traits of *nobilitas*, the striving for excellence in all endeavors, and *virtus*, the display of courage in dangerous situations, were imbued in his soul. Adding to his uneasiness was the long journey ahead of him. He was to be stationed on the northernmost frontier in Germania under the rule of General Publius Quinctilius Varus, governor of the province.

In his short life, Valerius had traveled to Capri to escape the heat of the Roman summers. That was it. Now he was about to sail through the gates of Hercules, along the coasts of Hispania and Gaul, and then on to Germania. This was a long way from home to a land whose people weren't overly fond of Rome, especially the imperial eagles of the legions. He'd heard some rather chilling accounts about these Germans. Based upon what he'd gleaned, the Germans were big men who liked to drink and loved to fight—if not with Romans, then with one another. The tribal feuds among the Germans were legendary and an ongoing problem for the military governance of the province.

As fortune would dictate, Valerius wasn't assigned to just any legion in the provinces. No, he was traveling to probably the most distant and hostile location in the empire. Just your luck, Maximus, he thought. You're not just going to the border of this belligerent land, you're going beyond it.

The Rhine was the established boundary for Germania, past which might be characterized as the abyss. The string of garrisons along the Rhine clearly noted the demarcation of Roman rule. All of the lands west of this river were firmly under the domination of Rome. He was to be stationed at the summer encampment east of the Rhine along the Weser in the dark interior of the country, where even the presence of Roman roads was sporadic. It was just recently that a series of forts, more aptly described as outposts, had been constructed along the Lippe River. There were no Roman settlements where he was to be stationed. The protection of the fortified camp of the legions was their only safe haven.

His posting to one of the provincial legions in Germania, though distant, wasn't considered that unusual. There were twenty-eight standing legions in the Roman Imperial Army garrisoned in the provinces. Across the sea to the south were eight legions—two in Africa, two in Egypt, and four in Syria. The remaining twenty legions were scattered from the Rhine to Moesia. By far, the heaviest concentrations were in Germania. If a tribune's family was connected by blood or friendship to a prefect of a legion, the commander could request his presence. Valerius had no such connection. In the end, while Germania wasn't a desirable assignment, it was logical that he was posted there. This was where many of the legions were stationed; thus, Germania was his destination.

His troubled thoughts were interrupted by a short knock. "It's time, Valerius," said Sentius through the door.

Valerius ceased his musings. Mustn't keep the guests waiting. He glanced one more time in the mirror to see that everything was in order. One didn't want to make a grand entrance with one's uniform out of place. He saw no loose threads, and the belts and straps were cinched tight. Just to be sure, he absently patted himself down and deemed all was in order. He could vaguely hear the murmur of various conversations and muffled bouts of laughter through his door. He had tarried long enough.

Valerius opened the door to his room, put on a brave face, and then strode purposely down the hallway to the open courtyard, where his family and friends awaited to see him off on his journey. Approaching the atrium, he glanced for a final time at the beauty of his home. It was a magnificent dwelling, a classic U-shaped house located on the Aventine Hill in the south section of Rome. They had a view of the Tiber to the west. One could see many of the structures on the Palatine Hill to the north. Best yet, the elevated location enabled the domicile to catch the cooling breezes in the hot days of summer.

The rooms were spacious and beautifully decorated with frescoes and carved furniture. The courtyard was the central feature of the house and open to the sun. There were beautiful flowering plants, a large fountain with tumbling clear water, and a tiled floor of exquisite work. He would miss these comforting surroundings. In the atrium just ahead was a receiving line of family and friends. He paused in his approach to the entranceway, drew a deep breath, and then proceeded onward.

He paraded in tall and erect, carrying his helmet in the crook of his left arm. His caliga made a distinct clacking sound as the iron hobnails on the soles struck the tiled surface. He made an impressive figure with his armor and trailing sword. As he emerged into view, there was a collective gasp from the gathering. They had never seen him in his full uniform. His aunts and uncles were there, along with his cousins. A few of his father's patrons were in attendance, and also some of the family's household servants who had known him since he was a boy.

Valerius attempted to clear his throat, but at the moment, it was as if he had swallowed a large rock. He waded into the group with forced bravado, hoping no one would see through his mask. He maintained a polite façade as he greeted everyone, exchanging the customary embraces and handshakes. He repeated his standard responses to many about his upcoming posting.

No, he'd never traveled that far away before. Yes, he was looking forward to the challenge, and no, he wasn't sure when he might return home for a visit. Yes, he'd heard that it got cold there, and yes, those Germans could be dangerous.

Valerius stood before his father's brother, his uncle Jallius, and his aunt Cornelia. His uncle, a former tribune, beamed with pride at his nephew. He slapped Valerius on the shoulder and spoke in a humorous tone. "You know, Valerius, Cornelia and I will sleep much better at night knowing you're guarding the empire."

Valerius quipped, "I imagine so. After all, I'm the ultimate weapon."

His aunt and uncle laughed at his retort.

"In all seriousness, Valerius, keep a sharp eye out up there in the north. You can never trust those Germans."

His aunt gave him a warm hug. "Do be careful, Valerius. You're a like a son to me." In a way it was true; Jallius and Cornelia were close family. They lived but several houses away. The two families were always sharing festive occasions together. He had enjoyed the company of his aunt and uncle and their two young children. He would miss sharing those celebratory events while he was away in Germania. Valerius, after assuring his aunt and uncle that he would stay in touch with them, politely disengaged from them and moved on among the guests.

As Valerius mingled, he was cornered by Flavia, the daughter of one of his father's fellow magistrates. She had been one of his parents' "chosen ones" as a possible match in marriage. She locked both of her arms around his neck in a show of affection. Valerius attempted to escape her clutch, but she continued holding him tight. He was able to release one arm, but, not to be deterred, she grasped his free hand with both of hers. Standing close to him so no one could see, she placed his hand firmly against her breast. Valerius could feel the hardness of her nipple through the thin material of her gown.

"Valerius, you're so handsome in that uniform. I shall miss you so much," she cooed. "Please come home early so we can resume our acquaintance. I shall make special sacrifices to the gods for your quick return."

Valerius attempted to disengage, but she would have none of it. She continued to pinion his hand against her breast. He looked about, hoping nobody had noticed. He grinned meekly back at her as she waited for a response.

Finally he relented and spluttered a reply. "Flavia, I'll think of you often. I, too, look forward to my return to Rome and seeing you once again."

She released his arm, smiling triumphantly at him. Flushing with embarrassment and hoping no one had observed what had just transpired, he broke away from her. He went a short distance toward two of his distant cousins who were in an animated conversation about the recent chariot races. Valerius continued to politely mingle among the invited visitors but stayed away from Flavia. He could feel the walls closing in on him. He had enough of this. He glanced toward his father, who smiled with pride, nodding in affirmation. It was time to leave.

Valerius approached his immediate family, who had gathered apart from the crowd. All were silent now as everyone watched the final exit. Some of the guests were already dabbing their eyes. His mother, Vispania, and his two younger sisters, Claudia and Diana, were in tears.

"Please don't go, Valerius. Stay here with me," Diana cried. The twelve-year-old had a bear hug around his neck and wouldn't let go.

Valerius gently disengaged her arms and brushed away her tears. "I won't be gone that long. When I come back, I'll bring you and your sister magnificent presents."

This did help a little, but the two sisters continued sob. He gave each a final hug. He moved on to his mother, giving her long hug. Roman law and customs dictated that the husband ruled the household, but in her own quiet way, she directed his father at what she thought was best for hearth and home. If she would just approve of Calpurnia, the tribune thought wistfully.

"I shall pray to the gods for you every night, Valerius. Please be careful. I'll miss you terribly."

"Mother, don't worry. Everything will be fine. I'll return home before you know it. I promise to write to you and Father. Farewell."

Valerius turned toward his father, but his mother wasn't quite finished with him yet.

"Oh, one more thing, Valerius."

"Yes, Mother?" He spun back to face her.

"Is there something else you want to tell me?"

Valerius hesitated in confusion, thinking he had committed some social blunder or other.

"Why, no, mother. I don't think so."

His mother fixed him with a deep frown. "I know about the drape."

Valerius spluttered. "Mother, it was an accident, you see. I was just testing my new sword, and..." He stopped when he saw his mother smirking.

"You have to get up pretty early in the morning to fool this woman. I'll forgive you this time, my son. But it had better not happen again," she chided. "Now give me a big hug and be on your way."

Valerius embraced his mother once more, knowing he was absolved. His mother, holding him close, whispered so no one else could hear, "Maybe when you return, we can discuss Calpurnia, just you and me. What do you say?" Without waiting for a reply, she continued. "You know, Valerius, I do like the girl."

He beamed back at his mother. So there was hope after all. Elated, he broke away, then stood in front of his father.

"What are you grinning about? Is there something your mother told you that was so funny?"

Putting on a bland expression, Valerius glibly replied, "Not really, Father. Mother just reminded me of some of the foolish things I did in my childhood."

Valerius stepped up to his father, grasped his right arm in both of his, and thanked him for all of his support. His father beamed back at him in pride. Valerius bade good-bye to all and began walking toward the front door. As he moved forward, away from his family and friends, out of the corner of his eye he spied a solitary figure standing by himself, his former tutor and mentor, Cato.

Valerius wondered why he hadn't seen him in the atrium. He'd known him for many years, developing a deep respect. He'd learned many things from his tutor beyond the typical classical studies. Cato and Valerius had spent much time together in the study of life. Valerius hurried over to his mentor, calling out, "Cato, so good of you to come." As he looked into the old man's eyes, he could see tears forming. This was probably the reason he'd not joined the larger gathering.

"Best wishes on your military service, Master Valerius."

He hugged the old man. "I shall remember everything you taught me, Cato. I'll miss the time we spent together. Thank you for all your imparted wisdom."

Cato responded, "I would be most honored if you'd find the time to send me a letter from Germania. I've never been there and would like to know more about it."

"So I shall. I'll relate to you the things I experience about the people, flora, and fauna. Take care of yourself, Cato. Farewell."

Valerius quickly moved toward the massive front door, hoping no one saw him wiping his eyes. He inhaled deeply, put on a brave face, and then exited into the bright morning sunlight of the streets of Rome. The servants had already loaded his baggage on the waiting wagon. He turned his head back one more time to look at his home with its massive marble columns. He waved to his family in the doorway. Valerius heaved a sigh and nimbly leaped onboard, then waved good-bye again.

The wagon passed ever so slowly through the crowded thoroughfares of Rome. There were masses of people everywhere amid the shouts and cries of vendors hawking their produce or other items for consumption. Dust swirled about the heated air of the late morning as men and women surged around the wagon, many carrying baskets filled with bread and vegetables for the evening meal. Valerius cursed himself for not insisting on an earlier start. At this rate, he wouldn't even get through the city gates by sunset, let alone the port of Ostia.

Valerius's ship sailed at dawn tomorrow, and he'd best be on it. For him to miss his transport to his first posting wouldn't bode well for him. His driver just stared ahead, totally unconcerned with their progress. Why should he worry? He wasn't the one who needed to catch a ship to sail at dawn tomorrow. Valerius craned his neck, looking ahead. The view was the same: streets crowded with people. He sat down again, staring ahead at the chaos of the streets. Above the noise of the crowd, he heard his name called.

"Valerius, Valerius."

He stood in the wagon, taking care to steady himself. He peered about as he heard his name spoken again.

"Valerius, over here."

He turned toward the other side of the wagon. Off to his left, the crowd parted. He saw Calpurnia running toward his him. Valerius leaped from his perch and embraced her. The two passionately kissed.

"I just had to see you one more time," she said breathlessly.

Valerius smiled at her, the frustration of his delayed journey temporarily forgotten.

"By the gods, what other woman in Rome would have come through a crowd like this on a hot day? Calpurnia, my thoughts shall always be with you. I'll return before you know it."

Calpurnia held him tightly. The two were oblivious that the entire market square had become silent as the people stared at the two lovers, smiling knowingly. Both looked away from each other, noting that they had attracted an audience.

"You two go get a room," a voice shouted from the crowd.

They turned back, grinned at each other, and then resumed their kissing.

"Calpurnia, you know I would love to stay here, but I must be on my way. I'm already far behind schedule. The ship sails at dawn tomorrow, with or without me."

Calpurnia nodded in understanding, tears streaking her face. "Go, my love."

Valerius kissed her one more time and climbed up on the wagon. Calpurnia blew him a kiss as the wagon began moving. Valerius continued looking back until she was swallowed by the crowd.

The cart continued to plod through the crowded streets of Rome, with many stops and starts. Finally, after much delay, the wagon exited the city gate and onto the Via Ostiensis. The hot sun of the early summer beat down upon the erect form of Valerius. The tribune mopped his brow with his forearm, glancing anxiously to see what was ahead. As far as he could see, the roadway was congested with traffic. At this pace, he would never make Ostia by nightfall. He now regretted wearing his full parade uniform. His metal breastplate was heavy and trapped the baking heat. He could have opted for a lighter cuirass made of leather, but his family had expected the full uniform for the reception in his house. He could rummage through his belongings on the wagon and put on something lighter, but it didn't seem military like. He would just have to put up with the heat of the discomfort.

At last, after a long day, they passed by the salt marshes on the edge of Ostia, then the necropolis with family crypts, and finally, they reached the city walls. The cart slowly lumbered through the gate and then journeyed past dwellings, a theater, the baths, the forum, and on toward the port. It was now late afternoon. The city was beginning to shut down for the day.

Valerius arrived at a massive stone quay. He noted numerous ships docked and secured with heavy mooring lines. He dismounted from his perch. He needed to seek out the office of the garrison commander. He didn't have to search far. The building was directly opposite the dock. He entered a small wooden structure. The interior was dingy, appearing more like some hovel than a military post. He looked about in the gloom, wrinkling his nose in disgust. This was the first legionary establishment that he had visited in his short military career. He expected something better. This *castrum* had seen better days.

He knew that during the period of Rome's wars with Carthage, the fort at Ostia had served a useful purpose, guarding the harbor and serving as a strategic base for the Roman warships. Those days were long past. Over the many years since Rome's defeat of Carthage, the purpose of the garrison had ceased to exist. Rome ruled the seas, with the exception of an occasional band of pirates. They were considered a minor nuisance and were usually caught within a short period of time and executed. There were no longer great warships moored in the grand harbor. Ostia's singular purpose was to serve as a docking for merchant ships. The military garrison was a mere shadow of the former castrum that had once protected the seaport. The naval fleets were now moored at Misenum and Ravenna, leaving the fort at Ostia but a crumbling ruin. Over the years, the walls had deteriorated. The barracks were no longer in use except for a few small buildings reserved for a handful of legionnaires stationed here.

He spied a solitary soldier, a centurion, seated at a wooden table, and he walked over. He silently presented his orders to the man, who, he guessed, was in charge. The centurion was attired in leather armor rather than the standard chain mail. He wore a military-issue belt with sword and scabbard. The centurion silently examined the rolled papyrus document that Valerius handed to him, squinting at the writing in the fading light of the late afternoon. Motes of dust floated in the air from the solitary shaft of sunlight that managed to penetrate the gloom. Valerius stared at the seated figure, who was engrossed for the moment with Valerius's travel orders. The tribune noticed several impressive gold and silver decorations for bravery in battle adorning the centurion's uniform.

There was a long, whitish scar snaking down the length of one arm. The weathered appearance of the man's face suggested that this was a person who had been outdoors quite a bit, given the dark hue of the skin and edged lines around the cheekbones. Valerius surmised that the centurion was a seasoned veteran, clearly no chair-bound warrior. This was a soldier of the line, the type of man who held the legions together. He seemed out of place in these rather grimy surroundings.

After a few moments, the centurion looked up. "We've been expecting you, sir," he said.

Valerius had never been addressed as *sir* before in the army. He admitted to himself that it did sound sort of distinguished. The centurion most likely knew immediately that Valerius was brand new to the world of soldiering, but he treated him with deference.

"The ship sails tomorrow at dawn. We'll load your baggage now. You can have the cart follow us down to the ship at the dock. You can bunk in one of the vacant rooms of the fort for the night rather than on the ship. If you'll follow me, sir, I'll guide you down to the dock and show you your transport."

The two men exited the building. Valerius gestured to the driver of the cart to follow them.

"So how is your duty, Centurion?"

The centurion stopped walking and turned to face the tribune. He appeared surprised and perhaps pleased that the tribune would take an interest in a veteran centurion.

"Ah, yes. Welcome to my post, Tribune. I'm lord and master of this garrison. Charming, isn't it?" He opened his arms wide in a magnanimous gesture.

Valerius wasn't sure how to respond.

The centurion smiled. "I know. This place is a dump, but it's my dump. I requested this duty, believe it or not. I'm at the end of the line. I'm retiring in two months. I was in Germania and wanted to get home to be with my soon-to-be wife. The first centurion owed me a favor, so I requested to come here. Really, it's not too bad."

The pair started walking again.

"Centurion, my congratulations on your years of service and your upcoming nuptials. I'm off to Germania. You appear to be a man of experience. Sure you don't want to reconsider and join me?"

The centurion stopped abruptly and frowned. "No, sir. That's most definitely not something I want to do again."

"You're sure?"

"Yes, sir, I'm sure." The centurion was silent for a moment. He paused in thought, searching for the correct words. "Listen to me, Tribune. You seem to be a decent sort. Be careful out there. It can be a little volatile, if you know what I mean."

"Come now, Centurion. It can't be all that bad."

"Sir, I imagine there are worse places to be stationed in the empire, but not many. Maybe I just got too old for soldiering, but the last time I was on patrol east of the Rhine, I never thought I'd see Rome again. I kept having these dreams of my corpse lying in some unknown woodland. I knew I had to get out of there. That country had a feeling of impending doom about it. I'm not trying to alarm you, sir, but..." His voice trailed off. "Shit, just be careful out there, sir."

Valerius smiled. "Thanks for the warning, Centurion. Once again, enjoy your retirement. Sounds like you earned it."

The centurion nodded in reply, obviously relieved that he wasn't the one going to the posting in Germania. The two men walked in silence the rest of the way toward the ship Valerius was to board.

Upon reaching the wharf, the two men walked a short distance along the seafront.

"There's your transport, Tribune."

The ship wasn't some worn merchant transport, but a Roman warship. It was one of the smaller, lighter versions, a Liburnian. Valerius gazed in awe at the vessel. It was over a hundred feet long and about thirty feet at the beam. Valerius wasn't a sailor, but he couldn't help but admire the sleek lines of the ship. The vessel pulled gently at her lines as soft swells coursed across the harbor in the late afternoon. Seabirds flew about the ship and called shrilly to one another while the vessel's pennants fluttered in the breeze.

He glanced around at the other ships moored in the protected dockings. They were all trade ships, ungainly in appearance, with squat ugly lines. Judging from the enormous size, these were no doubt all grain ships arrived recently from Egypt. It was spring, and there had been no traffic during the winter months because of the fierce storms that racked the seas. Gazing out over the harbor, he could see other ships waiting to unload their precious cargo. Valerius grinned in anticipation. He could hardly wait to reach the open sea on the Liburnian.

Valerius followed the centurion up a boarding plank and stepped on deck to meet the captain. The centurion guided Valerius toward the stern. He spied a man whom he assumed to be the captain. He was shouting at some of the crew to store some cargo. The man wore the uniform of the Imperial Navy. He was short in stature and appeared to be in his late forties, a bit older than most men of his rank. He had a dour expression on his weathered face. He continued his tirade at the sailors, ignoring the presence of the two Roman officers. The centurion waited a bit longer, then smoothly stepped in front of the captain, blocking his view of the crew moving the cargo.

"Captain Sabinus, may I present Tribune M. Valerius Maximus. He's one of the tribunes who will be traveling with you."

The captain sort of grunted in a surly tone when introduced, then turned his back on Valerius and the centurion. He yelled at one of the marines, "Junius, get your ass over here."

The man put down a coiled rope and sauntered over. "Yes, Captain."

"Yes, Captain, my ass. Now show this new tribune his quarters. He'll be traveling with us. His bunk is the one on the starboard side near the poop deck. You know the one I'm talking about."

"Sure thing, Captain. Right away."

The captain then abruptly turned and walked toward the bow of the ship. Valerius hadn't expected a warm welcome from the navy, but the captain's behavior was extremely rude. The tribune looked to the centurion for guidance.

In response, the centurion just shrugged. "Navy people," he said. "Never did like them much."

Valerius accompanied the marine, Junius, down a tight and twisted passageway to deposit his luggage and gear in his quarters. The marine, while continuing forward, turned his head back toward Valerius.

"Tribune, don't mind the captain. He's a decent sort. He's just pissed about his assignment. He's not used to having his warship serve as—let me remember how the captain phrased it—*a fucking transport*. But you won't find a better man in battle than the captain."

The centurion snorted at the marine's description of the captain. "He doesn't like his orders, does he? What a shock. Isn't that a first in the Roman military? Everything always made so much sense to me. By Hades, I always loved every one of my assignments."

The centurion laughed at his own barbed humor.

The three men stood outside a small space and peered inside the dark interior. Valerius frowned at the cramped nature of his new living quarters.

The marine quipped, "Not much, is it, sir?"

"I guess I was expecting something a little larger." Now he understood the centurion's offer to spend the night in the fort.

"Space is at a premium, sir. Even the captain's quarters aren't much bigger, but you'll get used to it."

Valerius stowed most of the gear he was carrying. The two men returned to the main deck. Valerius was curious and walked the length of the ship, accompanied by the marine. He noticed several areas on the planking of the deck where the wood was scored from a heavy weight.

"Catapults, sir."

Valerius looked back blankly.

"Those gouges you were staring at are where the catapults were. At least that's where they used to be. They were stripped off the deck, as this is a transport mission with no threat of pirates. Me, I prefer to have those little beauties on the ship. You can never tell who you might run into out on the open waters."

Valerius grinned back weakly. "I believe I'd prefer they be aboard also."

Valerius and the centurion exited the ship avoiding the captain, then walked back to the garrison. It was now past dusk. The watch torches were being lit all along the quay, illuminating the dock and waters close to the shoreline.

The centurion ushered Valerius into a small room and then silently departed. His quarters were constructed of roughhewn timbers featuring a solitary cot. He coughed as his feet stirred a small pile of dust from the floor. He looked about for a closet or rack to hang his uniform and sword. There was nothing. To Hades with it, he thought. He piled his gear in a convenient corner and rummaged through his kit to find some food his mother had thoughtfully packed for him. He guessed he could go out and search for a spot to dine, but he was tired and would rather stay right where he was.

After consuming his meal of bread, cheese, and olives, he lit a small oil lamp and stretched out on his cot, his hands locked behind his head. He thought briefly of penning a quick note to Calpurnia but discarded that idea. He would have no time to have the letter posted in the morning. He would have to wait until he reached Germania. He just wanted it to be tomorrow so he could be on his way. Valerius spent the night tossing and turning on the lumpy mattress. He was too excited to sleep and couldn't get comfortable. When he did start to drift off, some strange noise would jolt him awake. He finally slept. It seemed but a short while until there was a loud rap on the door.

"Tribune, your ship awaits you." He didn't know who spoke those words through the closed door, but the voice was tinged with sarcasm. Valerius didn't care. He eagerly jumped out of bed and hastily made preparations for his departure. He hurried to the dock and boarded the ship. Valerius stood against the railing with a sense of excitement. He didn't have to wait long. The captain bellowed orders as the lines were cast off one by one. Valerius had heard his share of foul language, but the captain had perfected his to an art form. The sailors and marines who served the ship paid little heed to the vulgar outbursts and continued on with their duties.

Amid the shouting and controlled chaos as the ship readied to sail, Valerius spotted a familiar figure in a tribune's uniform like him. The man's corpulent form couldn't be hidden by the cloak he wore around his shoulders. His hair was dark and combed back on his rather wide head. He had thick lips and mean, dark eyes. It was T.

Castor Nominatus, his antagonist from the drill field two weeks ago. Don't tell me of all the tribunes in the Roman army, I'm stuck with this pompous ass. No doubt there existed continued enmity between the two tribunes as a result of the confrontation.

Valerius decided to be on good terms with Castor. Besides, he could use the company. It was going to be a long voyage.

"Castor," he hailed across the deck.

The man turned his head and stared at him frostily.

Valerius walked across the deck. "How are you, Castor?"

"Fine, I guess," he replied in a somewhat cold manner. Valerius frowned. He realized Castor must have seen him already but hadn't acknowledged his presence.

"I see you're off to Germania like me."

"Yes, I suppose so," he replied in a laconic tone. Valerius looked for him to continue. Instead he turned slightly and looked out to sea.

Let me give this one more try, thought Valerius. "What do you know about our commander in Germania, this Varus fellow?"

Castor replied, "Do you mean General Publius Quinctilius Varus? He's a personal friend of our family and a great Roman. I'm honored to serve under him."

At least Valerius understood the nature of Castor's posting to Germania now. The legate—in this case, General Varus—often personally selected the senatorial tribunes he wished to serve under him. It was obvious that Castor's family and that of Varus were on close terms. Valerius, on the other hand, had no such connections. He was assigned there due to necessity.

Excuse me all to Hades, thought Valerius. This guy was definitely a pretentious asshole, but given his powerful connections, Valerius decided not to retort with some offending remark.

"I sure hope we have a smooth voyage. I'll see you later when we get out to sea."

Valerius turned, then walked away to the starboard side. So much for camaraderie. He leaned on the rail of the deck, holding back his anger. Valerius raised his eyes to the heavens and asked once again, why Castor? This long voyage had just gotten a lot longer.

All of the lines securing the ship were cast away, and, with a single command, the oars dipped into the waters and the ship slowly slipped away from the dock. In no time, they were out of the harbor and sailing swiftly through the calm seas. Valerius reveled in the refreshing breeze and the bright sunshine. The air was crisp and clean. The vast openness of the sea exhilarated Valerius. He went to the bow of the ship and stared at the blue sea, which was sparkling with the reflection of the bright morning sun. Seabirds chased the ship out of port with a cacophony of cries. It was on to Germania.

V

The eighty men of the training century gathered at midmorning in a loose semicircle on the parade ground to observe today's training demonstration. They had already completed their close-order drill. On this warm spring day, the recruits would begin their weapons training. The men had been had issued their swords, javelins, and daggers upon arrival at the base, but they had little idea how to use them.

"Let's move in a little closer." Centurion Longinius motioned with both arms for the group to edge closer. "Come on, closer. We don't have all day. Time's a wasting."

Lucius edged forward and frowned in annoyance as his helmet started to slide down his forehead. He quickly snapped the headgear back in place, silently cursing the centurion under his breath. Earlier this morning, the centurion had made a surprise inspection. He had flung Lucius's helmet across his room, apparently not pleased at its cleanliness. In doing so, he'd disturbed the cotton liner that had had been adjusted perfectly to fit Lucius's head. Now it was loose and wouldn't stay properly in place.

The sun blazed in the clear sky, baking the assembled men attired in their heavy chain mail lorica, helmets, shields, and their sheathed swords. Why was it always hot when they were in full armor? Was it possible the gods were in conspiracy with Centurion Longinius? The centurion motioned to a stranger standing off to the side to join him.

"We're fortunate today to have perhaps the finest weapons instructor in the legions, bar none, to instruct you how to fight like a Roman soldier. Let me introduce to you an old comrade of mine who'll teach you how to use the gladius properly. You'll give this man your undivided attention. Show him the same respect you do me. Understood?"

"YES, CENTURION."

"Good. Centurion Cluvius, they're all yours."

A short man outfitted in a leather muscle cuirass and no helmet approached. He had gray hair cut close to his scalp. His face, browned by the sun, had several noticeable scars of white, ridged tissue crisscrossing his countenance. He appeared fit and trim despite his advanced years. He smiled at them, appearing kindly, like someone's uncle. This was not to confuse Centurion Cluvius with being soft. The man had an air about him that suggested he was one tough customer who could be counted upon in a fight. He was just not the menacing type like Longinius.

"All right, lads, gather a little closer. Come on, close it on me so you can all see."

He drew his sword from its scabbard and held it up at chest level.

"This is the Roman gladius, the finest fighting weapon of any army. You all have one that's just like this one. I'll teach you how to use it."

Centurion Cluvius paraded slowly back and forth in front of the men, holding up the sword for them to examine.

"Notice that it's about two feet long, but that's all you'll need."

He returned to the center of the group. All eyes of the eighty men were riveted on the man.

"Follow me, if you please."

He turned and walked a short distance to a wooden post upon which was affixed a human form stuffed with straw. The mass of men dutifully followed after him like a herd of cattle.

"Can everyone observe me?" The recruits nodded in silent affirmation. "Good. Here we go."

Cluvius borrowed a man's shield. He fitted it to his left arm. He flexed his shield arm with a few quick motions as if the heavy shield was a feather, then stopped, satisfied with the balance of it.

"Now then, the first action you must take in combat is to thrust forward with your shield. Your shield is a weapon to be used in conjunction with your sword. Aim the metal boss on your shield at the center of your opponent's face. This will get his attention in a hurry."

There was nervous laughter among the men. Centurion Cluvius proceeded to savagely smash the shield quickly into the straw dummy with surprising force.

"Like that." He then repeated the technique with equal might.

"Observe how I step forward with my left leg for greater power. I use my entire body, not just my arms." He crunched the straw dummy again. The entire pole shook from the force, and straw flew out of the dummy figure.

"Note that my shield is just below eye level so that it protects my throat. You let your enemy get at your neck with a sword or spear, it will ruin your whole day. There's no armor there to protect you. Don't position your shield too high or you won't be able to see above the rim, but always keep it near eye level, not way down here."

To demonstrate, he dropped the shield to below the midchest area. "Now listen closely. One of the signs you're getting tired during combat is having your shield dip down below your face level. So always remind yourselves when your arm feels tired, how high is my shield, and is it where it should be? Keep that in mind. It might save your life someday. Now, after you lead with the shield, your enemy will be off balance. This is your opportunity. The second movement will be a thrust at the belly with the sword. Like this."

The centurion smashed the shield, then in a blur delivered a straight, low thrust at the straw figure. The blade exited out the dummy's back.

"Now, listen up. When you stab a man in the guts, you don't want your sword to get stuck in him, or you will end up with a similar fate.

So this is what you do. When withdrawing the sword, you twist the blade, either right or left. This serves two purposes. First, it inflicts maximum damage and ensures a quick kill. Second, it will free the blade from any bone or contracted muscles. Got it?"

He continued.

"Again, it's one." He smashed the shield at the figure. "And two." He stabbed the straw form.

"Now, if your opponent is protecting his belly, the secondary target is the throat, and if that doesn't work, go for the groin or the unprotected legs." He pointed to the straw dummy. "Here, here, and here are the spots." He touched them each with the menacing tip of the sword.

"Don't stab at the side. You'll just bounce the blade off the man's ribs, then he'll really be pissed at you. Try not to slash with this weapon. It's tiring. It also exposes your entire side when you raise the weapon above your head. Look at me in this position. Notice how my entire right side is exposed when I raise my sword above my head. I'm now off balance and subject to being knocked down. Also, when you slash, it is not necessarily a killing blow. When you stab a man, he is done. Remember, lead with the shield, then thrust with the sword. Questions, anyone?" The group was silent. "Good. Now let me see what you can do."

Each squad lined up behind one of the ten posts with straw dummies. Lucius stood before the post, shield at the ready, sword in hand. He approached the post and straw figure. Centurion Cluvius shouted out the commands.

"ONE."

Lucius smashed the shield heavily into the figure and felt the post rattle from the impact.

"TWO."

He thrust the sword savagely through the straw bowels.

"Excellent, men. Let's do it again. ONE." There was the sound of ten shields impacting. "TWO. I want strong, crisp blows with those shields, and stab hard. Remember, use your whole body when you lead with the shield. Again, ONE and TWO."

Each time Lucius slammed his shield into the post, his helmet slid forward, forcing him to move his headgear back in position with his sword arm. With every repetition, he became more annoyed. He vented his frustration on the straw figure. He smashed the post, then twisted his shield for extra destructive power. Straw flew everywhere as he continued to pound the figure. Finally, his group was told to stand down. In front of Lucius, parts of the straw dummy littered the ground.

Centurion Longinius walked by Lucius's position and stopped. He stared in silence at the remains of the figure, then back at Lucius. Lucius nervously waited for an explosion of anger. He warily eyed the vitis with which the centurion rhythmically tapped his leg, waiting for its swift descent upon his arms and back. Shockingly, the centurion smiled at him.

"Good show, Seventeen. That's the spirit. Now pick up that straw and stuff it back in there. We need the next man to have a go at this. Savvy, Number Seventeen?"

"Of course, Centurion." Lucius hurriedly stuffed the straw back, relieved he wasn't in the poor graces of Longinius, and returned to the back of the line.

The eighty men of the century took turns slaying the straw dummies under the watchful eyes of the cadre and Centurion Cluvius. Lucius stood in the shade, massaging his left arm, which held the shield. He could see a bruise forming under the skin from the repeated smashing of the shield against the post. He noted others performing similar ministrations to their black-and-blue flesh. Lucius took off his helmet, which was a forbidden act. He fumbled hopelessly with the liner. He glanced about to see if his transgression had been detected, then quickly put it back on his head. It slid back down on his forehead, obscuring his vision once again. "Stercus."

Cluvius gathered the men in again. He stared silently at the group for a moment.

"I'll now show you how to maneuver against your opponent. The most important thing is to maintain the proper balance at all times. Remember, your enemy is going to attempt to get you off balance so he can skewer you. We will not let that happen." He smiled encouragingly at the men.

Once again Cluvius walked over to the straw figure. He adopted a fighting stance with the sword and shield.

"When you maneuver to the left or right of your opponent, always maintain good balance. Make sure you keep your knees flexed, then slide your feet in the direction you want to go. Be braced for impact at all times. Like this. Notice I always maintain a wide stance for good balance."

Cluvius proceeded to hop with agility around the straw figure with quick, short steps, thrusting with the shield and the sword. Lucius was surprised at how nimble the centurion was for his age. He was like a cat. His thrusts were quick and violent. Cluvius had the men go through the same type of footwork. Lucius tried to emulate what Centurion Cluvius had done. He felt awkward as he shifted to the left and right. He attempted to move quicker and was rewarded with a stumble as his feet actually collided with each other. His actions didn't go undetected. Cluvius spotted him.

"You there, Number Seventeen, not so fast. Slow it down a little; your feet are getting ahead of your body. This is not a skill you acquire overnight."

Hours later, after numerous repetitions of the sword drill, Centurion Cluvius gathered the men around him in a loose semicircle for the next phase of instruction. He held a javelin, which he hefted and twirled about.

"Very good, men. Now, for your other weapon—and I'm not talking about the one in your tunic.

"This is the pilum." He held up the javelin for all to see. "This weapon will penetrate most armor at short range and will go through shields. The accurate range on these is about twenty-five to forty yards. This is what we soften the enemy up with before we have at them with the sword."

He suddenly pivoted and winged the missile at one of the straw dummies. The conscripts gasped in unison as the javelin went halfway through the target. He grinned back at them.

"That's how you throw these. I'll have your cadre demonstrate the proper technique for you." Cluvius nodded as a signal to the two cadre.

Both Allius and Terrentius were walking forward in a slight crouch, with shields sheltering their bodies toward the targets. The angled pilums were in their right hands, and the shields in the left.

The centurion explained, "Notice how they're fully protected by their shield at all times as they approach. The only vulnerable spots are the head and legs. They can shift the shield up or down as needed to deflect any objects hurled toward them. This is known as *tactical marching steps*. It is purely a defensive posture before the release of the pilum."

He issued the command, "JAVELINS UP." Both men brought the javelins up to a cocked position, with the right arms holding the javelins behind their heads. They proceeded forward, their shields protecting their bodies.

He continued. "Notice they don't anticipate the command. It could be several steps before the release command is issued."

The two legionnaires advanced with their arms cocked in the throwing position.

"They'll step forward with the left leg and shift the weight to that leg with the release. After the throw, they'll immediately draw their gladii. The reason for haste in the sword draw is simple. The effective range of the javelin is about twenty-five to forty long strides. Once the javelin is released, you are fairly close to the enemy lines. You must advance rapidly toward the enemy to take advantage of the havoc wreaked by the javelins. If the adversary has decided to charge or was already advancing, there is no time to spare for the sword draw. Any fumbling could have fatal consequences. If you can't have your sword ready almost immediately, you might as well have your dick in your hand for all the good it will do you.

"RELEASE."

With that, both legionnaires threw their *pila* at the straw targets, about twenty-five yards away. The javelins struck the targets, penetrating deeply. Their movement appeared so smooth and coordinated, almost appearing effortless. The two men promptly drew their swords and advanced.

Cluvius stood in front of the recruits. "Gentlemen, this is not difficult. I want of each of you to go to the rack of javelins," he gestured with his arm toward its location, "and select one." They are all about the same, so do not tarry. Just pick one."

Lucius selected a pilum from the rack and examined it. The wooden shaft was smooth and cylindrical in shape. It fit perfectly into his hand. The wood had a slightly oily feel to it, but not so that it was slippery. Lucius held the spear up to eye level and looked down the length of the shaft. It was straight and true. The pyramidal-shaped point was barbed and razor sharp. Lucius rolled his thumb along the edge of the tip. He was rewarded with a scarlet streak along his skin. He quickly drew his hand away.

They would be hurling their javelins from about twenty paces today. The objective of the training drill was simple. One eight-man squad at a time would approach on line in good order, in a slight crouch with the shield protecting the body, and then hurl the javelins at the targets on command. Centurion Cluvius and Centurion Longinius would observe the throws.

There was a subtle art to throwing the pilum. The weight was heavily loaded to the front end for greater penetration. One needed to compensate for this by adjusting the aim at a level higher than the expected point of impact. The first squad approached the targets, then released their pila. Most of the missiles went into the dirt, short of the intended target. Even though he had turned the training over to Cluvius, Centurion Longinius couldn't contain himself.

"What in Hades do you call those throws? A girl could throw better. What are you trying to kill, snakes?" Not satisfied with his outburst, the centurion picked up the javelin and proceeded to beat one of the unlucky conscripts about the body with the shaft.

"We're going to stay here all day and night if necessary until you girls learn to throw these things. NEXT!"

Longinius looked over to Cluvius and shrugged as if to apologize for interrupting the training. Cluvius grinned back at him.

Lucius's contubernium was stretched in a line, each man about five yards apart. Lucius and the members of his squad were all facing wooden posts to which were attached the straw dummies. Lucius nervously shifted the heavy shield back and forth. Cluvius stepped forward in front of the group. Lucius wisely stopped his fidgeting and became still. The others did likewise.

Cluvius bellowed his instructions.

"At my command, you'll advance toward the figures to your front in good order using the tactical marching steps. Remember what I said about having your shield covering as much of your body as possible. You should be in a slight crouch so that the shield covers most of you. In battle situations, there will be all kinds of shit coming at you. It could be rocks, javelins, darts, or arrows. The concept is simple. Let the shield take these blows, not you. At my command, you'll hurl your javelins toward the straw men and immediately draw your swords. Is that clear?"

"Yes, Centurion," the group shouted.

"ADVANCE."

Lucius proceeded forward in short, choppy steps as instructed. He stayed in a slight crouch so that his four-foot-long shield protected his body from chin to knees. At the same time, he glanced to his right and left to make sure he was in line with the rest of his squad and observed with some satisfaction that he was perfectly in line.

Cassius was to his left, moving at the same pace. The idea was not to be ahead or behind the rest of the line. Lucius was anxious and didn't want to make a mistake. He again eyed his position in the line. So far, so good.

"Not so fast. Slow it down. This is not a friggin' race," yelled Cluvius.

The recruits were spaced far enough apart laterally so they could heave their javelins without impeding one another in the act of throwing. Their pilums rested in their right hands, with the pointed ends angled forward at a diagonal fashion close to forty-five degrees. The only sound was the thump of their iron-clad sandals striking the compacted ground. Puffs of dust arose from the sunbaked earth. They advanced closer.

At about twenty-five yards away, the command was given to throw the javelins.

"JAVELINS UP."

Lucius drew the pilum back in his right arm. He stretched his arm back as far as he could. He could feel his muscles pulling as he cocked his arm.

"RELEASE."

Lucius heaved it toward the straw figure. This might seem an easy enough task, but it is more difficult with twenty pounds of armored mail and a bulky shield in the left arm. Lucius winged the missile. He was satisfied that he had good velocity with his throw. His whole right arm seemed to hum after the release. He followed the javelin's path. It barely missed the target at about chest height. He was now behind the others and had yet to draw his sword. To compound his mistake, Lucius fumbled with his sword and fell even farther behind his squad.

"RAPID ADVANCE," thundered the centurion. With that, the eight men roared and rushed forward in unison rapidly toward the enemy of straw.

Lucius knew he'd erred and wanted to make amends. He savagely smashed his shield with extra force into the wooden frame of the figure so that his left arm became numb with the force of the blow. The wooden structure reverberated from the shock. Lucius didn't want to disappoint the centurion. He thrust his gladius toward the straw foe.

"BACK!" Cluvius bellowed out staccato instructions to the recruits as they attacked the figures.

"FORWARD. You're lunging too far with the thrust. Remember, your right arm is exposed to the enemy the entire time you're stabbing forward. The thrust needs to be quick.

"NOW FORWARD." There was the sound of eight shields striking the posts in unison.

"Short thrust. Let's hear some spirit from you. I want to hear some killing yells."

Lucius screamed, "AAAARG," as he thrust toward the post.

"BACK!

"Now back again. Shield forward. Now thrust.

"STOP. MANEUVER RIGHT."

Lucius shifted to his right, always maintaining his balance and ensuring the shield covered his body at all times. He quickly thrust at the straw figure.

"MANEUVER LEFT."

Lucius slid to his left, repeating the drill with his sword thrust.

"HALT."

The recruits immediately ceased.

"Third squad, over here on me." Cluvius brusquely waved them over. He began his critique.

"First, your approach was fine for the first twenty-five yards. You advanced forward in good order, with adequate spacing and on line. After that, everything turned to shit in a hurry. When many of you threw your javelins, you either lowered your shield or turned it sideways. This will get you killed quickly. You open yourself to incoming missiles from the enemy. Keep the shield in front of you for maximum protection at all times."

The centurion paused, then continued.

"Next, I told you not to stop and admire your throw but to immediately draw your sword. Some of you followed the flight of your javelin. Don't look. Draw your sword. By the way, most of those throws were putrid. Last, your sword thrusts are too slow. You're exposed to attack when your arm is extended. It must be a quick thrust. Remember to stab at the belly. If you hit the chest or ribs, it'll glance off, and you'll be open for attack. If you're not successful, go for the throat. You must be quick and decisive when you move in any direction. Back in line.

"NEXT GROUP, ADVANCE."

Days later, they stood in formation in the weapons training area. Cluvius was now gone, and it was back to the usual. Centurion Longinius was speaking.

"We have a new drill. You've trained with your weapons. There's much more to be learned, but you know the basics. Today, we'll have our first individual mock combat, the *armatura*. You won't be fighting straw dummies on wooden posts, but each other. We'll pair individuals from the squads against each other. I want to hear you cheering for your squad mates as they face off against their opponents. Let's begin."

Lucius and his third squad were pitted against the fourth. The century would have three individual combats at one time, with the cadre acting as referees. Lucius was to be fourth in his squad for the combat. They were armed with the wooden training swords, which had leather buttons placed on the wooden tips, and the heavy wooden training shields. Antonius was the first of his squad to fight. He appeared evenly matched with his opponent from the fourth squad. Both men were a little tentative, unsure of what to do. The centurion let them know in a hurry.

"What are you two doing? Taking a stroll in the countryside? Is this what we have been drilling into your thick skulls the last two weeks? Get after each other now."

That got them moving. The two men hacked and stabbed at each other in a frenzy. Both participants were totally exhausted but continued to attack each other, too afraid of the centurion to even pause briefly. Finally, the centurion stepped in and declared it a draw. Lucius nervously fidgeted with the grip of the wooden gladius. He attempted to remember the lessons he'd been taught about the basics of sword fighting—maintain good balance at all times, no long thrusts exposing your arm and side, use the shield as a battering ram to knock your foe down for the kill.

Domitius was next. He was the slightest built of the squad and clearly overmatched against a much heavier and stronger man. In little time, he was lying in the dirt after being struck several times with the wooden gladius. He hugged his abdomen and rolled on the ground, gritting his teeth against the pain. The centurion, with a wolfish smile, held up the arm of the winner directly over the fallen Domitius. There was no doubt his purpose was to humiliate the fallen conscript even more. Flavius was next. As the two men paired off, Flavius had a huge grin on his face. This drove the centurion berserk.

"You think this is funny, Number Twenty? That man is your enemy. Fight him. Kill him."

Flavius attempted to put on a serious face, but the grin appeared again. Above it all, Flavius had a natural talent as swordsman. He moved like lightning, and his footwork was agile and smooth. Lucius looked upon him with envy, wishing he could be so good. Flavius appeared to toy with his man, not wanting to hurt his opponent. This wasn't lost on the centurion, making him angrier.

"Number Twenty, this is not a game. You're a soldier trained to kill. Now get after him." Flavius fought almost nonchalantly, with a complete lack of aggression, before easily defeating his opponent. The centurion wasn't pleased. He gritted his teeth, casting Flavius a baleful stare. Flavius, unperturbed, flashed a grin to all as he walked back toward the squad. The centurion didn't offer to hold up the arm of the victorious Flavius.

The next thing Lucius knew, he was in the ring circling his opponent. The man facing him smirked at him in a mocking fashion. He was slightly shorter than Lucius but of sturdier physique. Lucius stared at the man, contemplating his first maneuver. He knew he had the advantage in terms of reach, but in a power match, his opponent would definitely prevail.

"ARE YOU TWO GOING TO DANCE OR FIGHT? STOP CIRCLING AND DO SOMETHING."

The centurion, still angry from the conduct of Flavius, scowled menacingly at the combatants.

The man charged at Lucius and delivered a thrust at his legs. Lucius quickly blocked the blow, delivering a weak backhand slash that rattled harmlessly off the other man's shield.

"NUMBER Seventeen, THRUST; DON'T SLASH."

Now Lucius attacked. He smashed his shield into his opponent and thrust hard just as he'd been schooled, but his blow was blocked. Lucius followed with another charge. His opponent hastily retreated, stumbling in the process. Now was his chance; the entire left side of his adversary was wide open. Lucius lunged forward for the kill. His front foot hit a muddy patch in a small depression.

Despite his efforts, Lucius lost his balance and landed squarely on his back. He was helpless. He attempted to roll away, but his opponent quickly took advantage. He was dispatched with a painful stab to his midsection. The wooden swords were filled with lead to make them heavier. It was like being clubbed. Lucius pushed himself out of the mud, rubbing at the burning welt around his waist.

The centurion bellowed, his voice filled with scorn, "Number Seventeen, that was one of the worst displays of sword fighting I've ever seen and a sorry-ass exhibition of combat. You'd last about a heartbeat against the Germans. You won't get off that easy, Seventeen. You barely broke a sweat out there. I think I'll have you fight again. Next!"

Lucius was humiliated that he'd succumbed so easily. He stumbled back toward his squad. "Stercus," he exclaimed as he stood next to Cassius. Lucius looked at Cassius expectantly for some sort of solace, but he turned away.

His contubernium fared poorly against the competition. They had but two winners, Cassius and Flavius. The centurion was true to his word. After all the men in his squad had fought, Lucius was called out again.

"Number Seventeen, get your ass back out here. Don't think I forgot about you. You're fighting again, and you'll put on a good show this time."

Lucius was matched against the big man who had dispatched Domitius so quickly. His opponent was one of the few men who almost equaled Lucius in height, but he also had layers of muscles on his frame. His name was Marius. He was sculpted like a god. Lucius could hear the man's squad mates chanting his name.

"Marius, Marius, Marius."

As Lucius made his way to the combatant's circle, Cassius grabbed his forearm. "You can beat him, Lucius. You can do it."

Lucius appreciated the boost of confidence from Cassius, but he wasn't sure he would prevail against his opponent. Lucius appeared scrawny next to him. He guessed the centurion had selected this fellow because he had had such an easy time with Domitius. Marius appeared confident, and why not? He'd disposed of his opponent with little effort and noted how easily Lucius was defeated. He menacingly twirled his sword about in a show of bravado, no doubt eager to dispose of another adversary from the third squad.

Lucius eyed the man, wondering how he might possibly triumph. His previous opponent had certainly been less skilled than this man, yet he had lost badly. He tensed, readying for the command. The centurion gave the signal for the combat to begin.

With a rush, both men charged. There was a crash as the shields collided. They stabbed and slashed feverishly at each other. Marius advanced, thrusting hard at Lucius's groin. Lucius deftly slid to his right, avoiding the thrust, then stabbed at the man's neck. Marius blocked the blow with his shield, countering with a jab at the lower left leg of Lucius. The blow was barely deflected in time. Lucius charged, stabbing at his opponent's right side with a lightning thrust. Marius retreated swiftly.

"Marius, Marius, Marius."

There was a slight lull as the two men warily eyed each other, circling cautiously while looking for an opening. His foe took the initiative and charged. Lucius sidestepped the advance, delivering a whistling blow at Marius's head, barely missing. Then he counter-rushed the man, but too late to gain any advantage. Marius was quickly in a perfect defensive posture. Lucius delivered a hard blow at the man's side, but Marius threw his shield up in time. There was a loud crack as the wooden sword smashed harmlessly against the shield.

Marius circled guardedly, his sword pointed at Lucius. His arrogant grin was replaced by one of grim determination. The two men breathed heavily. They eyed each other, waiting for the next move. Before the centurion could yell for them to get at it, the two charged at each other. The shields crashed together. Lucius was almost knocked over by the force of the collision. He barely managed to regain his footing. He retreated to his left rapidly, adopting a defensive posture, ready for the next assault. "Marius, Marius, Marius."

The combat ebbed and flowed with no one able to deliver a thrust or slash that would be considered disabling. The advantage shifted with each charge and counter-rush. By now, all of the other squads had finished. Everyone from the cadre to the last pair of combatants was witnessing the savage duel. The two men repeatedly stabbed and hacked at each other. The blows were punctuated by grunts as each took aim at the other. The battle intensified, with neither opponent letting up.

"Marius, Marius, Marius."

Lucius shifted guardedly to his left, panting heavily. He slowed his movements, then edged to his right. His arms ached terribly from holding the shield and wielding the heavy wooden training sword. Gauging his opponent, Marius was in a similar state. Lucius felt the sweat running down his forehead, burning his eyes. Both men again circled, each trying to find a weakness.

The entire century was screaming encouragement, replacing the annoying Marius chant. He dared not acknowledge their shouts lest he let his concentration wane even for a moment. He noted that his shield had dropped to almost chest level, leaving his head exposed to attack. Centurion Cluvius had drilled them over and over to keep the shield up. Lucius observed his opponent had dropped his shield below chin level. It was time to end this. In a sudden gambit, Lucius feinted with a thrust to the lower leg. Marius lowered his shield to protect his leg. Lucius issued a wild cry and swung his sword at the man's head. Even Lucius was surprised with the swordplay. He had no idea where the clever maneuver had emanated from; it just happened spontaneously. It wasn't part of the sword routines that had been part of their instruction. Unfortunately for Lucius, Marius brought his shield to blunt the feint at his midsection, then stumbled downward, ducking his head, partially avoiding the blow. It was lucky for him. The strike would have knocked him silly even with the protective helmet. Some of the sword strike impacted Marius's head, forcing him back on wobbly legs. The centurion judged it not to be a killing blow and let the combat continue.

"Good move, Seventeen. You almost had him," bellowed Longinius.

The entire century was in an uproar over the sword maneuver; this was a fight. Both men charged, then separated, staring at each other, huffing for air. Marius rushed once more, but Lucius deflected the blow, stepping to the side. The entire left flank was exposed. This was it. Lucius aimed a clumsy thrust, missing badly. His arms and legs were like rubber. Under ordinary circumstances, it would have been an easy kill.

"You had him, Seventeen, and you let him get away."

Lucius barely heard the stinging rebuke. It took all his energy and concentration to maintain his fighting position. Bellowing, Lucius again charged. They collided, careening off of each other in different directions. The two swayed unsteadily back to the ready position, facing each other. The bout had lasted over four times the other combats.

"STOP."

The centurion walked between the two men, halting the combat. He held up the arms of both men, signaling a draw.

"By Jupiter, that's the way to fight. I hope you all watched these two combatants. Both of these men have the spirit and determination of Roman legionnaires. I want you all to fight like they did. They were tenacious out there." He stared at Flavius as he spoke, letting him know he hadn't forgotten.

The century broke for the midday meal. The squad congratulated Lucius. He was tired but felt redeemed. He walked over to Marius. They tapped each other's fists to show respect and there were no hard feelings. Lucius removed his helmet and wiped his forehead. He walked with Cassius over to the serving line for lunch.

Over the next week, they drilled, then drilled some more. If they weren't doing the century battle formations, they were performing individual sword drills with the wooden posts, always under the watchful eyes of the centurion and the cadre. They missed nothing. The slightest flaw in technique was corrected. The gods have mercy on the conscript who didn't give his full measure. Total effort was demanded from every man and at all times.

The recruits stood in formation on the parade ground. The centurion addressed them.

"Today we're going to further test the skills we've been teaching you over the past several weeks. We're going to have a mock combat exercise against a real opponent, not a bunch of wooden posts with straw figures or your own comrades. You'll get a chance to demonstrate what you've learned against a real enemy."

Lucius, like everyone else, was getting that queasy feeling in his stomach. Knowing the centurion, this had to be something nasty. The facial expressions of his fellow soldiers reflected the same apprehension.

The centurion continued. "Since you're going to Germania, we've assembled a small army about the same in number as you, equipped like Germans, and they'll fight like Germans."

The centurion pointed with his vitis at a group of men assembled in the distance.

"I expect they'll be no match for you because I've trained you to fight like Roman legionnaires. Don't disappoint me. Just remember that these are not wooden posts. They fight back." He laughed maniacally at his own humor.

"Oh, and by the way. Those people over there," he said, pointing with his staff off to the side at a group of men clad in gray tunics, "are medical orderlies in case someone gets hurt."

Legionnaires Allius and Terrentius rushed forward, each with a large bucket of a thick, white liquid. They went through each of the ranks and dabbed the white substance on the wooden swords and javelins of the recruits. The liquid was applied liberally to all of the training weapons. The men looked at one another with puzzled expressions.

A group of brutish-looking thugs proceeded forward to within a hundred paces. Many were sporting long hair and beards. Unlike the recruits, they had no body armor. They were equipped with small oval shields made of animal hides. They carried an assortment of wooden swords, clubs, and spears. A few had bags of rocks tied around their waists. The men were all different sizes and shapes, some large and powerful. Lucius could only guess where they got these dregs. Most were probably slaves who had been promised a few *denarii* to fight the recruits. Lucius surmised that these people probably didn't have happy lives and wouldn't mind beating up on some prospective legionnaires.

Allius and Terrentius finished their task, then went to the opposing force with their buckets of white dye. The centurion spoke to the recruits, pointing with his staff in the direction of the opposition.

"That's your enemy. You'll attack in formation as you've been drilled. The rules are simple. This century will advance on the foe within the area marked by the row of stakes you see to the right and left of you. No one from either force is permitted outside of these stakes. Anyone with white dye on a vulnerable part of his body will be considered a kill and out of the combat. Terrentius and I will be the judges of the casualties. Allius will be your acting centurion. If we deem you to be a kill, you'll go outside of the stakes and cease combat. Oh, one more thing: try not to disappoint me. I don't want to see a bunch of grown men pussyfooting about, just going through the motions. Those men over there are going to try to hurt you. Be aggressive. Show them no mercy."

Lucius stared ahead at the collection of miscreants, wondering what swamp they had dredged this bunch out of. The boundary stakes on either side looked to be about seventy-five yards apart. Lucius was praying he wouldn't be in the front ranks. This hope was quickly dashed. The first five squads were placed in front, with the remaining five in the second rank. Why was he always up front? Cassius was standing to his right. "Are you ready for this shit, Lucius?"

"I guess."

"We'll protect each other. Stay next to me."

Lucius nodded silently and swallowed the large lump now in his throat.

They assembled into their formation. The jeers and shouts started from the army of thugs opposing them. Allius and Terrentius finished the process with the white dye on the opposing force. Lucius felt a brief sense of panic envelop him like a thick cloud that wouldn't leave.

He turned about to view his fellow recruits. Judging by the other pale faces, Lucius sensed they were experiencing the same feeling. Lucius remembered the mantra of their centurion. He'd repeated it over and over: *Don't talk. Stare straight ahead at the enemy. Don't panic; you have nowhere to run anyway. Remember, you have comrades to either side and behind you to protect you. Above all, you're a member of the Roman Legions, the finest army in the known world, and it's rarely, if ever, defeated.*

Legionnaire Allius led them forward from the extreme right front of the formation. Centurion Rufus Longinius and Legionnaire Terrentius were over with the opposing force.

"TACTCAL MARCH, FORWARD."

The two ranks of legionnaires advanced in short, choppy steps, presenting a wall of shields. To Lucius, it seemed to take an eternity to approach within striking distance. As he got nearer, peering above the upped edge of his shield, he could make out more of their features.

They were truly an ugly-looking bunch. Their hair was ragged, and their clothes were dirty. They seemed to have no organization or leader. Some were screaming insults at the legionnaires.

They edged closer to pilum range. Lucius's anxiety seemed to heighten. He was thankful that he'd not yet eaten today, for surely that would be on the parade ground now. At about forty yards distance, the army of thugs began throwing rocks. Several of the missiles clattered harmlessly off Lucius's shield. He heard one or two screams of pain from within the ranks. Their boots thumped the earth solidly in unison as the century flowed forward toward their enemy.

"STEADY."

At thirty-five yards, Allius gave the command.

"JAVELINS UP."

After several more steps, "RELEASE."

The wooden training pila descended. Many of the opposing group crouched, putting their smaller shields up to protect themselves. This was an effective defense, but eighty javelins at one time are a lot to avoid. Perhaps as many as ten found their mark.

Centurion Longinius and Terrentius quickly attempted to cull as many as possible of those who were struck out of the force before the real combat began. In some cases, this was quite easy. Even though they were using the training pilum with blunt wooden points, they could still deliver a painful blow. Several members of the opposing force were on the ground withering in pain.

With a roar, both sides charged at each other. A particularly ugly brute of considerable bulk, who was missing most of his teeth, confronted Lucius. The man screamed at the top of his lungs what he was about to do to him. Lucius couldn't fully understand all of what he was bellowing, but it had something to do with shoving his shield down his throat and out his ass.

The two men pressed close together, neither giving way. Lucius could smell the man's putrid breath. It was time for action. He led with his shield, thrusting it forward in a powerful movement to unbalance his foe. To his amazement, it actually worked. The brute in front of him stumbled back from the force of the collision. Lucius felt the shock of the impact all the way to his shoulder. His arm became slightly numb from the force of the blow. Lucius hesitated slightly, thus losing his brief advantage.

Not to be deterred, Lucius advanced relentlessly, delivering a series of blows with his shield, driving his opponent backward several paces. The swagger and bravado of his foe was replaced by fear. The man attempted a swing of his wooden sword at Lucius's head, but he quickly lifted his shield and easily deflected the blow.

With a tremendous thrust from his powerful legs, Lucius smashed his shield into the man, almost bowling him over. Lucius then delivered a remorseless, hard thrust into the exposed midsection, followed by a slash across the back. The unfortunate foe screamed in agony at the hard thrusts, his torso smeared with white paint. The man weakly crawled on all fours away from the fracas. Fortune was smiling on Lucius. The centurion observed the mock combat not six feet away.

"Good kill, Number Seventeen. It appears we've made a legionnaire out of you. Now go get another one."

The conscripts were still in a ragged line. It wasn't a classic tactical formation by any means, but for trainees, not bad. Lucius glanced to his right and saw Cassius engaged with a muscular fellow. He appeared to have had some military training based upon the way he handled himself and gripped his weapon. Lucius immediately charged into the man, blindsiding him. The man went heavily to the ground. Both Cassius and Lucius delivered several heavy blows, thus disposing of another enemy.

Cassius and Lucius were now in a frenzy. Screaming, they charged into the flank of the next antagonist, who was engaged one-on-one with Domitius. The combined force of Cassius and Lucius smashed him with their shields. The man went flying through the air and collapsed in a crumpled heap, unmoving. Lucius searched for his next target. He was surprised that he was actually enjoying himself. This was much more fun than close-order battle drill.

Other recruits repeated the feats of Lucius and Cassius. More gaps were created. The lines of the opposing force buckled rapidly. Emboldened by the success of the first wave of legionnaires, the men in the second rank were now eager to get into the action. The pent-up frustration of their training was coming out with a vengeance. The recruits swept over the retreating force.

They were out of control, becoming more savage in their thrusts and blows to the now-cowering hoard. Lucius and Cassius simply ran over another foe, smashing him to the ground, and then hammered him with blows from their wooden swords. The man howled in pain, but Lucius didn't care. Before he could advance farther, the centurion grabbed Lucius.

"THAT'S ENOUGH. IT IS FINISHED."

All along the line, the centurion and his two legionnaire assistants attempted to stop the forward assault. They seized recruits, bellowing to cease the fighting.

Lucius stopped and looked around. What remained of the opposing rabble fled in terror from the crazed legionnaires across the empty field. Lucius surveyed the area to his rear, noting the crumpled heaps of bodies barely moving in the dust. He didn't see one legionnaire among them. He noted huge grins on the faces of Centurion Longinius and both Allius and Terrentius. The centurion raised his arm high in the air and spoke. "Recruits, on me."

The group quickly trotted over and gathered in a semicircle around the centurion. There were a few noticeable injuries, including some facial gashes and some arms and legs that appeared to have some minor damage. For the most part, the century appeared relatively unscathed. Their foes had fared poorly. Medical personnel and other staff were tending to several prone bodies.

The centurion began: "It appears we've made legionnaires of you after all. In my many years of training recruits for the legions, that was the best exhibition of fighting I've ever witnessed. The discipline was superb. You rolled over that group of riffraff and exploited their weakness. By Jupiter, I'm proud of this group."

The conscripts were in shock. They had never heard the centurion issue compliments to the century. Every man was wearing a wide grin from ear to ear.

The centurion continued. "Tonight, I'll have double wine rations for every man, and you'll feast. Tomorrow, you're off from training for the entire day. Dismissed!"

With a shout of joy, the group disbanded and headed toward the barracks.

The next day was a needed respite. Now on their own free time, Lucius and Cassius went into the small village near the fort, purchased a container of wine, and headed for the river to relax. Under a large, shady tree on the banks of the river, they lay back on the cool grass and enjoyed their freedom. They passed the wineskin back and forth, laughing and chatting about their experiences.

Lucius, who was getting a little drunk from the wine, decided to relay his story about his visit to the sibyl.

"Cassius, I don't believe this sorceress foretold my future. She says to me, 'Lucius, you'll be going on a journey far from home and be among strangers.' Next thing I know, I'm in front of the centurion with the rest of you sorry bastards soon to be headed for Germania."

Lucius paced in front of Cassius and waved his arms in animation. "I don't believe in that shit. I'm not superstitious. But this woman was so damn accurate about what happened. Then she tells me I'll meet a woman who'll capture my heart."

"Doesn't sound so bad," said Cassius.

Lucius didn't even pause. "The worst part was she lied to me at the end. She gets this look like I don't know what. The woman appeared scared. I get chills just thinking about it. I guess every man has his ordained fate, but no bloody witch can foretell that future."

"Lucius, so she got lucky about this going-away thing. She guessed right. What about her other prophecies? Have you met the woman who'll capture your heart? I don't think so. None of us have even seen a woman except for that innkeeper's wife who sold us the wine. I don't think that hag would be your choice. She wouldn't be mine; that's for sure."

Lucius couldn't help but laugh. Indeed, the woman at the inn was quite ugly.

"Look at the bright side. You've endured the rigors of the training of a legionnaire like all of us. True, it hasn't been fun, but what about the friends you've made? You wouldn't have met me, Flavius, Domitius, or any of the others. Am I right?"

Lucius responded, "You're right, I've made great friends. I just feel so unsettled about this life in the army. I never dreamed I'd miss my old life so much. When will I ever see my family again? And what about Germania?"

"What about it?" intoned Cassius.

"The reports we've heard aren't exactly encouraging. I don't even know how far away the infernal place is," said Lucius.

Cassius responded, "Lucius, you're starting to whine about all of this."

"I wasn't—"

"Yes, you were. You have to be a little more positive. Listen up, my friend. It can't be that bad. Think of it as an adventure. I hear most of our journey will be by boat. We'll sail west downriver to the sea and from there, north. Have you ever seen the large sea?"

"No, I obviously haven't."

"And you probably never would have. Here you go, Lucius. This could be fun."

Cassius continued. "Besides, do you think we're going to spend our whole career in Germania? Once they see our talents, it's straight to the

Praetorian Guard in Rome. Can you imagine us marching in Rome? I heard they have many people who live in the city, with great buildings made of stone. The rich live in palaces of unbelievable size. Maybe we could be guarding the emperor. Lucius, it's you, me, and the emperor. I can see it now. I'll bet the sibyl didn't foresee that possibility."

"Pass me the wine, Cassius. You've obviously had too much."

"I'm telling you, Lucius, this is going to be much better than you thought. Stop the gloom-and-doom shit."

Several weeks later, the entire century was gathered in the armory, with its vaulted ceiling and stores of weapons. On their right side were wooden racks filled with javelins. On the surrounding walls were pegs on which shields were hung. To their left were rows of swords and daggers. Mounted torches blazed away to provide light in the windowless building. The place smelled of oiled metal and fresh-cut wood. This wasn't their usual place of assembly, but then again, this wasn't a normal, everyday event. Tonight was something special.

There was a large open space in the center of the armory, where they stood in a tight formation. In front of them was Centurion Longinius. The torchlight flickered on the walls, illuminating the faces of the men. Amazingly, all eighty men had completed their training without any losses. The empire had selected satisfactorily. It wasn't surprising. The legions liked their men big and strong. This was why the legions did most of their recruiting from the small towns in the countryside, where men were accustomed to hard, physical work. Rarely did the legions venture into the big cities for their soldiers, especially Rome.

Centurion Longinius addressed them. "Legionnaires, you've performed well. You're about to take the sacramentum. It's an oath you may never undo and must always uphold. It's a sacred oath that you'll be swearing on your life. There's no more hallowed vow in the empire than the sacramentum."

The men grinned openly. They understood immediately that they'd achieved a new measure of respect. They had never been addressed as legionnaires before. It had always been "conscripts" or something more demeaning.

The centurion continued. "I'll administer the oath to the first man in the first squad. He'll repeat the oath. As I stand in front of you, each of you will individually repeat the words *idem in me* (the same for me) while raising your right hand with the palm open."

The centurion stood before the first man in the first squad. "Raise your right hand with your palm open. Now repeat after me."

"I WILL SERVE THE EMPEROR AND HIS APPOINTED DELEGATES.

"I WILL OBEY ALL ORDERS.

"I RECOGNIZE THE SEVERE PUNISHMENT FOR DESERTION AND DISOBEDIENCE.

"I SWEAR ALLEGIANCE TO THE LEGIONS AND WILL DEFEND ROME UNTIL MY DEATH."

The centurion began the process of approaching each of the remaining seventy-nine men. As he stood in front of them, each man raised his right hand with an open palm and stated, "Idem in me." Lucius dutifully waited his turn, then the centurion was in front of him. Without a thought, he raised his right hand and repeated the fateful words. He was now truly a soldier of the legions.

When the centurion had finished with all of the men, he returned to the front of the formation.

"Congratulations. You're all officially legionnaires. You're no longer on your probationary period."

The men cheered. Lucius and Cassius beamed proudly at each other. All of the soldiers congratulated one another with back slaps and handshakes. The centurion held up his hand for silence.

"Listen up, Legionnaires. I'd like to say I'm proud of every man in this room. I know you dislike me. That's expected. I completed my training eighteen years ago. I still hate my training centurion. He was a son of a bitch."

This elicited a few chuckles from the men. The centurion chuckled, then continued in a somber tone.

"The training you received wasn't done out of malice, but of necessity. Being a soldier requires toughness, both mental and physical. The legion thrives on discipline. That's why we were so hard on you. As a legionnaire, you'll face great danger and tremendous physical hardship that will tax your last reserves. You must overcome whatever obstacles confront you. Your survival will depend upon it."

He paused before continuing.

"Tomorrow you'll receive your orders and travel money. You're going to Germania as replacements. This is no secret. I told you this the first day. You'll be assigned to the Seventeenth, Eighteenth, or Nineteenth Legions of the Army of the Northern Rhine. Your destination will be the summer encampment on the Weser River. This is the most northern outpost in Germania. There are no frontiers beyond where you're going."

The centurion stared at the newly sworn-in legionnaires for a moment before he continued.

"Soldiers, I don't envy you. These Germans are a nasty bunch and not to be trusted. Remember what we've taught you, and live. In the morning, you'll march with all of your gear under the direction of legionnaire Allius. Before you leave, you must verify your home address with the clerk in the building to my right. The legion will send a letter to your next of kin informing them you're now officially legionnaires and on your way to your assignment with the legions in northern Germania.

"Allius will be in command of your detachment and guide you overland on a short journey to the Loire River. There you'll embark on transport boats to the sea. You'll be given three gold denarii as traveling money. May you serve the legion well.

"DISMISSED."

VI

*V*alerius perched near the bow of the ship on the port side, gripping the handrail. The rigging hummed as the following wind caught the sails, thrusting the ship onward. The battering ram on the bow caught the slight chop on the water, sending the spray skyward. Valerius licked the salt from his lips, then wiped his face as another splash of sea water rained upon him. He shaded his eyes from the glint on the ocean surface with one hand, gazing ahead at the open sea.

The crew scampered about, securing lines and performing other assorted duties. The deck was filled with containers and pallets of all sizes tightly strapped down for the voyage. The tribune preferred topside, as his quarters below decks were more like a cage. There was barely room to stand up and so little area between the hammock and bulkhead. One could hardly turn around. He gleefully pictured Castor in similar quarters. Maybe that pompous ass might get hopelessly wedged between the bulkhead and the deck. Valerius laughed out loud, the sound of his mirth lost in the wind.

He had never sailed the open waters of the Mare Nostrum. His father had warned him of the bane of sea travelers, the sickness of the stomach. Now that the ship was under full sail, he was feeling terrific. Furthermore, his trepidation of his future assignment with the legions of the Rhine evaporated as the ship sliced through the waters.

It was as if the sea had cleansed his soul. So far, this tribune stuff was going pretty well—that is, with the exception of Castor. Why did I have to get that arrogant prick traveling with me and to the same province? Valerius inhaled the clean air. It was a good day to be alive. He would write to his tutor, Cato, and share his exhilaration. Perhaps he also had experienced this feeling.

His thoughts ventured to the commander of the garrison, General Publius Quinctilius Varus. What kind of man was he? Varus was the military governor, connected to the ruling family by way of marriage to the emperor's grandniece. He was formerly the governor of Syria. He knew that much about his future commander but little else. Valerius had never crossed paths with the man or met him socially. He must know his stuff, thought Valerius, or he wouldn't have been selected to rule over a turbulent province such as Germania. It was somewhat disconcerting that Valerius had little knowledge of his commanding officer. He ruminated briefly, wondering if other fresh tribunes had knowledge of their superiors.

The day passed quickly. After consuming an evening meal of salted pork and biscuits, Valerius remained up on deck to gaze at the stars. A single lantern hung near the stern of the ship, casting a faint glow. The main deck was deserted, with the exception of a few solitary crew. He could barely make out their silhouettes as they steered the vessel steadily onward. The ship's passage was silent with the exception of the creaking timbers.

To his rear, he could hear faint fragments of a muted conversation. Valerius was content to lean on the rail, observing the night skies. It was so peaceful. The heavens blazed a great deal brighter out on the open ocean, much more so than in Rome. Horizon to horizon was replete with shining stars. Regrettably, he was completely ignorant of even the basic knowledge of the positioning of the heavens.

His cogitations were interrupted as the captain abruptly sidled up next to him. "What's the matter, Tribune? Never seen the stars before?"

Valerius was taken aback that the captain was actually speaking to him. He assumed he was on the man's stercus list, along with the rest of the military cargo bound for Germania.

"Not like this. I never realized how many stars there were. I've heard that sailors navigate their ships by the movement of the stars. Can you tell me about them?" he said eagerly.

"Tribune, let's start with the most important, Ursa Major."

Valerius was silent.

"You've got to be shitting me, Tribune. You never heard of Ursa Major?"

Valerius grinned back sheepishly. "Actually, no."

"What in the Hades do they teach tribunes these days?"

"Let's see. I was tutored in oratory, mathematics, the classics, of course, and Roman law."

"That learning won't do you much good out here on the open sea, will it, Tribune?"

"I guess not."

"All right, Tribune, follow my arm. Now see that group of stars shaped like a great ladle? If you look at the bottom of the ladle..."

Valerius nodded.

"And follow the star to the top of the bucket and keep on going, that star above always points north. It's the one star that doesn't change position."

Valerius turned from his skyward gaze and faced the captain. "So as long as that's on our right side, we must be going west?"

"Very good, Tribune. You catch on quickly."

Valerius beamed back at the captain's compliment.

The captain continued his tutorial on the positions of the stars. He seemed pleased to share this knowledge with the tribune.

"Now, Tribune, follow my arm again. See those three in a row? Those are the belt of Orion, the hunter. Watch my arm as I trace the outline of his form."

"Captain, I do see it. By Jove, there it is, just as you said it was. Tell me more."

Valerius was an eager pupil, soaking up the captain's dissertations like a sponge. When the captain was finished, Valerius proudly pointed to the night skies, reciting to the captain the stars and constellations he'd learned. There were the scorpion, maiden, bear, fish, crab, and many others.

"Excellent, Tribune. You should have joined the navy. If you want, I'll see what I can do to have you posted on a good fighting ship."

Valerius laughed. "Thanks, but no thanks. I must confess I'm enjoying this voyage much more than I had imagined, but I've trained all my life to be a ground pounder in the legions, not a navy man."

"Are you sure, Tribune? I do have some influence," he said in half seriousness.

Valerius laughed. "Positive. But if I were to serve in the navy, it would certainly be on your good ship. Thanks for the lesson, Captain. I'm going to my berth now. Good night."

"Good night, Tribune."

Valerius stopped in midstride on his way to his berth. "Oh, by the way, Captain Sabinus."

"Yes, Tribune?"

"Do you think we'll have smooth sailing like today all the way to Germania?"

The captain paused in thought. "Who in Hades knows? But not to worry, Tribune. I can smell it when a storm is coming." He tapped his nose with his index finger to dramatize his point. "And if there's a tempest brewing, I'll head to the nearest port."

Valerius was astounded at this. "Really, Captain?"

Captain Sabinus snorted in derision. A wide grin creased his countenance.

"I tell people that shit to make them feel better. Most actually believe it. Know what I mean, Tribune? Anyway, in all my years at sea, I've yet to meet the mariner in this man's navy who can smell a storm coming. It's a bunch of crap, Tribune."

Valerius laughed. "I have to admit, you had me going there. Good night again, Captain." Valerius turned and departed.

Sabinus shouted at the retreating figure of Valerius. "Don't worry, Tribune. I'll get you to where you're going, dry and intact."

Valerius waved an arm in acknowledgement without turning around.

The captain stared as Valerius disappeared into the darkness, shaking his head in dismay.

Valerius stripped off his tunic, then stretched out in his hammock in the dark cabin. He pondered again what his life would be like when he joined the legions in Germania. What would his fellow officers think of him? He was unsure of what would be expected of him. He'd trained in the art of Roman warfare, which would provide a foundation and knowledge base. It would help, but his standing and conduct as an officer would need to be carefully shaped and refined over the coming months. He didn't know how he should deal with the centurions, the real backbone of the army. He'd heard that some centurions often resented the tribunes and the authority they carried.

They were two different classes from different worlds. For the most part, the centurions had earned their positions through blood, sweat, and tears, while the tribunes were appointed based upon their wealth and family name. Should Valerius let them run the show? They knew far more than he in matters of the legions. What was his role? Perhaps more concerning, how would he react in a battle situation? Germania wasn't a conquered province. These people had a history of fighting. The possibility of hostilities was real. So many questions, he thought, but nothing I can't deal with. He smiled in self-assurance, listening to the sounds of the ship as the timbers creaked and groaned. He could feel the ship knifing through the waters. With a contented sigh, he fell into a dreamless sleep.

Over the next several days, the weather remained favorable, so Valerius spent almost all his time on deck. He liked to observe the workings of the crew aboard the ship as they scurried about in their duties, usually accompanied by the curses of the good captain. After a few days, the deckhands accepted his presence. Valerius asked questions of the crew as to why they did this and that, how they trimmed the sails and navigated the ship. They had been wary of him at first, but the tribune's warm manner and sincerity prevailed.

The crew seemed pleased that someone of Valerius's social standing would seek them out, asking questions of them. In turn, Valerius humored them with his self-effacing stories of his training as a tribune. On one occasion, he related how his fellow tribunes had played a practical joke on him by wedging his wooden sword into its scabbard with a soft piece of wood jammed strategically in the right place. He was paired against another tribune in mock combat. When he attempted to draw his sword, it wouldn't budge, no matter how hard he pulled. The training centurion screamed at him to advance into combat while Valerius made futile efforts to free the weapon. His fellow tribunes were having a good laugh at his expense.

In another incident, they had been on parade in front of dignitaries, including some senators. Valerius had imbibed of the grape heavily the night before. His fogged brain missed the command, and he marched in the opposite direction from the formation. He had to run to catch up with the other marchers. His training centurion had a few words to say about that episode.

As for Castor, Valerius would occasionally see him on deck. When the two men made eye contact, Castor would deliberately turn away and stroll to the opposite end of the ship. It was humorous. The crew of the ship noticed Castor's behavior. They didn't like him and his haughty manners. He treated the crew with disdain, as if their sole purpose on the ship was to serve his needs. They made up special names for him, none of which were complimentary. Valerius's favorite was tribune lard-ass. He was beginning to enjoy the confrontations with Castor. Each time Castor would avert his gaze, Valerius would smirk in derision. The crew waited in anticipation for when the two tribunes were on the deck at the same time, then laugh at Castor as he spun away.

After several days, the captain informed him that they had cleared the Pillars of Hercules and were now sailing north. In about a week, he was told, they would stop along the coast of southern Gaul to resupply the vessel and bring on more cargo for the ship. They would refresh the ship's stores of food and water and bring on more supplies for the legions. This would be past the halfway point to their destination, and it would offer the opportunity for the tribune to go ashore if he so desired.

The ship anchored at the wharf late in the afternoon. Valerius prepared to go ashore and get some decent food and a room. He fervently hoped that when he arrived at the base on the Weser, the army rations would be better than the fare served aboard the ship. He quickly emerged from his berth onto the main deck, eager to leave the confines of the ship. He wore his standard tunic, leather cuirass, and military cloak. Valerius slung the overnight bag over his shoulder, preparing to depart. The captain looked up from a chart he was studying.

"Going ashore, Tribune?"

Valerius nodded in reply. "When do we sail again, Captain?"

"In the morning, Tribune, so be here not long after sunup."

"I'll be here. For now, I need to feel solid ground under my feet."

"Tribune Valerius," said Captain Sabinus in a more formal tone.

Valerius was moving toward the gangway. He stopped and looked up expectantly. "Yes, Captain?"

"Just remember this isn't exactly the Palatine. I don't know what you're expecting, but my advice is to be careful. Make sure you bring that fancy sword I always see you sharpening. You may need it. Things can get a little rough and tumble, if you get my drift. Those of my crew who choose to leave the ship do so in numbers. They are required to return to the ship at night."

In response, Valerius grinned at the captain, patting the sword attached to his belt. "I can take care of myself, but thanks for the warning."

"Suit yourself, young tribune, but heed my advice. Be careful out there."

Valerius walked down the plank and onto the quay. He puffed out his chest and, with a jaunty stride, exited the dock area and went into the town. Just to feel the earth beneath his feet again was a relief. He surveyed the collection of houses and shops along the main avenue.

He was a little disappointed. The captain was, indeed, correct. This was not the Palatine Hill in Rome. It was plain awful. The shops would better be characterized as hovels. It didn't take long to walk the entire length of the town. There wasn't much to see.

He stopped at the only inn that appeared to offer some semblance of hospitality. Even at that, it was a shabby-looking affair. On the outside, the bricks were weathered, and, some places, pieces were missing. The door to the structure was leaning to one side. The wooden frame to which it was attached had long ago rotted from the sea air. Inside, the dwelling reflected little improvement. He inspected one room and rejected it; too small. He went to another that was larger, but it smelled terribly from the last occupant. Finally, he found one that was acceptable, but barely. He never would have stayed in such an establishment in Rome. He would have to lower his standards if he was to find any accommodation at all.

He dropped his bag off, then sauntered down the street in search of a place that served food. Anything had to be better than the hard biscuits and salt pork on the ship. He spryly strolled down the middle of the narrow street. Valerius found an establishment about two blocks away from his quarters. The place had an amphora that was supposed to be suspended lengthwise by two chains. One of the lengths of chain had broken off from the amphora, causing it to hang in a lopsided manner. Valerius looked up at the object and frowned. "Just charming," he muttered. He walked into the open doorway of a darkened room. Some small oil lamps provided some illumination. A short man wearing a stained apron approached him.

"What can I get for you, Tribune?" he said in an obsequious tone.

"Get me your best wine and some bread and cheese. As fast as you can, if you please."

He didn't even bother asking for a Setinian or Falernian. These were the best wines of Rome. There was no chance they would be in this place. Who knew what sort of swill they would serve as an excuse for wine? His order of bread and cheese was one of caution. Better to be safe and stick with the basics at this place and not order anything that needed to be cooked.

114

"Of course, Tribune. Right away."

The innkeeper hurried off, shouting for someone in the kitchen to get his ass moving. Valerius grinned inwardly. Being a tribune in the Roman Imperial Army commanded respect. People hurried to do his bidding. Minutes later, the man returned with a large cup of wine. Valerius took a tentative taste. The proprietor looked on anxiously.

"It'll do. Bring another as soon as I finish this one."

Not bad stuff for the provinces, he thought. Of course, he reasoned, anything would have tasted good at this point.

Valerius quickly finished off two cups. Feeling somewhat mellow, he stretched his legs out from his seat, put his arms behind his head, and leaned back against the wall. Other patrons had since entered the inn, perhaps twenty. He reasoned that if the place was this crowded, the food couldn't be too bad. Then again, maybe it was the only establishment in town.

The room echoed with quiet conversations punctuated occasionally by some raucous laughter. He briefly surveyed the clientele in the room, then sampled his third cup of wine. Shortly thereafter, his platter of bread and cheese arrived. Valerius inspected the contents of his meal and judged it to be safe to eat. He wolfed down his food. It was a notable improvement from the meals onboard the ship. No wonder all those sailors and marines are thin, he thought. If I had to eat that stuff every day, I'd be nothing but skin and bones.

He raised the cup to taste the wine once more. As he did so, he noted, out of the corner of his eye, two men seated in the corner openly appraising him. He turned toward them. They quickly avoided his glance. He didn't like the looks of these two. They had an unsavory appearance and an air of menace about them. Both were swarthy in complexion, their clothes unkempt. This description might fit a lot of people, but these two had an aura about them that said danger and avoid if at all possible.

Valerius had developed a kind of savvy when it came to judging people and their intentions. His street smarts stemmed from a lifetime living in Rome. The wondrous city had law and order, but there was a criminal element that sometimes ruled the streets. One learned to exercise caution, especially at night. Mindful of the captain's warning, he realized he'd best stop drinking. He had no intention of being an easy mark for a pair of local thugs. He turned slightly in his chair to get a better look at the two men. He noted that neither was imposing physically. He had no doubt that in a confrontation, he and his sword would prevail over these two. But their furtive glances told him that their attack would be stealthy and one of surprise.

Valerius lingered at his table, hoping his head would clear a bit from the wine. When he glimpsed again toward where the men had been sitting, they were gone. With a sigh of relief, he quickly paid his bill, then ventured out the door. He didn't, however, finish his cup of wine, leaving it almost full. As he exited the eating establishment, it was now dark—in fact, almost completely black. The night had turned chilly, and a fine mist blew off the sea.

There was little in the way of light. He looked about to get his bearings, then made his way down the darkened street toward where he believed his accommodations were located. There was no moonlight or torches to guide him, just the illumination that filtered from the shuttered buildings along the avenue. Valerius was alarmed that there was no one else about. He expected some activity on the street, but all was silent. Where was everyone? He cautiously began to stride in what he believed was the general direction of his room. There was open space to his right, so that had to be the sea. By his reckoning, his lodging should be somewhere off to his left.

He'd proceeded about half a block when he thought he heard a scuffling noise behind him. With his heart beating wildly, he spun around. He saw only billowing vapor, nothing more. Valerius was feeling panic now. He should have stayed in his room or, better yet, on the ship. The tribune cursed himself for his stupidity. The next time, if there was a next time, he would listen to the advice of the captain.

He reached down and touched the hilt of his sword, still in its scabbard. He patted the grip reassuringly, then proceeded farther down the street. He glanced nervously to the rear once more, but there was nothing there. *Probably my imagination.* He continued his hurried pace through the gloom. He reckoned that he was now about halfway back to his room. He considered bolting down the street, but he couldn't see where he was going. Who knew what he could run into in this fog? He had visions of himself running headlong into a brick wall and getting knocked senseless. He looked about for familiar landmarks but found none. He'd devoted little attention to his surroundings in his urgent quest to find some decent food earlier that evening. It would have made little difference anyway, for the entire landscape seemed to have changed with the onset of darkness.

He ventured onward. All he could hear were his solitary footsteps as his hobnailed boots struck the uneven stone pavement. If someone was behind him, there was little chance he could hear with the noise the boots were making. He muttered a curse in frustration, attempting to walk softly, almost sliding his feet along the street surface, but to no avail. The sound of the hobnails continued to reverberate on the cobbled street.

A woman suddenly burst out with a raucous screech in the building fronting the street to his left. Valerius jumped at the sound. His heart thumped wildly in his chest. His head quickly swiveled in all directions. The silence returned to the empty street.

He hurried past the house with the woman's laughter. Couldn't be much more to go. He again heard a scuffling noise behind him, like someone running. This was not his imagination, but real. Without any hesitation, Valerius whirled around and instinctively drew his sword in one fluid motion. The weapon cleared the scabbard and swept in a blur toward his rear. The sword's descent was interrupted as the blade struck something solid.

There was an agonized cry, then a burst of warm liquid sprayed on him. In a moment of clarity, he saw a man holding his face, then two men running away down the street. As quickly as they had come, they were gone in the mist. He looked down toward the ground and saw an ugly-looking dagger lying on the pavement. It was long and narrow. This was not a knife used for dining; it was designed for murder. There was a trail of large, dark splotches leading away from the scene.

With trembling legs and his sword extended in front of him, Valerius dashed down the darkened street. He swatted at the fog with his sword. He ran, hoping to see a clearing in the mist. He halted in the middle of street, his heart thumping in his chest. He stared at the building to his right. The place looked vaguely familiar. He hurried closer to the house front. He remembered the door was red and sagged to the right. Yes, this had to be the place. By some miracle, he'd arrived at his lodging. Valerius said a quick prayer of thanks, then rushed inside, slamming the door behind him.

Valerius rushed up the flight of stairs, ignoring the stare of the proprietor on the landing. There was an oil lamp in the hall, which he carried into his room. He shut the door, and the light of the lamp illuminated a dark liquid on his arm. He realized that he was coated with blood. His sword was a dark crimson along the bladed edge. With trembling hands, he took a cloth from his bag and wiped his face and hands, then his sword. He tried to calm himself, but it was difficult. He needed wine. He exited his room and yelled down the stairs. "You there, innkeeper, fetch me a cup of wine if you please."

The proprietor stared back at him without saying a word.

"Are you deaf, man? Get me some wine."

After a pause, the man hurried off to get the wine. When the proprietor returned, Valerius slipped the man several coins, paying way more than was customary. He drained the cup in seconds and lay down. Not the best way to start a career in the legions. He was on edge despite his efforts to calm himself. His mind went back over the flash of his sword in the dim alley and the sickening sound as it met human flesh. His arm continued to tremble. He attempted to lie down and sleep, but that was a fruitless endeavor. He tossed all night, haunted by faces appearing out of the dark. At dawn, he groggily hurried back to the ship.

Valerius walked up the boarding plank, attempting to appear as if nothing had occurred out of the ordinary. He hurriedly proceeded across the deck toward the entrance to his cabin, hoping no one would notice him. There was no such luck. The captain was standing directly in front of him. He gave the tribune his full scrutiny. He spoke in a sarcastic tone.

"Have a good time ashore, Tribune?"

He gave Valerius a knowing look as if he were aware of everything that happened to him. Valerius said nothing. He rushed past him toward his berth, hoping the captain wouldn't spy any blood spots he'd missed cleaning up. He cursed the nosy bastard under his breath. Valerius quickly changed clothing. He emerged back on deck, then casually ambled over to the ship's railing. Looking up, he saw a rather burly man of wide girth in a long cape approaching the ship. The individual hurried toward the ship, flanked on either side by two other men. The trio stopped short of the gangplank.

The bulky man shouted across the short distance to the crew. "I need to speak to the captain of this vessel. It's an urgent matter."

The captain strode over to the railing. The entire crew stopped what they were doing to hear the exchange.

"I'm the captain of this good ship. State your business, if you please."

The man stared back at the captain and replied, "I'm the constable. A man was killed last night in town."

Before he could continue, the captain interrupted. "What's so unusual about that? When isn't that a man killed at night in your town?"

The entire crew laughed at the captain's wit. The constable, flustered at the captain's response, blurted, "The person who was killed has lived here for many years. I knew him well. His face and neck were split open like a melon."

"Constable, what makes you think it was one of my crew who killed one of your fine, outstanding citizens?"

"You're the only ship at dock. The man was obviously struck with a sword."

The captain was silent for a moment, choosing his words carefully. "Don't you think it's a bit of a leap thinking that it had to be one of my crew? Are you telling me that none of your town's inhabitants owns a sword?"

The constable wasn't used to being challenged like this and was clearly agitated.

"People aren't killed by swords in this town. I demand to board your ship and question any of your crew or passengers who were ashore last night." For emphasis, the constable and his two thugs opened their cloaks to reveal large wooden clubs. They approached the boarding plank.

"Constable, you take one foot forward on that boarding plank, and I'll have my crew cut you into little pieces. I'll delight in feeding those pieces to the fish. Are we clear on that?"

The man froze in his tracks. He stared back at the captain, at a loss for words. "Captain, I would remind you that I represent the law in this town—Roman law—and I demand you let me board."

"You may represent the law in this sewer you call a town, Constable, but on my ship, I'm the law. This is a military vessel of the Roman Imperial Navy. You have no authority here. Of course, you may, if you so desire, pit those puny clubs you have against my crew and their cold steel, but I don't believe that would be a wise choice."

The ship's crew guffawed once more.

Valerius stood, unable to move. He realized that he had killed a man. If the constable had talked at all to the proprietor of the inn where he had stayed, there would be little doubt as to the guilty party. He edged away from the rail to blend in with the rest of the crew, all the while attempting to maintain an impassive composure.

The constable was ruffled by the captain's refusal.

"I insist you let me board." His words had lost some of their bluster. He again approached the plank, but his two henchmen stood unmoving. The ugly rasping sound of weapons clearing their scabbards pierced the morning air. A dozen swords materialized among the crew. The constable froze in place.

"Not one more step, constable. If you think I'm bluffing, try boarding my ship. Now get out of here before I throw you in the drink. My ship is about to sail."

"If your ship ever docks here again, I'll be watching for you. Do you hear me?"

"Constable, I hope we never do dock here in this dung heap you call a town. Now leave us. You're interfering with the emperor's business."

The constable did an abrupt about-face and quickly walked away. The captain watched him in silence before turning to Valerius.

"Any idea what that fool was talking about, Tribune?"

Valerius shrugged in innocence. "None at all, Captain. None at all." Valerius turned and walked away, aware of the captain's stare on his retreating form.

VII

The ship's arrival at the mouth of the Weser River in northern
Germania was greeted with brilliant sunshine and a cloudless
sky. The vessel advanced cautiously upriver under power of her oars
in the shallow waters. The captain stood tight lipped on the bow looking straight ahead, his shoulders tense with anxiety. Occasionally he
would raise his right or left arm, indicating a slight course correction.
The sailors stood about, waiting to do his bidding. All was quiet, with
the exception of the faint splash of the oars, which dipped in unison as the boat glided up the river. After they turned a slight bend in
the river, a pier came into view. The captain barked an order. "Make
ready to dock."

The crew instantly swarmed to their stations. Leather hides were
flung over the rail to protect the sides of the ship. Docking ropes were
played out, ready to throw ashore.

Valerius shielded his eyes with his hand from the glare of the sun
on the water. Two other merchant ships were moored at the wooden
pier, and supplies were stacked on the wharf, ready to be transported
to the huge fortress upriver. As the ship edged closer, he could make
out figures carrying sacks from the tethered boats. Off to the side
were numerous smaller craft that bobbed lightly against the river

current, secured to the dock with taut lines. He assumed these would be his transportation farther upriver to the fort.

With delicate precision, the bow of the ship lightly kissed the pier. The oars on one side were taken in, while the others churned the water, thus swinging the entire length of the ship closer to the wooden dock.

"All stop," roared the captain.

The side of the vessel pivoted, then lightly nudged the dock. Heavy lines were heaved over to waiting slaves, who secured the boat. They had arrived.

Minding his manners, Valerius walked over to the master of the ship.

"Nicely done, Captain Sabinus. Many thanks for the safe voyage, and of course the astronomy lessons."

The captain actually smiled at him. Valerius knew Sabinus was relieved that his craft would no longer be a merchant ship.

"Good luck, young tribune. You be careful out there. I hear these Germans like to fight."

"If it gets too bad, I'll quit and join the Imperial Navy. Of course, I'd request a posting to your ship, Captain."

"Anytime, Tribune. You know you're always welcome on my ship."

With a final wave, Valerius turned and started to walk down the plank and off the ship.

"Oh, Tribune."

Valerius stopped and turned. "Yes, Captain?"

"Someday you and I need to share a jug of good wine. You can tell me what really happened back there in that seaport town in Gaul and what got that constable so riled up."

Valerius sensed his face beginning to flush. Doing his best to maintain his composure, Valerius replied, "I'm not really sure what you mean, Captain, but I'd gladly share a jug of wine with you any time or place. I'll even pay for it."

The captain snorted in derision. "If I ever get back this way, maybe I'll take you up on that offer, Tribune."

Valerius gave him a casual wave and departed the ship.

Valerius stood on the pier, watching the baggage and assorted crates being unloaded first to the dock and then onto the small fleet of light draft barges. For lack of anything better to do, he paced back and forth. A grizzled-looking centurion and a handful of legionnaires stood idly by, lounging in whatever shade was available. They seemed unconcerned with the entire process, waiting for the navy to finish its job.

As Valerius passed by the group of soldiers, the centurion addressed him. "What's the matter, Tribune? In a hurry to get upriver?"

Valerius stopped and walked toward the group, anxious to take the opportunity to move into the shaded area, as the sun was getting quite warm. He wiped his forehead with his hand, looked into the centurion's eyes, and grinned. "Is it that obvious?"

The centurion smiled back at him. "Pardon me for saying so, sir, but you're making my men and me nervous just watching you. But don't worry; we'll be getting underway, and soon. We need to wait until all of the barges are loaded, then we'll move out together. For security, you know."

Valerius looked back at him, puzzled.

"It's like this, Tribune: we go as a group. All the transport craft leave the dock together as one so the Germans don't pick us off. They are a bunch of thieving murderers as far as I'm concerned, so we don't give 'em a chance to act up. They won't attack a group this size—at least I hope not."

Valerius replied, "I had no idea the situation was that precarious."

"Don't worry, Tribune, we'll get you there in one piece. We haven't been attacked in a while." The centurion turned his head and nodded to his men.

"Right, men?"

One of the soldiers quipped, "Not this month anyway, Centurion."

The group of soldiers smirked at the last remark. The centurion directed an icy glare at his soldiers. The last thing he needed was to have some tribune complaining about him and his men failing to give the tribune the proper respect. There was a moment of tense silence.

Valerius realized he was the butt of their humor. He was also aware of the awkward situation he now found himself. Should he be offended at the remarks of common soldiers to a tribune, or should he let it slide? He needed to decide quickly. Valerius reasoned that he did look kind of silly pacing about. The soldier's quip wasn't meant to belittle him. He laughed. "Centurion, let's hope the peace and tranquility of the river remains intact for this month, anyway."

The centurion, now clearly relieved, smiled back at Valerius. "We'll do our best to ensure your safety, including your fellow passengers. Saying all of that, I do believe it's almost time to get underway."

The centurion addressed the men. "All right now, get off your arses, gather your gear, and let's make haste. You know the drill."

The soldiers grabbed their weapons and assorted belongings for the voyage ahead. The centurion gestured for Valerius to proceed before him down to the waiting barges. There were six oars to each side of the barges, manned by twelve strong-looking men. They pulled the oars effortlessly against the current. There was little sound except for the grating of the metal in the oarlocks and the near-silent grunts of the rowers. The flotilla of barges progressed steadily upriver toward the awaiting legions in their summer camp.

The early-summer sunlight glinted off the river, and sporadic breezes blew across the water. Towering trees lined the banks. Valerius stared into the foliage looking for hostile Germans, but after a while, he gave up, noting that the various crews and the soldier escorts appeared almost nonchalant about any hidden menace.

Occasionally they would pass a small village with mud walls and straw roofs. Valerius peered ahead anxiously, craning his neck, hoping to catch a glance of the Roman encampment, but each turn of the river yielded the same view—more forested shores. At last, the barges rounded a sharp bend into slower-moving waters, revealing a series of wharves on the right side, the western bank, of the river. The Roman fortress was several hundred yards back from the water's edge. It was every bit as massive as he had imagined. A plank road of split timbers led from the dock to the wooden gates set in the huge walls of the military compound.

He exited the pier, noting a formation of what looked like new recruits getting ready to march into camp. They were probably feeling a lot more anxious than he was at the moment. An *optio,* who appeared to be in charge, came up to him and spoke. "Sir, are you new to us at this camp?"

Valerius cleared his throat. "Yes, I am."

"Your name, sir?"

"Tribune Valerius Maximus. Can you direct me to where I should be going?"

"Sure thing, sir. Where's your baggage?"

Valerius walked back toward the wharf, pointing to it. The satchels rested with the multitude of crates and supplies that had been unloaded. The optio yelled to a couple of legionnaires standing nearby to come over.

"Sylvus and Gaius, get the tribune's baggage loaded and taken to headquarters. The officer's name is Tribune Valerius Maximus. Make sure it gets to the right place. All of it had better get there in one piece, or you'll have latrine duty for the next month. Understood?" He glared at the two men. Both soldiers nodded in bored acquiescence. The soldier turned back to Valerius.

"Don't worry about your baggage; it'll be waiting for you when you arrive at your quarters. If you'll follow me, sir, we'll move out with this contingent of newbies to the fort. I'll direct you from there."

Valerius walked off to the side of the formation. They marched down the road. The group approached the entrance of the fort. The earthen walls were about ten feet high with a V-shaped ditch at the base probably six or seven feet deep. Atop the walls were iron palisade stakes driven into the earth and pointing outward. A massive wooden gate with twin towers made of rough timber bisected the ramparts.

The towers, manned by a contingent of legionnaires, rose eighteen feet high. The gates swung slowly open. Valerius had his first look into the fortress. There was a sea of leather tents as far as he could see. Directly in front of him was a wide road that bisected the entire length of the camp. The optio halted. "Sir, I need to take these soldiers to their new cohorts, so we're parting ways here." The optio extended his arm and pointed down the *via principa*.

"Sir, if you'll follow this road, it'll lead you to the headquarters. You can't miss it. It's where this road intersects another one of the same size."

Valerius walked alone down the broad avenue observing the sights and sounds of the legionnaire camp. He passed a water point where fresh water was brought in from the wells. Men filled large containers to be carried back by mules to other areas. He heard the clanging of metal from the forges as iron was hammered into weapons and armor. He smelled the cooking fires and the bakeries of the legions. Small formations of soldiers passed by on their way to their duty posts.

Valerius continued down the road in the summer afternoon. After several hundred yards, he reached the intersection of the two main thoroughfares. Tents of huge proportions occupied the area, with big wooden frames for support. This had to be the headquarters. Soldiers dashed to and fro from the tents and to the road outside. The one in the middle was the most significant and probably the one he should try first. He strode to the center tent and entered. The scene before him was a beehive of activity.

There were numerous clerks seated at wooden tables busily scanning scrolls and wax tablets. Several uniformed soldiers were shouting instructions to messengers. Valerius waited, hoping someone would notice him. He wasn't sure how he was supposed to report in and announce his presence or, for that matter, to whom. Seeing no one was coming to his rescue, he walked over to a civilian clad in a long gray tunic. The individual appeared to be someone of importance. He issued a staccato series of orders in rapid succession to various clerical staff before finally looking up at the tribune.

"May I help you?" he stated somewhat brusquely.

"I'm Tribune Valerius Maximus reporting to the camp for duty. Am I in the right place?"

The clerk stared at him, gesturing impatiently to the parchment Valerius held under his left arm. "Orders, please."

"Oh, yes, of course. Here you are."

He handed the clerk his parchment scroll that contained his orders. The clerk eyed the papers, rose from the table, and indicated for the tribune to follow. They went into another tent that was connected.

"Centurion, here's that new tribune you've been waiting for to arrive."

The officer was seated at a table surrounded by several other clerks processing wax tablets, or in some cases, scrolls of papyrus. He was outfitted in a shiny breastplate and was immaculately groomed. There wasn't a speck of dirt on his uniform. His hair was carefully barbered and oiled. The clerk turned abruptly and was gone.

"Welcome, Tribune," said the centurion. "We've been expecting you. Please wait here while I check with the general's secretary."

Valerius tried to maintain his patience while he stood and cooled his heels. After quite some time, the centurion returned.

"Sorry for the delay, sir. You're scheduled to meet with General Varus in one hour. He likes to meet all of the tribunes and personally give them their assignments. I would suggest you clean up and make yourself presentable. The general is a stickler on appearances, especially for the officers. I'll have one of my staff show you to your quarters." The centurion looked around and, seeing no one, yelled out. "Dionysus." There was no answer. "Dionysus, you damned Greek, where are you?"

A rather diminutive man wearing a rough woolen tunic appeared from around the corner of the tent. "Here I am, Centurion." He smiled sheepishly. "How may I be of service?"

"Why is it that you're never around when I call for you?"

Not waiting for a reply, he continued. "Take Tribune Maximus and show him to his quarters."

"Is he to lodge with the other tribunes?"

"No, I'm having him bunk with General Varus," he said heavily. "Of course he's with the other tribunes. Now be useful to me and show the tribune where his quarters will be."

"As you wish, Centurion," the clerk said softly.

Valerius was led out of the connecting tents by Dionysus. He followed him down the thoroughfare about fifty yards. The man appeared to be smirking. He probably enjoyed annoying the centurion. There was no conversation between Valerius and Dionysus as they walked. He was ushered into a large tent sectioned off into individual quarters. It had a common area that had several campstools and tables.

He saw no one else around. Valerius was led to a small section of tent, perhaps six feet by eight feet, where, miraculously, his baggage was sitting. His room had a cot and a small table. Dionysus departed without a word. Valerius feverishly went about the task of making himself presentable after the long journey. He smelled under his arm, wrinkling his nose in disgust. He could have used a bath, but that was impossible at the moment. He quickly changed into a fresh tunic. There was a large pitcher of water he'd noticed in the common area. He went back and retrieved it. He looked into the container, sniffing the contents. It looked fresh. He washed his upper body as best he could, shaved himself with his bronze razor, careful not to nick himself, and tidied up his uniform.

He was about as presentable as he was going to be. He needed to get moving. Time, in his estimation, was short. He proceeded toward the legate's tent, checking his uniform along the way for the third time to ensure he hadn't missed anything. He entered a spacious area. From there, he was directed through a series of rooms bristling with activity. Tribunes, centurions, common legionnaires, and clerks appeared, moving in all directions with frantic energy. Orders were shouted as men hurried back and forth to accomplish their tasks.

A centurion noticed Valerius. "Tribune Maximus?"

"Yes, I'm he."

"This way, Tribune."

Valerius followed a centurion who pointed toward a partitioned space to his right. Valerius pushed the flap to the opening aside and entered a quiet area removed from the chaos of the alcove he had just left. The small room was filled with wooden benches. A civilian secretary sat at a single wooden table. He looked up at Valerius. "Tribune Maximus, I presume."

"You are correct."

"Please be seated. The general will be with you shortly."

The man motioned to a wooden bench off to the side. Valerius sat and waited.

Tribune Castor was seated in front of General Varus. The general spoke in a booming voice. "Castor, it's so good to see a familiar face. I was pleased to hear that you were joining us. I personally requested that you be assigned to my command. You know that, don't you?"

"Yes, sir. Thank you for placing me on your staff. It's truly an honor to serve under you."

Castor was laying it on thick, and he intended to capitalize on his good family connections.

"Are you going to help me govern these unruly barbarians up here in the north?"

"I'll help you in any way possible, sir."

"Good. Good. So tell me, how are things in Rome? I miss it. This place is like the end of the earth. Even Syria seemed like a paradise compared to this wilderness."

"Sir, Rome is Rome. It's the same wondrous place. By the way, my father and mother send their regards."

"Do they now? And how are the noble senator and your mother, the lady Diana?"

"Sir, they're doing fine. My father complains of his work in the Senate. I believe that in his heart he loves it. He even met with the emperor the week before I departed."

"Did he? Your father is moving up in the world. You'll need to update me on all of the latest gossip. I'm sure there's some juicy stuff. Am I right, Castor?" He winked to get his meaning across.

"Yes indeed, sir."

"Castor, I'll make it a point to schedule a private dinner so you can update me on all that's going on in Rome. Just the two of us, and perhaps one of my staff. What do you say?"

"That would be fine, sir."

"Enough of Rome now. Tell me, how was your journey? I trust it was uneventful."

"Actually, sir, it would have been much better if not for the problem I had with another tribune, but I managed to prevail," he added. He looked to Varus, hoping for a response. He got it.

"What kind of problem? Who was this tribune?"

"He was insulting to me, but, sir, it was nothing. I don't mean to trouble a man of your great responsibilities with such a trivial matter. It's just that his arrogance was a bit much."

"Nonsense. What's the name of this man? I'll make his ass sorry for any indignation he heaped on you. Listen, Castor, your family and mine are close, and we need to look out for one another. How would it appear if I did nothing to help you in this situation?"

Varus answered his own question. "I'll tell you. Not very good. We must stick together up here in the north. What do you say?"

Castor grinned inwardly. He'd get back at that Maximus through the general. This was even easier than he had thought. He decided to draw it out a little more.

"Sir, really, it wasn't—"

"Give me his name," the general demanded.

"Sir, his name is Valerius Maximus."

"Ah, yes, Maximus. I believe I'm supposed to meet with him sometime today." Varus rose and shouted out for the chief clerk. "Balbus, get yourself in here now."

The clerk appeared at the entrance. "Yes, General."

"Don't I have an appointment with this Maximus tribune sometime today?"

"Yes, sir, immediately after Tribune Castor. In fact, he's waiting outside. Do you need me to reschedule him, sir?"

"Oh, on the contrary. I will meet with him as soon as I'm through with Tribune Castor."

"Anything else, sir?"

"No, that will be all. You're dismissed." Varus turned back to Castor. "I assume he's not a senatorial appointment. Is he of the equestrians?"

"Yes, sir, he is."

Varus offered a malevolent grin. He now had no political impediment to bringing his wrath upon Maximus. His family wasn't of great importance.

He continued in a vehement tone. "You leave this tribune to me. I'll bury him so deep in the bowels of the legions that he's going to wish he were never sent here. I know just where to assign him. Oh, do I have a duty for this impudent tribune. And if he messes up in any shape or form, which I'm sure he will, I plan to come down on him so hard he'll have wish he never joined the legions."

"Yes, sir." Castor didn't protest any of this.

Varus summoned the clerk again. "Balbus, I need you back in here."

The clerk reappeared. "Yes, sir?"

"After Maximus enters here, I need you to find Tribune Calvus and inform him that Tribune Maximus will be responsible for the legionary pay records. Is that clear?"

"Most definitely, sir. Legionary pay records for Tribune Maximus. I'll see to it."

"Very good. You are dismissed." He waited until the clerk exited. "Now then, Castor, leave this matter to me. As to your duties, you'll be on my personal staff, assisting me on various administrative matters." Varus then went on to explain to Castor his responsibilities.

Valerius pondered the waiting area of General Varus. Not much to look at and little in the way of any furnishings. He could vaguely hear some muffled conversation from what he guessed was the legate's headquarters. Valerius looked up at the secretary. The man pretended to be busy. The secretary's table contained a few wax tablets and a water clock. He shifted several items about with no apparent purpose, barely acknowledging the presence of the tribune. Suddenly the clerk was called into the general's inner sanctum. He returned a short time later but was ordered back. When he returned the second time, he gave Valerius a quizzical look.

Valerius heard laughter from the other side of the partition. Emerging from the general's quarters were none other than Castor and a high-ranking officer Valerius assumed to be Varus. The general had his arm around Castor's shoulder as if they were the best of friends. Varus was speaking in a hearty tone.

"It's good to have you here, Castor. I need men of your character to help me govern these uncouth barbarians. As I said, I'll arrange for you to dine with me this week. You can relay to me all the news from Rome."

Valerius eyed Castor. He had a smug expression on his face. It was a *look at me and see how friendly I am with General Varus* expression.

"I should like that very much, General," replied Castor.

"Excellent. This is not Rome, but we can put on a proper banquet from time to time."

"I'm looking forward to it already, sir."

I'll bet he doesn't ask me to dinner, thought Valerius. The secretary cleared his throat as Castor exited without as much as a glance at Valerius. "Sir, your next appointment, Tribune Valerius Maximus," voiced the secretary.

The general turned to face Valerius. At first glance, he didn't appear to have much of a military-like appearance. He was of medium height, with a thick waist and a crown of oiled hair that was curled. His nose was thick and his eyes watery. Varus gave him a cold look, then a frown creased his lips. Valerius was somewhat taken aback by his expression. Was that hostility?

The general looked to be in his fifties. He wore a magnificent cuirass of armor that shone even in the dim light of the tent, but even the armor couldn't overcome the shortcomings of the man's physical appearance.

Valerius stood at erect attention. "A pleasure to meet you, sir."

Varus studied him for a moment, then replied curtly, "Come with me, Maximus. We'll talk."

Valerius followed Varus into his chamber. Varus indicated a stool for him to sit on in front of the general's field table. The table was on a dais, so Varus looked down on all who appeared in front of him. Valerius respectfully waited for Varus to sit first.

"I like to meet all my new tribunes and get to know them."

"Yes, sir."

"I understand you come from a good family and are well educated."

"Yes, sir."

"Good. Now then, the army will be staying here in our summer encampment for a few more months. We'll then proceed to our winter quarters at Vetera. I expect you to serve me and conduct yourself like an officer at all times. Is that clear, Tribune?"

"Yes, sir."

"As for your assignment, you'll be in charge of the legion's staff of clerks who take care of our payroll records. You'll have a centurion to help with this task."

"Yes, sir," he said dutifully.

Valerius tried not to let his disappointment show. He had been hoping for some type of responsibility with the actual soldiers. He didn't want to be buried in a pile of records. He could have stayed in Rome and done that. He'd traveled halfway across the empire to supervise some clerks.

Varus must have read the expression on his face. "What were you were expecting? The command of a legion? You tribunes must learn you'll serve where and when you're told."

Valerius managed to blurt out, "I understand, sir, but I—"

"Do not *but* me, Tribune. Who do you think you are, interrupting me and telling me you don't like your assignment?"

This was going downhill fast. Valerius needed to smooth this situation over. "Sir, I wasn't suggesting—"

"Yes, you were, Tribune. I didn't get to be a military governor by being any man's fool. It's time you learned some military courtesy. How dare you question your assignment?" Varus was shouting now. "This is your duty. You'll perform it to the best of your abilities. Do we understand each other, Tribune?"

At this point, Valerius realized the meeting couldn't be salvaged. It was best not to say anything more. "Yes, sir," he responded perfunctorily.

"Very well. You'll report Tribune Calvus, who's senior on my staff. He'll direct you to where you'll be assigned. Understood?"

"Yes, sir."

"You're dismissed," he said frostily.

Valerius rose from his stool, his face burning in humiliation. He performed an about-face, then began walking. He hesitated slightly. He thought that maybe he could clear the air but quickly dismissed that as futile. He needed to get out of the general's presence as soon as possible. What was all that about? He'd been verbally assaulted for little or no reason, without provocation. Why? He was just a tribune, but this couldn't be the way senior officers treated the junior staff. He numbly exited the tent.

There were several senior staff officers waiting outside. They must have heard the entire conversation and the shouting by Varus. Were they smirking? Probably so, he thought. He looked straight ahead, trying to make some sense of the conversation that had just occurred. What had he done to upset Varus?

He passed through the tent. Valerius stopped and dazedly asked an officious-looking clerk where he might find a Tribune Calvus.

The man looked up and gestured with his thumb. "Two tents down and to the left."

Valerius numbly exited and followed the directions he thought the clerk had told him.

He entered a rather large enclosure with armed guards in front of it. He took little notice as he entered an open space with a peaked roof. Inside were numerous oil lamps burning. On the right side of the tent was a kind of altar. It was covered with a fine white cloth with small oil lamps sitting on top of it. In front of the altar were three wooden poles embedded in the earth. On top of each pole was a silver eagle of exquisite craftsmanship. Each of the figures was about a foot and a half tall. These were the sacred eagles of the three legions in the encampment, the Seventeenth, Eighteenth, and Nineteenth.

The eagles gleamed in the flickering light. Valerius gaped at the sacred birds. The legions held these symbols in such high esteem that they were constantly guarded day and night. Their location was central to the location of the legions. They were placed in a shrine like this when not in front leading the legion to battle. Under each eagle, embossed in silver, was the identification of the particular legion with the word *legio* and the number. He'd never seen the standards this close, as his previous glimpses had always been at victory parades in Rome, and those views had been from a distance. He edged even closer to admire them.

"Can I help you, Tribune?"

Valerius turned, startled. A centurion, the captain of the guard, was addressing him. Several large soldiers flanked the centurion.

"They're magnificent, Centurion," he replied.

"Yes they are," replied the centurion. "They're our most prized possessions."

"I hope you don't mind my gawking at the eagles. I've never seen them this close before. I'm new here."

"I guessed that, sir."

"Actually, I am looking for Tribune Calvus and came in here by mistake."

"I believe you'll find the good tribune in the tent next to us on the left."

Valerius thanked him, still in a state of awe from the standards. He turned, gave the legion's eagles a final glimpse, then strode on in search of Calvus.

Tribune Calvus was seated at a camp table reviewing records. He was rather tall with wavy brown hair. He had a handsome profile. Other men were seated in the room recording entries or reading documents.

"Tribune Calvus?"

The man looked up from his reading and nodded in affirmation.

"Tribune Calvus, my name is Maximus. I believe I'm to report to you regarding my assignment."

"Yes, Maximus. In fact, I just got word about you from General Varus. You'll be handling the payroll records. You need to find a Centurion Marcellus. He'll be your right-hand man and show you how things work. He's a good soldier. Pay attention and learn from him. Any questions?"

Valerius couldn't think of anything and shook his head. "I don't think so."

"Good. You need to hook up with Centurion Marcellus right away. I believe he needs your assistance on some matters. The centurion should be three rows from my left and five tents down to your right." Calvus offered a warm smile. "Welcome to the staff, Maximus."

"Thanks. See you around."

Valerius was feeling somewhat better. This Tribune Calvus seemed decent enough. Valerius walked down the avenue a short distance, this time counting the rows, entered another tent, and was directed toward Centurion Marcellus by a seated clerk. Valerius headed down a cluttered aisle and spotted a soldier in the uniform of a centurion. That had to be him. The man was big, much larger than Valerius. He wore his hair short and had a short, trim beard. His brown hair and beard were laced with gray. Valerius guessed his age to be over forty. His arms and legs were heavily muscled. Valerius approached the centurion, noting a rather handsome countenance. He had that weathered look from being outside all of the time. His face had the texture of tanned leather. He looked up as the tribune entered and smiled. It was a cheerful smile and sincere.

"Ah, let me guess. You must be the new tribune. Welcome, sir."

"Yes, I'm Tribune Valerius Maximus. You must be Centurion Marcellus."

"Indeed I am, and we're glad to have you here." His voice was almost a cheerful bellow that immediately put Valerius at ease. He didn't know what to expect or what kind of reception he might get.

"You're new to the legion, Tribune?"

"Yes. How could you know?"

The centurion laughed. "Your uniform and armor, Tribune. You stand out. Looks like you're about to go on parade."

"Oh, I didn't realize I was out of place."

"Not a problem, Tribune. We were all new at one time."

The centurion continued, "I'll get you informed on all that we do here. If you don't mind, we can do that later. For now, how about we get some food? I'm starved. What about it, Tribune?"

Valerius suddenly realized how hungry he was. He could use some real food. It had to be better than the ship's rations he'd been eating. It was getting late in the afternoon. He wasn't sure about the appropriate protocol in terms of eating with a centurion, but what the Hades.

"That's fine with me, Centurion. Lead on."

Valerius observed a noticeable limp with the centurion's right leg. Valerius began to put on his helmet.

"No need for that, Tribune. Camp rules. Unless you're on guard duty, outside the fort, or performing drill, you don't need to wear the helmet."

Feeling somewhat foolish, Valerius placed the helmet in the crook of his right arm. "Oh."

The centurion spoke as they advanced down the street. "We eat the same food as the common soldiers of the legions. The difference is we have our own serving area and shorter lines. Rank does have its privileges."

They entered a line and received a heaping plate of wheat porridge, boiled vegetables, and bread. Valerius was handed a cup of the sour wine mixed with water. They walked past groups of officers and centurions and found an isolated table out of hearing range from the others.

"To your health, Tribune." The centurion raised his cup.

"And yours, Centurion."

"Tribune, do you come directly from Rome?"

"I'm from Rome, Centurion Marcellus, but don't hold that against me. I'm most anxious to learn the ways of the legions."

"Relax, Tribune. We've had some damn fine tribunes from Rome over the years. So tell me, have you met our esteemed general yet?"

"You mean Varus?"

"None other."

Valerius stared at the centurion. He couldn't tell if there was any sarcasm in that remark. The centurion maintained a blank expression. Was he fishing for some kind of response? There was no way he could know about his confrontation with the general this soon.

"As a matter fact, I have. Not too long ago."

"And?"

"And what?"

"What did you think?"

Valerius was silent. He looked down at his plate. He attempted to mask his feelings and compose a suitable reply. What the Hades; I should tell him, he decided. Probably half the staff had heard of his difficulties by now. Marcellus would eventually learn of it.

The centurion rescued him. "By that look on your face, I would make an educated guess that it didn't go well."

Valerius blurted, "Not go well? It was a disaster."

"Tribune, I've been in this man's army for over twenty-five years. Care to lay it on me? I'm just a centurion, but I know a thing or two about the workings of the legions. I might be able to help. It's up to you."

He didn't add that Valerius was just a green tribune not wise to politics of an army camp, but Valerius knew that's what he was thinking. He began to convey his encounter with the general.

"I don't know what I did to provoke him. I was on time for my meeting. I looked presentable, at least as best I could in the short time available to me. I tried to observe military courtesy, but apparently not to his satisfaction. Maybe I should have just said 'Yes, sir' to everything he said. It was as if he was looking to be provoked. He was screaming at me. It was humiliating. Are all generals like him, Centurion?"

Marcellus was silent for a moment. He stroked his short beard in thought.

"All generals aren't like him." He pondered a moment in silence. "I believe there are two possibilities. One, he was in an extremely bad disposition. This happens. Generals get in pissy moods. Or two, you have a powerful enemy in this camp. You might have been set up."

Valerius contemplated those comments.

"When I was waiting, he came out of the room smiling, with his arm around Tribune..."

Valerius exploded.

"It was that fat fuck, Tribune Castor."

The centurion laughed heartily.

"I'm sorry, Tribune. I didn't mean to make light of the situation, but your graphic description of this Tribune Castor fellow was amusing."

Valerius relayed his account of his problems with Castor, beginning with the sword drill while in training and ending with his behavior on the ship. He also noted the prominent family that Castor came from and their powerful connections, especially with Varus.

"I'll get that bastard if it's the last thing I do."

"Whoa, slow down, Tribune. You're not going to get anybody, at least not just yet."

"What would you suggest I do?"

"My advice, Tribune, is to do nothing for the moment. You must do your duty. Stay away from Varus and this Castor. Become invisible for now. Lie low. They're powerful people. You mentioned that Tribune Castor's father is a senator. We both know that Varus has family connections to Augustus Caesar. No, Tribune, it would be no contest. You'd get plucked and slaughtered like some fowl served for the evening meal. We can't have that now, can we? You may get an opportunity someday for some retribution, but not for the present."

Valerius pondered the wisdom of the centurion's remarks. Of course, his logic was correct.

"I guess you're right. All I wanted to do was my duty and make my family proud."

"Tribune, there'll be time for you to serve the legions. But my advice is to avoid them like the plague."

Valerius needed to change the subject. He would think about his problem with Varus and Castor later.

"How about you show me what's involved with the pay records tomorrow?"

"First thing in the morning, Tribune. I'll go over what you're responsible for in the legions. Welcome to the world of clerks and records."

VIII

*L*ucius and friends stood in formation outside the walls of the summer encampment on the Weser River in Germania. Their sea journey in bulky troop transport ships had been uneventful other than the mass-scale puking that occurred when they hit some heavy weather. Fortunately, no one had fallen overboard. The eighty men plus optio Allius had arrived intact.

A centurion from the fortress addressed the new arrivals in a bored and laconic manner.

"My name is Centurion Marcus Quietus. Welcome to the summer encampment of the army of Germania. I'll lead you into the fort. Make sure you have all your gear. You'll be processed into the army and assigned a unit. You'll stay with me at all times. You'll not talk or break formation for any reason. After we process your records, you'll join your new units. Any questions?" The centurion didn't even wait for anyone to ask. "Good. Let's get moving."

The centurion formed them up in ranks. Lucius noted a tribune in resplendent armor standing by the side of the road speaking to an optio. Lucius bet his reception would be a lot better than what they were going to receive. The group proceeded inside the gates and down a broad avenue until they reached a large intersection. Then they marched to an assembly area deep within the fortress, where a centurion and several optios were waiting for them. They stood dutifully in formation as their assignments were called out. The centurion announced each man's name and unit, and then an optio handed the man a wax tablet with his orders and told what unit he was appointed to. The particular unit was designated by legion, cohort, and century. Cassius had already received his placement. He was in the Eighteenth Legion, Tenth Cohort, and Third Century.

Lucius stood at attention in nervous anticipation. Names were shouted and men assigned their units. Cassius, Flavius, and Domitius were assigned to the same century. Odds were he wouldn't be with them. He mentally performed the calculations in his head. There were three legions in the camp, the Seventeenth, Eighteenth, and Nineteenth. Each legion had ten cohorts, and each cohort had six centuries. That made a total of 180 centuries. No, it wasn't likely he'd be teamed up with any of his friends. I'll be the odd man out, reasoned Lucius. He was already feeling sorry for himself. He was so deep in self-pity that he was half startled when his name was spoken.

"Lucius Palonius."

"Here, Centurion."

"You're assigned the Eighteenth Legion, Tenth Cohort, Third Century." He handed Lucius his orders.

Cassius, standing at rigid attention, turned his head slightly so no one would notice and gave him a large grin, like *I told you so.* Lucius tried to keep from smiling. It was uncanny that they would be assigned together.

The group spent the next several hours getting their pay records in order and having a physician poke and prod them. Lucius, Cassius, Flavius, and Domitius were directed to their unit's location. After walking in circles for what seemed like hours, they finally found their way through the sea of tents. Embedded in the ground in front of a large tent was the standard of the Tenth Cohort, replete with medallions of past conquests. The four men entered the enclosure. They were directed toward a centurion who was sitting at a small day table. They came to attention in front of him and handed him their orders.

The centurion fixed them with an icy glare. Finally, he spoke. "My name is Centurion Frontinus. I take it you're the replacements that I've been anticipating for so long?"

Not knowing what they were expected to do or say, they remained silent.

"Answer me. Are you?"

"Yes, Centurion," they answered in unison.

"I understand you're all conscripts, not volunteers. Almost the entire legion is composed of volunteers. They don't like conscripts. They believe it sullies the reputation of the unit. I must say that I'm in agreement with them, but I'm willing to let that slide. You men must do your share. In fact, you may have to do more than your share to overcome the stigma of your conscription. I'll not have any shirkers or troublemakers in my unit, because if you are, I'll make your life miserable. Understood?"

"Yes, Centurion," they replied dutifully.

"Excellent. We understand each other. You're all assigned the fourth squad. You'll need to draw gear in addition to what you brought with you. Just go straight down the avenue here, and you will find the cohort supply point. From there, they will direct you to your quarters. You have the rest of the day off, so I would suggest you make good use of your time and familiarize yourselves with the camp. Dismissed."

The four men performed a ragged about-face, then exited the tent. They walked aimlessly among the tents of the various centuries. They didn't get far. A group of five legionnaires dressed in gray tunics and marching boots approached them. The man leading the faction whispered something to his comrades. They sniggered at his comment. The group approached Lucius and friends.

The one out front of the others spoke. "What do we have here?"

Lucius hesitated, uncertain as to who these men were and how he should respond to them.

The leader spoke, his tone demeaning. "I'll wager these are the conscripts that we're getting as replacements."

Word spread quickly, thought Lucius.

Domitius smiled and said, "We just finished our training in Lugdunum."

Domitius had a voice that was slightly high pitched. The leader of the group harped on it right away. "We just finished training in Lugdunum," he mimicked in a falsetto voice.

The others laughed, egging him on.

"They don't look like soldiers to me. More like a bunch of girlies," said another of the pack.

Lucius wasn't sure if this was just good-natured harassment of the new guys or something else. He was willing to give them the benefit of the doubt, but he didn't like the looks of the leader. He was an ugly-looking cuss with large, protruding lips that made his mouth look cruel. He was of medium build with short brown hair. There was a nasty scar on his left jaw that seemed to accentuate the perpetual sneer he had on his face. Lucius heard one of the men refer to him as Decius. He experienced a visceral loathing of him. He could sense this guy was bad news, not to be trusted at all.

"What are your names?" the man called Decius demanded.

Lucius and friends gave their names. There was no return introduction.

"I guess we'll see you around," said Decius good naturedly.

Domitius, in the lead, was starting to go past them when Decius stuck his leg out and tripped him, sending him sprawling in the mud. It had rained the day before, leaving patches of brown goop everywhere. The pack thought this was hilarious.

Lucius had his answer. This was no longer some innocent poking fun at them. It figured they would go after Domitius, the slightest one of the group.

Domitius began to rise from the mud. He was halfway up when Decius propelled him back into the slime with a shove of his foot. This set the band of legionnaires into laughter once more.

This was enough for Lucius. He'd run into his share of bullies from his hometown. He'd learned the hard lesson that one needed to react decisively and with force. Otherwise, they would continue their behavior. Lucius sensed a rage building in him. Decius was intent on repeating the shove into the mud again.

He moved between Decius and Domitius. "That's enough." He stared into the eyes of Decius, his gaze not wavering. Up close, Decius's face was even more repulsive. Cassius and Flavius remained frozen, too petrified to do anything. Decius stared back.

Decius broke eye contact first. He shrugged as if it were just a mistake.

"Sure, we were just having some fun. No hard feelings." Decius turned away from Lucius and toward his cronies.

"Right, guys?" He suddenly whipped around with his right fist hurtling toward Lucius's face.

Lucius was anticipating the sucker punch. He blocked it with his left arm, then delivered a savage right cross that sent Decius reeling into the mire. Decius wiped his bloody mouth with the back of his hand.

"Get him, Decius. Make him pay," urged one of the band. Decius cursed, then charged. Lucius edged slightly to his left, evading the rushing figure, then delivered a right hand to the face once again. Consumed with rage, Decius again came at Lucius. He feinted with a punch, then attempted to kick him in the groin. Lucius sidestepped the kick and grabbed the leg. Decius was now completely off balance. Lucius propelled him up and back, sending him sprawling into the sludge.

Decius slowly got out of the mud and whipped out his dagger. "Let's see how tough you are now, conscript."

Lucius, unsure of what to do, reciprocated, drawing his dagger. The legionnaire-issued dagger, the *pugio*, was about eight inches long, wickedly sharp, and capable of inflicting significant carnage. Lucius didn't know much about knife fighting. This wasn't part of the standard weapons training of sword, shield, and javelin. All he'd been instructed to do was use the dagger if he lost his sword, and by the way he'd been drilled, above all, he should never lose his sword. So here he was facing another man with a dagger in his hand. Now what? Lucius held the weapon out in front of him. The two men warily circled each other. Time seemed to slow down. Lucius heard his own ragged breathing.

Decius charged, slashing wildly. Lucius slid to the side. He knew Decius would be the aggressor, but his blind rage might work to Lucius's advantage. He edged around, positioning himself so that the next time Decius charged, he would have to come through the muddy patch of ground. Decius paused with his knife in front of him. "I'm going to cut you up real bad."

Lucius stared back at him blankly, further enraging Decius with his silence. The half-crazed legionnaire lunged, whipping the weapon in front of him. Lucius's strategy worked to perfection. The dagger missed Lucius's face by a hand's breadth. He could feel the passing of the blade. Decius was totally off balance in the mud as he charged awkwardly past. Lucius slammed into him, knocking him over.

Decius sprawled on the ground on his back. Lucius advanced quickly toward the sprawled figure and kicked the hand that held the knife. Decius screamed in pain as the iron-shod sandal connected with full force. The dagger went flying out of his grasp. Lucius jumped on Decius, smashing him in the nose with his fist. He pinned him in the mud and placed his dagger point at his throat. A single bright-red drop of blood appeared and slowly ran down his throat.

"WHAT IN THE NAME OF FUCKING JUPITER IS GOING ON HERE? DROP THAT WEAPON NOW."

Centurion Frontinus towered above them. He saw Lucius with the dagger.

"Stand up, both of you."

Decius rose slowly, attempting to stop the flow of crimson from his shattered nose. The centurion looked at Lucius. He was the uninjured one.

"You're one of the replacements I just spoke to not long ago."

"Yes, Centurion."

"Did I not warn you of being a troublemaker? What was your name again? Palonius, I believe. Right?" He didn't wait for a confirmation.

"You're not here but an hour, and you're attempting to skewer one of my legionnaires."

"Sir, he started it."

"I don't want to hear this shit."

"Yes, Centurion."

"You'll have latrine duty for the next two weeks. If you had injured that man severely, you'd be in for it. Consider yourself lucky I don't have you flogged. I'm going to be watching you like a hawk, Palonius. You screw up again, and I'm going to put a serious hurt on you. Do you understand me?"

"Yes, Centurion."

He walked over and held Decius's face up. The centurion snorted. "I've seen worse. Decius, go to the aid station and get that face attended to. Now get out of my sight, all of you."

Walking away, the centurion continued his lament to no one in particular. "Why did they send me these fucking conscripts? They're worthless. I always get the dregs,"

Moving away, Lucius and friends looked back over their shoulders briefly at their antagonists. Decius, holding his injured nose, gave Lucius a parting malevolent glare as the two groups separated.

Domitius turned toward Lucius. "I appreciate what you did for me, Lucius."

Attempting to control the trembling in is voice, Lucius replied, "No problem. I've seen his kind before. They understand one thing, and that's force."

Cassius chimed in. "Holy shit, Lucius. I thought you were going to skewer the him."

"I was definitely thinking about it, but we'll all need to be careful. He and his friends will come at us again."

Domitius asked, "Lucius, how did you know he was going to try to sucker punch you?"

Lucius stopped walking. Everyone looked at him expectantly.

"Back home, there was this big, nasty guy in my town. This miscreant was pure mean. I made the mistake of trying to be nice to him.

It doesn't work with these types. They'll keep pushing and tormenting you. Nobody would stand up to the guy. He scared the Hades out of everybody.

"One day, I was unloading some containers from my father's wagon at a wealthy Roman's villa outside of town. Next thing I knew, this guy showed up out of nowhere. His name was Brutus. I stopped unloading the wagon because I knew this was trouble. I had no idea why he was out there. I said hello to him, looked him right in the eye. I could tell he was looking to pick a fight.

"He asked what I was doing, and I told him. I was delivering these containers. He went over to the wagon, picked one up, and dropped it on the ground. It smashed. He looked at me, waiting, to see what I was going to do. I didn't say a word. I charged right into him. Caught him by surprise. We both unloaded on each other for what seemed like hours. By this time, we were both bloodied. I mean, I got some good shots in on this guy, and he nailed me a few times.

"So we were both standing, dripping blood into the dust and panting away, staring at each other. He offered to shake my hand and call it a draw. I let my defenses down and offered my right hand, and Brutus brought a roundhouse into my nose. I heard it break. I was in agony and fell onto the ground. This guy kicked me in the ribs for good measure and walked away laughing. The good news was that he never bothered me again. The bad news was that my nose was a mess. It's been crooked since. Here, take a look at it."

"It's crooked, by Jove. It adds charm to your handsome face. The women probably love it," said Cassius.

They all laughed at the sick humor.

Lucius continued, "I'll never let anyone bully me again, and I'll never trust one either."

IX

*C*ursing the foul weather, Valerius hurried down the camp street, eager to get out of the early-morning rain. It was streaming down, creating huge puddles on the uneven ground. Valerius nimbly jumped sideways to avoid a particularly large pool. His momentum carried him into an even larger puddle, soaking him to his ankles. Cold ooze splattered his uncovered legs. Muttering another oath, he hurried onward.

He congratulated himself for having the wisdom to wear his heavy red cloak. What kind of weather was this? It was supposed to be summer. His mind drifted briefly back to the warm sunshine beaming into the atrium of his home in Rome. He pictured himself sitting on the cool marble bench, surrounded by fountains and beautiful plants in his courtyard with the morning sun caressing his face. He quickly dispelled those thoughts. He needed to focus on his assigned duties in the legion. Besides, what was a bit of rain? He could certainly handle that.

Today Marcellus was to give him the grand tour and explain exactly what he was responsible for. Valerius increased his gait, for it was now raining even harder. He passed a century of legionnaires marching by in the opposite direction. Their faces were grim. It would be a miserable day for a soldier outside in the elements today. When compared to the plight of those unfortunate legionnaires, Valerius didn't feel as bad; at least he'd be inside.

He dashed into the tent, shoving the flap aside. He mumbled an oath at the rain as he took off his cloak and shook the water out. He wiped his muddy sandals as best he could on the wooden slats of the floor as close to the entrance as possible, then stomped them to rid his feet of any stubborn remains. Marcellus was waiting for him, sitting on a campstool, entirely at ease, munching on a biscuit.

"Morning, Tribune. Getting a taste of our fine German weather, I see."

"It's coming down in buckets."

"As they say in the legions, Tribune, it's raining shit and stones to splash it."

Valerius laughed. "I've never heard that one before, but it appears to be an apt description."

The centurion dusted the crumbs from his hands. "Ready?"

He didn't wait for an answer. He entered into the spacious interior of a large tented area. Valerius quickly hurried to catch up. Inside, a small brazier filled with lighted charcoal was in one of the corners. Valerius approached the hanging vessel, rubbed his hands together, and reveled in the warmth.

"Ah, that feels good."

Surveying the room, he noted numerous scrolls and wax tablets piled in orderly arrangements on wooden tables. Flickering oil lamps hung from poles, providing additional illumination. Even at this early hour, some of the tables were already occupied by clerks. They barely looked up from their duties and continued their work, oblivious to the new tribune. The centurion gestured with his arm at the expanse of the tented room, then began his tutorial.

"Sir, let me introduce you to the staff." He turned and addressed the staff. "Listen up. This is Tribune Valerius Maximus, recently assigned to oversee our small enclave. Over there is Claudius, this is Petrus in front of us, and back there is Artorius. They're a good group, and they work hard."

Valerius just nodded in response to the introduction, which probably appeared snobbish, but he couldn't think of anything to say. He would need to get to know them better in the coming weeks.

"This is the way it works, sir. There are about eighteen thousand soldiers, auxiliaries, and civilian employees here at the summer encampment. You, Tribune Valerius Maximus, are now responsible for their pay records. Congratulations, sir."

"I can do without the sarcasm, Centurion. Continue on if you please."

Marcellus offered a mocking smile.

"Certainly, sir. As you can see, there are a lot of records. Now, let me tell you about the pay. The salary of each man is based upon rank. The legates make the most, naturally, followed by the tribunes and centurions. The more senior your position on any of these levels, the more pay you're entitled to. The starting salary for an entry-level centurion is about 3,750 denarii—way underpaid, I might add—and 6,000 denarii for a tribune."

"They pay centurions that much. No wonder the empire is going broke. What about the common soldier?"

"The ordinary legionnaire has a salary of 225 denarii. If he has a particular skill or has been decorated in battle, he may get more. He may get double or even triple the standard pay. Sometimes the entire legion gets special donatives from the emperor. Hasn't happened recently, though. In any event, we have to maintain a record for each soldier. Got that, Tribune?"

"I think so. How often does everyone get paid?"

"I was just going to tell you about that. The legions are paid three times a year. Their *stipendium* has deductions for food, uniforms, and weapons. They also receive a special allowance for their shoes. At least a fourth of their pay goes into the regimental savings. These funds are for their retirement and funeral expenses. They'll get to keep at least thirteen denarii for spending every four months. We get to maintain the records for all this. We also send these records to Rome so the disbursement can be made."

"We need to keep all those records?"

"You got it, sir. We're entrusted with the safekeeping and security of these records."

Valerius did some quick mental calculations on the soldiers' regimental savings.

"Let me ask you something, centurion. It appears that those men who serve their full term have nice retirement savings."

"That's not all, sir. They get a bonus when they retire in either hard currency or a land grant. Also, if there's any booty on the campaigns, they get a share of that. There hasn't been much in the way of plunder over the last few years, but you never know when opportunity will strike. Life is hard in the legions, but the pay is good. You don't see many deserters. Most of these men couldn't make this kind of money outside the legions, and you're guaranteed to be fed every day."

"Show me how we keep records on all of this."

"Indeed, Tribune. Follow me; right this way."

For the better part of the day, the centurion explained in excruciating detail all that was required of the clerical staff to maintain the proper records now under the tribune. The organization and magnitude of the operation was impressive. Valerius was in a precarious situation. If something went wrong, he would be blamed. There would be no excuses available for him. He was, by all accounts, extremely vulnerable. Varus could discipline him, so he needed to be on his guard. By late afternoon, Valerius had a throbbing headache. The two men were so busy they had skipped the midday meal. Given the late hour, the tents were now deserted of the clerks. Valerius's belly was beginning to grumble.

"Centurion, enough. I'm famished. Let's get some food."

"Good idea, Tribune. We can bring our plates back here. I can still hear that rain out there."

The two brought back heaping plates of food with some wine and sat down. Marcellus inhaled the aroma from the food as it steamed in front of him.

"Tribune, I hope you like stew, because that's what we serve. We got stew, stew, and more stew. I'm not complaining, mind you, for it's not half bad. Of course, it sure beats the Hades out of our winter rations. Eventually the river freezes, cutting off out supply lines. We're usually down to just barley before spring arrives."

Valerius dug his spoon in and shoveled in a mouthful. He paused as he tasted the concoction. Surprisingly, it was quite good. Maybe not standard fare for a proper Roman banquet, but he wasn't in Rome anymore. He could see all kinds of vegetables and some meat in his portion. He ate another large portion. He broke off a piece of bread and chewed on that. Both men ate quickly with little conversation. Valerius stared up from his empty plate. He was curious as to how the centurion had been selected for his assignment. It was obvious that this wasn't the path to future advancement. He decided to broach the subject.

"So tell me, Centurion, how did you get this duty? You know how I got here."

A scowl appeared on the face of the centurion. Valerius thought he might have offended the man somehow.

"I'm sorry. Perhaps it was impolite to ask."

"No, it's all right. It's common knowledge what happened. I'll tell you the story. Last year, we got into a skirmish with some of these Germans, not a huge battle by any means. I was unlucky enough to get one of their throwing spears in my leg. It hurt like fucking crazy."

"You were a centurion on the line?"

"Yes, I was indeed. I was of the Fifth Cohort of the Seventeenth Legion. It was a good unit, trained to the highest standards of the legions. We made those German bastards sorry they ever attacked us. We put a giant hurt on them. Slaughtered them in the end. Anyway, I went to the hospital. The physician sewed me up real good. He said to me, 'Centurion, you'll heal up in time if you do exactly as I say, but you'll always have a limp.'

"I said to him, 'Will I be able to go back to my unit and function as a centurion?'

"He said to me, 'I don't see why not. The leg will over time become strong, but again, you'll have this slight limp.'

"I went to this physician every single friggin' day. He spread this foul-smelling crap on the wound so it wouldn't mortify. I wasn't permitted even the lightest duty during the healing process. I mean no weapons practice, lifting, marching, running, no nothing. I guess it worked, 'cause my leg is fine. Four months later, I was pronounced fit by the physician for return to duty. In the meantime, I was replaced. I understand that. They needed to have someone to fill in that role in my absence. Every century needs a centurion, and all we had was a green optio recently promoted, so they had to get an experienced man in there right away. I was also with that unit for five years, so it was time to move on. The legions like to change centurions around every five years or so. I was expecting a new posting. I was being considered for the top slot in the cohort as my next assignment. You know, the first centurion. The next thing I knew, here I was."

"What happened?"

"It seems a few months before I was wounded in the German ambush, I had this run-in with a young tribune. Some of the men from my century and I were out scouting for a place to have a bridge crossing on some small river. This young tribune—Plautius was his name, a senatorial tribune at that—was with us. Yeah, Tribune Plautius. Ever heard of him?"

Valerius shook his head. The name wasn't familiar.

"He's gone now, back to Rome where he belongs. As I was saying, the river was high and angry looking that day from the rain. Next thing I knew, this asshole tribune—no offense, sir—was ordering my men to wade into the river to see how deep the water was and determine what kind of bottom was on the river. You know, mud, gravel, whatever. He said that he needed this information to complete his report. I saw that to enter that water was death. That river was moving fast and deep. I countermanded the order. The tribune and I got into a pissing contest about this. Of course, my men listened to me. They didn't want any part of that river. No way. Most of these guys were savvy veterans. They knew better than go into that raging torrent. Let me tell you, if that tribune ever gets command of an army, the empire is in some serious trouble."

Valerius interrupted. "So the tribune got back at you?"

"Yeah. I found out later from a fellow centurion in headquarters I knew pretty well. This tribune went up the chain of command and put the word out on me. Wouldn't surprise me if it went all the way to Varus. When the opportunity arose to screw this old centurion, they did. Bastards."

"Appears you and I have a lot in common."

"Now that you mention it, Tribune, it surely does."

The two finished their meal and cleaned up the dishes. Valerius was curious as to what to do after duty. He didn't feel like going back to his tent and dealing with the other tribunes just yet.

"Centurion, what do you do after hours? I mean, how does one relax and get away from this?" Valerius gestured with his arms at the piles of records and tablets.

"I have a special interest. Want to see, Tribune?"

"Lead on, Centurion."

The two men walked down the camp street, their boots oozing in the mud. Remarkably, the sky had begun to brighten a bit, and the rain had ceased. The sun was setting in the west, but there was probably an hour or so of daylight remaining. Marcellus hailed two centurions approaching from the opposite direction down the avenue.

"Hey, Fabricius, Pollio, how are you? Keeping out of trouble and saving the empire?"

The two men stopped in their tracks and turned toward Marcellus and Valerius. The one named Fabricius spoke. "Marcellus, you old dog, how's the legion treating you? When are you going to stop by and bring us some good wine?"

Marcellus paused for a moment before speaking.

"Fabricius, you should be buying me wine, considering the number of times I covered your butt. And you, too, Pollio. You should buy me some good wine and not that cheap swill you're accustomed to drinking." The three men smiled at their own wit.

Marcellus turned toward Valerius. "By the way, let me present Tribune Valerius Maximus, new to the legions by way of Rome. Tribune, these are Centurions Fabricius and Pollio, two of the finest centurions in the legions. Of course, I'm the one who taught them everything they know about soldiering."

The two men grinned back, indicating there was probably some element of truth in Marcellus's remark.

"A pleasure, Tribune," said Pollio. "I hope you enjoy your tour of duty here."

Valerius nodded back. "Thank you. Marcellus is educating me on the finer points of the legionary pay system."

Both centurions nodded. "Good luck, Tribune. Marcellus, we have to be going, but give us a shout sometime."

They stopped in front of the tent Marcellus shared with others. Marcellus emerged from his tent holding a long leather satchel with a carrying handle.

"Follow me, Tribune."

They proceeded to exit the camp walls and went down past the river. In the distance, there were straw bundles set as targets for javelin practice. Marcellus proceeded to take out the object in the satchel. He held it in front of him for inspection. It was a magnificent war bow made of dark polished wood with a lacquered finish. The bow was huge, almost five feet in height, much larger than the bows the auxiliaries used in the legions. Next he withdrew a quiver of feathered arrows, each about as long as a man's arm. The tips were bronze and razor sharp, and three feathered fins were at the base of each projectile to ensure the arrow spun true during flight. The heads were cylindrical in shape for greater penetrating power.

"Tribune, the Roman army is the best fighting force in the world, no exceptions. I've been all over the empire and no army can match up to us, but one thing we've never been able to master is this weapon. We have no expertise. None. The legions employ auxiliaries from the east who serve as the *sagittari*, but they're utilized primarily for the defense of permanent encampments. They're just a token force and frankly not especially good. Their bows lack range and killing power. They're puny compared to this one." He held it up for inspection.

"When I was in Egypt, I learned about this weapon. I got a couple of their old warriors to show me how to master this thing. This used to be their primary weapon, years and years ago. It's a forgotten art. This bow, Tribune, is called a compound bow. It's made from a horn from some kind of antelope. The horn material is bound to this black wood. It grows in certain places in the east, apparently quite rare. I don't know the name of the tree, except the wood is black."

"You're a fountain of knowledge, Centurion."

"Ain't I now? You know, those Egyptians were closed mouthed about the whole thing and the process of bonding the two materials. But I didn't care as long as I got my hands on the bow. Together, these two materials, along with the size of the bow, provide the source of the power. Thank the gods none of these Germans know anything about archery. For the most part, they're strictly sword-and-spear guys. Let me show you this thing."

Marcellus leaned on the bow at a certain angle and strung it. He did it effortlessly. He notched an arrow and smoothly drew the feathered end back to his lips. He paused briefly, sighted down the length of the arrow, then released the string. The arrow was a blur as it reached the straw target in a heartbeat. The shaft buried itself in the center of the target, over a hundred yards from where they were standing. Valerius couldn't believe the power of the weapon. He could hardly follow the flight of the missile. Back in Rome, on the field of Mars, he'd seen demonstrations of bows and arrows, but they were nothing compared to this.

Marcellus continued. "Some call this a coward's weapon. To me, whatever works in battle is a good weapon. We're not engaged in some wrestling match. This is life for the winners and death for the losers. What kind of horse's ass would call this a weakling's weapon?"

"Centurion, this is one impressed tribune. What's the range of that thing?"

"I'm not sure; a long way, though. These arrows can go through a man at close range."

"I don't suppose you'd mind teaching me to do that."

"Not at all, Tribune. It would be my pleasure. That's why I brought you here."

Valerius was ready to try the bow. He picked a perfectly balanced arrow from the quiver and notched it. He went to draw it back and got to about three-quarters of the way. He struggled to pull it back farther but gave up. He stopped, rested, and looked quizzically at Marcellus.

"How in the Hades did you draw that back all the way?"

The centurion laughed. "It's all in the technique, and I practice it every day. Here, let me show you how."

The centurion demonstrated.

"One uses both arms in drawing the bow. The left arm pushes while the right pulls. The key is keeping your left arm fully extended at all times while gripping the bow. Like so." He showed the tribune the proper technique for gripping the string. He used three fingers to pull the string back.

Valerius did much better after studying and practicing the maneuver over and over. The centurion now explained the shooting phase.

"What you do is bring the feathered part of the arrow even with your lips, almost as if you were kissing it. You center the arrow on the target and let out about half your breath, then hold it. All you have to do is release the string with your fingers. Make sure you release all three fingers at once."

Valerius drew the arrow back to the proper position, held his breath, and let the arrow fly. He jerked the bow upward, a common mistake for beginners. The arrow streaked downrange, a blur in the fading light of the evening. His shot missed the target by a wide margin, about six feet above the straw bale. Valerius was amazed at the power he'd been able to generate with the bow. Eager to try again, Valerius let another missile fly. He missed again, although a little closer.

"Concentrate on your breathing and your posture, Tribune. The less movement the better when you release the string."

Valerius focused, remembering what the centurion had demonstrated. He fired again and again, all misses, some left and others right. A few of the shots were dead on but were either too high or too low. He was close on several occasions, but they were still not in the target. The centurion said little. He stood to the side, carefully observing the tribune.

Valerius's arms were fatigued, but he was determined to hit the target before retiring. He had one more arrow in his quiver. He set up and drew the string back, sighting down the shaft in the deepening gloom of the evening. He sighted the arrow up slightly. His last few shots had been direct center, but the trajectory was a bit low, causing the arrows to strike the ground in front of the target. The muscles in his arms and shoulders ached with the tension. He let out half a lungful, then released the arrow. He attempted to follow the flight but lost the missile in the fading light. Then he saw it. There was a splash of straw from the target, dead center. He let a whoop to celebrate.

"By Jove, that's the way, Tribune. I've made an archer of you after all."

The two men walked toward the straw bale to retrieve the arrows. Valerius reached the bales. He had to tug and twist to extract the feathered projectile. It was buried half its length into the straw. Valerius shuddered involuntarily. He could imagine what these would do to human flesh.

"Not bad, Tribune. As you can see, it takes practice with this weapon to master it."

"I'd like to do this again. Would you mind if we pursue this some more?"

"Anytime you want to practice, let me know."

It was getting near dusk. They had to get back within the walls of the camp before the gates closed. "How about some wine, Centurion? My treat."

"Best offer I've heard all day. Let's go."

The two men sat alone at a small field table illuminated by torchlight. The evening was warm with a slight breeze. Valerius stretched his legs out, pleased with his latest efforts on the archery range. The centurion did most of the talking as they shared a small clay container of wine. He spoke of the commanders he'd known and places he'd been.

"Let me tell you about Centurion Junius, whom I served under in Germania. He was one hard-assed son of a bitch, but I loved him. He started my eventual promotion to centurion. That man could lead. He got every last ounce of energy from his men. He led by example. Centurion Junius could outmarch, outfuck, outfight, and outdrink any man in his century. He was a man of iron, but he cared about his men. I owe a lot to him."

The centurion continued. "Junius took me aside one day. He looked me right in the eyes. He said, 'Marcellus, you're a fine soldier. You could be a centurion one day if you'd stop screwing around so much.'

"I just looked at him real stupid-like. He let me know that if I'd stop drinking and whoring and concentrate on soldiering a little more, I could be a real leader. He then told me I was to be promoted to optio. I kind of took his words to heart, because I cut back on my social activities, if you know what I mean."

Valerius spoke. "Looks like Junius made a good choice."

"Ha. The man would puke if he could see what I was doing now."

"So how long have you been with the legions?" inquired Valerius.

"Over twenty-five years. My career began in the east. I served with distinction despite my intense dislike of the heat. I was originally from a small town in the hills far north of Rome, the mountainous Aemilia, or eighth district. I could never get used to the hot climate of the east, especially in the heavy armor of the Roman soldier. Initially I was stationed in Syria. Then, after several years, I was transferred to Egypt. It was there that I became interested in the bow. After Egypt, it was on to Germania, where I've spent most of my career. Unlike most in the legions, I kind of like it here. The air is crisp and clean. There is an element of danger always present, but I don't mind that. Many complain it is cold and gloomy here. I would take this over the searing heat of the east in a heartbeat.

"I received his first award for bravery in Syria. Surrounded by bandits while on a night patrol, I kept a cool head, saving several of my comrades. My second and most prestigious award was the Mural Crown, or Corona Muralis."

"You were awarded the Corona Muralis?" A tinge of awe in his voice.

"Yes indeed. Opportunity beckoned in the Batavia region of Germania. It was a major campaign under the late Drusus, brother to Tiberius, now adopted son of Augustus Caesar. The Roman army had made considerable headway, pushing the German opposition farther east of the Rhine. But on this particular day, it was the Romans who were stymied. Volleys of German throwing spears were blunting our forces, ripping them to pieces. The advance of several cohorts on the German fortified position was mired down. Legionnaires were being killed one after the other by the hurled javelins. Our lines were stationary targets, unable to mount an offensive because of the constant barrage of spears."

"So what happened?"

"I went crazy. Don't ask me why; I couldn't tell you. I waved my sword in the air and then charged the German fortifications, screaming at the top of my lungs. The others realized this was the right thing to do. They followed my lead. The German defenses of the redoubt buckled under the onslaught and fell apart quickly. The goddess Fortuna smiled upon me that day. Not only did I survive, but the legate of my legion witnessed my bravery. The commander was so impressed that he asked the name of the brave legionnaire. The next day, I was informed that I was getting the Corona Muralis."

"And here you are now with me, a green tribune."

Marcellus offered a grin. "Don't worry, Tribune. We'll get through this together."

Valerius rose from the campstool, bidding the centurion good night. He walked a short distance toward his quarters.

He entered the common area. Several tribunes were sitting around a table drinking wine. He nodded hello as he walked into the room. He heard one of them snigger.

I wonder what this is about? Valerius thought. He started to walk past the table.

"Hey, Maximus."

He turned. "Yes?"

The ringleader of the group, a tribune whose name Valerius had forgotten, spoke. "I understand you'll be working quite a bit with a trusty stylus in your duties."

"It looks that way. Yes."

"Do you have a scabbard for that thing?"

The others burst out laughing at the remark.

Valerius grinned weakly at them, attempting to conceal his annoyance, and proceeded into the next room. To Hades with them, he thought. I really need to hear their crap about this asshole assignment.

Marcellus ventured back to his tent, staring morosely at his quarters. In the past, he would have been sharing a cup of wine with his fellow centurions, telling war stories and talking about what they were going to do when they retired. Not so anymore. He knew many of the centurions and was still connected with them, but it was different. He was no longer part of the rank and file of the legions. He was a glorified leader of clerks, an outcast. He could tell by the way the other centurions interacted with him now. They were polite but distant. He wasn't part of their inner circle anymore, nor was he invited to or welcome at any gatherings. If they had a problem involving the pay records, they would come see him. That was it. Sure, Pollio and Fabricius had offered to share some wine with him earlier this evening, but that was more out of politeness. He knew the two centurions still liked him, but their friendship could go so far.

Marcellus didn't blame them. This was the order of things in the legions. He'd been at the wrong place at the wrong time and had been punished severely. He'd acted in the best interest of his men. Perhaps he should have been more politically astute in dealing with the tribune named Plautius, but that was over and done. His ostracism by his fellow centurions was bothersome, but what was far worse was his assigned duties. He was a warrior, by Jupiter. Nothing would ever change that. He was now one of the people he used to mock, the rear-echelon pukes. Putting him with the clerks was a cruel fate.

Fate could be so fickle, he mused. He could retire from the legions if he chose to do so. He had more than enough years of service for his pension, but what would he do? He had no skills other than soldiering. He'd be damned if he was going to molder away in one of those legion retirement communities. Never! He continued to hold out hope that by some chance the legions would come to their senses, and perhaps he could get command of a century again. Not bloody likely, he thought.

Marcellus reflected on the new tribune. He seemed a decent sort, not pretending to be the next Julius Caesar. Many of these tribunes from the aristocratic class were resented by the men of the legions. Their haughty airs and condescending manners created enormous friction. Not this one. No, Tribune Maximus appeared to be down to earth and had a good wit about him. He seemed eager to learn and had a good head on his shoulders. Marcellus kind of liked him. To say that Valerius wasn't off to a good beginning in the legions was an understatement. He had powerful enemies and was on dangerous ground. Marcellus guessed that the other tribunes would steer clear of him.

Both of them were outcasts in the legion. What the Hades; he was up for the challenge. There was an unwritten rule in the legions concerning the social divide between centurions and tribunes. The two were of distinct and separate social classes that didn't mingle. He thought about it a bit but decided it was all a bunch of crap. Ha! What could they possibly do to him? Make him a clerk? It was the two of them versus Varus and his ass-licking cronies. Besides, he enjoyed sharing his love of the oversized war bow. The tribune appeared smitten with the instrument. He hoped the tribune would ask for more instruction, as he had said he would.

X

The sun slid lower into the west, coloring the sky in bright hues of red and purple. Colorful pennants gently fluttered in the wind. Lucius, Cassius, Flavius, and Domitius walked aimlessly along the tented avenues. They eventually arrived at the south gate. Its massive wooden frame and watchtowers rose above the earthen walls of the fortress. The foursome looked on as a cohort—six centuries, or about five hundred men—entered. They stared in fascination at the column of men approaching them.

The *signifier*, the legionnaire carrying the cohort standard, marched proudly in front. The man was clad in the customary animal pelt, in this case a wolf skin, and hefted the cohort standard replete with medallions and decorations from past victories. The first centurion of the first cohort, the overall commander of the five hundred men, plus his staff, were followed by the six centuries. The legionnaires walked by slowly in a lethargic fashion, each with a hollow stare. They were powdered in a layer of fine brown dust, appearing as tan apparitions moving past.

The men carried their shields, weapons, and forked poles loaded with gear. Their faces portrayed extreme weariness coupled with grim determination. Rivulets of sweat streaked their faces where it had cut through the accumulated grime. Shuffling by, a few nodded numbly in silent greeting at Lucius and friends. Several were hobbling, supported by their comrades, determined to see the journey through. A few hawked some saliva from their dry mouths and spat upon the ground.

Cassius leaned toward Lucius and spoke. "I sure as shit am not looking forward to wherever they went."

"Me neither," said Lucius.

Unnoticed, a centurion had wandered up beside Lucius and friends. He was a squat figure, layered in muscle. He laughed at the last several remarks.

"New to the legions, gentlemen?"

They all turned toward the unexpected voice. Cassius replied, "We just arrived from our training base in Lugdunum, Centurion. We don't know too much of what the training and drills are like. Where were these men?"

The centurion replied, "This cohort was out on patrol. Everyone gets a turn; I'm sure you will also. It's like this. Each week, the legions rotate units, sending ten cohorts outside the walls into the countryside in full armor with mule trains. The cohorts operate independently of one another, heading in different directions. The units patrol seven to ten days. There are thirty cohorts, ten for each legion, in the encampment, so about every three weeks, each cohort will take a turn. There are two purposes for these military excursions into the countryside. First and most important, we are making the presence of the legions known. The Roman Imperial Army is a superior fighting force. We are reminding the local populace of exactly who is in charge. The second reason for these maneuvers is to keep the soldiers sharp and in shape. These marches into the territory aren't pleasant strolls, but forced marches in full gear. The commanders want to ensure the men don't become soft and lackadaisical."

Lucius spoke up. "Centurion, how far do they go, and do the Germans ever attack us?"

"As to the first question, each cohort has a different route, but I can assure you it's not a stroll out for a picnic. Get my drift?"

"An ass breaker, right, Centurion?" replied Lucius.

The centurion laughed deeply. "That would be an apt description. As to the second point, this summer has been free of any hostilities. The Germans appear to be under control, but me, I don't trust them." He hawked and spat to the side to make his point. "We've been fighting them off and on since the days of the great Julius Caesar. Have we made progress? Yes, but I don't think these people consider themselves conquered. When we go out on these excursions, it's considered a tactical situation where the threat of enemy attack is imminent."

Nobody said anything in response to the centurion's sobering words.

"To what unit are you men posted?"

Domitius spoke. "Centurion, we've been assigned to Legion Eighteen, Tenth Cohort, Third Century."

"Ah, Centurion Frontinus. He's a good man. I know him. Listen to him. You can learn a great deal from the man. I'm Centurion Nilus. I'm also in the Tenth Cohort. I command the Sixth Century. I'll see you tomorrow at the cohort drill. The march, by the way, is coming soon. My advice is to not drink too much wine the night before. You'll need all of your strength. Good luck and good fortune."

The centurion strode away.

For lack of anything better to do, Lucius and friends wandered toward their unit's designated mess area. The four men entered the serving line and returned with steaming platters. Most the tables for their cohort were already packed with soldiers. Lucius looked around for some empty spaces. He spied a half-vacant table with four legionnaires seated at it and pointed. "Over there."

The seated men at the table barely acknowledged the newcomers. They were preoccupied with wolfing down large quantities of bread and boiled vegetables. A legionnaire glanced up from his platter of food. He appeared puzzled at their presence. "You the new guys in the third?"

"Yeah, we are. How can you tell?" said Lucius.

"Never seen your faces before, and your uniforms look brand new."

"Which one of you kicked Decius's ass? It had to be one of you."

Lucius hesitated briefly, not sure whether he should volunteer that information. He just wanted to blend in with the others without the notoriety of beating someone's face in.

"That would be me."

In unison the other men at the table stopped eating, then looked up from their half-finished meals. Unknowingly, Lucius had become somewhat of an instant hero. Apparently, word had spread like the plague among the men of the Tenth Cohort about the confrontation with Decius. One of the new guys, a conscript, had put Decius in his place. Indeed, he'd pulverized his face into a bloody mess.

The man continued. "He deserved it. He's a nasty one. Never much liked the man. If I were you, I'd lie low, watch my back. I believe he's out to get you in any manner possible. I overheard him talking. He and his cronies might be hunting for you now. So my advice is to be careful. Oh, by the way, the name's Drusus. I'm of the Fourth Century." He stuck out his hand to them.

Lucius replied, "I'm Lucius, and that ugly-looking fellow is Cassius. That's Flavius, and this is Domitius. Thanks for the warning, Drusus. I kind of expect him to try something."

"I got to go, but I thought I'd warn you. Good luck."

The other men at the table quickly followed, leaving Lucius and friends alone. Cassius looked over his shoulder for any sign of Decius and his posse.

"Lucius, did you hear what that guy said?"

"Yes."

"What are we going to do?"

Lucius munched on a piece of bread as if pondering the question.

"Listen, we need to stick together on this. We don't wander off alone. We stay armed at all times. He'll not attack us openly. He's too smart for that. My guess is he'll try to ambush us or isolate one of us alone. He's after me, but if he gets the opportunity, he'll go after any one of you. So we stay together, and we stay vigilant. Agreed?"

Everyone nodded solemnly.

Lucius and friends hastily finished their meal, then ventured off to explore the camp some more. It was twilight, and torches were burning along the main avenue. They came upon a large congregation of soldiers with cups of wine and beer. Laughter and shouted conversation echoed in the evening air. Dice games flourished everywhere. They found a large tent that had a plank upon which rested numerous jugs of wine and drinking goblets. They each purchased some wine. It wasn't the best quality wine, but it tasted wonderful.

The group lounged about trying to fit in with the rest of the soldiers, sipping their wine. Flavius held his empty wine goblet up, glancing quizzically at Lucius and Cassius. Lucius frowned in thought.

"Guys, I don't want to spoil the party, but tomorrow is our first day of drill. I'm already on the centurion's stercus list. So no more for me, but you guys can have some more."

Cassius replied, "I guess you're right, Lucius. As much as I would like another cup, I think we should quit now. We need to be on our toes in the morning. Tomorrow is our first real full-duty day. I'm not exactly sure what to expect. I don't want to blunder and have the centurion on our collective ass."

The four departed the area. With the exception of the main thoroughfares, the camp was in total darkness. They headed in the general direction of where they believed the tents of Tenth Cohort were. They got lost. Everything looked the same in the dark. They wandered aimlessly in the maze of roads.

"Cassius, do you know where we are?"

He turned, surveyed the camp in all directions, and rubbed his chin in thought. Lucius and the others waited expectantly. He finally answered. "No, do you?"

Lucius swore an oath. "By Pluto's cock, I have no idea."

"Sorry, Lucius, but I don't know. Anyone else?"

They all looked blankly at one another.

"Let's go this way," said Flavius. He pointed to his right down a narrow avenue of tents. The group wandered down several avenues, unsure of where they were.

Finally they spied a solitary legionnaire walking their way.

"Can you direct us toward the Eighteenth Legion?" Cassius asked sheepishly.

"Lost, are you?" The man snorted in derision. "What kind of soldiers are they sending to us who can't even find their own way to their tent? Stupid-ass newbies—that's what you are."

The man laughed at his own barbed humor. Lucius didn't reply. He just wanted to get back to his quarters.

"I'll help you out this time. Just go down this road and turn in the third street on your left, then follow that for a bit and turn right."

The man quickly departed, muttering about the dumb-ass legionnaires who couldn't find their own tents. By Lucius's reckoning, they weren't even close to where he had thought they were. So much for his navigating skills. They made their way toward their cohort zone area, approaching by means of one of the side streets. Lucius saw a furtive movement off to their right side. It was hard to tell in the dark, but he definitely saw something. He held his hand to his lips for silence.

"Come on, let's get out of here," he whispered.

The urgency in his tone was enough to propel them forward without asking why. They ran in a zigzag pattern between tents, careful not to trip over any tent ropes. Lucius spied a tent that was of a shape, almost square, not like those used to house the men. He ripped the flaps open and ushered the others inside. Lucius held up his hand for silence, then secured the flaps. He saw racks of javelins, helmets, and chain mail. Lucius yanked a javelin out of its rack and held it at belly level toward the tent opening.

They heard a group of men approaching. Lucius quickly identified the muffled voice of Decius.

"I know I saw him and his three friends. It was them I saw. They must be around here somewhere."

Another voice spoke. "Maybe it was them, but we won't find them in this darkness. They could be anywhere. Maybe they're in their tents by now, and we're wandering out here in the dark. We can get them another time. Besides, I'm getting tired of this."

Lucius heard Decius speak again.

"You can leave us anytime, Colvus. We don't need you anyway. I want this Lucius now. I'm going to whack his sorry brains out with this club."

Lucius held his breath, gripping the lance tighter, willing the figures outside to move away. Then the voices faded as Decius's group walked away.

"Whew, that was close," said Lucius. "We need to get to our tent now, before he finds us. As I said before, we need to be armed and ready for this asshole. Agreed?"

The others nodded in the darkness. They exited the tent. Lucius continued to hold the javelin in front of him at belly level, its wicked point ominous even in the darkness. The men hastened toward their tent, occasionally glancing over their shoulders for any sign of Decius. The four paused in the shadows. They scanned the darkened area for any sign of Decius and his followers but detected no movement. The four men waited awhile before they assumed it was safe. Lucius heaved a sigh of relief. They were secure for the night. Decius wouldn't dare attack them in the tent with other legionnaires around.

Lucius, clad in his tunic and full armor, stood in the assembly area and shivered in the early-morning mist. By the gods, it was much colder here in Germania than his native Gaul. He wished he could be wearing his cloak, but that wasn't the uniform of the day this particular morning. The vast multitude of soldiers gathered about in their respective assembly areas, waiting for the signal to form up. He spied Decius, perhaps twenty paces distant, his face deformed from the pummeling Lucius had delivered. In turn, Decius stared back, giving him a look of pure hatred.

A group of soldiers wandered between the two men, cutting off eye contact. Lucius moved away from the vicinity, mindful of the centurion's warning about another confrontation. Enough of Decius, Lucius needed to concentrate on his duties within the century. Fortunately, Decius was in the seventh squad and not in close proximity to Lucius in the third squad. The men mulled about a few more moments, and then the *cornicens* blew for the men to stand in their places in formation. The soldiers formed up quickly to their assigned spots, where their centurions and optios awaited them.

In a short time, the three legions were in their unit formations, an impressive spectacle. Over fifteen thousand men were assembled into the thirty cohorts and subdivided into the 180 centuries. There was absolute silence. The rolls were checked, and the centurions quickly but thoroughly reviewed the men in formation. The cornicens blew once more, and the three legions prepared for a full-scale battle drill.

Lucius's cohort, along with all of the others, marched to the wide-open drill field to the south and east of the fortress. Each man was fully armored, with the full complement of weapons. Helmets were worn and securely strapped down. Towering above the open area was a wooden platform upon which stood the senior officers, where they could observe the troop movements.

Lucius's century began to go through its paces in coordination and as part of the Tenth Cohort. It was familiar stuff. They had done this over and over in training back in Gaul. Lucius was mindful of Centurion Frontinus. He appeared to watch their every step, waiting for the chance to deliver a stinging rebuke. The cohort deftly executed battle drill, turning the formation left and right, then charging straight ahead. Lucius was amazed at how good these soldiers were. The men were ready for every command and change in formation. Lucius guessed that they had done this often enough to do it in their sleep.

Lucius was in the front rank as his century advanced with javelins at the ready.

"RELEASE."

He quickly drew his sword and marched forward as he'd been instructed in his training in Gaul. They did things a little differently here. The line of soldiers was already running at full speed, leaving Lucius far behind the front rank. The centurion picked up on it right away, and he was on Lucius's ass. He ran up to him screaming, "What are you waiting for, Palonius? Get a move on it."

Lucius didn't utter a word and hurried to catch up with the others.

They drilled all morning. After a quick meal, it was back to the drill field. The repetitions were endless as the cohorts flowed back and forth across the drill field. Formations changed based upon signals from the horn blowers. Lucius didn't quite understand the various horn calls or some of the tactical formations employed by the legions. This hadn't been part of their training under Centurion Longinius. So Lucius concentrated as the century went through its paces. He followed the lead of the other men. He did what they did.

Finally the soldiers stood down, taking a much-needed break from the drill. Lucius, next to Cassius, wearily removed his helmet. His hair was soaked with sweat, as there was no ventilation in the helmet. Like all the others, Lucius jabbed his javelin into the earth and eased the shield to the ground. Lucius wiped his face, and, as a matter of caution, looked about him for Decius. There was no sign of him or his followers.

Relief flooded Lucius's features. He didn't figure Decius would risk a confrontation out here with everyone present, but given the man's rage, one had to be careful. The ranks of soldiers congregated around the area drinking water, conversing about what they were going to do tonight. Coarse banter and an occasional laugh filled the air.

Lucius guided Cassius away from the others and in a low tone spoke so others couldn't hear. "They're watching us. The centurion and the optio have had it in for us all morning. It's like they hope we screw up."

Cassius replied, "Don't you know it. They yelled at me once for being out of formation. I wasn't. I know when I'm not covered to the man in front of me or dressed to the man to my right."

Lucius responded, "This, too, will pass. Right, Cassius? Just remember the log races."

"You got it, Lucius. We'll hang tough."

The centurion bellowed for them to form up. It was time for more drill. Everyone quickly recovered their weapons and gear.

XI

*I*t was late afternoon. Valerius sat hunched over a wooden table, examining a parchment document. He slowly rubbed his forehead in concentration. Suddenly, he hurled the piece of paper to the ground, then pounded his fist on the tabletop.

"By Jupiter's balls, enough of this crap."

There was silence among the several clerks seated nearby. Marcellus arose from his table off to the left. He laughed heartily. "I see these records are getting to you, Tribune. I also thought that tribunes were trained to be gentlemen and not swear."

Valerius continued to seethe. "Marcellus, this tribune does swear and enjoys doing it. This payroll business is maddening. Let's start with the one first thing this morning. Tribune Scribonius departed the legion's rolls many months ago. Do you think any of those scholars in headquarters bothered to communicate with us? They have the gall to tell me—with a straight face, mind you—that they sent the information to us. Of course, they don't know who wrote it up or when, but they were sure it was sent. Then we have the unfortunate case of legionnaire Arctus, poor soul. He died over six months ago from the plague, yet we were never advised. Someone has been receiving his pay. Please explain that to me, Marcellus."

The centurion stroked his chin in thought. "It's one of the most common scams there are, Tribune. Each legionnaire is supposed to be identified and sign his mark for the pay, but there are always those who find their away around the regulations. Trust me on this. There are some real creative folks when it comes to swindling money."

Valerius wasn't finished his ranting yet. "What about those three men who were promoted to optio within the last several months, yet we have no word about it? I personally spoke today with the three centurions who promoted the men. They all swore they sent the proper paperwork to headquarters for approval. So here we sit, the target of the three men's wrath—not that I blame them. They didn't receive their new pay raises. I believe their centurions. The problem is with headquarters. How about I go over there and ram my foot up their collective butts?"

Marcellus frowned. "Tribune, remember what I said to you about keeping a low profile? I don't believe that would fit the description. Look, it's late in the afternoon. I'm as fed up as you. How about we go out to the archery range for a little practice? I do believe you are getting better with the bow. What do you say?"

Valerius nodded. "Lead on, Centurion. Let's get out of here."

Earlier in the week, Marcellus had let Valerius use a second bow, slightly smaller than the one he'd previously shot, although by comparison with other bows, it was still much larger. The weapon was better suited for Valerius. The weapon Marcellus had initially let him shoot required an inordinate amount of strength to fully draw. Valerius had struggled to bring the bowstring back to his lips before releasing, and his ability to do this on a continuous basis was limited. The somewhat smaller weapon still required strength to draw, but it was less demanding.

Valerius was a quick learner. With the slightly smaller bow, he was hitting the target about four of every ten shots. He certainly didn't qualify as a skilled marksman or come close to the capabilities of Marcellus, but he was getting there.

It was almost dusk. They had been practicing for some time.

"All right, Tribune. How about a new drill to end the evening? Do you still have a little arm strength to finish out the evening?"

"Of course I'm game. What do you have in mind?"

"Here's the tactical situation. We have an enemy force advancing toward us. We need to release a volley of arrows to stop them. We'll each rapid-fire ten arrows at the targets to see what damage we can do."

"Bring them on, Centurion."

"Tribune, remember what I told you about the single fluid motion. Bring the arrow out of the quiver, then shoot it in a single motion. Discharge the arrows rapidly, but not in haste."

"I remember what you've taught me. Let's get on with it."

In turn, Marcellus gave him a mocking grin.

"On my mark...are you ready, Tribune?"

"Hold on. Give me a moment, Centurion." Valerius proceeded to adjust the position of the quiver so he could easily access the arrows without fumbling.

"Whenever you're ready, Centurion."

"Begin!"

Valerius smoothly drew an arrow out and notched it on the bowstring. He drew it straight back, then steadied his aim, holding it momentarily, and let fly. He was already reaching for another arrow as the first missile streaked toward the straw target. He could see Marcellus out of the corner of his eye doing exactly the same thing. Both men discharged their arrows. Between the two of them, there were feathered shafts constantly on the way to the target. As expected, the experienced Marcellus finished his allotted arrows first. He looked on as Valerius released his last one.

"Not bad, Tribune. Let's go see the damage."

The two men walked up to the targets about a hundred yards away. Marcellus had scored nine hits out of a possible ten. Valerius had hit the mark six times.

Marcellus spoke. "By Venus's pert arse, I believe we have made you an archer. We would have successfully deterred an enemy force. Don't you think so?"

Valerius could not believe he'd been that accurate. He grinned back at Marcellus. "The empire is saved! Centurion, I believe we need to celebrate our success. Let's get some wine. I'm buying."

The two men pulled their arrows from the straw target and walked back to the encampment, both satisfied with their mastery of the bow this evening. Marcellus was in an ebullient mood, pleased with their success. As they walked, he began to recite:

There was a legionnaire who slept in the sun.
Woke to find his tunic undone.
He remarked with a smile,
By Zeus, it's a sundial
And now it's quarter to one

Valerius couldn't help but laugh at the limerick.

"What's the matter, Tribune? Never heard Livy recited before?"

"Not that particular verse. No, that's a new one for me."

"I have lots more. I must educate you on some of the finer verses of our Roman poets."

"My tutor, Cato, would be tied in a knot if he heard your classical verse."

"You had a tutor, Tribune?"

Valerius was embarrassed. He'd unintentionally flaunted the huge social gap between the two. He knew his world growing up had been a lot different than the centurion's. He bit his tongue, cursing himself for his stupidity. He needed to change the subject.

"Sort of," he said dismissively. He returned to Marcellus's poetry. "I must hear more of your verse over the coming weeks."

The centurion grinned back at him. "Be my pleasure, Tribune."

After enjoying several goblets of wine with Marcellus, Valerius returned to his quarters. Entering, he spied Calvus, the senior tribune of the general's staff, the man Valerius reported to in the chain of command. While Calvus was his immediate superior, Valerius rarely saw him. Calvus was content to let Valerius take care of business with respect to the pay records. He had little interest in getting involved in that facet of the legions. In fact, he made it a point to steer clear of Tribune Valerius and his records. Not in an unfriendly sense, but Calvus was politically astute. He knew Valerius was in the bad graces of the legate. Any association with him would bring down the ill will of General Varus on his unfortunate ass. If there was a problem with the pay records or a shortage of funds, it would be Valerius's fault, not his.

"Hey, Maximus, what are you doing tomorrow afternoon?"

"The same stuff I usually do. Why?"

"General Varus is holding court with some of the German tribal chiefs. It could be quite a show. Why don't you come? All of the senior staff will be there."

"I'm invited?"

"What are you, dense, Maximus? I just did. Consider yourself invited. Now try to get there. It should be a real spectacle."

Valerius thought about the big event the next day. He'd never been invited nor asked to participate in anything since his arrival. He didn't know what to expect, but he wanted to be there. He had little idea what these German warriors looked like or how they dressed or behaved. It was time he found out. He'd come all this way to serve in Germania, yet he hadn't even had contact with the German people.

He entered the large common area of his quarters, walked past several seated tribunes, then collided into Castor, who had been lurking unseen off to the side. Valerius understood at once that it had been a deliberate ploy on the part of Castor.

"Ah, Maximus, there you are. Haven't seen much of you. I heard they have you taking care of the pay records. Did I tell you I have a place on General Varus's staff?"

Valerius could feel the heat rising. It would be so gratifying to punch his face in, but heeding the warning of Marcellus to lie low and avoid any confrontation, he remained composed. Valerius replied in a calm voice, "Good for you, Castor. I hope you find the experience rewarding."

He turned to avoid Castor, but he jumped in front of him, blocking his path.

"Imagine coming all the way from Rome to supervise some clerks. Are you required to wear a uniform, or can you dress in civilian garb?"

Valerius could take so much. The other tribunes had overheard the exchange and were listening intently, though they pretended not to. Their idle chatter had ceased abruptly. The perfect response came to Valerius in a flash.

"Hey, Castor, since you're assisting and protecting General Varus, perhaps you should take your corpulent self to the drill field and practice your sword fighting skills. I recall your abilities were somewhat lacking. Perhaps I can give you a few pointers. What do you say?"

Castor was shaking with anger. He bit off his words. "I'm not finished with you yet, Maximus. You'll pay for that remark."

Valerius stormed past him, but not before ramming his shoulder into Castor, staggering him several feet sideways. His momentum carried him into a campstool at about knee level. Castor went sprawling on his ample butt.

Valerius knew he should have backed off, but the tribune's lard ass had provoked him beyond his limit. If there was any doubt at all as to who had poisoned Varus against him, that was now clearly evident. Anyway, he rationalized, he hadn't provoked this exchange, Castor had. He walked away triumphantly. He could hear Castor shouting after him from the floor.

"I'll get you for that, Maximus. You'll be sorry you ever crossed paths with me."

Valerius returned to his quarters and sat on his campstool, repeatedly clenching and unclenching his fists, furious more at himself for letting Castor goad him. His brief elation over knocking Castor on his ass had evaporated. No doubt this would spur Castor into other maneuvers against him. He inhaled deeply to dispel his lingering rage. He decided to write a letter. Maybe that would help assuage his anger. His sleeping area was illuminated by a single candle. All was quiet, with the exception of a faint pattering of rain on the leather tent. Valerius pulled his cloak around his shoulders to ward off the chill. He picked up the stylus and parchment, then composed his letter. He needed to ensure his grammar was perfect, because if it wasn't, he would hear about it from Cato.

Cato, I trust all is well with you and this epistle finds you in good health. I am sorry I did not write sooner, but matters have been somewhat eventful here in Germania. My sea journey here was a learning experience for me. The good captain of the ship tutored me in the art of the seamanship and an understanding of the stars. How is it you never taught me that? I had a rather unpleasant encounter in a small port in Gaul that I shall refrain from writing about at this time. I believe it needs to be told in person.

Let me get on to the legions. This encampment is huge. It is surrounded by massive earthen ramparts and is heavily fortified. I never saw so many soldiers before. There are three legions, the XVII, XVIII, and XIX, here on the Weser. They are supposed to be the cream of all the legions in the Northern Empire. We will all live in tents until autumn, when we will journey to our winter quarters on the Rhine. The climate is decidedly cooler here than in Rome and with much less sun. More to the point, it is often miserable and gloomy. Saying all that, the land has a certain rustic beauty. I have not seen much of the Germans yet, but I believe there is a large council meeting with the legate and some of the German chieftains tomorrow.

I will confide in you some serious business about what has happened to me. My first meeting with the legate, General Quinctilius Varus, was a disaster. Apparently a fellow tribune poisoned him against me. I believe you know the family of Castor Nominatus. Apparently they are in tight with the Varus family. Castor holds a personal grudge against me. He is a worm. I remember you telling me that the most dangerous and deceptive animal in this world was the two-legged variety. I have come to appreciate that wisdom. The good general has exiled me to the pay records, which I loathe, by the way.

I am maintaining a low profile, staying out of the general's way. I would ask that you keep this in the strictest confidence. Please do not convey any of this news to my family. I have told them nothing, and for good reason. Between Varus and Nominatus, those are two powerful families who reach all the way to the imperial household. I do not want to have the ripple effects from this situation carry over to Rome. I am sure my father has sense enough not to interfere with these people, but it is better he not know of it.

On a positive note, I have befriended a veteran centurion who is teaching me in the art of the bow. Marcellus is his name. He quotes some of the most vulgar verse you ever heard, attributing it to the classics. I am sure you would enjoy it. Maybe not.

It is time I ended this letter. I will write again when I have seen more of this country and learned more about the ways of the German people. I wish I could be there to talk to you. I hope that time will come soon enough. You will be in my thoughts, and, remember, no word to my family about this Varus mess—not a word.

Your favorite student,
Valerius

The next afternoon, Valerius went to the large headquarters tent for the council meeting. He arrived a bit early to see what was going on and who was there. All of the tribunes and the senior officers were just beginning to file into the spacious chamber. Various small groups were engaged in polite conversation before the meeting. Off to the side, Valerius spied Calvus. Not really friends with anyone else, and owing to the fact that Calvus had at least shown him a little respect by inviting him, he decided to engage him in some dialogue. Valerius walked up to the tribune. He was occupied in discussion with a German. Even better—he would get to meet one of the indigenous people. The German had his back to Valerius, so he could see little of his features. From the rear, the man was wearing cloth trousers fastened at the waist. A leather jerkin covered his upper body. His arms were bare, revealing heavily muscled shoulders and biceps.

Calvus turned to Valerius. His greeting was more of an announcement. "Tribune Valerius Maximus, glad you could come. I want you to meet Arminius. He's commander of the auxiliary cavalry and has been awarded the rank of equestrian."

Arminius turned to stand squarely before the tribune, then stared at Valerius face to face. Valerius, not sure of the customary greeting, nodded coolly at the man, returning the intense gaze. Arminius spoke Latin in a guttural tone. "A pleasure to meet you, Tribune."

Valerius had never seen such eyes. They were a blazing blue that fixed him with a piercing stare. The man had a handsome face. In the custom of the Germans, his hair was worn long, accompanied by a short beard. Valerius judged him to be in his midtwenties. He was an imposing physical warrior. I wouldn't like to cross swords with this one. I'm glad he's on our side.

Calvus spoke. "Arminius distinguished himself as a friend of Rome in the Pannonia revolt. The emperor's stepson, Tiberius, personally knighted him after the campaign. He's one of the good Germans."

Valerius thought he saw a flash of anger in the man's eyes. Arminius tried to hide his animosity, but Valerius saw it. The words had grated upon the man, no doubt about it. This German held contempt for Rome.

Arminius glared at Valerius, no doubt aware that Valerius had seen the flicker of rage that he had unsuccessfully attempted to cloak. Valerius returned the stare, not willing to be the first to break eye contact.

Calvus, sensing a socially awkward situation, continued. "Valerius is one of our new tribunes. Be nice to him, Arminius. He is responsible for the pay records."

Arminius finally spoke in a heavy accent. "Welcome to Germania, Tribune. I'm sure you'll do a good job with the pay records."

He nodded slightly and turned away.

Valerius wasn't sure whether the man had spoken with contempt or not. Probably, yes. He stared after Arminius as he blended into the crowd.

Valerius turned to Calvus. "Are they all like that? You know, the Germans."

"Don't worry about Arminius. He's been with us for a number of years. He's completely trustworthy."

Valerius continued staring in the direction Arminius had gone. "If you say so, Calvus."

Their attention turned toward the front. A Roman officer entered, wearing a spectacular gold breastplate. He strutted about, greeting acquaintances loudly so the entire gathering knew he was there. He was of average height with a large chest, which he puffed out. He appeared to be bowlegged as he paraded about. Valerius gazed at the man and followed him about with his eyes. He turned to Calvus. "Who's that?"

Calvus gave a knowing chuckle. "That is Vala Numinius, commander of the cavalry."

Valerius continued staring at the antics of the man. "A bit taken with himself, isn't he?"

"I guess you could say that. He likes to promote his image and that of his precious cavalry units."

"Are they any good?"

"So I've heard, Valerius. I'll let you be the judge of that."

The tent began to quiet. Two legionnaires entered carrying Roman standards on long poles. They were placed to both sides of a large chair situated on a dais.

As protocol demanded, the visiting German chiefs arrived first, each with a small retinue. They were all big men with long, flowing hair and beards. Each wore trousers made of crude cloth. On their torsos they wore a variety of garments, some of hides and others of rough wool. They all wore multiple armbands of gold and silver.

Valerius noted that the Roman officers were adorned in their finest armor. The gold breastplates gleamed in the light. There was probably enough gold in this room to sink a grain ship. The Germans stood in a small circle warily eyeing their Roman hosts, occasionally speaking in quiet tones among themselves. More time passed.

It was becoming warm in the enclosed space. Men shifted about, uncomfortable with the delay. Some of the lower-ranking Roman officers looked about, politely exchanging nervous looks. Valerius wondered if this was some grand scheme of Varus to throw the Germans off balance.

There was a bustling outside. At last, Varus and his retinue of legion commanders entered. The adjutant called the Roman officers to attention. They immediately stood erect, ceasing all conversation. Varus, clad in his purple cloak, or *lacerna*, which identified him as the legate, strode immediately upon the raised dais to a lavish chair of ornate wood, almost a throne, then sat gracefully. He beamed at everyone as if nothing were wrong and the long wait was of no consequence.

"Welcome, everyone. Let us get down to the proceedings. I believe several of the chieftains have requested an audience with me."

A tribune who served as Varus's aide de camp cleared his throat. He spoke more as a formality, since everyone knew who was there and for what purpose.

"Sir, representatives of the Bructeri, Sugambri, and Marsi tribes are here to speak with you today concerning the tribute that has been levied upon them."

Varus spoke in a magnanimous manner. "I'm always willing to meet with the German leaders. Bring them forth and let them state their case. I'm a fair and reasonable man. Everyone knows that."

A German interpreter communicated this to the three chiefs. He spoke loudly in harsh guttural sounds. Valerius listened intently to the exchange. He had no idea what the interpreter had said. It all sounded like gibberish. The three German leaders approached the dais along with the interpreter. The largest of the three—Valerius didn't know of which tribe—spoke to the linguist in German. In turn, the translator turned and spoke to Varus in slightly accented Latin.

"Greetings, General Varus. We hope you're in good health. We wish to speak to you today about the tribute levied on our tribes."

Varus spoke. "Welcome. I hope you and your people have prospered over the warm summer. Please continue."

The translator addressed the German leaders. In turn, each of the chiefs spoke briefly back to him.

"Sir, the leaders don't know why they must pay so much tax to the Roman. The assessment is almost double that of the previous year."

Varus replied, "Have I not instituted Roman laws in this savage country? There's a Roman peace. Ask if any of them has had his lands raided by marauding tribes since I've been here. There's Roman justice with Roman law. What about all of the roads my legions have built in this wilderness? It costs money to build these roads. Look at all of the wares from the four corners of the empire that have come to them. Commerce is good here, is it not? Go ask them."

The men huddled together, speaking in low tones in their harsh tongue, sometimes arguing with one another. At last the linguist emerged from the conference.

"General Varus, it's true there are Roman laws and many new roads bring in trade, but they don't understand why they should pay such high levies."

Varus frowned, obviously displeased with the German response.

"They're better off for it. They just don't want to admit it. It's that stubborn German pride. Have I not also bestowed upon the leaders generous gifts of land and horses?"

The interpreter went into a conference again with the leaders. The tone of the conversation was now loud and accompanied by wild arm gestures.

"General, they appreciate the gifts, but the tribute far outweighs them."

Varus scoffed. "The roads have generated prosperity, making many of you rich men beyond your wildest expectations."

The translator conferred with the chiefs in a terse exchange. Somewhat flustered, he turned toward Varus and continued. "Sir, they say they have little gold to pay the tribute. Their only wealth is their cattle and horses."

Varus had a vulpine gleam in his eyes. He spoke loudly. "Tell them to sell their cattle and horses for gold. I'll generously extend the terms for delivery of my gold by ten days. That should give them plenty of time."

The interpreter returned to the Germans and spoke. The exchange was loud, with several scathing looks directed at the general. The situation was getting ugly. Arminius, who was strategically positioned off to the side so that he could observe both parties, stepped toward the German contingent. He put his arm around the shoulder of one of the men and conferred in a soothing tone. The men listened to him, losing some of their anger. Muted conversation followed.

Arminius turned to General Varus.

"Sir, the leaders have agreed to collect the gold you requested. They promise to pay you in the time span you've graciously extended to them."

"Arminius, thank you for making them see the wisdom of my ways. I know I can always depend on you to help me. You're truly a friend of Rome. I'll talk to you later about these matters. This meeting is adjourned."

The German contingent quickly exited the tent, not looking back. A group of fawning officers swarmed toward Varus, congratulating him on his handling of the barbarians.

"Exceedingly well done, General. That should put these barbarians in their place," shouted one of the staff.

"Now they understand Roman power," spouted another.

Varus preened for his audience.

"This is just like Syria. You have to show them the wisdom of Roman law and who's in charge. These people are no different than in the east. These barbarians must understand that they live in a land ruled by Rome. Their old ways are gone. Like the other provinces, they must pay their share of taxes."

Several other sycophantic officers approached Varus, including Castor, offering their plaudits of his handling of the situation. This prompted Varus to continue his soliloquy on Roman law and order.

Valerius studied the scene unfolding before him. Now, these were first-class ass kissers. They were so obvious it was enough to make one puke. I will never be one of those.

Outside the tent, Arminius was walking with the German leaders, talking in quiet tones. He quietly spoke to the chieftains.

"We'll talk of this later outside of this camp. It's not safe to discuss matters here. Be patient, my friends. We'll have that dog's head, and soon. Are you with me?"

One of the chiefs, his face crimson with outrage and still seething over the encounter, was about to release a stream of invective aimed at General Varus. Arminius grabbed the man's forearm tightly and gave him a warming look. Arminius gritted his teeth and spoke in a low, menacing tone. "I said, not here."

The chieftain glared at Arminius in anger, then turned his head and shrugged, his rage spent for the moment. The other men nodded to Arminius in silent agreement.

"Good. We'll speak of this tomorrow."

Arminius walked away from the others, grinning inwardly. Things couldn't have gone better had he planned it. This latest act by that fool Varus would draw even more of the German tribes to his plan. He and all the Germans would have their revenge, and soon.

Valerius hurried from the tent, eager to share what he had just seen with Marcellus. He wasn't exactly sure what he'd just witnessed. Was it a victory for Roman diplomacy or something else? He found the centurion sitting alone mulling over some wax tablets. The clerks had been dismissed for the day. He looked up as Valerius entered.

"Ah, the tribune is back from the council meeting. Did we put those fierce Germans in their place today?"

"Marcellus, it was strange." Valerius now addressed the centurion by his familiar name, although Marcellus continued to refer to Valerius as Tribune.

"How so?"

"It was quite a performance by our noble general. He arrived late. He was very demeaning to the German chiefs. He demanded a large tribute from them in gold. It got extremely contentious. This German auxiliary—I think his name was Arminius—stepped in and smoothed things out. If not for him, I believe we would've had a sword fight right there in the tent."

"You said he demanded tribute from them in gold?"

"Yes. It didn't appear they had a lot of gold to pay the general."

"You know what they say about our esteemed legate?"

"What?"

"You're aware that he was the former governor of Syria."

"Yes, I know that, Marcellus."

"They say he went into a rich province a poor man and departed a poor province a rich man."

Valerius laughed. "Marcellus, I'm not sure this was best way to handle these Germans. Of course, I'm not a legate, but I have to believe these people were irate. They were humiliated."

"Tribune, better watch what you say here. These tents have ears, if you know what I mean."

Valerius leaned closer and spoke in a softer tone. "You mean people would report back on these conversations."

Marcellus nodded. "There are informers everywhere. Best not to let any of this get back to you know who. You're already on the stercus list."

"I guess we should continue this conversation at the archery field. I know we're alone there. I wonder if anyone else has doubts about our supreme commander."

"There are others who question his ability to govern this territory, but they keep it to themselves. Just remember, the emperor appointed this man. That should say enough. Who are we, a humble tribune and lowly centurion, to question the man? As I said, we can discuss this outside the walls."

Later that evening, Castor entered the general's quarters. He'd been invited to dine with Varus. This wasn't the sharing of army rations; it was to be a feast. Castor licked his lips in anticipation. This army food was dreadful—wheat porridge, bread, and boiled vegetables supplemented occasionally by some unknown meat or fish. His slaves ate better back in Rome.

Castor was ushered by the servants into a spacious tent with oil lamps illuminating the area. Soft carpets had been placed on the floor. Small tables had been set up, surrounded by plump cushions. Although no food was in sight, Castor could smell all sorts of delicious aromas wafting through the general area. Varus was in animated conversation with another officer. He looked up as Castor approached.

"Come in, Castor. Come in," boomed Varus. He was in an ebullient mood. "You've met General Caecina, my deputy and chief of operations."

Castor nodded. "Of course. How are you sir?" He continued, "Thank you for inviting me, General. Something smells delicious. I hope I didn't keep the two of you waiting."

"Nonsense, Castor. You're right on time. Tonight we feast, Castor. This is not Rome, but we manage to put on a proper banquet now and then. What do you say, Caecina?"

"You're correct, sir. I've been looking forward to it all day."

Varus spoke. "Let us begin. Castor, you go to my left over here, and General Caecina, you go to my right."

Varus nodded to the servants waiting in the background. Wine was poured into their goblets. Various fruits and vegetable were brought in for the men to nibble on while they gulped down the wine. The men chatted briefly about the hardships of army life. At the insistence of General Varus, Castor began imparting the latest gossip from Rome.

"Let me see, where should I begin?" Castor stroked his chin in thought.

"Oh. Come on, Castor, tell us the juicy details of who's in bed with whom," said Varus. "Don't you agree, Caecina?"

"Quite right, sir. I'm sure there's enough going on to keep us entertained."

"Stop toying with us, Castor," said Varus jokingly.

Castor gave him a knowing grin. "There's Senator Antonius's wife, Flavia. What a piece of work she is. I think she's bedded half of the Senate."

Varus interrupted. "She's that little dark-haired one with the enormous chest."

"That would be her, sir."

Varus laughed. "I wouldn't mind a go at her myself. What about you, Castor?"

"No, sir. I wouldn't mind either."

Castor continued with his recital of transgressions in the city of power and wealth.

After a time, enormous platters that contained almost an entire wild boar, a variety of fishes, and roasted venison followed. The steam rose off the large silver plates as the succulent meats and fishes were presented the three men. They tore into the food, stuffing it into their mouths. There was little in the way of conversation; they were too busy gorging themselves. The men grunted as they ate. Their faces were covered in grease as they washed the food down with more wine.

At last Varus spoke. "I've arranged for a little entertainment for us tonight. Please continue eating. We have all sorts of sweets and delicacies yet to be served." He clapped his hands.

A flute player emerged, accompanied by three young women, imported from the eastern provinces, given their darker appearance. The women wore diaphanous garments that left little to the imagination. They began swaying in time to the melodic notes. The three men grinned knowingly at one another. As the women danced, the men lusted after them with their eyes. As they continued their sensuous motions, bits and pieces of their costumes fell to the floor. In no time, the women were lying with the men on the carpets, practicing their trade.

XII

*J*ulia hummed happily and made her way to her tent. Her long legs carried her gracefully down the worn path. Despite her weariness, she had a bounce to her step. A bright sun in a cloudless sky warmed her face, for which she was grateful. The weather in Germania, as she knew from experience, could be fickle. She'd learned to enjoy a balmy day, for tomorrow could bring forth torrents of rain and wind. From her vantage point on the low hillside on the outskirts of the army encampment, she had a panoramic view of the massive fortifications. Like some immense eruption from the earth's surface, the walls of timbers and dirt emerged from the grass plain along the river.

The animal pens and shelters from which she'd just emerged were situated outside the fortress. It would be impractical to have the beasts that served legions enclosed within the fortification walls. This would create all sorts of hygiene problems, with the troops up to their knees in animal dung. There was ample room for the beasts to graze here on the grassy outskirts. The animals and the staff who watched over them were close enough to be protected by the men of the encampment if the need arose. With the exception of a few isolated thefts of horses by some local bandits and some isolated attacks on the mules by wolves, all was pretty much secure.

Julia was exhausted. She'd been up half the night assisting her father in the delivery of a new foal. It had been a difficult labor, but just as the dawn broke the morning sky, the new colt had made his way into this world. She didn't have to be there. Her father, the camp veterinarian, had plenty of staff to assist him with the several thousand animals, mostly mules and oxen, plus the horses for the cavalry squadrons. Julia helped her father because she liked being with him and caring for the beasts.

She'd inherited her father's gift of sensing an animal's mood and knowing when things weren't right. Julia was almost as good as her father, Petrocolus. He'd taught her everything he knew. Over the years, he had patiently schooled her, demonstrating the proper ways of caring for the beasts. She'd soaked up the knowledge like a sponge.

Julia had grown up in the presence of the legions. Her mother had died from one of the plagues that swept through the countryside when Julia was but a little girl. Her father had no other family or friends with whom he could place the young child, not that he would want to part from her, for she was his pride and joy. But bringing up a daughter in the camps of the legions wasn't the most desirable of places. The two had made do as best they could. Julia had become the willing apprentice of her father. She wasn't unhappy with her fate. She loved her life with the animals. She was good at it and couldn't even contemplate anything different.

Even with her fatigue, Julia carried herself straight and tall. Like her father, she was long in stature and almost as tall as many of the soldiers. Her hair was a soft brown, and she wore it short. Long hair was a luxury she couldn't afford in her line of work. It got in the way, and there was no time for care and grooming. The women of Rome could wear their hair in the latest coiffures, but not so out here on the German frontier; plain and simple was the rule. At twenty years of age, she was a fully mature woman with a stunning figure.

Julia entered the tent and stripped off her soiled garments. She washed as best she could in the basin of water and put on a soft cotton shift. She was going to grab a few hours of needed sleep. Later in the afternoon, she'd decided, she would journey upriver and bathe in a large, cool pool she'd discovered earlier in the summer. The water would be refreshing. The soldiers of the fort had constructed a makeshift bath for themselves by cutting out sections of the bank in the river. While this might serve the soldiers, it was hardly a place a woman could venture. Julia reclined on her cot and was asleep almost immediately.

It was a beautiful day made even better by the fact that the cohort commander of the Tenth Cohort, Eighteenth Legion, Centurion Clodius, had given the entire unit the afternoon off. Soon it would be the cohort's turn to patrol the German territory outside the safe confines of the walled encampment. It was good for the men to relax and rest before the grinding physical march into the German countryside.

Lucius and Cassius were in high spirits, especially Lucius, who had just completed his two long weeks of latrine duty as punishment for his altercation with Decius. Latrine penance was considered one of the worst sentences. Cleaning and emptying the waste from the privies was a truly disgusting job. This task was always reserved for the transgressors and rule breakers. Some would say that they even preferred physical punishment. In any event, Lucius had served his time.

Centurion Frontinus had inspected his work and grunted his approval, not yet ready to give any praise to the newcomers. In the past few days, the centurion had mellowed somewhat toward the recruits, but he still kept a wary eye on them all, especially Lucius. Frontinus was not yet ready to give them equal status with the unit's veterans. The smallest infraction or hesitation during battle drill would merit his rebuke. But lately, there were fewer reprimands.

Lucius and Cassius had purchased a flask of wine and some bread and cheese. They were venturing upriver for a refreshing swim. It was common sense that one always ventured upstream from the encampment to swim or bath. All of the latrines flushed downstream from the fort. The beauty and clarity of the river above the encampment was pristine. Below the camp was a place not to venture. They had invited Domitius and Flavius, but they had the bad luck to be assigned guard duty.

Both soldiers wore their gray tunics, but no armor or helmets. They did, however, have their gladii and daggers secured from their belts. The general rule was for the men to wear their armor and weapons outside the gates. But even this code was relaxed, given the current peaceful state of the surrounding region. There had not been the slightest hint of hostilities from the Germans. So the legion's revised doctrine was that a legionnaire could venture forth outside the gates without armor, but sword and dagger must be carried at all times.

"Cassius, I heard in the early fall we march out of here to our permanent encampment at Vetera. I asked some of the guys about it. They said the duty isn't bad. We have a roof over our head. They a have a bath facility and some fine drinking establishments outside the fort. The main complaint that I heard was that it gets cold enough to freeze your ass off. They said that we're expected to drill even in the cold and snow."

"I heard the same thing. It doesn't sound too bad except for the part about the cold."

Cassius continued walking, not saying anything. That was unusual for him.

"Why so glum, Cassius? I thought I was the melancholy one."

"Lucius, I'm concerned about this business with Decius. After we break camp here, how's this going to play out when we're all in the same barracks? I keep looking over my shoulder for him."

"What the Hades, Cassius? You are beginning to sound like me. I'll take care of Decius. Am I concerned? Yes, but I'm not overly worried. I know we new guys aren't exactly accepted by the veterans. But the others don't like Decius either. He's a deranged asshole. You heard them the other night in the mess area. They told us he had it coming. I know the centurion keeps a close eye on us. He has some doubts about us as soldiers, but I can't believe he favors Decius and his cronies. Listen, as I said before, we need to stick together on this— you, me, Flavius, and Domitius."

Cassius stopped walking to consider Lucius's remarks.

"Hey, you're right. Let's get going. We're wasting our time walking so slowly. I can taste the wine already."

Julia, refreshed from her brief nap, walked along the river, heading upstream. She carried a coarse towel draped over her arm. Earlier in the summer, she'd discovered a secluded spot on a feeder stream that emptied into the main river. About fifty yards into the woods from the creek's entrance into the main river was a deep pool surrounded by trees that sheltered the view from anyone walking along the riverbank. It was her secret grotto. It was hard for a woman to find any privacy in a fortress with twenty thousand men, but incredibly, she'd discovered this spot.

Julia slowed her pace, recognizing the large thorn bush with multicolored leaves. This was her beacon for the hidden track from the path along the river. Here a small game trail broke through the thickets and trees that led to the bathing pool. She glanced in both directions to be sure she wasn't observed, then darted into the foliage. She crouched down to avoid the overhanging vines and turned toward the stream.

She reached the tranquil setting and smiled at the beauty of her secluded spot. On her side of the stream, the land sloped gradually down toward the creek, ending in a small sand-and-gravel beach at the water's edge. On the opposite side, perhaps thirty feet across, a huge rock over ten feet high bordered the creek. One couldn't see the bottom in the deep pool sheltered by the boulder and the overhanging tree limbs. Rays of sunshine slanted through the tree branches, warming the still waters of the creek.

Julia glanced about again to see if anyone might possibly be around. She saw nothing suspicious. The only sounds were from the songbirds nesting in the surrounding trees. With a smile, she untied her sandals, shook off her cloak, and unfastened the pin that held her linen shift on her shoulders. She was totally naked under the shift. She stood on her toes and arched her back, stretching her joints.

She waded into the pool, exhilarating in the clean coolness of the waters. She floated on her back, motionless, blissfully unaware of the world around her. She giggled to herself as several small minnows surfaced to nibble on her toes.

Lucius and Cassius wandered upriver, not far from a place where a small stream entered the larger river. Both men quickly shed their weapons and clothes and dashed into the water. They found a slough in the waterway where the current was minimal. Both men floated dreamily in the cool waters. After a time, they withdrew, put on their tunics, and sat down to enjoy some wine and cheese. The two men stared out over the water, content to listen to the comforting sounds of the river as it splashed over the rocks.

"Cassius, have you ever thought about taking a wife and having a family?"

"I did before all this happened. My future is somewhat spoken for over the next twenty years. You know we're not permitted to marry while in the legion. Why did you ask?"

"Nothing. Just idle curiosity."

"Lucius, I know you won't marry and have a family."

"How do you know?"

"The sibyl didn't tell you."

"You had to bring that up, didn't you?"

"Of course. How could I pass up that opportunity?"

"Always the wise ass, eh, Cassius?"

"Lucius, you overstate. By the way, I heard some of the veterans talking about a celebration festival when we get to our winter quarters at Vetera. They sacrifice a few animals to consecrate our arrival, then it's time to feast. They said that there are roasts of wild boar, venison, ducks, and geese, with plenty of wine. I get hungry just thinking about it."

"Hey, I'm up for that. When was the last time we had something above and beyond our standard rations?"

"Start counting the days, Lucius. We'll be gorging ourselves before you know it."

Lucius grinned back. "Pass the wine, Cassius."

Julia exited the pool refreshed. The sunlight glistened off the beaded moisture on her body. She arched her back and stretched. Her skin tingled with pleasure. She felt wonderful. She patted herself dry with the rough cloth. She paused in her ritual and stood still. She thought she heard a rustling in the thicket. It was difficult to hear above the gurgling of the water. Probably a small animal. She listened again, then looked around her, but saw nothing. She decided it was best to dress quickly. She was alone. Nobody knew she was here. Julia raised the linen shift over her head and slipped into the garment.

She was startled as three legionnaires led by Decius emerged out of the brush, leering at her. She backed up but realized there was nowhere to go. The creek was to her rear. The three men had her hemmed in on every side. She was trapped.

"Leave me alone, you slime." Julia cursed herself for not bringing her dagger with her. She retreated even farther down toward the creek. She looked around in panic, searching for a safe haven, a place to flee.

"Why don't you shed your clothes, missy? You looked just fine before," the ugly one in the middle with a deformed nose said to her. The others gave a chuckle at his remarks.

"Get away from me," she shouted.

The legionnaire to her left, a large man with a long scar on his face, reached toward her and ripped her shift, exposing a plump breast. "I'll even help you." The man grinned at the other two for approval, taking his eyes from Julia. It was a mistake. Julia booted him square in the groin with all of her strength. The man went down, screaming in pain.

The other two quickly rushed her, but Julia was agile and quick. Decius attempted to grab her, but she sidestepped his advance, then raked the side of his face with her nails. Decius backed off, holding his face. He brought his hand away from his face. It came away with blood on it. He snarled at her.

"You're going to pay for this, bitch. I'm going to hurt you bad." He advanced toward her with an evil grin. Julia yelled piercingly again.

The other legionnaire, a tall, thin man with bad teeth and a hooked nose, grabbed her from behind. Julia screamed shrilly as the man twisted her arm. Her shift fell to her waist. She managed to break away briefly but was quickly overcome by the man's strength. She shrieked once more.

Lucius and Cassius were sitting by the river enjoying their wine. Cassius was expounding on the feminine beauties of his hometown.

"Claudia was the most beautiful of the bunch, Lucius. She had hair of gold and a figure like Venus."

"Cassius, the next time you'll get to see her, she'll probably be an old hag, so stop thinking about her."

"Lucius, she was stunning. I remember this one—"

Lucius held up his hand. "Shhh. What was that?"

"What?"

They both heard the yell above the rushing waters. Lucius grabbed his sword and ran downriver toward the sound. Cassius fumbled with his marching sandals and leaped up after Lucius. After about fifty yards, Lucius stopped and listened again. The scream was repeated, but shriller. Lucius charged off the trail through the thick brush toward the direction of the high-pitched shriek.

Julia screamed once more and tried to kick Decius in the groin. It didn't work. He was wise to her now. One of her arms was pinned by the thin legionnaire. She continued to flail with her free arm at the approaching Decius. She attempted another kick in his direction. She was rewarded with a savage punch to her stomach. Decius then slapped her in the face, stunning her momentarily.

Lucius charged through heavy brush, ignoring the long thorns that tore at his tunic and exposed skin. He burst into the edge of the clearing unseen by the three assailants. He sized up the situation before him. Decius was in the act of striking a young woman—quite beautiful from his brief glance—while a second man held the poor girl. A third legionnaire was prone, curled in a fetal position moaning and holding his crotch. Two against one with a third man incapacitated.

Not bad odds at all. He had no idea how far behind him Cassius was, so Lucius decided to act quickly.

Decius was about to hit Julia again when he was smashed to the ground by a hurtling figure out of the brush. Lucius charged into him full bore with his entire weight behind him. Decius went flying in a heap. Lucius quickly drew his gladius.

"Let her go," Lucius yelled at the tall, thin man holding her. For emphasis he waved his sword and pointed it directly at the man's face. The legionnaire immediately released her.

Decius was groggily attempting to get to his feet. Lucius rushed over. He savagely kicked the prone figure in the face and placed the gladius at his throat. "Well, well, Sir Decius. We meet again. Picking on women this time, I see."

Decius answered in a croak.

Lucius stood over the fallen man. "How about if you and me have it out right now? There's no centurion around this time to stop us. What do you say, Decius?"

He didn't answer. He woozily looked up at Lucius, not quite registering what had happened to him. Lucius placed the point of the sword on his throat and deliberately drew blood. He grew angrier just looking at Decius.

"You slimy piece of shit. I should cut your head off now."

Cassius crashed through the brush, sword in hand. He surveyed the scene before him. Lucius was standing over the prostrate form of Decius with his sword at his exposed throat.

"Not again. Lucius, you must back off. You can't kill him."

"I should finish him now."

"Report him to the centurion."

"What's he going to do? Unless he killed the lady, he'll ignore it."

He looked in contempt at the two men on the ground. Decius was sprawled in the dirt not saying a word. The other man continued to moan softly, still clutching his family jewels. Lucius glared at the three. Seeing that Lucius was preoccupied with Decius, the tall, thin legionnaire with the bad teeth inched his hand toward the hilt of his sword. Lucius took notice and raised the point of his sword away from Decius and directly at the standing legionnaire's face.

"You just go ahead and draw that thing and see what happens."

The man quickly dropped his hand away.

Lucius glared at the man. "Get your two asshole friends out of here." Lucius gestured with his sword for added emphasis. "And be quick about it."

Julia was standing with her arms across her naked breasts, blood trickling from the corner of her mouth. The unscathed legionnaire helped the two figures from the ground. The three men hurriedly stumbled through the bushes, exiting the area without looking back. Lucius rushed over, grabbed Julia's clothing, and handed it to her. She quickly wrapped it around her shoulders, covering her exposed flesh.

"Are you all right, lady?"

Julia responded, her voice trembling, "Yes, I think so."

"My name is Lucius, and my friend over there is Cassius."

Julia had recovered some of her composure by now, although she was shaking.

"My name is Julia. I thank you for rescuing me from those thugs."

"We've clashed with that group before, my lady. They're a bad bunch. We're not all like that."

"Would you mind turning around while I adjust my shift?"

"Of course. Sorry about that."

Lucius and Cassius turned their backs while Julia adjusted her garments. She fastened her clothing about her as best as possible.

"You can turn around now." Julia stared at the tall one, liking the figure before her. Her father had told her over and over to stay away from the soldiers. They were a rough, uncouth lot, but there was something about this one that captivated her. She couldn't explain it.

Lucius, aware of the awkward silence, tried to make the best of the situation. "We would be pleased to accompany you to wherever you need to go."

Somewhat recovered, Julia giggled. "I'm going to the same place you are. My father is the veterinarian for the legions."

"In that case, we'd be glad to escort you back. Right, Cassius?"

"By all means."

"Will those three be lurking along the way?" Julia's voice quivered a bit as she spoke.

"I think not. I believe they've had enough for today, but Cassius and I will keep an eye out just in case."

They walked back along the river. The two men stopped briefly to recover the rest of their gear. Lucius racked his brain to think of an appropriate subject to converse with the young lady. He certainly didn't want to discuss the attempted assault. He was sure she didn't want to relive that experience again.

Julia began speaking, her voice still trembling from the recent encounter. "So tell me, how long have you been with the eagles?"

Cassius responded, "Julia, in truth, we just arrived a few weeks ago."

Lucius jumped in. "Cassius and I are from Gaul. We were conscripted in the early spring. We met each other at our training garrison. They sent us here."

He continued in a self-effacing tone. "I'm sure the northern borders of the empire are now safe with Cassius and me."

Julia laughed at his wit. "Yes, I knew I felt more secure beginning a few weeks ago. It must have been because of the two of you. I've been with the legions all of my life. Most of the time, we were in towns near the forts to which my father was posted. My mother died when I was young. I've been living with my father since. I have no other family nor any place to go."

Cassius cleared his throat. "Not to offend you, Julia, but the encampment of the legion is no place for a young woman."

Julia laughed.

"True, it can be dangerous, but I manage. I love helping my father and his staff with the animals. It's the only life I've ever known. I've made friends with some of the families of the soldiers who live outside the camp."

Lucius asked about the upcoming exodus to the permanent garrison. "I assume you've been to Vetera. How do you find the quarters there?"

Julia thought about it a minute. "I love the warmer weather here, even if we live in tents. The march to Vetera is hard, but it's nice to have a solid roof over your head, especially in the cold winters."

They continued strolling downriver, talking about the legions, Julia's animals, her father, and some of the families who lived outside the garrison. The conversation was light and easy. They soon arrived at Julia quarters. There was an awkward silence as the three stood there. Lucius wasn't sure what to say, but he didn't want to turn his back on the beautiful woman and walk away.

Julia spoke first. "Thank you both for helping me."

Lucius wasn't sure how to respond, so he just nodded. Julia was hoping he might say something about coming back to meet her father or something, but no such luck. There was silence. Feeling bold, she said, "Come around sometime. I'll have you meet my father. I'll show you how we care for the animals." She said it to both Cassius and Lucius, but there was no doubt that she was addressing Lucius. She was staring straight into his eyes.

Lucius responded quickly. "I'd like that. How would I find you in all of this?" He spread his arms to indicate the vastness of the area.

"Just ask anyone around here. They all know who I am and where to find me."

Lucius and Cassius said good-bye, then started walking back toward the fort. Julia stared at the retreating forms, wondering if the tall one known as Lucius would come back to see her. She hoped so. Julia smiled to herself. It had been like a bolt of lightning exploding through her when she'd looked upon his face. It was something she couldn't understand. Nothing like this had ever happened to her before. Perhaps this was what her mother had experienced when she first met her father.

She would speak with her father about it later this afternoon. She couldn't avoid the subject. Her face was swollen where she had been struck. Her father would want to know what had happened. It would be a difficult discussion, as it involved a legionnaire. He had made it clear that she should avoid the soldiers at all costs, which she had for most of her life. She gazed after them once more, turned, and went to her quarters. I hope he got my message.

XIII

*L*ucius stared out into the darkness from the palisade. He pulled on his heavy cloak, known as a *sagum*, to ward off the evening chill and the driving rain. He peered to the ground below from his elevated perch. Nothing, that was what he saw. What a waste of time. But he had best be alert. The duty centurion would be checking the night watch. It was a matter taken very seriously by the legions, no matter how unlikely the possibility of attack. The punishment for sleeping or lack of attentiveness while on guard duty was severe.

It was a boring night, and he was expected to participate in his unit's drill and training the next morning. The fact that a soldier had little or no sleep was unimportant. One was counted upon to be there in formation at daybreak, no excuses. As Centurion Frontinus said, "The emperor pays you for a full day of service. He wants his money's worth."

No one appreciated his humor. Centurion Longinius had said the same thing. He wasn't funny either. These centurions all had the same wit, or lack thereof.

To pass the time, Lucius thought of Julia often. In fact, that was all he thought about. She captivated his mind. Lucius reveled in her words, visualizing her image from his brief encounter. Her laugh was infectious. It would make anyone smile. He couldn't explain his attraction to her. He was totally mesmerized. He had met a few beautiful women before, but he'd never been this overwhelmed. He was waiting for the chance when he would have some free time. There was no doubt that she'd extended an invitation for him to come and see her. He intended to follow through on that. The question was, when? He had no idea, but he hoped it would be soon.

A week later, by some strange quirk of fate, he was free for the afternoon. It was indeed peculiar. Almost everyone in his century was assigned some sort of duty or other. Cassius and Flavius were assigned to a water detail and Domitius to gate guard. Lucius was relieved in that he need not explain to anyone where he was going.

He put on a clean tunic and fastened his belts so he could wear his sword and dagger. Inhaling deeply to calm his nerves, he ventured out of his tent, then rushed, almost at a run, to the south gate. He passed several units performing drills and various small working parties. Not today, not me. He was free of the legion's grasp, if just for a short while. Lucius picked up the pace, hurrying through the gate, waving to the sentries as he exited. They barely acknowledged his presence.

He ventured to the area where the animals for the legions were penned. There were beasts everywhere. Many were massed in corrals, others were by themselves in individual stalls, and some were being herded out in the open to graze. The cacophony of animal sounds was overwhelming. They seemed to feed off one another as to which could make the most discordant sounds. The mules were braying nonstop. The oxen bellowed the loudest. He could hear horses in the distance, with their distinct whinnying sounds.

Lucius stopped and looked around for some assistance. He spied several men to his immediate front tossing armfuls of hay toward the penned oxen. He asked them where he might find Julia. One jerked his thumb and shouted something about the sick pen. Lucius wandered another hundred yards toward a small fenced-in area. There she was, inside the corral with several men, attending to a horse. Julia knelt and applied some type of liniment to the horse's right foreleg. She spoke in a soothing voice to the animal. The horse remained totally calm while Julia delicately smeared the concoction up and down the leg of the animal. It was as if the horse knew that she would take care of it. When she'd finished, she bound the leg tightly with a woolen cloth.

The men holding the colt let go. One might expect the horse to go careening around the pen, bucking and kicking. Instead, the animal went immediately over to Julia and nuzzled her with his long nose. Julia stroked the animal's face, whispering to it. She held up a bundle of oats for the horse to eat. Lucius had some experience with horses. He knew them to be unpredictable and often excitable, especially young colts. He'd never seen anything like what Julia had just done.

Lucius edged closer to Julia and the horse. He nervously cleared his throat. "*Salve*, Julia."

She looked up at him, smiling brightly. Lucius gave an inward sigh of relief. She appeared glad that he was here and not the least bit self-conscious given that she was in the middle of a horse pen and wearing a garment splattered with mud and other undesirable material usually found around animal pens. She was in her element and not ashamed of it.

"Lucius, you came to see me. How nice."

She ducked through the wooden enclosures in the pen and came next to Lucius. "Come with me back to my quarters so I can change out of these clothes."

The two started walking side by side. Now that she was closer to him, Lucius could make out some puffiness around the corner of her mouth where Decius had struck her.

"If you don't mind my asking, how did you manage that?"

"Manage what?"

"You know, bandage that colt's leg without him kicking up a storm."

Julia laughed. "A lot of people ask me the same thing. I know these animals. They understand I won't harm them. It's hard to explain sometimes, but it's like we're one."

"You've never been kicked or stomped?"

"A few times, but I've learned when to be careful in certain situations. There's usually a reason for their behavior. The trick is to recognize their mood."

"That was truly remarkable. You must be gifted."

"That's what my father says."

The two arrived at a modest-looking structure, a slightly larger version of the eight-man tent Lucius shared with his squad, but this one had a wooden platform for a floor. Julia parted the flaps.

"Wait here. I'll just be a moment."

Lucius caught a brief glimpse into the interior as she pushed the flap aside. He noted some actual furniture, including some throw rugs, and all in all, it appeared quite comfortable. It was certainly better than the quarters he shared with seven others. Lucius stood outside cooling his heels, congratulating himself for coming here. He'd made the correct decision. Julia seemed pleased to see him.

She reappeared after a brief time clad in a clean woolen shift. Her hair was combed, and the mud spatters were gone from her face. "Are you hungry, Lucius?"

"Sure, I could go for some food. A soldier is always hungry."

Julia went to another enclosure and returned with a small bundle and a container holding some wine. She handed them to him. They started walking.

"Lucius, I assume you're off duty and have some free time."

"Yes, I have the rest of the afternoon off. Where are we going?"

"You'll see when we get there," she said teasingly.

The two strolled upriver for some time. They finally came to a spot where the riverbank opened to an area almost like a small beach. The current was slow here. The river made a wide curve around the shoreline. Julia broke out the food. She'd brought some bread, cheese, and fruit along with the wine. She spread the cloth on the ground and laid out the food. They were both famished. Lucius made an effort to put on his best table manners, trying not to dribble wine down his chin and make a fool out of himself. Dining etiquette was something not practiced to any extent in the legions.

"Julia, this is a beautiful spot. How did you find it?"

"I like to take walks. I need to leave the camp at times, just to get out. I explore the woods around here. I know lots of places."

Lucius decided to drop the subject. He didn't want to revisit Decius's attempted assault of last week.

"Lucius, do you have a family?"

"Yes, I do. I miss them very much."

"Tell me about them."

Lucius spoke carefully and distinctly, lest he lapse into the lexicon of the soldier. Words that were commonplace in the vocabulary of the legions weren't proper around the likes of Julia.

"I come from a small town in Gaul. My father has a business. He transports amphorae. I was his number-one helper until I was conscripted by order of the emperor into the legions."

"You didn't volunteer?"

"Not likely."

"Maybe it was your fate."

Lucius paused, his thoughts going back to the sibyl and her prophecy. "You're probably correct. I'll speak about that later. I have a younger brother, Paetus, and a younger sister, Drusilla. She'd like you. She never had a sister, just my brother and me. We were good at tormenting her."

"Lucius, how could you? Teasing your little sister."

"I didn't say tease. I said torment."

"You should be ashamed. Do you really torment her? I find that hard to believe."

"It was all in fun. I wish I could see her again. I have no idea when I'll ever get the opportunity to be with any of them," he said wistfully.

"What about your mother?"

"She's a beautiful lady. She's a friend to everyone in the village. I sure miss her cooking, especially her baking."

"Were they sad to see you leave?"

"Yes, it was hard on them. My father didn't say too much, but I could tell he was upset." Lucius frowned, recalling the sadness of his departure some months ago. He could still see with great clarity the tear-streaked faces of his mother and sister.

"My parents understood that I had no choice on the matter. My fate was sealed. If the emperor calls, you'd best go."

"Do they know where you are?"

"Yes, I think so. I was told the legions sent a notice of my assignment and location to the town where I live. I'm sure the magistrate told them the news."

"It must be difficult for them without you."

"It was not easy for them to accept. I know it was certainly hard for me. During the first few weeks of training, all I thought of was my family. I desired to be back with them in the worst way. Call it homesickness, or perhaps the unpleasant training regimen; I wanted out."

"Lucius, I know a way to get mail sent to your family. If you don't mind my asking, can you write?"

"Yes, of course. I had schooling, even a tutor for a little while."

Julia raised her eyebrows. "A legionnaire who had a tutor. That's a strange combination, Lucius. No offense, but that is uncommon."

Lucius grinned back. "No offense taken. But it's true."

Lucius said a silent prayer for his mother, who was the one who'd insisted he have private schooling.

"My mother wanted me to do something besides assist my father. She thought that someday I'd become someone of importance as a result of my education. The legions sure put an end to that." There was a brief pause in the conversation as both munched on some bread.

"Back to the letters, Julia. How can I get letters sent? I thought it was only the rich people and official business of Rome who could send letters, scrolls, and the like."

"Ah, I see I've piqued your interest. My father has an official position in the legions. Who's to say that official and privileged correspondence can't be sent to...where's your home again?"

"It's called Belilarcum."

"Belilarcum," she repeated.

"Julia, to think you'd take advantage of your father's position in the legions to send mail," he said in mock seriousness.

"Yes, precisely. I know a few other tricks too."

"I can't wait to hear about these."

"Maybe later. Let's change the subject."

"What about you, Julia? Tell me of your life."

"As I told you before, when we first met, my mother died of the fever when I was young. I've lived with my father, Petrocolus, all my life. I have no other family. My father is the head veterinarian for the legions," she said proudly. "I have lived around soldiers all my life."

"It must be hard for you."

"It's sad not having a mother, but I love helping my father with the animals. My days are pleasant enough. My father has a network of friends. We've dined with some of the legates' families in the past, but not with this Varus. We've spent time in Gaul and Hispania. It was a little more civilized there."

Lucius spoke. "I imagine it's difficult getting used to living in a tent."

"It is, but it's for a short time. Once we get back to Vetera on the Rhine, our accommodations are much improved. We have a solid roof over our head and a wooden floor. There's clean running water in many places. There are constant supply boats bringing all sorts of good food to the fort. Of course, the rations do become a little sparse in the dead of winter, when all of the rivers freeze. We even get visitors from Gaul on occasion. You'll see when we get there."

"Julia, tell me of your future. What do you see for yourself?"

Julia sighed. "My mother told me when I was a little girl that someday I'd have a family of my own. She said she consulted a seer, who charted the positions of the stars the day I was born. She said I'd lead a happy life with many children. Do you believe in fate, Lucius? Can someone read the stars and tell you of your fortune?"

Lucius paused in thought. Julia looked at him expectantly.

"I never believed in that stuff. I thought it was just so much garbage. Then, one night I was out with some of my friends, and I drank too much wine. I went to see a sibyl. She foretold my conscription and posting to Germania."

Lucius didn't tell her about the rest.

Julia laughed. "Maybe it was a lucky guess."

"Maybe it was, but it was damn uncanny." Lucius reddened slightly as he realized his vocabulary was becoming coarse. "Uh, sorry about the language, Julia. You know how soldiers talk."

Julia seemed pleased that he had corrected himself.

"What else did this sibyl say to you?"

"Oh, not too much else. Nothing of importance."

There was a brief lull in the conversation as both sipped their wine, staring at each other's faces. They talked the rest of the afternoon, enjoying the tranquil scene by the river. Lucius tried to keep his eyes on Julia's face and not the gentle curves under her shift. The shadows were lengthening toward the end of the day. Lucius offered his hand to Julia to help her up. She grasped his hand and didn't let go. Lucius felt a tingle go up his arm. They walked leisurely, hand in hand, along the river.

"I want you to meet my father when we get back. He would like you."

"And I'd like to meet him."

"Good. I'm sure we'll find him engaged with some sort of problem with the beasts."

They wandered back to the area where the animals were sheltered. They found her father supervising the attempted yoking of two massive oxen. The beasts were unwilling participants despite the efforts of several men. The oxen were clearly agitated, resisting any attempt of the two men to place the heavy wooden yoke on them. They stomped and churned the earth with their hoofs. They bellowed, turning their heads violently side to side. Julia approached her father, waiting for him to look up. After several moments, he saw his daughter.

"Lucius, this is my father, Petrocolus. Father, this is Lucius, the soldier I told you about."

"A pleasure to meet you sir." Lucius was putting on his best manners.

The father nodded tersely at Lucius. From his demeanor, he was clearly not thrilled to have his daughter in the company of a legionnaire, or maybe he was just preoccupied with the task at hand. Lucius regarded the man in front of him. He was middle-aged and fairly tall, with a slight paunch around his middle. His hair, which he kept short, had a generous mixture of silver interspersed with the brown. There was some facial resemblance to Julia, although not a lot.

There was an awkward silence. Lucius decided to act.

"I have some experience with these animals. If you don't mind, let me see what I can do."

Back at his home, this was an everyday task. Lucius had handled and cared for the two oxen that they used to pull the heavy wagon loaded with amphorae. The animals projected an aura of stupidity, but Lucius had come to understand that they were more intelligent than their appearance. Most of all, they responded more to kindness than threats. Their size made them impervious to most physical persuasion.

Lucius spied a feed bag and grabbed it. He calmly approached the two animals. The two assistants were barely holding their own. They struggled mightily with the ropes tethered to the oxen. The beasts eyed the newcomer warily. They began once again to churn the earth with their hooves. Lucius halted his forward motion, standing still.

The oxen seemed to accept his presence, ceasing their agitated actions. Lucius resumed advancing ever so slowly toward them. He cautiously fed the beasts and stroked their necks while gently talking them. Lucius edged backward ever so slowly. The two animals migrated toward Lucius. He nodded to the two men to let them go. He continued pampering them, then gestured with his arm for the helpers to come forward with the yoke. The rest was easy. The oxen submitted to the yoke while Lucius attached the traces.

Petrocolus was impressed. "Very good, young man. I see that you have some experience with these animals."

"I did this almost every day. My family's business required the use of oxen and cart."

Lucius grinned at Julia, knowing he'd scored some goodwill with her father. She grinned back at him, pleased with his performance.

Lucius glanced upward toward the approaching darkness filling the evening sky, then looked at Julia. "Time to go. I'll come again when I'm free from duty."

"I'd like that very much. Come as soon as you can."

As he passed by the penned oxen, Lucius hailed her father. "A pleasure meeting you, sir."

Petrocolus nodded. "And you also, young man."

With a casual wave to Julia, Lucius headed toward the camp gate with his heart soaring.

Several days later, the goddess Fortuna smiled on Lucius again. The century drill lasted until early afternoon. It was cut short for some unknown reason. Perhaps it was the upcoming patrol into the German hinterlands, for drill was seldom excused early. Without so much as a word to his friends, Lucius sprinted away from everyone else. He dumped his gear in his tent and was off to the south gate.

Julia and Lucius went out again on another walk. They spoke of many things—the present, past, and future. Lucius found it so easy to talk to Julia.

"Lucius, what would you do with your life if you hadn't been conscripted?"

"I suppose I'd be working in my father's business. It's not as if I had a lot of options, you know, despite my mother's desires that I find a different profession that uses more brains and less brawn. The prospect of working in my father's business never thrilled me, but that was before I experienced the life of a soldier."

"It doesn't agree with you."

"It's a hard life, but it appears that's my destiny. It can be brutal. That's the truth of it. Of course, if I didn't become a legionnaire, then I would never have met you."

"Why, Lucius, if that was a compliment, it was a stretch."

"I never said I was eloquent."

"I guess a lady takes what she can get."

The two laughed and walked hand in hand along the riverbank. It was a peaceful summer afternoon, and the world belonged to them.

The only sounds were the chirping birds and the gentle melody of the flowing waters. They stopped and looked into each other's eyes, then kissed. Lucius felt a surge through his body as he pressed his mouth against her soft lips. After a time, they broke apart for a moment, then started again. Lucius could feel all of the enchanting curves under her thin shift as they clung to each other. He delighted in the heavy swell of her breasts pressing against his chest. Her loins pressed closely against his. They broke apart again. Julia's face was flushed. She held him at arm's length.

"I think we'd better get back."

Lucius grinned. "If you say so."

"I say so. Let's go."

As the two walked back, Lucius broached the subject of his up-coming march.

"Julia, I'll be unavailable for the next seven or eight days, maybe longer."

She looked back at him with disappointment, which in a way thrilled Lucius. She did care about him, he thought.

"Why?" she asked, alarmed.

"Duty calls, as they say. It's our cohort's turn to patrol the countryside. I'll be out of the fort on patrol for at least six days, maybe more. I'll let you know when I can visit again."

She squeezed his hand. "Just don't be too long."

XIV

Strictly observing military protocol, following the chain of command, Valerius went directly to Senior Tribune Calvus, his immediate superior. Valerius had been mindful not to appear as if he were asking for a favor or requesting any special treatment. Calvus reported directly to General Varus, his commanding officer. He was certain that Calvus knew precisely the details of Valerius's encounter with Varus. Privately, Calvus might be sympathetic with Valerius's plight, but for him to support Valerius in any shape or form would be political suicide. Calvus wasn't about to risk his own future for the sake of a junior tribune. Therefore, Valerius was circumspect in his approach. He'd gone to Calvus in his quarters on the pretext that he needed his signature on some pay records. Getting his authorization on the documents and tucking them under his arm, Valerius turned to leave, then stopped.

Calvus looked at him. "Yes, is there something else?"

"Just that I was thinking about going along with one of the cohorts on one of their forays. Would you mind if I join one of the units for a patrol outside the walls?"

Calvus looked at him as if he were crazy. "Why in Hades would you want to do that?"

"Calvus, I know it sounds kind of foolish, but I'm a soldier. I've trained for years to be a soldier. I'd like to experience life outside these four walls. Listen, all of my records are up to date. The section can survive without me. It certainly functioned satisfactorily before I arrived here. Centurion Marcellus is more than capable of filling in during my absence. After all, I will be gone for just about a week."

Valerius watched as Calvus silently weighed the consequences of his decision. He held his breath, hoping for a favorable decision.

"Fine. If you want to risk your neck and sweat your ass off, be my guest. But I want you back with the records the day you return. Clear?"

"Understood, Calvus. Many thanks for your consideration on this matter. I promise to get back to the records as soon as we return."

Calvus nodded, letting Valerius know he was dismissed. He hastened out of Calvus's quarters before the tribune changed his mind. He was already prepared for the next step. He'd previously inquired as to the name of the senior centurion of the Tenth Cohort of the Eighteenth Legion. It was this cohort with whom he was to tag along with on patrol. He'd been informed that the man's name was Centurion Clodius. He was the centurion who would be the overall commander on the upcoming patrol.

Valerius rushed over to the headquarters area of the Tenth Cohort seeking the centurion. He entered the vicinity and noted a cluster of soldiers. He was disappointed. The man he presumed to be Centurion Clodius was surrounded by a host of other centurions and messengers. The scene was chaotic. There were several discussions occurring at one time, all centered on the upcoming patrol.

Valerius, waiting patiently for a break in the hectic activity, stayed to the periphery of the group. The centurion appeared to know his business. He was an older man, probably close to fifty, of medium height with a chiseled physique. The centurion coolly and with an air of confidence directed what he wanted done in preparation for the coming march.

"Centurion Fulvius, I need you to go over and speak directly to the assigned commander of the cavalry scouts for our little expedition into the badlands. I don't know who he is, and frankly, I don't care, but they'd better be outside the fort walls and formed up at sunup tomorrow. I haven't heard a word from those people since the warning order was issued for our upcoming foray. I'll personally go over and stick my gladius up someone's butt if they're not there at dawn. Clear?"

Centurion Fulvius grinned back. "Oh, I'll make sure they get the message, just like you told me."

The crowd of men around the Centurion Clodius suddenly dissipated. Valerius seized the moment, darting toward the centurion.

"Centurion Clodius, a moment of your time."

The man turned to observe Valerius. His expression was neutral, but Valerius could guess what the man was thinking. Here comes some green tribune to fuck up my day.

"Yes, Tribune, what can I do for you?"

"Centurion, my name is Tribune Valerius Maximus. I'm in charge of the pay records."

"Is my pay in error?"

"No, nothing like that, Centurion." He grinned reassuringly at the centurion, who looked back in puzzlement at Valerius's presence.

"I've been given approval from Senior Tribune Calvus to join the Tenth Cohort out in the field. I'd like to ask your permission."

Valerius need not request the consent of the centurion. He had the acquiescence of a higher-ranking officer, but it was a tactful ploy on his part. It would make the centurion feel that he wasn't being forced upon him. Clodius stroked his chin in thought, staring fixedly at the tribune, attempting to measure him, and trying to fathom why the tribune wanted to join the cohort on the patrol.

"I guess so, but this won't be any parade, Tribune. You'll be on foot like the rest of us."

"Understood, Centurion. I'm just an observer. I know you'll be busy. I promise to stay out of your way. If I can be of any assistance, let me know."

The centurion appeared mollified.

"You're welcome to come, Tribune. See Secundus, my optio, over there for the details."

He motioned with his thumb to a legionnaire to his right, who, without a doubt, had been privy to the entire conversation.

"Many thanks, Centurion." Valerius, smiling smugly and congratulating himself on his political skills, turned and walked toward Secundus. His ploy had worked. Maybe there was a career in the Senate for him after all, as his father desired.

Secundus spoke. "It works like this, sir. Wear your armor and bring your weapons with you. We move out at sunup from the west gate. Don't worry about rations; the cohort will take care of that. Any questions, sir?"

"No, I understand. I'll be there at dawn tomorrow. Thanks."

Valerius, elated at his victory, hurried toward Marcellus's location. Entering the tent, he spied the centurion. He was engrossed in his work, not bothering to look up as Valerius approached.

"Marcellus, guess what?"

Marcellus continued to stare at the records in front of him.

"What?" he said blandly.

Valerius blurted, "I'm going out with one of the cohorts on their next march into the countryside."

Marcellus fixed him with a gaze for a moment before replying. "Are you, now? Good for you, Tribune. It should be a rewarding experience for a young officer. But just remember that this is not a drill out there."

Somewhat defensive, Valerius replied, "Nothing has happened all summer. All appears calm."

"Listen to me, Tribune. It's hard to understand these Germans. You don't know when they'll get a bug up their ass. If they're not fighting us, they're fighting one another. Trust me on this, Tribune. I've been here for a while."

"Fine. I hear you, Marcellus."

The centurion wouldn't let go of the topic. "Tribune, I know you want to experience what being a soldier is all about. I'd feel the same way if I were you. Hades, I'd go if they let me. But heed my warning. Be careful out there. It can be extremely volatile. These are not wooden swords people are carrying beyond these walls. Saying all that, it'll be a fine experience for you to partake of a real military operation, not this horseshit we're engaged in on a daily basis. Let me know when you're departing; I'll see you off."

Valerius threw himself into his work with renewed vigor. He finally had something to look forward to, and he was excited about it.

It was near dusk as red hues colored the sunset. Slanted rays of sunlight pierced through the clouds, bathing the camp in a golden aura. Amid this tranquil setting, the legionnaires, in preparation for the upcoming march, worked feverishly. The single objective for each legionnaire was to have his gear ready upon awakening. The cohort would march out early in the morning, and there would be no time for further preparation. Each man needed to be prepared and have his weapons razor sharp. A dull or rusty dagger or sword would earn one additional duty.

Rumors were flying around the encampment as to where they were going and how far. Most of the stories of the upcoming march lacked credibility, or, in the vernacular of the military, they were pure crap. Some said forty miles this way, while others said twenty miles that way. One said north, the other said south. Each rumor was allegedly based on firsthand knowledge from the legion headquarters. They knew a clerk or had overheard a centurion.

The truth of the matter was that the cohort would venture west for approximately twenty-five miles. The route of march was designed to pass three large German villages. They'd be taking a circuitous course on the way back, crossing a broad area from west to east. This was no better or worse than other routes. The areas surrounding the encampment in a thirty-mile radius could be equally dangerous.

In the dim light, Lucius and Cassius settled into the mindless rhythm of sharpening their weapons with sharpening stones. It was a long process that took patience. Lucius had a habit of sticking his tongue out of the side of his mouth as he slowly stroked his sword.

The cohort area was filled with the rasping sound of sharpening stones sliding the length of steel. As a result of yesterday's sword drill on the wooden posts, everyone's sword was full of nicks and dull edges from hacking and stabbing at the wooden foe. The men hurried to finish the task before darkness descended.

As Lucius worked, he thought of Julia and how she looked and how she spoke. Perhaps, he reasoned, this journey wouldn't be as arduous if he thought of her as he marched along with a load of gear. Typical of most soldiers, when faced with a bad duty assignment, he was already beginning the countdown of the days until he was back again. Breaking it down, there would be seven days and six nights. If they had bad weather, he supposed it might stretch into eight days.

At last Lucius held up the gladius and examined it in the fading light. He angled the blade in different directions so he could better see its edges. He nodded in satisfaction with his handiwork. The twin cutting edges were razor sharp even at the widened base of the blade. Lucius firmly held the bone grip, which fit his hand like a glove. Stepping back from the others, he swung the blade through the air. It made a menacing hissing sound. He was ready.

The next day, legionnaires were up before dawn. A heavy mist hung in the air, and drops of dew coated the grass. Men hurried silently about in the semidark with their gear to the assembly area. Lucius positioned himself into his assigned spot with his gear and weapons strapped and hung securely to his person. He could sense rather than see the other centuries of the cohort off to his left and right.

Flavius, Domitius, and Cassius stood next to Lucius, chatting idly to pass the time before they ventured out. Lucius noted Decius in the half darkness, his face still swollen from his latest encounter. His lip was puffed out. And one side of his face reflected faded scratches courtesy of Julia. The two exchanged hated glances at each other. Lucius braced for the confrontation, not exactly sure what to expect. Decius seemed to hesitate in front of Lucius, but then proceeded onward.

The soldiers shivered in the early-morning chill. The coarse banter and shouted insults that usually accompanied the men was absent. They all knew they were about to experience a difficult week. It would be physically exhausting, and the element of danger would be present. There was no griping nor whining. They knew what was expected of them. It was time to be a soldier. With a hand signal from the senior centurion at the front of the column and a blare from the trumpet, the centurions gave the command to load their gear. All of the men purposely cinched their belts and straps. Each man hefted his single javelin and forked pole laden with gear, then made ready.

The Tenth Cohort smartly exited the encampment. The standard bearer, accompanied by Centurion Clodius, led the way, followed by the First Century. The cohort exited through the west gate. The sentries stared in silence from the twin towers. They nodded grimly from their perch to the soldiers below, thankful that they weren't going out with them. The pack of mules, along with several carts and wagons burdened with assorted gear and supplies, awaited the advancing cohort on the outskirts of the encampment. Off in the distance, to the right of the mule trains, was a detachment of cavalry, perhaps forty riders, fidgeting on their mounts, waiting for the plodding mass of five-hundred-plus men to reach them.

Lucius walked under his heavy burden. He twisted slightly to the rear, grunting with effort under his heavy load, to see how far they had come. The faint silhouette of the walls was still visible. He glanced farther to the right, toward the now-distant animal pens, thinking once more of Julia. He wondered if she was up yet, what she wore, or perhaps what she didn't wear, when she slept. Lucius lingered on this delicious thought as he plodded farther down the road.

His thoughts drifted to his home and family. What would they be doing right now? He could picture his mother and sister baking something delicious in the kitchen. His father and brother were probably loading the wagon for the day's deliveries even at this early hour. He smiled, thinking of his old life. It seemed so long ago. He'd been transformed. He was the same person, yet he was drastically different.

He'd crossed a wide chasm between legionnaire and civilian. He had become a toughened and hardened soldier. He wasn't sure whether the change was for the better, but he accepted it. He wondered what his parents would think if they saw him now. His father would beam with pride and slap him on the back. His mother would be mortified, hating the uniform and weapons of a soldier.

Lucius's thoughts returned to Julia. She was beautiful, with her soft brown hair and long legs, and the way her heavy breasts moved under her shift. Her kisses had enthralled him. He could hear her laugh echo in his head. His mind wandered back to the fortune-teller. What about that damn sibyl? She was right again. He'd met Julia, "a woman who would capture his heart," as the sibyl had so aptly put it. How was this possible? Could these people really foretell the future? He never believed any of that stuff, but why that panicked look by the sibyl at the end? Why had she lied? Lucius was haunted by the images of the sibyl and what she'd said—or, better put, what she hadn't said. Despite the heat of the day and his exertions, he experienced a chill up his back. Maybe he would speak to Julia on the subject when he returned. Perhaps she could cast some wisdom his way. Cassius was hardly sympathetic to his tale of the sibyl, not taking him seriously on the prophecy. He guessed he needed a woman's perspective. Yes, he'd bring it up with Julia and hope she wouldn't make fun of him.

The men had marched all morning when the word came down to break under the trees. The legionnaires went off to the sides of the road in the shade but remained vigilant. Guards were posted to ensure there was no unwelcome visitation by the Germans. With a collective groan, the men collapsed, followed by the usual flow of curses about life in the legion. The soldiers were allowed to remove their helmets long enough to cool their heads and dry their hair. They'd been marching for several hours at a rapid pace, draining their energy. There was muted laughter among the ranks. The men relaxed on the ground, thankful for the respite, no matter how short in nature.

Cassius spoke. "Lucius, at least we don't have Centurion Longinius shouting and kicking our ass. I can still feel the sting of that wooden staff. I thought he was going to break that thing on my back."

"I suppose we should count our blessings. Another couple of hours, and we can break for midday meal. I'm starved already."

Domitius spoke. "Why in the Hades are we out here? I haven't seen anything but trees, some scattered farms, and small groups of mud hovels along the side of the road. Who's going to attack us? The birds? There's no one out here but us."

Flavius spoke. "Seven days from now, this will just be a bad memory. We'll spend a night drinking wine and maybe some of that German brew. What do you say?"

"I'm in."

"Me, too."

"Count me in."

"EVERYBODY UP."

So much for their plans. Centurion Frontinus fixed a baleful glare at Lucius and friends. He wasn't going to cut the new guys any slack. He followed them with his eyes as they dutifully made their way to their assigned places. With a groan, everyone refastened their straps and shouldered their burdens. The cohort marched onward.

Later that morning, the soldiers arrived at the first major village. The hamlet was a sprawling affair perched slightly back from the main road. A palisade of pointed logs and branches surrounded the cluster of buildings. The gates were wide open. The cohort was positioned strategically just outside the entrance.

From what Lucius could see inside, there was a concentration of mud huts with thatched roofs. This is what we're worried about, Lucius thought. What a pathetic collection of houses. You've got to be joking. These people are going to attack us? He'd pictured masses of German warriors waving spears and demanding Roman blood.

"LINES. SHIELDS UP."

As they had been so thoroughly drilled, the six centuries quickly formed battle lines, presenting a wall of shields. There was a crash as the shields locked within the lines. Swords remained in their scabbards. The centurions and optios went to the front of the formation to ensure everything was in order.

As Lucius peered toward the front of the village, he didn't un-derstand the need for such an intimidating show of force. Was this necessary? He stood motionless, waiting for the next set of com-mands. As he looked to his front again, he noted a contingent of soldiers, including a tribune and several centurions. Some of the vil-lage inhabitants ventured out of the stockade to stare at the legion-naires. The glances weren't warm and friendly. They simply looked on in morose silence at the soldiers. Even the children gave them blank looks.

Thus far, Valerius was thrilled with the patrol. He was attached to the First Century as an observer. He attempted to be as unobtrusive as possible. He made a conscientious effort not to get in the way. He realized he served no useful purpose with the unit, but it didn't mat-ter. He intended to make the most of this opportunity to be with real soldiers. Valerius stood apart from the others, staring at the palisade in front of him. Not much to this place. It was certainly no match for the fortifications the Roman legionnaires prepared for their encampments.

His thoughts were interrupted by someone calling him. "Tribune, are you coming with me into the village, or are you just going to stand there all day and gawk?"

Valerius offered a smile at Centurion Clodius, pleased that he was considered part of the leadership. "Sure, I'll go with you."

He proceeded over to the centurion, then accompanied Clodius plus some of the other centurions and several veteran legionnaires acting as bodyguards into the settlement. He'd been told that these people were part of the Sugambri tribe. Valerius was unsure how to act or what they might encounter, so he kept his right hand on the hilt of his sword.

Centurion Clodius eyed Valerius. "Relax, Tribune. No need for that right now. You might get the locals nervous. Know what I mean?" The centurion grinned mockingly at Valerius.

Feeling somewhat foolish, Valerius nodded, quickly dropping his hand away from his sword. Once inside the village walls, he took a closer look at his surroundings. The crude huts were scattered everywhere in no pattern or organization. Livestock and chickens roamed the village, creating an even more chaotic atmosphere. Most of people he saw were dressed in an assortment of different garbs. The men seemed to favor leggings of animal hide with a cloak. The women were clad in rough woolen garments that extended down to their ankles. Many of the children were naked.

The village chief, a large man dressed in deerskin britches and no upper garment, approached them, smiling. In heavily accented Latin, he welcomed them to the village. He announced himself as the headman of this particular clan. Valerius couldn't understand the man's name. It was too guttural of a pronunciation for him to distinguish. The leader smiled as he spoke. He was missing his two front teeth. The chieftain gestured for them to follow him. They all adjourned to the main building to get out of the sun. The earth floor was covered in fresh-cut rushes. The men all sat. The chieftain, through the legion's German interpreter, translated the words for Centurion Clodius and his staff.

"He says his clan has been here about two years and numbers about eight hundred men, women, and children. Their cattle and horses are thriving. The harvest is expected to be bountiful. They welcome the Roman soldiers to their village."

Valerius silently wondered if these Germans would have the same feelings for Rome when additional taxes were collected at the end of the summer.

Other tribesmen had wandered in to view the proceedings. They appeared to accept the presence of the Roman soldiers with calm detachment. Valerius studied their faces and couldn't detect any animosity. The German headman gestured with his hands, offering refreshments of a fermented concoction from a large wooden pot. After a brief hesitation, Centurion Clodius nodded in assent.

The chieftain smiled at the centurion, no doubt pleased that the Romans were drinking the home draught. Small bowls of the liquid were passed around. Not knowing the strength of the concoction, Valerius exercised caution by taking but a small quantity of the liquid. He had been forewarned by Marcellus of these German brews, and a good thing. Even though he consumed but a small quantity of the liquid, he fought to hold back the choking reflex. His face turned crimson. Aware that Centurion Clodius was watching him intently, he looked back, offered a weak smile, then politely cleared his throat. In a show of bravado, he took another taste. He noted that the other centurions had likewise taken but small nips. Centurion Clodius nodded, relieved that the tribune hadn't embarrassed the group by spewing the brew over everything. The headman appeared disappointed, no doubt hoping one of the Romans would disgorge the contents on his fellow officers.

The men drank in silence. Valerius glanced around off to the side. There stood a solitary woman clad in a long white cloak of fine weave. She was much different from the rest, aside from the fact that she was the only female present. She was tall, perhaps taller than Valerius. Her long blond hair cascaded down upon her shoulders. She stood perfectly straight, almost regal in her bearing, staring at the men with bright-blue eyes that seemed to shine even from a distance. I wonder who the lucky guy is who gets to bed her, he pondered. On second thought, she was beautiful, yet there was something cold and aloof about her.

The chieftain rose, mumbled something about coming right back, and then departed the premises. The interpreter, whose name was Balsix, looked at Clodius and shrugged. Valerius leaned over to the translator, attempting to be as discreet as possible, and whispered, "Who is the woman?" He nodded in her direction.

The interpreter openly stared at the white-clad figure. "She is the priestess of the village. Very powerful."

The woman, knowing the two men were discussing her, stared boldly back.

Valerius could feel his face redden from the woman's penetrating gaze. He turned back to Balsix. "Priestess of what?" he asked in a low voice.

"She's the holy one in the village. She's the link to their gods. Their deities are not very nice. Tiwaz is their god of war, and Donar the god of thunder. They demand sacrifice of their prisoners. Best not to be captured by one of those, young tribune. Your end wouldn't be pleasant." The German laughed at his own humor.

The headman returned with another bowl of home brew. The dialogue between the Romans and Germans began again. Valerius continued to sneak glances at the priestess. He vaguely recalled a story he'd heard about the mighty General Drusus, late stepson of the emperor and, it was acknowledged, the most capable commander since Julius Caesar. On his campaign in Germany, Drusus had been so unnerved by the prophecy of one of these priestesses that he'd halted his advance and changed his plans.

What sort of witchery were these strange figures capable of performing? She was certainly an imposing figure one wouldn't easily forget. Despite the heat of the day and his heavy armor, Valerius shivered involuntarily. He returned his attention to the conversation between the senior centurion and the village headman. Valerius had missed some of the exchange, preoccupied with his musings of the priestess. He silently chided himself for not paying attention and thinking with the part of his body below the waist. That could get one into trouble every time.

The polite discussion continued for a while longer. Centurion Clodius decided they had spent sufficient time with their German host. He gestured for the group to rise. He expressed his gratitude for the hospitality. The Roman command contingent then exited the village.

The men in the ranks outside the village walls had been allowed to stand down, given the absence of any threat. Centurion Clodius signaled with his arm for the column to load up. All at once, the various centurions were in front of their men, bellowing for them to get their gear on and form up. There was a clatter as the men adjusted their straps and weapons.

The column marched on, the day turning warmer. The cohort stopped for a midday meal of hard wheat biscuits, *bucellatum*, and sour wine, *acetum*. The men greedily wolfed down the meal. Not the most filling or tasty of food, but it would have to do. They advanced in a northwest direction for the remainder of the afternoon, stopping at several villages that were about the same size as the first one they'd encountered. There were no signs of belligerence.

The afternoon dragged by. The heavy armor, weapons, and assorted gear took its toll over the course of the day. The legionnaires attempted to hide their fatigue, but some men were now staggering, their steps no longer orderly. Every soldier was silently asking the same question: When do we stop for the night? They all fervently hoped it would be soon.

Finally, Clodius halted, pulled out his map, and nodded in silent affirmation. He yelled for the lead elements to proceed forward to a nearby hill and pointed for emphasis. The cohort immediately began to build their marching camp. They were in luck. They were digging in the foundations of a previous Roman excavation, probably constructed some months ago. The erection of the camp was easy. The men had little trouble preparing the ditches and ramparts. In several hours, they had completed the mini fortress, including palisade stakes, and pitched tents. Water was secured. The men cooked their wheat porridge for their evening meal.

Lucius, Cassius, Domitius, and Flavius sat around a small fire within the ramparts. Flavius was lying on his back, staring at the sky. Cassius was busy massaging his aching and callused feet. Lucius stared into the flames thinking of nothing in particular. He tried to ignore the knots of pain in his neck and shoulders, knowing they would get worse tomorrow. They were exhausted but comforted, knowing the day was at its end, with just six more to follow.

Cassius, still ministering to his feet, spoke. "What are you thinking about, Lucius?"

"Nothing. Perhaps how good the main encampment is going to look when we get back."

Cassius stared back at Lucius. "Who do you think you're kidding? I know of whom you were thinking. It was sweet Julia."

Lucius stared back and grinned. "I wasn't at the moment," he said defensively.

"Oh, come on, Lucius. You've spent every free moment chasing after her."

"So what?"

"At least you're now admitting I'm right."

"Tell us about Julia," the others chimed in.

Lucius spoke. "Hey, guys, cut me a little slack here. How about changing the subject?"

"Oh, we do have a shy one here," opined Flavius. "When are you going to introduce her to Domitius and me?"

"Soon." Lucius grinned back in defiance.

Cassius spoke. "We'll let you off the hook for now, but you will tell us, even if we have to beat it out of you."

Flavius quipped, "Lucius, sooner or later we want the details, and I mean all of them. You got it?"

"Yeah, sure. I hear you."

Domitius entered the conversation and mercifully changed the subject. "Hey, at least it's not raining. Can you imagine that road we traveled in the rain? We'd be up to our asses in mud."

"Can we talk about something a little more pleasant?" said Lucius. "Don't remind me of our march. Cassius, tell us more lies about the women you've known."

"Yeah, we want to hear," everyone chorused.

Cassius didn't disappoint them. He loved an audience and had them laughing at his stories. For the next half hour, they were entertained before hitting the tents. Tomorrow would be a long day. For some, it would be their last day on this earth.

Early the next day, the young German chieftain, Jurus, crouched amid the trees off from the side of the road, concealed in the thick foliage. He had an unimpeded view of the Romans. Some might describe Jurus as impetuous and foolhardy. He didn't care. He had enough followers who thought like him. He wanted to draw Roman blood and do it soon. His passionate boasts had attracted many other young warriors to his cause. Besides, Jurus was more than just talk.

He looked like a warrior, tall and muscular, with handsome facial features, a natural leader.

Crouched upon one knee, he watched the cohort of Roman soldiers march past. He and a contingent of his warriors had been shadowing the cohort since yesterday. They observed the Romans, looking for weak spots in the formation. They wanted to kill these Roman soldiers.

Various chiefs and elders had warned him not to attack the Romans, that a massive attack was being planned for in early fall. A Cherusci nobleman, Arminius, was taking charge of things. Jurus had heard of how Arminius had persuaded the tribal leaders to back down to the Roman general, Varus. They were supposed to be servile, accede to his wishes. This great plan was to lull the Romans into a false sense of security, then strike a colossal, unexpected blow when the Romans were out of their camp. Why should he listen to the likes of Arminius? He was a Cherusci. Everyone knew they were inferior to his tribe, the Sugambri.

Jurus would attack today. He had no doubt that his actions would displease some of the chieftains, but once they learned that he'd massacred the Roman column, they'd sing a different tune. He'd be famous among the German tribes. They'd praise his name.

Jurus planned to strike toward the end of the day, when the soldiers were most weary from their day of marching in the sun. He also knew the Romans would most likely choose a place for their night encampment where a previous legionnaire base had been located. They were so predictable. He'd staked out a spot not far from where he expected the cohort to break for the day, a site situated so that his men would be hidden from view anywhere on the road. His warriors would quickly be upon them, and too late for the legionnaires to defend themselves.

He'd attracted over eight hundred warriors to his cause, anxious for battle and ready to spill Roman blood. They heavily outnumbered the Roman cohort of five hundred men. His men were ready to prove themselves. He would show this Arminius and the others how to fight and destroy these soldiers. Now, all he needed to do was wait for the sun to sap the strength from these marching soldiers. His plan, while bold, had been conceived with care. The Romans would be too far from the base camp on the river to receive reinforcements. Jurus turned back toward his scouts. He motioned with his outstretched arm and pointed. It was time they advanced to the ambush site, a good distance up the road on which the cohort would be traveling.

It was long into day number two. Valerius's legs hurt, and he was fatigued. He silently chastised himself for becoming so soft. The cohort had been marching hard all morning and now into the afternoon. He wasn't used to this physical activity. It was embarrassing. He didn't even have to bear the burden of the ordinary legionnaire. The gear he carried with him besides his helmet and armor were his long sword, dagger, and supply of water. He reckoned he'd spent too many hours behind a table rather than out on the drill field.

He thought back to the previous day, when the cohort was preparing to march out of the gate. In the early light of dawn, Marcellus had accompanied him to the parade ground. He'd again cautioned the young tribune to be careful. Valerius was a little annoyed with this vigilance thing. He could take care of himself. He realized that Marcellus was just trying to help. Not wanting to hurt the centurion's feelings, Valerius had hidden his irritation, nodding in acquiescence to Marcellus, assuring him that he would be alert at all times.

He was somewhat disappointed at what he'd witnessed thus far. The German villages they'd come upon weren't impressive. The numbers of warriors present didn't appear overly large, nor did they appear formidable. The villagers had been almost placid.

He had no misgivings, aching legs aside, about his decision to come out with this cohort. He wasn't trying to impress his superiors or anyone else. He was here because this was what he wanted to experience—life as a soldier, not a clerk. So what if his ass was dragging? Better this than the pay records. He was no longer a rear-echelon stool sitter. He would make this trade any day. He was trained to serve as a soldier, not a bureaucrat. He mentally began composing what he would write to Cato, his tutor, about this experience and how to embellish his words to make it sound like a true military operation.

Lucius trudged on in the heat of the afternoon sun, inhaling in gasps, hoping they would find another camp like last night. It had been another boring day. After rising early before dawn, he had marched all morning. Now late into the afternoon, he could feel the dust and grime that had accumulated on him and found its way under his armor. He, like every other legionnaire, wondered why they had to march with their heavy helmets fitted snugly on their heads. It was extremely uncomfortable and hot. All appeared to be peaceful, so why not let the soldiers march with the helmets suspended from their necks? But this wasn't a question that a legionnaire dare ask his centurion, so he marched onward, the helmet baking his head.

The six centuries of the cohort were in a column of fours, not the usual six men abreast. The narrowness of the dirt road prohibited the standard marching formation. Lucius was on the right inside file. Cassius was behind him. Each man concentrated on putting one foot in front of the other, hoping it would get them that much closer to their evening rest. The road was winding through stands of trees and heavy brush. The sky was clear and full of white, fluffy clouds. Judging from the angle of the sun, it was probably about three hours past midday. Puffs of dust rose up as the men's feet struck the dry, packed earth. They would no doubt be stopping soon.

Jurus gazed intently at the approaching Roman column from his concealed position amid the heavy bushes. He slowly brushed aside a small tree limb to better view the soldiers. He could make out the standard bearer at the head of the column. Yes, that would be his soon. He would parade proudly into his village carrying the Roman cohort standard for all to see. Jurus easily identified the centurion commander by his distinct helmet with the horizontal crest. And what was that next to the centurion? This was even better. He spotted a tribune in his fancy armor on the perimeter of the century, trailing slightly behind the standard bearer. Perhaps he would add a tribune's head as a trophy.

Jurus waved his arms for the men to rise. The Roman column was almost abreast of their location, entering the kill zone. Jurus hefted his spear, his palm slippery with sweat. With a howl, he charged out of the brush. The forest erupted. German warriors emerged from the trees and brush. War cries burst forth from the mouths of the attackers. A volley of javelins descended upon the unfortunate soldiers. Many legionnaires instinctively raised their shields to ward off the threat, but some were too late. Roman soldiers throughout the entire length of the column fell. Some writhed in agony, while others lay still in widening pools of blood soaking into the brown dirt of the road.

Lucius was stunned by the onslaught. A soldier two ranks ahead of him fell, a javelin piercing his chain mail as if it were papyrus. A spray of iron links exploded into the air from the force of the throw. Out of the corner of his eye, Lucius saw a blur. Something struck him a fierce blow on the upper left side of his head. He staggered from the impact, feeling wetness on the side of his face. He was half blinded as blood poured into his eye.

Lucius, ignoring the pain from the wound, took action. He dropped his forked pole and javelin, then drew his gladius. He clutched his shield protectively, covering most of his body. With the exception of his head and feet, he was no longer exposed. His heart was pounding. He attempted not to panic. The blood cascading down his face bothered him, but he'd worry about that later. He was still standing, so he couldn't be hurt that bad. All of this had occurred in a matter of a few heartbeats. The centurions and optios were now bellowing orders. Amid the bedlam, the commands registered.

"FORM SHIELD WALL. FORM THE SQUARE."

The legionnaires of the century responded in a disciplined manner. Lucius moved with the men to tighten the formation. The ranks formed a compact rectangular mass facing outward toward the threat. The century consolidated into a defensive position featuring two sets of lines on both sides of the road, squared off on the two ends. They formed their lines with speed and fluidness, almost as if executing an exercise on the parade ground.

Lucius was in the second row and could see little of the attack, but that changed suddenly. The man in front of him screamed, dropping hard. Lucius didn't look at what fate had befallen the unfortunate soldier. He stepped into the breach without hesitation. He was now in the outside rank, fully exposed to the German onslaught.

A warrior in cloth leggings and a bare chest charged at Lucius with a stabbing spear. The man appeared to be about the same age as Lucius but shorter in stature. Remembering the words of Centurion Longinius, he violently extended his arm, smashing his shield forward with all of his strength. He heard a satisfying crunch as the heavy shield struck the man's face. The warrior wobbled back toward the forest holding his head, blood pouring through his fingers from his ruined nose and cheekbone.

Centurion Frontinus coolly directed his men, seemingly oblivious of the mayhem and deafening shouts around him.

"TIGHTEN IT UP IN THERE. NO GAPS. SHIELDS AND SWORDS AT THE READY."

A full-bearded German jumped at Lucius with an axe-like weapon that had an elongated handle. Lucius deflected the blow with his shield, feeling the shock over the entire length of his arm, then retaliated with a short thrust of his sword. He connected with the man's right arm, creating a large gash in the flesh. The warrior gasped in pain, dropping his axe from nerveless fingers, then hastily retreated into the woods. That was two Lucius had sent packing back to the forest. Temporarily free of any assailants confronting him, he looked around for the next threat.

Time seemed to stand still. Strangely, he noted the smallest of details. Amid the clamor of battle, he could hear his own breathing, feel his heart pounding. Several escaped mules ran by, braying in fright. A spear deflected heavily off Lucius's shield with a resounding thud. A legionnaire three men to his left collapsed screaming, impaled by a javelin. A helmet rolled by in a lopsided manner across the road.

Lucius swiveled his head from side to side, but he was having difficulty seeing to his left as a result of the steady flow of blood from his head wound. He angrily wiped his face with his right arm, which was holding the sword. His arm came away from the wound covered with blood. The scarlet liquid continued to cascade down his face. Grunts and shouts punctuated the individual combat, creating a deafening roar. Hurled javelins filled the air. The formation of soldiers shifted in mass slightly to the right, and Lucius carefully stepped over a fallen legionnaire, careful not to trip over him and suffer the same fate.

The initial assault of the Germans had ebbed. Despite the ferocity of the attack and the advantage of surprise, they'd not breached the cohort's formation. Sensing failure, the Germans renewed their assault with greater savagery upon the Roman formation.

A massed group of Germans charged at the area where Lucius stood. He braced for the attack, but the impetus pushed him back. Off balance from the thrust of the enemy, he allowed a gap to open between his shield and his right side. A German stabbed at Lucius with his spear. In a lightning move, Lucius swung his shield to the right. He deflected most of the force of the thrust, but the javelin glanced downward off his shield and struck his left leg. Lucius experienced a burning sensation where the spear had sliced his flesh.

In a rage, Lucius counterjabbed viciously with his sword at the man's exposed midriff. The blade slid in without resistance. The man screamed as Lucius impaled him, the sword point exiting the man's back. He savagely yanked the blade out with a twisting motion, inflicting maximum damage. The man collapsed onto the ground. Lucius stared briefly at the fallen figure, then looked up for any new threat.

Tribune Valerius looked toward the front of the cohort. He was now about ten paces behind the ranks of the First Century. His thoughts turned to the comfort of sitting by a fire with his armor off, perhaps with some wine to slake his thirst, easing the aches he now felt over most of his body. He eyed the winding road that disappeared over a slight rise, hoping that their night encampment would be just beyond.

Suddenly, all Hades broke loose. A collection of armed men rushed the front and sides of the First Century.

He was too startled to react in any meaningful fashion. He stared with his mouth half open. Spears filled the air, descending upon the Roman cohort. A horde of Germans, screaming battle cries, emerged from the forest. Valerius whipped out his long Spanish sword, its blade gleaming malevolently in the sun. A man attacked Valerius from his left. He prepared to meet the threat, but before he could act, a veteran soldier from the First Century stepped in front of him, confronting the German. The hulking legionnaire quickly smashed into the figure with his shield, then almost severed the man's head with a vicious sword stroke to the man's unprotected neck. He nodded briefly to Valerius, then assumed his place in the defensive formation.

Valerius rushed forward and inside to the protection of the ranks of the leading century. A second wave of Germans attacked the front of the cohort. Through the mass of entangled men, Valerius witnessed a group of four Germans break through a small gap in the Roman lines, heading for the standard bearer of the cohort. There was no one but Valerius between the four charging Germans and the cohort standard.

Without hesitation, Valerius charged at the enemy, his sword flashing in a long arc. He intercepted the Germans and sliced the leading man's shoulder open. The unfortunate warrior went down screaming. Two of the others who were closely following stumbled over the wounded man. Several other legionnaires noticed the threat to the standard and came to the aid of Valerius. They rapidly closed ranks to seal the breach in the lines. The Roman reinforcements dispatched the two. The surviving German managed to evade the legionnaires and headed directly toward Centurion Clodius. The centurion had his back turned to his assailant, directing troops to shift to their left to meet a surging attack. The German leveled his spear. Valerius rushed forward, stabbing the attacker. His sword thrust was so hard and clean it went all of the way through the man, almost to the hilt of the sword, killing him instantly. The startled centurion turned as the man fell near his feet. He nodded his thanks to Valerius, then coolly turned back to directing the counterattack.

Jurus was furious that his men weren't collapsing the ranks of the legionnaires. He could see his men repulsed repeatedly. They hurled themselves repeatedly at the Roman lines but made little progress. He stepped back from the fray, frantically motioning with his sword for more of his warriors to attack the head of the Roman column. He knew his only chance for a victory was to kill the Roman leaders and capture the standard. He grabbed one of his lieutenants and yelled into the man's ear to break contact and bring his entire force to attack the front of the Roman column. In response to Jurus's urging, waves of Germans charged the command element and the First Century.

Lucius's century repulsed another assault, leaving more Germans dead in front of the Roman lines. There was a temporary lull as the pressure eased. Centurion Frontinus glanced about, noting that the First Century and the headquarters element were now separated from the main body of the cohort. They were holding their own, but they were effectively cut off and surrounded. He waved his sword and motioned for the century to shift to their left toward the cohort standard and Centurion Clodius.

"ADVANCE FORWARD TOWARD THE STANDARD."

The century broke contact and double-timed, shields facing outward, toward the threatened command group. Lucius and his comrades were only a short distance from the ranks of the First Century when another concentration of Germans attacked in a wedge aimed at the cohort standard. The battle swirling around him, Lucius witnessed the headquarters element surrounded. Moving forward, Lucius and several others smashed into the flank of the attacking Germans with a resounding crash, the heavy shields booming at the contact. Several of the enemy were skewered by the advancing soldiers, but the Germans didn't break off. More Germans filled the void of those slain. They surged forward, hacking and thrusting at the Romans.

Lucius advanced steadily through the melee as he thrust his shield forward, followed by his plunging sword. He didn't think they would break through quickly enough to save the surrounded group.

Valerius gripped his sword tightly, grimacing as he deftly deflected several spear thrusts by two Germans. It had happened so quickly.

He and a small group of legionnaires were holding their ground with Centurion Clodius and the cohort standard. In a few heartbeats, they were cut off and surrounded by a rushing band of the enemy. He had no idea where they had come from; they were just there. The legionnaire to his left suddenly went down with a gurgled cry, leaving just the three of them to defend the cohort standard.

Off to his left, through the swirling mass of combatants, he saw Roman reinforcements desperately attempting to rescue his beleaguered group. He wasn't sure they would arrive in time. Valerius screamed an oath, then slashed his sword in a wide arc to buy more time. He knew he couldn't hold on much longer. His sword arm was weary. Germans continued to press relentlessly at them. He hacked again with his sword. He didn't make contact, but the Germans recoiled slightly. One of the remaining soldiers of Valerius's besieged group groaned, then went to his knees with a shoulder wound. Valerius desperately swung his sword again, knowing he was exposing his entire left side. The Germans surged in for the kill, but then the reinforcements of Lucius's century broke through.

Lucius and a small group of legionnaires charged into the flank of the attacking Germans, their swords plunging and slashing at any exposed flesh. A German was in the process of thrusting his spear at Valerius's open side when Lucius stabbed the foe in his right arm. Lucius could feel the blade strike the bone through the pierced flesh. The German gasped in pain and dropped the spear from his useless right arm.

Valerius turned just in time to witness a German drop his weapon almost at his feet. The man had been thwarted by a legionnaire's sword strike to the arm. He caught a quick glimpse of the soldier who had saved him. The figure had blood freely flowing down his face. He disappeared from view as others shifted in front of him.

The German attack wavered. They had failed to capture the cohort standard. Many looked about to see what their comrades were doing. Some began to fall back. The initial trickle of retreating men soon turned into a mass exodus. They fled to the shelter of the surrounding woods, ignoring their wounded. The cohort, at the direction of the shouting centurions, quickly dressed up their battle lines. Centurion Clodius motioned with his arms to tighten up the ranks even more. There would be no pursuit of the Germans into the surrounding forest. The centurions quickly consolidated their units into a defensive posture. Stillness descended on the battlefield, punctuated by the moans of the wounded.

The medical staff hurried to each of the centuries to triage the wounded. Cassius turned to see how Lucius was doing. What he saw appalled him. The entire left side of Lucius's face was covered in blood, while his upper left leg streamed crimson from a nasty wound.

"Uh, Lucius, you're bleeding like a stuck pig. You better get over to where they have the wounded."

Lucius didn't even feel the wounds. Perhaps a little, but he was charged from the fight and remained on edge. He wiped blood from his face with his hand, frowning in annoyance at the thick red smear on his sleeve. "I'm good. At least I think so."

Centurion Frontinus came upon the two of them. "You, Palonius, get over there with the wounded." He pointed to a collection of bleeding legionnaires, some standing, others supine on the ground.

"I'm fine, Centurion. I can stay."

"You don't look fine. Now get your ass over there like I told you to."

"Yes, Centurion." Lucius began to move, then swayed slightly off balance. The pain was kicking in now. He gingerly went to one knee. He started to see spots and was feeling dizzy.

He wobbled toward where the medical staff was treating the injured. Seeing Lucius in distress, Cassius ran over and supported him with his arm and shoulder. Lucius didn't object.

A medicus, an elderly man, materialized in front of him, waving Cassius away. He pushed Lucius all the way on the ground. "Be quiet and try to relax while I have a look at you."

He expertly examined the wounds, starting with the head. He made some clucking noises in his throat. He gazed downward toward the leg wound. "Nasty cuts you have there, Legionnaire. I've seen worse. Corpsman, over here," he shouted.

A younger man approached with an armful of linen bandages.

"Bind these wounds tightly to stop the bleeding. That'll do for now. We'll sew him up later."

The orderly proceeded to wash the wounds and truss them snugly. Lucius felt a little better. He decided he needed to sit rather than lie on the ground. He tried to ignore the moans from the men seriously wounded around him. Lucius grabbed his goatskin water container and drank deeply. This seemed to clear his head a little.

Cassius came over. "Lucius, are you feeling better?"

"Yeah, yeah, I don't feel real great, but it's not too bad." He noticed that Cassius had a tight-lipped expression. Something was wrong. He knew Cassius, and this wasn't a typical expression. "What is it, Cassius? Why are you looking that way? Is my face that bad? Come on, out with it."

Cassius looked over toward his right. He blurted, "It's Flavius. He didn't make it."

Lucius stared back in stunned silence, trying to comprehend what he'd been told.

"Help me up, Cassius. Where is he?"

Cassius assisted Lucius, raising him to a standing position. Lucius hobbled over, attempting to ignore the throbbing in his leg, to the spot where Domitius was sitting. He was holding the limp hand of Flavius, whose body was sprawled in the dust. A huge, gaping wound was present on his neck. The dark-brown earth was saturated with blood. Domitius looked up at Lucius, his eyes brimming with tears. "I don't know what happened, Lucius. He was two men away from me. When it was over, this is what I found."

Lucius felt both a terrible anger and a deep sorrow. He was numb; his wounds were forgotten for the moment. He stooped down next to Domitius and put his arm around his shoulders.

"There's nothing you could have done. Come with me away from him. He's beyond our help now."

Cassius and Lucius gently led Domitius away from the corpse of Flavius. Lucius turned his head back toward the collapsed figure of Flavius for a final glimpse of his former comrade. Flavius, a talkative young man who had always had a smile for everyone, was no more. They had gone through so much together. Flavius, laughing at the absurdity of the training, smiling at his opponent during the mock combat, and driving the centurion into new fits of fury. They had been no more than boys when they arrived at the training base in Lugdunum. A tight bond of camaraderie had been forged that was now broken. The three men shuffled over to a shaded spot and sat in silence. One of their group had been taken in a bad way.

Valerius was in a state of shock. He walked around with his bloody sword, not sure of what he was supposed to do. He glanced at his sword arm and noticed it was shaking. He tried to remain calm, but he couldn't. His stomach was doing flip-flops as he viewed the carnage around him. Bodies were sprawled everywhere. Some lay separately, while others were in piles, draped over one another. The pungent odor of death was pervasive. The air was filled with the moans of the wounded.

Valerius hurried to the side of the road and vomited. That made him feel a bit better. He looked around, hoping no one had noticed. He grimly wiped his mouth on his sleeve. He looked at his bloody sword, wondering why he was still holding it. He hastily cleaned it on some grass and returned it to its scabbard. He needed to find the legionnaire who had saved his life and thank him. He shouldn't be too hard to find with a face wound like that. He was about to begin his quest when Centurion Clodius strode purposely in front of the assembled mass, then waved his sword.

"I want all of the centurions here now. That includes you also, Tribune." He motioned for the leaders to join him. The centurions quickly flocked to Clodius. They formed a loose circle around him. Clodius nodded in satisfaction, noting that all of the officers had survived. The men silently eyed the senior centurion, waiting to hear his orders.

"This is the situation. I've been informed that at last count, we've lost seventy men killed and another eighty wounded. I don't know if there'll be any more attacks, and I have no intention of waiting around to find out. We move out and return to the main camp as soon as we burn the bodies. Strip all of the armor and weapons from the dead. I want you to assign men to get enough wood for the task. Make sure you have proper security, and take precautions for any further attacks. I want to march until dusk, then construct a fortified camp for the night. I know the men are exhausted. My ass is dragging too, but we all need to suck it up and carry on. I've sent some of the cavalry ahead to alert General Varus of the events of today."

Clodius paused, eyeing each of them for a moment, a grim expression on his face.

"I believe this was an isolated attack, but you can never be sure with these Germans. That's why I want to beat feet back to the camp as quickly as possible. Any questions?"

One of the centurions spoke. "What about the German wounded?"

Clodius frowned before replying. "You know what to do. Keep one alive to take back to camp with us." The centurion nodded to the men in dismissal.

The column began moving, but not quickly enough. The smell of the burning bodies wafted through the air. From his perch on the back edge of a cart, Lucius attempted to breathe through his mouth. The odor of burning flesh was sickening. He tried not to think of Flavius back there. Each jolt of the wagon on the rutted roads jarred his throbbing wounds. He gritted his teeth, considering himself fortunate compared to some of the more seriously wounded, who were prone on the floor. Some men were in a heap, as there were too few carts to carry all of the injured men. Lucius could see blood oozing through the linen bandages. A few moaned in pain. Others were completely still, perhaps dead.

The cart bounced down the road in the late afternoon. Several times, Lucius passed out, only to wake when he began falling over. The cohort traveled hurriedly until near dark, then encamped for the night by a small stream. The wounded were immediately tended to by the medical staff. The same physician who had examined Lucius at the site of the ambush handed him a gourd containing liquid. "Drink this; it'll help with the pain while we suture your wounds."

Lucius gagged at the foul-tasting liquid. A corpsman, arm raised above his head, held a torch for illumination. Another assistant held Lucius's head while the physician sewed. It hurt like Hades as the physician sewed the ragged edges of his head wound. Lucius attempted to be stoic as the sharp needle entered his flesh. He wasn't entirely successful.

Lucius grimaced involuntarily each time the needle entered his flesh. This earned him an admonishment from the physician to be still. He finished the face, then shifted to the injured leg. After each stitch, the physician looked at him expectantly, as if to ask if that hurt. Of course it hurt. The medicine he'd been given to drink to dull the pain was about as useful as mule piss and tasted about the same.

At last they were finished. He proceeded to wash both areas liberally with strong vinegar. The physician motioned for the torch holder to bring it closer so he could examine his handiwork. Lucius shielded his face with his arm from the heat of the flame. The physician grunted in satisfaction at his efforts and nodded to the corpsman.

"It'll have to do."

"May I join my comrades now? I don't want to be here alone."

The physician stroked his chin in thought. "I don't see why not. Go ahead, but try to stay off your feet."

Lucius limped a short distance, then sat wearily against the base of a tree, joining Cassius and Domitius.

Cassius looked up. "Are you all right?"

"I have had better days, but I guess, overall, I will get through this."

The three sat in silent reflection of the events of the day. A small fire flickered, casting a faint light. Their tranquility was interrupted by the arrival of Decius and friends. The seated men looked up in disgust.

"Still with us, Palonius? I was hoping the Germans would have taken care of business for me. Of course, that would have deprived me of the pleasure of personally killing your ass."

"I'm not that easy to kill. How did you escape? Hiding behind your cronies again, you lump of shit?"

"We're not through yet. I'll have my day."

Cassius spoke. "Until then, kindly get the fuck out of here. You're stinking up the place."

"I'll get you also," retorted Decius.

Cassius started to rise, with bad intentions written all over his face. His right hand touched the hilt of his sheathed gladius. "I've had about all I can take of you, you ugly fuck."

Lucius held Cassius back with an extended arm. "Let him go, Cassius. He's all mouth anyway. We can deal with him later."

Tribune Valerius entered the area. He glanced in confusion at the two groups of men squared off against each other. He realized he'd entered a tense situation. Those were angry faces he was seeing. Decius stared at the tribune, then quickly motioned with his arm for his men to follow. The group disappeared into the dark. Valerius stared after them.

The tribune recognized Lucius by his face wound, which looked hideous even in the dim light of the campfire. The left side of the legionnaire's face was swollen and discolored along the sewn-up gash. Yes, this had to be the man.

"My name is Tribune Valerius Maximus. You were the legionnaire who saved my hide today. It was you, correct?"

Lucius nodded. "Yes, sir. I do remember that foray into the Germans. It wasn't just me. There were quite a few of us."

"I know, but you were the one who saved me. Thanks to your intervention, that German wasn't able to skewer me. I live to fight another day. My heartfelt thanks."

"Sir, no thanks are needed. We were all just trying to survive. My name is Lucius. That one over there is Cassius, and this is Domitius." Lucius grimaced in pain, as it was difficult to talk with the stitches on the side of his face.

"I am glad to meet all of you, especially you, Lucius. One more moment, and I would have an iron spear in me. I trust your wounds are being cared for?"

"Yeah, I guess so. I can't say I enjoyed having my face sewed."

"Lucius, I'm sure it'll heal fine, and the ladies will love that scar. By the way, I do have something that might help with the pain."

The three looked at the tribune inquiringly.

Valerius produced a skin of wine that he'd been holding at his side.

"Now, that's an excellent idea," said Cassius. Valerius handed him the wine.

Cassius held up the wine. "I'll make sure our friend Lucius gets a liberal dose of this stuff. I know the physician would approve. Don't you think so, Lucius?"

"Just don't keep it all to yourself," replied Lucius.

Valerius grinned at the three men, glad he could give them a little comfort. "I wish I could join you, but I need to meet with Centurion Clodius. I'm indebted to you, Lucius. It was nice to meet all of you." The tribune turned to go, then abruptly stopped. "It may be none of my business, but what was that all about when I first got here?"

Cassius spoke. "Bad blood, Tribune. We have some problems in our ranks. That group you just observed is no good. We'd be better off without the likes of them."

"If I can be of any assistance, let me know." The tribune turned about and departed the area.

Lucius remembered little of the agonizing full day it took to return to the main encampment. He was passed out in the baggage cart. Lucius had feverish dreams of Centurion Longinius, Decius, the sibyl, and his German foes. In one scenario, a grinning German held the bloody head of the sibyl. In another, Decius and Longinius were tormenting him, laughing at his efforts to carry one of the heavy logs used in his training. Occasionally, Lucius would awake from his semistupor, then collapse into another nightmare.

The battered cohort hobbled into the camp with the wounded. Their return was subdued compared to their departure several days ago—no bounce in their step. The expressions on the faces of the men were grim. They were covered in dust, filth, and blood. The cavalry scouts had arrived ahead of the cohort, reporting the ambush to Varus's staff. The word of the ambush had spread like the plague over the camp. Many turned out to witness the haggard survivors stagger through the fortress gates. Centurion Clodius and his centurion commanders were met by Senior Tribune Calvus.

"Centurion Clodius, General Varus requests that you and your centurions come at once to the *principia*, where the senior officers are waiting to hear your report of the battle with the Germans."

Centurion Clodius nodded politely to the tribune. "Tell the general I'll be there shortly." Clodius turned away from Calvus, then called for his centurions to assemble on him.

"Centurions, on me." The leaders quickly separated themselves from their men, moving toward Clodius.

"Listen up. I've been informed that General Varus and his senior staff want to meet with us now, as in right away. They're waiting for us. Have your optios take care of the stand-down and care for the wounded."

Valerius looked quizzically at Clodius.

The centurion nodded and spoke. "You too, Tribune. You were out there with us and got a taste of German hospitality."

The officers of the cohort walked proudly, almost defiantly, toward the assembly of Varus and his officers. The unit had acquitted itself in fine fashion, all things considered. They entered the large tented space. The staff officers were all seated. They were fastidious in appearance, adorned in their finest armor. They looked on in silence as Clodius led the men to an open area with vacant seats reserved for them. Valerius for the first time noticed the condition of his uniform. He could see blotches of blood on his armor and underlying tunic. He could smell himself in the enclosed space. He could taste the dust in his mouth. Ah, what he wouldn't give for a cup of iced wine right now. He licked his lips as he saw many of the staff officers with goblets in their hands. Clodius beckoned for Valerius to sit next to him, so he was visible to all of the senior officers present.

General Varus addressed the lead centurion. "Welcome back, Centurion Clodius. I'm pleased to see you're unharmed. I understand you encountered hostilities on your expedition. We need to understand what happened and who was responsible for this outrage. The idea that these barbarians dare attack the legions of Rome is disturbing. Please report and tell us what you know."

All eyes of the assembled officers focused on the centurion. Clodius, a twenty-five-year veteran, stood, then paused to compose himself before he began. One didn't want to misspeak in front of this audience. Any display of weakness or miscalculation in his choice of words could have disastrous consequences.

"Sirs." He paused again, looking around the room for effect. "We were ambushed by a body of Germans about a day and a half from here by a force much larger than ours. In my opinion, this wasn't a spontaneous act, but one that was carefully planned."

Before he could continue, Varus interrupted. "How so, Centurion? Please tell us how you come to that conclusion."

Clodius was ready for that question. He raised the index finger of his right hand for emphasis.

"First, sir, the cohort was too far away from the camp to receive any assistance." He raised his next finger. "Second, the attack occurred in the later part of the afternoon, when the men were most exhausted from the day's march. Third, the site of the ambush was selected with care. They chose terrain that suited them. The Germans charged out of hidden positions that were close to the road, assaulting our flanks. And fourth, they greatly outnumbered us. This was not hit and run. Their intention was to annihilate us. Of this I am certain." He was about to continue with a description of the battle.

Varus interrupted again. "Centurion, do you have any idea what tribe might have been responsible?"

"Sir, I'm not really sure. They all look alike, if you know what I mean. Some had these blue markings on their arms, some kind of tattoo, I think. Don't know if that might help identify them."

"You took no prisoners, Centurion?"

Clodius cringed inwardly. He had known that question was coming. He had, in fact, brought a wounded German with him, but the prisoner had somehow come in possession of a sharpened tent stake and driven it into his throat. That was one scenario. Most likely a legionnaire killed him out of revenge for his comrades. In any event, he had no prisoner to present for questioning.

"We did, sir, but he died on the way here from a self-inflicted wound."

Varus nodded coolly. "I see."

By order of his elevated position, Arminius was in attendance. He stepped forward.

"I'll find out who's responsible for this outrage. Leave it to me, General Varus. I will make inquiries. I have my sources. I have my suspicions already, but I'll confirm them. I promise you'll have your vengeance for this attack upon Rome."

Varus replied, "Very well, Arminius. I want to know as soon as you find out. I want the man's head on a platter who was responsible for this. Understood?"

Arminius grunted in reply.

The commander of the Eighteenth Legion, who was responsible for the Tenth Cohort, General Artorius Chaerea, spoke. "Your cohort suffered losses, Centurion Clodius?"

The centurion grimaced. Typical of Varus, he thought, to not even inquire about the losses of men. At least General Chaerea cared.

"Yes, sir, we lost men in the battle. I believe the latest tally is seventy-five men killed and a large number of wounded. Seventy of the men were killed at the ambush site. We lost five more on the way back. I was informed by the medical staff that some of the wounded aren't expected to survive. But I'll tell you one thing. The men fought bravely. We were punished from the initial assault, but we drove the barbarians away with their tails between their legs. We killed a large number of the enemy. I didn't count them, but there were piles of their dead back at the ambush site. The lines held despite the initial shock of the attack. The cohort performed as if it were a battle drill right here on the parade ground. One almost killed my ass except for Tribune Maximus, sitting next to me here. He put his entire sword through the man. Thank the gods this tribune came along. This officer and a handful of my legionnaires held off a cluster of Germans who were about to separate the command group and capture the standard. The tribune can march with me and my cohort anytime he pleases." Clodius grinned at Valerius in thanks.

Varus noticed Valerius sitting with the rest of the combatants.

A dark frown creased the face of Varus. "Tribune, I thought you were assigned to the headquarters staff for the pay records."

"Yes, sir, you're correct. I received permission to accompany the cohort." He looked briefly at Senior Tribune Calvus, who maintained a neutral expression. Valerius cringed inwardly, hoping he hadn't gotten the man into any political trouble with Varus. Valerius needed friends, not more enemies.

General Chaerea of the Eighteenth Legion joined in. "General Varus," he said, partly in jest, "it's not fair that you keep all of the good tribunes at the headquarters and not assign any of them to the individual legions. I could use a good man like Tribune Valerius by my side."

There was an awkward silence in the room. Varus stroked his chin, somewhat flustered. "I see. Well, good job, Tribune."

Varus quickly turned back to the centurion, unconcerned about Valerius for the moment. Somebody else was, though. Valerius glanced to his right, behind where the general was seated. He saw Castor, his eyes glinting with hatred, a gash for a mouth. He looked as if someone had shoved a sharp stick up his ass. Valerius smirked. That should serve him right, he thought. He fixed Castor with an insolent stare before returning his attention to the proceedings.

Varus continued his grilling of Clodius. "Anything else you can share with us, Centurion?"

"No, sir, just that there didn't appear to be hostile intent from the other villages that we encountered. The people seemed peaceful."

"Very well." The general looked about among the assembly of officers. "Arminius, where are you?"

Arminius strode forward. "Here, General Varus."

"Arminius, I'll repeat myself." The general spoke succinctly in anger, biting off his words. "I want the name of the rogue and the tribe that was responsible for this outrage. Do you understand?"

Arminius nodded to Varus.

The general spoke to the other officers. "Any more questions for the centurion?"

There was silence. The meeting was over. The officers began to file out of the room. Valerius stared again directly at Castor, giving him a smug smile. He grinned to himself. I got one up on you. Castor looked up briefly, then stormed out of the room.

Valerius went back to his tent, shed his armor, and washed his face. Despite his weariness, he decided to seek out Marcellus. He needed to talk to someone about the ambush. His mind continued going back to the battle over and over. Had he acted as a tribune should? Had he done what was expected of him? There was no doubt he had been scared. What about that vomiting at the end? He needed to talk the whole thing out.

He found Marcellus where he usually was, among the pay records.

"Tribune, back from the hinterland, and in one piece."

"I guess you heard, Marcellus?"

"I did indeed, Tribune. I saw one of the centurions just a few moments ago. He said you made it through intact."

"I expect you're going to tell me, 'I told you so.'"

"No need for that, Tribune. The important thing is you survived."

Valerius stood in front of the seated centurion not knowing what to say. He couldn't put into words the turmoil he was experiencing.

Marcellus rescued him. "The first time in battle is hard for any man. Thinking back, I believe I wet myself."

Valerius couldn't help but laugh. "I think I was close to that."

Marcellus paused for a moment before replying. "I remember it was all screams, shouts, and absolute pandemonium. There was no order to things; it was just draw your sword and do the best you could. Tribune, why don't we get some wine, and you can tell me all about it. I heard some stuff already, but nothing firsthand. What do you say?"

"If you let me buy."

Marcellus replied with his customary refrain: "What are we waiting for?"

The two men retired to an open area of the camp with a small table and several campstools. It was not yet time for the evening meal, and most of the men were on duty. They would remain undisturbed here. Marcellus waited patiently for the tribune to begin; best to let him tell it on his own terms. To break the tension, Marcellus raised his goblet. "To your health, Tribune."

Valerius raised his goblet in response but wasn't ready to speak. He swallowed hard to keep his emotions in check. He composed himself as best he could.

"I'm not sure I can explain what happened. It came upon us so quickly."

"The Germans ambushed you and came out of forest, right?"

Valerius nodded. "Yes. All was calm, and then, in a few heartbeats, there were bodies all over the place. I drew my sword and started swinging it like a wild man. I'm not sure I followed the steps of proper sword drill."

Marcellus laughed at the tribune's description. "Listen, Tribune. The centuries of the legion practice sword drill almost every damn day, and the centurions still need to remind the troops in battle to thrust and not hack. A common enough mistake."

There was a pause in the conversation. Valerius looked at the ground as if in concentration.

"I killed some men out there, Marcellus. I know I'm a soldier and everything, but it keeps bothering me. After the battle was over, I vomited in the bushes."

"You killed some men? I believe there was more to it than that. The way I heard it, you saved old Centurion Clodius's ass and maybe the entire cohort. One of the centurions told me you were an army of one. Everyone in the camp knows by now. A green tribune—no offense, sir—saves the senior centurion from certain death and stops the Germans in their tracks. Pretty impressive for a new tribune, wouldn't you say?"

Valerius grinned back modestly.

"As to the killing, Tribune, no shame there, sir. Most men feel the way you do. Killing isn't a pleasant business, but it's sometimes necessary. You'll get over it; we all do. The important thing is you survived. You did your duty."

Valerius looked at the centurion. "You think so?"

"You'll feel better tomorrow. By the way, how did our esteemed general act when he was notified of your bravery?"

"I believe he was a little flustered, but in the end, I don't suppose it bothered him much. He had greater concerns with the ambush and the tarnished image of Roman authority. I saw Castor's face. He was furious."

Marcellus snorted in derision. "Serves the odious prick right."

XV

*W*here was he? Lucius could hear orders shouted and sensed people around him. He felt several pairs of arms lift him from his prone position. He'd passed out some time ago, delirious with fever and exhaustion. I can stand, he thought. But he really couldn't.

His bloody outer garments were stripped off his person. Lucius felt cool sponges soaked in vinegar and water cleansing his body of the road grime that had accumulated over the past two days. He was half carried to a cot with wonderfully soft blankets. From far away, he heard someone asking questions about his name and unit. Lucius mumbled something in reply before collapsing into a deep sleep.

Cassius trudged back to his tent. He had volunteered to help carry Lucius to the hospital area. He and the others were abruptly dismissed once they had placed Lucius in a cot. No words of thanks from the medical staff, just get out and we will take care of it from here. Cassius was too tired to take offense. He would go see Julia first thing in the morning and inform her about Lucius's injuries. He assumed word had spread about the ambush, and Julia would be concerned about Lucius. He couldn't go now, as it was almost dusk and the gates would be closed for the night.

The next morning, Cassius woke from a deep sleep, noting with some surprise that he'd slept with his full armor on. He hazily remembered that last night, he was just going to lie down for a few moments. Stepping outside, careful not to stumble over the other forms passed out in dreamless oblivion, he greeted the day. From the angle of the sun, he realized that it was almost midmorning. Cassius cursed himself for his laziness. He hurriedly shed his armor and changed into a clean tunic.

There was a large pot of water outside the tent that he scooped up in his cupped hands and washed his face. The water was chilly from the coolness of the night, refreshing him. He poured the remainder over his head and ambled on to the cohort mess area. He grabbed two large biscuits, each as big as his hand, then rushed toward the gate. In midstride, he changed direction. He decided he'd make a quick detour on his way to Julia for a quick visit with Lucius to see how he was coming along. Besides, he reasoned, the hospital was located kind of on the way he was headed, so it seemed the sensible thing to do.

He hurried along, cramming the biscuits into his mouth one after the other. Cassius approached the tents that housed the injured. They were easy to identify, with their high wooden platform floors. In all, there were four enormous shelters. He knew Lucius was in the one to the far left. Brushing the bread crumbs from his hands and tunic, Cassius approached. A rather stern-faced orderly blocked his way. The scowling man was huge.

"You have business here?" the man demanded brusquely.

Cassius presented his most disarming smile. "I was hoping you could help me. My best friend, Lucius Palonius, was wounded yesterday. I promised I would look in on him this morning. Is he in here?"

The man consulted a wax tablet with names scrawled upon it.

"He's here, but you can't see him. No visitors. Standing orders. No exceptions." The man crossed his arms in front of his chest defiantly.

"Look, I understand the need for camp regulations, but this is different. It'll be a quick visit, I assure you. You can even accompany me to make sure. I won't even bother the other patients." Cassius continued smiling at the man.

"No exceptions. Now be on your way."

"I'm not asking for a lot. Can't I see him for just a moment?" Cassius was pleading for reason.

"I said be on your way, soldier. Now, if you know what's good for you, you'll move on."

The man stepped forward in a threatening fashion as he spoke. The orderly must have expected Cassius to step back. He didn't. The smile disappeared from Cassius's face. The two men were now close to each other. While the other man was bigger, this didn't intimidate Cassius. If he could deal with armed Germans, he could handle this brute.

"You come one step closer to me, sir orderly, you fucking hump, and I'm going to take my dagger and shove it up your fat ass. You got that?"

To prove his point, Cassius drew his dagger. The blade made an ugly rasping sound as it cleared the scabbard. He now regretted that he had not brought his sword, as required by regulations when departing the camp. In his haste to rush toward Julia, he had forgotten his weapon.

The orderly, his face etched with fear, edged backward. Before things got really serious, another orderly of similar dimensions appeared. Cassius, although outnumbered, didn't back down, continuing to stare at both of his antagonists. He realized that this wasn't a battle he would most likely win. Even if he did, the punishment could be severe, regardless of his good intentions to see his friend. The legions wouldn't take kindly to this; they frowned upon a soldier stabbing medical orderlies.

Without breaking eye contact, Cassius slowly retreated. The hulks grinned mockingly at him. He was considering going back at them, but instead turned around and hurried toward Julia's location. He vowed he would one day get the opportunity to even the score. Cassius rushed out of the gates in the direction of the animal corrals. Despite his weariness, he ran. After asking five different people of her whereabouts, he finally found Julia with several other staff working with the mules. Approaching Julia, he tried to keep his expression neutral so as not to alarm her.

She saw Cassius. Her face immediately brightened. "Cassius, how nice to see you again. Lucius has told me what a good friend you are to him. But what are you doing here? I thought you were out on patrol with Lucius."

Cassius didn't respond. He stood there rigid and tight lipped, unable to utter his rehearsed lines about Lucius. It was obvious Julia was unaware of the ambush. Suddenly Julia's face turned ashen. Cassius, for all of his efforts to portray a neutral expression, had failed miserably.

"Oh, no. What's happened to Lucius?"

Cassius moved to her and put his hand on her arm for reassurance.

"He's all right, Julia. He's been wounded," he said quickly. "There was an ambush when our unit was out on patrol."

"Where is he?"

"He's in the hospital. He has a cut over his eye and a slight leg wound."

Cassius tried to downplay the injuries as much as possible. A cut and a slight leg wound made it sound insignificant. In truth, Lucius looked like the loser in an axe fight, and the other guy had the only axe.

"Can you take me to him now?"

"I guess so. I'm not sure they'll let us see him. You know how fussy those physicians are. They wouldn't let me enter when I stopped on the way here. I had a rather nasty confrontation with some pea-brained dolt of an orderly." Cassius silently congratulated himself for keeping his description somewhat clean in front of a lady.

Julia used a nearby cloth to wipe her hands clean, then smoothed out her hair. She turned to Cassius. "Let's go. We'll get in. I'll see to that."

Lucius awoke from his long sleep. He felt like Hades. His face was swollen where the physician had stitched his wound. His leg ached, and he had a terrible thirst. He noted he was on a cot on a wooden floor and naked with the exception of a blanket that covered him. From his limited vantage point, Lucius observed the place was exceptionally clean and smelled strongly of vinegar.

To one side, there was a rack that contained all sorts of hanging dried plants, which he presumed were used for medicinal purposes. Immediately to his front was a table covered with a fine cloth on which rested all kinds of shiny metal instruments. He shuddered involuntarily, thinking about the purposes of these tools. There were other cots in the large tent, occupied by wounded legionnaires. Some of the men moaned softly in pain. Hanging oil lamps provided illumination.

Lucius tried to shift his position without moving his wounded leg. He was unsuccessful, wincing in pain as the stitches pulled against his flesh. He lay back, closing his eyes, waiting for the throbbing to go away.

Lucius opened his eyes, sensing a presence near his cot. Turning his head to the left, he saw Tribune Maximus standing there observing him.

The tribune smiled. "Sorry, Lucius. Didn't mean to wake you. I just wanted to check in and see how you were getting along. Your eye looks a bit frightful, but other than that, you appear satisfactory. How are you feeling?"

Lucius's attempt to speak came out as a croak.

Valerius spied a pitcher of water on the nearby table. He looked inside at the contents and sniffed it. "Looks good to me." He proceeded to pour some water in a clay cup and handed it to Lucius.

"Here you are. It's not every day a tribune waits on a legionnaire." Valerius beamed at his own humor.

Lucius drained the contents. "Thank you, sir. I'm so thirsty."

"More water?"

"If you don't mind, sir, that would be wonderful."

The tribune poured more water into the goblet, which Lucius quickly drained. He wiped his mouth with his arm, then looked back toward the tribune.

"I promised to look in on you to see you were cared for properly. I saw one of the physicians on the way in here. He said you were recovering satisfactorily. He seemed a bit cranky that I came to check on you."

"Thank you, sir. I'm feeling better than when I arrived here; that is for sure. I haven't spoken to any of the physicians yet."

Julia and Cassius approached the medical tents. Cassius pointed out the one Lucius occupied. The same corpsman was standing at the entrance. The man looked back at Cassius and spoke in disdain. "You again. I see you brought reinforcements." The man smirked at his own humor.

Julia, ignoring the barb, took the lead and spoke. "Is Lucius Palonius in this tent?"

"Yes he is, but you can't enter," he said officiously. He stood up to block their path. "Physician's orders. I told this one"—he gestured at Cassius—"the same thing this morning. He doesn't listen."

"But we're his friends."

"Doesn't matter."

Julia took a step forward. "How silly. We won't stay long. Can't you let us in for a brief visit?" she pleaded.

"Look, lady, nobody is supposed enter."

Julia was not to be denied. "Don't you 'lady' me. Where's this physician who won't let a patient's friends see him?"

She started to go around him. The corpsmen extended his arm to stop her. That was a mistake. She was in the man's face now, raising her voice. "Get your hand off me. Get the physician in charge, now!"

A balding older man appeared through the tent flaps. He was dressed in a linen gown stained and spattered with blood. "What's going on here in my hospital? Mistress Julia? What are you doing here?"

"Marcus Vitellius, how are you?" She deftly edged around the bewildered corpsmen, then sidled next to the physician, putting her hands on his arm. Marcus Vitellius was a good friend of her father. They frequently dined together. She smiled warmly at him.

"Julia, what's all this about?"

"I'm here to see a legionnaire who's a friend of mine. He was wounded the other day in the fight with the Germans. This mule head won't let me pass." She pointed her finger directly in the orderly's face.

"Sir, your standing orders are for no one to be admitted," the orderly stammered.

The physician looked at both Cassius and Julia, then turned toward the orderly. "It's fine. We'll make this one exception. You may let them pass."

With a triumphant smile, Julia led Cassius into the tent. Cassius flashed the orderly a triumphant grin as he passed.

"Thank you, Marcus. I'll tell my father of your kindness."

Lucius and Valerius turned their heads at the sound of a commotion to their left. He heard a female shriek followed by some gruff male responses. Lucius recognized those voices. Then Cassius and Julia came parading in toward his cot. He started to smile, which in turn pulled his stitches. That really smarted. Lucius involuntarily put his hand to his face, wincing.

Julia hurried to Lucius's side, gasping at the sight of his face. It was heavily swollen on the left side near the eyebrow. The color was a purplish red. The gash extended all the way to the lower earlobe, marked by the tight stitches.

Lucius, despite his current physical state, remembered his manners. "Tribune Valerius, this is Julia. She's with the camp veterinary staff. And you remember Cassius from our meeting a few days ago."

"Certainly I remember Cassius. Julia, it is an honor to meet you. Here I thought all of the pretty women were in Rome."

Julia blushed at the compliment. "Thank you, Tribune. It's a pleasure to make your acquaintance." All eyes turned back to Lucius.

Julia grasped his hand. "How are you?"

"Better than I was."

"What about your leg?"

"It's sore. The damn stitches pull every time I turn over."

"Let me look."

Lucius, realizing he had nothing on underneath the blanket, tried to put her off.

"No, really, Julia, I'm fine. It's just a scratch."

"Like your face is just a cut."

Cassius decided to come to the rescue. "Come on, Lucius, go ahead and show her." He pulled the blanket aside, revealing Lucius in all his glory. He grabbed futilely at the blanket to cover himself.

"Uh, sorry, Lucius," said Cassius.

Lucius's entire face turned a bright crimson to add to the purple and red hues from his wound. "Thanks, Cassius. I owe you one."

Julia put her hand to her mouth and stifled a laugh.

"Lucius, don't be so ashamed. I've seen enough of those on all of the mules and horses of the legions." She added, "Except they're bigger."

Cassius and Valerius laughed.

"I'm sure glad you three are having a good time at my expense," said Lucius.

Julia continued to giggle. She grabbed Lucius's hand and held it in her own. "We're truly sorry. We came to see how you're doing. We're both worried. Right, Cassius?"

"Indeed. I don't see any other visitors here. You're lucky we care about you."

Valerius chimed in. "I sure wish my girlfriend was here to care for me. You're indeed a fortunate young man."

Marcus, the physician, entered.

"How are you doing, young Palonius?" He brushed the visitors aside, then proceeded to quietly examine the two wounds. He put his hand on Lucius's head to check for signs of a fever. The man's eyes narrowed as he studied Lucius. Everyone looked on, anxious to hear what he had to say.

"Those are some pretty nasty cuts you have there, soldier, but there's no sign of mortification. All in all, the wounds look like they're healing, and your fever is gone from last night. I'm going to keep you here one more day. After that, you'll present yourself here twice a day without fail, once in the morning and once in the evening, to have the wounds washed properly and dressed. You must try not to get the wounds dirty. I don't want you bathing in that cesspool of a river, either. You'll be excused from military duty for three weeks while these wounds heal. Understood?"

"Yes, sir," replied Lucius.

"I'll write a note to your centurion excusing you from duty. What's his name?"

"Centurion Frontinus."

The physician noted the name on a wax tablet he'd secured around his neck with a thong. "And unit?"

"Eighteenth Legion, Tenth Cohort, Third Century," replied Lucius.

"Very well. Furthermore, you'll limit your physical activities. I don't want those stitches to break."

"Yes, sir."

Julia and Cassius stood at his side, beaming. Cassius was envious. "Lucius, you dog. Three weeks without drill."

"Marcus, I'll make sure he follows your directions religiously," said Julia. She smiled smugly.

Marcus nodded to Julia. "I'm counting on it. By the way, tell your father he's welcome to dinner anytime."

"I'll do that, Marcus. It's been too long."

"If you'll excuse me, I have more patients to attend to."

He turned and exited, muttering curses about the damned Germans. Valerius decided that it would be a good time to leave.

"I need to be going also. It appears that I am leaving you in good hands. Julia, once again, a pleasure meeting you. Make sure this young man follows the physician's instructions."

Julia grinned back at him. "I shall. A pleasure meeting you, Tribune Valerius. Good day."

Cassius and Julia chatted with Lucius for a while longer. Julia promised to fix him lunch midday tomorrow if he was able to walk to her quarters outside the gate. Julia gave Lucius a good-bye hug and left him alone once more.

It was midmorning of the next day. Lucius painfully limped out the gate. His leg ached and his head throbbed, but he felt totally alive and free. He walked toward Julia's quarters, moving slowly. Every time his leg exceeded its capacity to stretch, it would remind him in an uncomfortable manner. Lucius was accustomed to a long gait, so it was difficult to limit his stride. He couldn't get in the rhythm of a smaller, almost dainty stride. He had to stop several times and rest on the way there. It took a while, but he eventually arrived at Julia's quarters. She was waiting for him and gave him a warm hug.

"What took you so long? I've been here by myself all morning."

"I had to stop at the hospital and get everything checked out. They washed the wounds and rebandaged the leg. I hurried over as soon as I could. I can't walk too fast. It hurts when I do."

"I'm glad you're here. Look what I've prepared for you." She gestured magnanimously with her arms toward the small table laden with food. There was fresh-baked bread, olives, cheese, smoked fish, and fresh fruit, along with a container of wine. Lucius was famished. The two of them spent little time talking. In the middle of the feast, Julia's father entered. He was taken aback by the condition of Lucius's face.

"My goodness, Lucius. Julia told me you were wounded. Are you all right?"

"Yes, sir. It looks worse than it is."

"I heard about the ambush. You can't trust these bloody Germans. They're so unpredictable. I understand Varus has tripled the guard around the animal pens and the fortress. Prudent thing to do, if you ask me. The sooner we get to winter quarters at Vetera, the better. At least there we'll be safe within the fortress walls and a have a decent roof over our heads."

"I'm also looking to moving to the winter base on the Rhine. This living in a tent is getting to me," replied Lucius.

"I think you'll like it there, Lucius. I believe you'll find it much more comfortable. Julia told me you were treated by friend Marcus Vitellius."

"Yes, sir."

"Damn good man. One of the finest physicians in the army. You're fortunate to have him take care of you. Trained in Greece. His mind is sharp. He remembers everything, knows his stuff, by Jove. Enough about your face. I'm sure you'd rather change the subject. Mind if I join you for some food?"

"Father, you need not ask. Of course you're welcome. I've prepared a feast to help Lucius recover. Look, I managed to purchase some of your favorite goat cheese."

"So Julia tells me you have family back in Gaul?"

"Yes, sir, and I miss them. My conscription wasn't a happy event in our household."

Julia's father paused to smear more goat cheese on a piece of bread.

"Damn unfortunate, your conscription, if you ask me. The ranks of the legions have been filled with volunteers for a long time. I hear that these days, they take men from all over the empire. If I could give you any advice, it would be to make the best of it. Anyway, there isn't a lot you can do about it now."

"I've reconciled myself to my fate. I've enjoyed seeing new places. I hope to see more of the empire in the coming years."

"That's the spirit. I've lived with the legions for a long time now, and Julia also. It's not all that bad."

Petrocolus stuffed another piece of cheese in his mouth.

"I have to go now. Julia, I may need you later this afternoon to help with some of the horses."

"Going so soon? You hardly ate very much."

"I have matters to attend to."

"Anything that you need me for?"

"No. Just the usual routine."

"Very well. I will see you later today, Father."

After lunch, Lucius sat with Julia at a small table. She produced a piece of parchment and a stylus. "Look what I have here for you, Lucius. Remember I said I could have a letter delivered to your family? This is the perfect time to write that letter to your parents. My father will ensure that it arrives by military courier."

Lucius nodded gratefully, then examined the parchment.

"Want to give it a try?"

"Sure, why not?"

Lucius placed the parchment in front of him and dipped the stylus in the ink. He thought for a moment and began crafting the letter to his parents. He knew his family would be elated when they received it. He carefully chose his words and began to write deliberately.

Salve, Mother and Father,
No doubt you are surprised at this letter. I will tell you more of that shortly. I hope you are well and that Paetus and Drusilla are behaving in my absence. You know I miss you all terribly. I was told that you were informed of my posting to the legions of the northern Rhine. I am on a river called the Weser. This is the northern frontier of the empire. There are three legions here, the XVII, XVIII, and XIX, so I am well protected. Please do not be concerned for my safety. The land here is strangely beautiful but rugged. I managed to survive my training in Gaul and journeyed by boat on the large sea. That was quite an experience. I have made many friends, including one known as Cassius, who lived some ten miles from us. You would like him. He is quick of wit and a true friend. The people appear peaceful in Germania, and I look forward to our journey to winter quarters on the Rhine sometime in the fall. I will be comforted knowing that I will be that much closer to you. I have also met a young woman, the camp veterinarian's daughter. Her name is Julia. She is responsible for this letter being sent by military courier. I would hope that someday you could meet her. I look forward to the day when I can see you all again. So to you, Mother and Father, and little brother and sister, I hope the gods are smiling upon you, keeping you safe. Please know that my thoughts are of you every day. I can almost see you and hear your voices. Know that I am fine and look forward to our reunion.
Your son, Lucius

Lucius examined the letter and was pleased with his work. Julia, looking over his shoulder, frowned.

"The people appear peaceful? After what they did to you, this is what you write?"

"There's no need for them to know about the ambush and worry about me. Why should I alarm them?"

Julia grinned. "Of course. You're correct. Some things are better left unsaid."

He waved the parchment back and forth to get the ink to dry. Lucius tried to imagine his family's reaction when they got the letter. He grinned in anticipation.

"Julia, how long do you think it'll take to get there?"

Julia thought for a moment and did some calculations in her head. "I would guess a little over two weeks," she replied.

"I can hardly wait for them to get this letter. They'll be so surprised. Many thanks, Julia."

She grinned back at him in pleasure.

Every morning after having his wounds washed and examined, Lucius was off to visit Julia. He returned to camp late in the afternoon to have the same process repeated by the medical orderly. His visits to Julia were limited to the confines of the animal compound. It was painful to walk any great distance. One day, he and Julia were enjoying another fine lunch. Lucius decided he needed to broach the subject of the sibyl to Julia. The encounter continued to haunt him. In fact, it was driving him crazy.

"Julia, remember I mentioned to you about the sibyl?"

"Yes, of course. She foretold your conscription and journey away from home. I remember you telling me all about that. What about it?"

"There's more."

"Tell me."

"She prophesized I would meet you."

"No way! That's not possible."

"She absolutely did."

"What did she say?" Julia leaned toward Lucius in anticipation.

"She said I would meet a woman who would capture my heart."

Julia got a mischievous look in her eyes. "And have I stolen your heart?"

"You know you have."

"How sweet of you." She leaned over and kissed him.

Lucius broke off. "That's the good part. You know, about us. She wouldn't finish the prophecy. She had this horrible look on her face. She avoided my eyes. I know she lied to me at the end."

"Maybe she had a vision of how your face looks now."

"Julia, come on. I'm a little worried about this. Too many of her prophecies have been right on the mark. This is beyond coincidence."

Julia could see that this was troubling Lucius.

"I'm sorry, Lucius. Perhaps she had a vision of the battle and how seriously you were hurt."

"Do you think that's it?" he said wistfully.

"It's possible. A sibyl wouldn't want to tell a customer he's going to get stabbed or cut, now, would she?"

"Maybe you're right. Why don't we change the subject? I get the chills just visualizing the expression on her face."

Julia moved closer to Lucius and kissed him. Lucius was conscious of only Julia as they wrapped their arms around each other. Julia moaned with pleasure. After a while, Julia stood and unfastened her garment, letting it fall to her feet. Lucius just took in the sight before him.

"Julia, what about your father?"

She laughed at Lucius. "What about him?" She proceeded to drag him toward her bed.

XVI

*T*wilight was deepening in the sacred grove. It was chilly for a late summer evening, more so in the gloom of this heavily shaded copse. A large fire burned and crackled, casting an eerie glow over the assembled faces of the various German tribal leaders and their subordinates. This was no ordinary gathering. Tonight, many of the most powerful and influential chieftains were assembled. The men's faces were expressionless, waiting for the discussion to begin. They sat on wooden benches that had been excavated into the sloped surface of the small, bowl-shaped hill. The seating area was semicircular, in shape almost like a natural amphitheater.

Towering oak trees surrounded the grove. The fire illuminated their massive trunks. As long as anyone could remember, this had been a hallowed location for ceremony and ritual sacrifice. The gathered leaders considered this a holy place. A huge stone altar of ancient origin occupied the center stage. The audience was all men, with the exception of two women priestesses clad in long, flowing, white robes. They weren't seated like the men but remained standing off to the right of the stone altar. Each priestess carried a sacrificial dagger with a jeweled silver hilt tucked into the sash around her middle. Because of the sanctity of the location, it was necessary to have the women present. They stood to the side staring into the fire, waiting for the proceedings to begin.

Many of the tribes were represented here tonight. There were the Sugambri, Suebi, Cimbri, Angrivarii, Teutons, Cherusci, Tencteri, Segni, Chatti, Bructeri, Marsi, Trevari, Nervii, and the Batavians. Other, lesser tribes were also present. There was little talking except for snippets of muted conversation or occasional muffled laughter.

An older man rose from the front row, clad in a long purple cloak of exceptional quality. Underneath, he wore a woolen tunic, tan in color. The man was partially bald and wore a long beard that was liberally dosed with gray. Despite his age, he was still an imposing figure. The man was probably in his midforties, yet he retained a large muscle mass on his upper torso. He gazed about at the assembled throng, then decided it was time to proceed. Proud and erect, he boldly strode to the front of the gathering. He faced the waiting audience and raised his arm for silence. The grove became quiet, with the exception of the crackling fire.

"You all know me. I'm Charus of the Trevari tribe. I've been selected to host the discussion tonight concerning certain recent events with the Romans. These are serious matters. You're my guests, and I welcome you all, even the Segni," he quipped.

This drew a large roar of laughter from the men, breaking the tension. The Trevari tribe of Charus and the Segni were always feuding about something. As long as anyone could remember, they had been fighting. If they had nothing to feud about, which was rare, they would invent something. It could be stolen horses, booty, women, cattle, or blood feuds. For this evening, at least, this was cast aside.

After the laughter died away, he continued. "You all understand the reasons the council has been assembled. Let us begin. The first to speak will be Jurus of the Sugambri tribe." Charus nodded slightly to the seated figure in the front row, then returned to his place. Jurus, the leader of the failed ambush of the Tenth Cohort, rose from his seat, then strode purposefully to the front of the natural amphitheater. He confidently faced the assembly. Jurus, in his early twenties, looked like a warrior, with his muscled physique and flowing hair. He spoke in a loud voice.

"We've been told all spring and summer to act the part of the docile people to the Roman legions and their arrogant general. The same Romans, I would remind you, who have killed many of our friends and brothers and enslaved our people. I look around me tonight and see the sorrow on your faces for the losses we've taken. I note the troubles in your eyes. It's a terrible burden we all bear. No, burden isn't the right word. It's not a burden; it's shame. We've been humiliated." He paused for a brief period to let his words sink in.

"Be patient, we're advised. Our time will come. When will that be? Soon, the Roman armies will depart to their winter quarters on the Rhine. They'll stand behind the huge, impregnable walls of their fortresses, where we can never defeat them. All the while, their haughty general demands gold and silver tributes from us. This Varus humiliates each and every one of us with his actions." He paused for effect and paced a few steps in front of the gathering.

"I could take no more. Five days ago, my men, my *comitatus,* and others who are sick to death of the Romans, struck a blow for all Germans, a blow to free us from the Roman yoke. We attacked one of their cohorts, slaying many Romans. They retreated quickly to their base camp, cowering in fear. Now they know they'll never be safe as long as German warriors hold spears or swords in their hands."

Jurus walked the length of the natural stage, peering into their faces. He would now begin his personal attack on Arminius. He'd rehearsed these lines many times. To embellish his point, Jurus pointed directly at Arminius, then raised his voice.

"One of our own, Arminius, would have us believe that we must submit. We must bow to these subjugators like slaves. That this will serve us in the long run. How can this be? Arminius tells us that we'll have our day. He says this while he's paid by the Romans to do their killing. He's proved that in Pannonia, where he served under their generals. His very own brother, I would remind you, has become a friend of the Romans, even adopting a Roman name. Can we trust this man who serves the Romans? He even urges us to pay the tribute the Roman general demands of us. We should follow him? When will be the time to attack? When we're all in shackles?"

He now raised his voice for his final words. "I say we strike a blow for Germania now, while they're here at their summer encampment. They're not invincible. I've proven that. We shall attack and destroy them!"

He punctuated his remarks by striking his fist into the palm of his other hand. He was finished. His lieutenants gave him encouraging shouts. The remainder of the gathering was silent, expressionless. Jurus returned to his seat, attempting to mask his disappointment. He had hoped for a more enthusiastic response.

Charus stood, waited for Jurus to be seated, then nodded silently toward Arminius.

Arminius rose from his seat and slowly approached the gathering. He wore a long, drab cloak over a thin tunic and deerskin leggings. His reddish-blond hair shone in sharp contrast to the neutral shade of his cloak. His blue eyes blazed with frantic energy. At his side, he wore a long iron sword of exquisite craftsmanship. Arminius's choice of clothing was no accident, but carefully planned and chosen with care. Gone were all the vestiges and accouterments associated with his Roman uniform as liaison commander of the German auxiliary forces. This included his sword, which the Romans traditionally wore on the right side but which was now on his left, German style.

No, tonight he was just Arminius, a German chieftain of the Cherusci tribe. Even his dress as a German chieftain reflected plain clothing, not the attire usually worn by of one of his considerable standing. He was one of them. Arminius knew he had the strong support of some of the tribes, but if his plan was to work, he needed more of the clans to join the German coalition that he was attempting to unite. Once that was accomplished, then he would make war on Varus and his army. Arminius understood that the Roman legions were a tough bunch, not to be underestimated. It was no accident that they had been victorious over lands far and wide. Those armies that opposed the legions usually lost badly. Yes, he would need as many warriors as possible if he was to succeed with his plan. Jurus's blundering attack would aid him in his pursuit of defeating the Romans. Rather than view Jurus's ill-conceived ambush as a setback to his ploy, he would use it to his advantage. It was time to start his quest.

"Greetings, fellow Germans. You all know me. You know my father, Sigimer. I've spoken to many of you before. You understand that I hate these Romans as much as you do. You just heard the account that Jurus gave you about the mighty victory he and his men achieved over the Roman legions. Did he not tell you how the Roman soldiers fled in panic back to their summer encampment?" He paced to the left and stroked his chin in thought, then snorted in derision.

"I believe the facts may be a bit different from Jurus's account. From what I've heard, it was Jurus and his friends who fled the battlefield. Shamefully, I would note, leaving their dead behind and the wounded to be executed by the Roman soldiers. Oh, there were Romans slain. I'll grant you that, but at what cost? How many Germans died?"

Jurus, seeing that he was being mocked by Arminius, rose to protest. "You weren't there. How can you possibly know what happened?"

Charus, as host and moderator, quickly interceded. "Jurus," he chastised, "it's Arminius's turn to speak. You already had your say. Don't interrupt him."

Jurus frowned and reluctantly went back to his seat. He dared not argue with one of such stature as Charus in front of all these chieftains.

Arminius glared in annoyance at Jurus before returning his attention to the assembled congregation of Germans.

"Yes, men were slain on both sides. Probably a lot more Germans than Romans, from what I'm told. But what did we accomplish? I'll tell you what. Nothing! Not a thing. What's more, the Romans will now be on their guard and dare not trust us."

Arminius stood still, then paused, letting his words have their effect on those present.

"Leaders and chiefs, listen to me. I tell you, we'll have the opportunity to rid ourselves of these arrogant conquerors. Their commander is a lawyer who knows little of war. Varus is a gullible fool.

We can defeat them, but we must select the time and place when the advantage will be ours. I've explained my plan to many of you. We'll lure the Romans away from their normal route of march on the way to their winter encampment. The Chatti tribe has agreed to stage a false rebellion on the fringes of their territory. In the thick forest, the Teutoburg, we will spring the perfect ambush. The Romans will take the bait. I know they will. Their foolish pride, their vanity, and their sense of Roman superiority will be their undoing. I've studied these Romans over many years. I know how they think. They have no respect for us as a people and consider us subdued. That is, they believed we were subdued until Jurus pulled his stupid stunt and ambushed the Roman cohort."

Arminius took the opportunity to give Jurus a disparaging glance, then turned away from him dismissively.

"As I was saying, the Romans will see the staged Chatti rebellion as pure insolence, a transgression that'll warrant retaliation and punishment. Once they're in the forest, they'll be trapped. Our forces will surround and destroy them all. Please note, fellow warriors, that I stated *our* forces. This is not my army, it is yours. I am merely hatching the plan that will rid these arrogant creatures who have occupied our lands. At the same time, we'll attack all of their forts from here to the Rhine and wipe them out. We have to wait a few more weeks. Is that too much to ask? Just a few more weeks until we have their heads."

A German chieftain of the Cimbri tribe rose and spoke. "Arminius, how can we possibly surprise the Romans in the Teutoburg Forest? Will they not have their cavalry out to the front, rear, and flanks for security? We'll surely be discovered."

Arminius grinned back at the man. The question solidified his point. In fact, he was counting on someone making that inquiry.

"The German auxiliaries of which I am in command will have full responsibility for the security of the Roman column."

There were scattered shouts of exclamation from the assembly. He had them now. Arminius continued on in a subdued tone.

"Jurus would have you believe we should attack them now by luring them out in the open. We've all seen the results of these forays.

We Germans have lost every time. The weapons and tactics of the Romans were designed to use shock and to maneuver against their enemies. We dare not oppose them on open ground. Brethren and comrades, listen to me. I'm beseeching you. Varus believes I'm his friend. Their commander trusts me implicitly. I'll lead him to the area of the Chatti rebellion deep in the Teutoburg Forest. The Romans can't use their tactics in the thick woods. The advantage will be ours. We'll chop them up piecemeal and kill them all. I've seen this tactic work when I was with the legions in Pannonia. The Romans were almost defeated there. Now, who's with me on this?"

There were shouts of agreement from the assembled men.

Arminius raised his voice almost to a shout. "I say again, who stands with me on this?"

Arminius had discussed his speech before with his followers, requesting them to jump to their feet showing their approval. They were planted in strategic locations through the audience so that the assembled chieftains would see the strong support for Arminius.

"I'm with you, Arminius."

"I also," shouted another.

The effect was instantaneous. Many of the men were now standing, screaming their approval.

Jurus realized that his position was all but lost. He leaped to his feet, trying to be heard. He quickly approached Arminius in front of the audience.

"Arminius will get us all killed. He's too close to his master."

No one paid attention to Jurus.

Arminius waved everyone to be silent. He glared at Jurus.

"We do have a problem now, don't we? We must regain the trust of the Romans. They'll want vengeance for the death of their soldiers. What are we to do?"

Arminius answered his own rhetorical question. In the blink of an eye, he drew his long sword and savagely ran it through Jurus so that the blade protruded half a foot out his back. Jurus gasped, vomiting a gout of blood, gaping in disbelief at the offending sword that had pierced him.

Arminius smoothly withdrew the blade. Before Jurus could fall, Arminius swung the sharp-edged blade with two hands, nearly severing the head. Blood flew in all directions as the lifeless body of Jurus collapsed to the ground. Those seated nearest the front were showered in crimson gore. The audience sat in stunned silence. Arminius reached down and finished the job, sawing through the remaining bone and gristle of the neck, freeing the head from the body.

"I'll deliver this," he said as he reached down and picked up the grisly object, "to the Roman commander. He'll trust us once again."

Arminius stared at the men seated on the hillside.

"I know that some of you find it difficult to believe in this plan, one that's conceived by a Cherusci chieftain. We've had our differences in the past. There's mistrust. This I understand. I ask nothing from you if we succeed—no cattle, no land, no gold. I say again, nothing. You must believe me on this. Like many of you, all I want is to see our lands liberated of these would-be conquerors. We must put an end to this subjugation. I believe we're now in a position to do this. Our children's children will sing our praise around the council fire."

There were shouts among men in the audience now.

"Kill Varus and his soldiers."

"The Trevari are with you."

"Hail Arminius. Death to the Romans."

Arminius grinned a wolfish smile in triumph. He had the allegiance of five of the larger tribes—the Cherusci, which was his own, plus the Angrivarii, Trevari, Bructeri, and Chatti. He knew that he'd garnered more followers tonight from the smaller tribes, but there were still some who were uncommitted. He needed them. He must leave the door open for the others to possibly join later. He held up his hands for silence.

"I thank you for your support. I understand that some of you still have your doubts and are reluctant to pledge your forces. To be clear about this, there are no hard feelings. If you choose not to join me, I don't look upon you as enemies. What I did tonight to Jurus was the right thing to do. You all know that. The man was an arrogant fool. For those of you who are undecided about what course of action to take, know that you're welcome to join at any time. It's not my cause;

it's yours. This is a hard decision for many of you. I respect that. But know this, fellow warriors. I believe with all my heart that we can drive these Romans out of Germania. We'll have their precious eagles they prize so highly. I hope that all of you will find the wisdom to join me. Our time is coming. It will be soon!"

XVII

*I*t was officers' call, mandatory attendance, no exceptions. At the summons of General Varus, all of the general officers, tribunes, and centurion cohort commanders were to meet in the large council tent. The word had been put out the day before that they were to assemble two hours before the evening mess. It was standard military protocol in the Roman army for the commanding general to convene his officers from time to time. It would be ill advised for anyone whose presence was expected to be either late or absent.

The subject of the meeting was no surprise. It was almost time to depart to their winter quarters, located at Vetera on the Rhine. The distance of the march was about a hundred miles. The logistics of such an endeavor were enormous. Everyone and everything would be moving southeast toward the Rhine River. This included fifteen thousand legionnaires plus auxiliaries, cavalry, and support staff; hundreds of mules, oxen, and horses; baggage carts; supply wagons; food; water; and anything else that was part of the three legions. Nothing would be remaining at their summer encampment except the earthen ramparts and wooden watchtowers. If the army could figure a way, they probably would transport them. The legions wouldn't return to the banks of the Weser until late next spring.

Despite the coolness of the early fall, it was beginning to get stuffy inside the tented area. Valerius milled around with the other officers, waiting for the senior staff to arrive. He recognized various faces and nodded politely or exchanged brief greetings. It was strange. He knew his fellow tribunes, but then again, he didn't. The tribunes were names he put to faces. It was clear his brethren ostracized him. They stayed clear of Valerius as if he had the plague. He was never invited to join them for any dining or drinking. When he entered the common area adjacent to his quarters, conversation ceased immediately, followed by an awkward silence. His brief moment of glory after he'd returned from the ambush accompanying Centurion Clodius, who had all but credited him for saving the entire cohort from annihilation, had been short lived.

Varus and his entourage entered the tent. The general's aide called the officers to attention.

"OFFICERS, *INTENTE*."

Varus, his finest gold breastplate polished to a bright hue, strutted in with his aides and the senior officers. He appeared to be of an angry disposition, a hint of annoyance in his features. Valerius was surprised when he noticed that Arminius was now included in the elite group of the senior staff. His official position, now clearly elevated after bringing back the severed head of the rebel, Jurus, was deputy liaison for the German people. The general stood in the front of the room. Behind him was a tripod upon which was propped a large map of Germania.

"Take your seats, gentlemen. We have important matters to discuss." He glanced around the room, taking in his audience. He went right into it.

"As you're aware, gentlemen, we'll soon exit to our permanent quarters for the winter. I can't say I'm disappointed to be leaving our present residence."

This elicited some chuckles from the group. It was no secret that General Varus loathed the primitive living conditions imposed upon him in the summer encampment.

Varus's features darkened.

"Unfortunately, we have some unfinished business. Yesterday it was reported to me that there's a revolt brewing among the Chatti due northwest of our present location. There have been confirmed intelligence reports that several outposts were overrun. Those individuals friendly to Rome were massacred, including one of my tax collectors. Traders and other civilian personnel have fled the area."

He walked over to the large map and smacked the spot with a wooden pointer, upon which a tip of ivory was affixed.

"They're in this general vicinity."

The commander of the Seventeenth Legion, Vitruvius Licinus, the senior and the most capable of all of the military officers present, stood facing Varus. General Licinus was a man of iron who had dedicated his life to the legions and the honor of serving. He looked the part. Licinus had a powerful, muscular frame without an ounce of fat. His head was shaved. He wore a black eye patch to cover the empty socket, injured many years ago in battle. His acts of bravery were legendary. He led from the front, always at the head of his legion regardless of the danger. The men of the Seventeenth Legion adored him, a fact that wasn't lost on Varus, who didn't command the same level of veneration.

"Sir, do we have any idea of the enemy's strength?"

Varus was clearly annoyed at the question. "We'll get to that shortly. Be seated," he commanded laconically.

He continued. "I'll not tolerate any civil disobedience from the German peoples while I'm governor and the appointed consul of this region. Have these fools not learned their lesson? They should know by now there's no gain to be had in attacking the Roman Imperial Army or its citizens. I had a similar situation in Syria. I resorted to crucifying thousands of them."

Varus turned to his left and sought his German ally. "Arminius, tell us what you know."

The German advanced and stood next to Varus. He began to speak in accented guttural Latin.

"I'm not surprised that the Chatti would be at the bottom of this uprising. They're always causing trouble. I, for one, have never liked them much. They talk about doing this or that, but seldom do they back up their words with deeds. To many other German chieftains and me, they're contemptible. You might ask, will other tribes join them? I think not. No one cares for them. I believe their strength to be no more than four thousand warriors. They're poorly organized and led."

If only they knew, thought Arminius. The troop strength of the Chatti was more like eight thousand, and they were a formidable foe. If Arminius's plan unfolded as planned and the other tribes joined, the total number of warriors would exceed thirty thousand, maybe even many more.

Varus began speaking again.

"There you have it from Arminius. He's a friend of Rome who's helped us many times. He brought us the head of the last rebel who challenged our troops in an ambush weeks ago. What was the rogue's name again, Arminius?"

"Jurus, sir. His name was Jurus."

"He is no longer of consequence, is he? His lieutenants were also rounded up and dispatched. We thank you for your assistance, Arminius."

Varus walked back to the large map.

"Now then, gentlemen, here's my plan for dealing with these criminals who dare challenge Roman authority. As you know, our normal route is to proceed south along the Weser River, then swing west along the Lippe River until we reach the Rhine at Vetera, from here to here."

Varus's aide indicated the two locations on the map with his pointer.

"Because of the uprising, we'll change course. My orders are as follows. We'll move our forces north a short distance along the Weser, instead of south as originally planned, and then swing due west to the land of the Chatti. It is about fifty miles from here. You'll note that our new course, after we pivot to the west, is somewhat parallel to our established route of march to Vetera."

The aide traced the revised route with the pointer to indicate the new course.

Varus seized the pointer, then smacked the map for added effect, as if this would somehow cause the enemy pain.

"Gentlemen, here's where we'll go. I intend to make war upon these rebels and teach them a lesson they won't soon forget. After making things right again, the army will then proceed due south toward the Lippe and intersect the established route to Vetera. It'll be a minor inconvenience. We mustn't let these rebels go unpunished. It might give others the idea they can do as they please. This is a challenge to Roman authority. I'll deal with these...what did you say their name was, Arminius?"

"Chatti, sir. They're the Chatti tribe."

"They're going to rue the day they messed with the power of Rome and her legions. I'll surely make an example of them and show no mercy. None."

General Licinus rose. "Sir, I concur that this tribe must be taught a lesson. We can't let them go without punishment. Others will question our resolve if we fail to act. But, sir, is it necessary to bring all the supply trains and other staff on this mission? This is unfamiliar territory, and we have little knowledge of the roads—or even if there are any, for that matter. As I recall, the terrain in this vicinity is most inhospitable. There are many hills and steep ravines."

"General Licinus, are you questioning my orders?"

"No, sir. I was just pointing out the potential logistical problems with the baggage trains."

Varus interrupted, his voice rising with each word. "It sounded that way to me. Just because you have more military experience, you think you know it all. Don't you? You think I'm not capable of commanding this army?"

"Sir, I was respectfully pointing out—"

"Enough of this. Not another word. My decision is final. You're dismissed. Vacate the premises at once."

"As you wish, sir."

There was complete silence as General Licinus rose from his seat and exited the tent. He looked neither right nor left as he strode away from the assembled officers. Most of those present looked uncomfortably down at the floor.

Varus continued.

"Gentlemen, you've heard my plan. Let me make this clear. I'm in command of this army, and this is what we'll do. We'll now make plans to execute it."

Valerius had positioned himself in an unobtrusive place on the periphery of the gathering. He was inconspicuous, yet he could clearly observe the proceedings. He was shocked at the dressing down Varus had given one of the senior commanders. General Licinus was a soldier through and through, a man of honor, yet Varus had publicly chastised him in front of all of the other officers. The points raised by Licinus were valid. Why was the entire army with baggage trains going into unknown territory replete with thick forests and marshes that were absolute quagmires? What kind of shit was Varus getting them into?

Varus motioned for his deputy commander and chief of operations, General Caecina, to speak. Like Varus, he was a political appointee with little military experience. He was also a first-class ass kisser. He would never question the orders of Varus. General Caecina was from a wealthy and politically strong family. He was unremarkable in appearance and, like Varus, he was overweight. He began to speak.

"The situation is what was described to you by General Varus and Arminius. There's a revolt in progress that requires our presence. We'll depart at daybreak seven days hence, in standard column formation. The army will advance due north on the unimproved road near the river. The engineers and their pioneers will head the column. They'll clear any obstacles obstructing our path. The order of march will be the Seventeenth, Eighteenth, staff and baggage trains, and last, the Nineteenth Legion. The German auxiliaries will provide rear and flank security. Our mission is to close with and suppress the indigenous populations in the area of the uprising through whatever force is required."

Varus interrupted.

"I intend to use maximum force and crush this revolt. I don't care if I must crucify every man, woman, and child of this tribe. I'll show no mercy. Continue, General."

Caecina droned on. "We'll attack all known fortresses and villages in the area, inflicting severe punishment. Once we've cleaned up this region, we'll proceed due south toward the Lippe, perhaps forty miles, and resume our journey toward winter quarters. All commanders will have their order of march by cohorts in to me by tomorrow morning, with plans for linking up to all units in front or to the rear of their legions. Food stores will be drawn the day before the march and no sooner."

Varus stood, nodding to his deputy to sit down.

"Thank you, General Caecina. Gentlemen, it appears we all have a lot of work to do. I suggest you all begin the necessary preparations immediately. Any questions?"

There was polite silence in the room. No one dared speak after the treatment of General Licinus.

"You're dismissed."

Valerius ambled back from officers' call along the muddy thoroughfare, eager to inform Marcellus of General Varus's new plan. He wanted to know what the centurion thought, although he was pretty sure what Marcellus would say. He found the centurion hunched over, squinting at a wax tablet, munching on a biscuit.

"Marcellus, wait until you hear about this one."

The centurion looked up from his study with an exasperated sigh, wiping the crumbs from his hands.

"And which one would that be, Tribune?"

There he goes with that Tribune crap again, he thought. He'd told the centurion that he need not address him as sir or Tribune. He'd insisted that Marcellus call him by his name, Valerius. This didn't follow military protocol, as it was not proper etiquette for a subordinate centurion to address a tribune by his official title or sir, but the two of them had a relationship that extended way beyond that. The pair had formed a bond of trust and friendship in the few months that they had known each other, transcending even the rigid military code of the legions. Every time Valerius had requested Marcellus to drop the formality in the address, all he received was a blank stare or a retort, "If you insist, Tribune." It was infuriating, but he guessed there was no way he was going to break Marcellus of this habit.

"Marcellus, in case you haven't heard yet, we're not—and I emphasize the word *not*—returning to winter quarters at Vetera by the normal secure route. It seems there's a bit of trouble brewing in the land of the Chatti. They've killed several civilians, including some of Varus's precious tax collectors. Marauding parties of warriors have been spotted by our scouts. Varus wants the return march rerouted to the territory of the Chatti, where he intends to teach them a lesson. If I recall his words correctly, he wants to 'crucify every man, woman, and child in the area of rebellion.'"

With a frown, Marcellus stooped down on the floor and opened a rather large rectangular wooden container. He began rooting around in the papers, occasionally glancing at a document before putting it carefully aside. A pile began to form outside the box that was larger than the contents that remained inside.

"I know that bloody thing is around here somewhere."

"What bloody thing is that, Centurion?"

"The map, of course. The bloody map."

Now scrolls and parchments were being tossed out of the box as Marcellus became even more agitated.

"Ah, here's the bloody thing." Marcellus held the rolled-up document in triumph. "Now show me what Varus is planning."

Marcellus spread the map on the table and moved the oil lamp closer. Valerius grabbed the outer edge and helped spread the map on the table.

Valerius stabbed his finger on the parchment.

"We're here, of course." Valerius pointed at a spot on the map where the river bent. "Now, this is the normal route we would take." Valerius traced with his finger the southwesterly course that snaked along the Weser, then the Lippe River.

"Varus is going to take this direction."

He traced his finger along a course almost due north of their present position.

"He'll then swing the army in a northwesterly direction here. It leads to this place marked as the Teutoburg Forest. After he takes care of business and slaughters some Germans, he'll then proceed due south and intersect the road along the Lippe."

"What about the baggage and supply trains?"

"Everything. The whole army will advance to the Chatti territory, no exceptions."

Marcellus appeared visibly shaken. He spoke tersely. "That is the Teutoburg Forest. He is taking the entire army into the Teutoburg, is he? By Jupiter's gray beard, the man must have taken leave of his senses. Tribune, didn't anyone point out to our esteemed commander that we'll be venturing through primeval forest and bog?"

"Yes, General Licinus attempted to warn Varus about the potential logistical problems in relation to the terrain. He was chastised in front of the entire officer corps and dismissed from the gathering for being insubordinate. I can't believe he did that." Valerius was about to continue when Marcellus interrupted.

"Tribune, listen to me. I've been in the Teutoburg. It's pure wilderness. We don't even send patrols in that direction because of the terrain. There are huge stands of timber, ravines, and marshes. A detachment went out a couple of years ago with the engineers to survey the land. I'll tell you that in all my years of service, that was one time I was scared shitless. A small group of us was alone in unfriendly territory. That land is so rugged that nobody has settled there in any great numbers. We got ourselves turned around, wandering for days and not seeing a soul except deer and wild boar."

Valerius interrupted. "Hold on there, Marcellus. Turned around? You mean you were lost?" Valerius offered a mocking grin.

"Tribune, there's something you need to understand. We centurions never get lost. Perhaps a bit misoriented, if you know what I mean, but never lost."

"I see," said Valerius with a knowing grin.

"Now, as I was saying, Tribune, we went through forests so forbidding there was almost no light. The trees were friggin' huge. Sometimes the bogs would extend for miles."

"Are there any roads?"

Marcellus snorted in reply. "Roads? At best, you could call them trails, but certainly not like the surfaced roads we've built along the Weser and Lippe. I can't even imagine the baggage trains getting through that territory. Tribune, tell me how in the name of the gods are we going to find these rebellious souls?"

"Apparently, Arminius knows their whereabouts. He will lead the army to them."

"The whole Imperial Army of Northern Germania is going to be following a Cherusci chieftain into the unknown?" The centurion grunted in derision.

"Marcellus, sarcasm will get you nowhere. Besides, Arminius is now a deputy to Varus. He's the liaison officer for the German tribes. His standing was certainly elevated when he brought the head of that German responsible for the ambush to Varus. I've heard he even joins him in his legendary feasting and gluttony. By the way, I'm still waiting for my invitation."

"What were you saying about sarcasm, Tribune?"

Valerius offered a weak smile in reply.

Marcellus thought for a moment before speaking.

"Let me ask you a question, Tribune. Did you ever hear of the ambush at Arbalo?"

Valerius replied, "Certainly. The exploits of General Drusus Caesar, stepson of Augustus, are celebrated and chronicled. His campaign against the Germans reflects brilliant military strategy, especially his success at Arbalo. It was required reading for all tribunes."

Marcellus stared back at Valerius. "And what did they teach you about Arbalo?"

"As I recall, the expeditionary legions under Drusus were ambushed by a collection of German tribes while on a march through a narrow pass. Drusus, despite the tactical adversity, calmly directed the legions to valiantly fight their way out of the ambush and save the day."

Marcellus grunted. "Is that what they taught you? Let me tell you what really happened."

Valerius replied in amazement. "You were there?"

Marcellus spoke quietly. "I was. That was my first year with the legions in Germania, about twenty years ago. We were swarmed upon from all sides by the Germans in a forested pass. The front and rear of the marching column were hopelessly blocked. The baggage trains were destroyed. The legions couldn't maneuver. Despite our efforts, we were beginning to sag from the relentless pressure on our flanks. Then, for some unknown reason, the Germans withdrew. Some say the Germans didn't believe that destroying an enemy in this fashion was manly. Who knows? But I believe they would have defeated us if they had continued to press. Drusus was one lucky Roman that particular day."

Valerius replied, "I never knew that version of the battle."

"And another thing, Tribune. You know the name of one of the tribes that almost cooked our ass that day?"

"No, just that they were Germans."

Marcellus replied, "It was the Cherusci."

"So?"

"So think about this, Tribune. Arminius is a Cheruscan, and his father was rumored to be one of the German ringleaders. Furthermore, Arminius, when a young boy, was shipped off to Rome as a hostage to make sure his father behaved."

"What should we do, Marcellus?"

"We'll follow orders. We're soldiers and must obey. Besides, there's nothing that will change the mind of Varus. But I'll tell you that if we get caught in that terrain with our tunics down by a large force of Germans, we'll be in deep trouble. The legions weren't designed to fight in heavy forest or sinking bog. May the gods have mercy on us if the Germans attack us in there."

Marcellus turned away from the map and went toward the back of the chamber. He reached down and picked up a leather case.

"Tribune, I've been meaning to give this to you. Here, please take it."

Valerius looked at the satchel containing the ebony Egyptian war bow with which he'd become so familiar over the past several months. He was stunned.

"Marcellus, how can I accept this? It's priceless."

"I want you to have it. I don't need two of them. I can't possibly shoot two of them at the same time, now can I?"

"I have nothing to give you in return."

"None is expected. Tribune, take the bow. You're wearing my patience thin."

"Many thanks, Marcellus. It's a beautiful gift. I'm honored."

"One more thing, Tribune."

"Yes?"

"If I were you, I'd have that bow accessible on this goat-fuck expedition Varus has planned. Bring it!"

General Varus sat hunched over the small camp table, rubbing his forehead in frustration as he pondered the pile of dispatches before him. A junior tribune who functioned as one of his aides stood silently by, hanging on his every word. Several clerks and servants moved quietly about so not to disturb the general's concentration. Varus finally vented his displeasure.

"Damn these papers anyway." For effect, he hurled one of the rolled pieces of parchment into a corner. Staring at the tribune, he gestured with his arm. "Enough of this. Give these to the deputy commander and have him finish this for me."

Varus was about to continue with his tirade when one of his aides appeared, clearing his throat. Varus glared at the man, giving him a withering stare. "Yes, what is it?"

"Sir, sorry to interrupt you, but there's a German national named Segestes requesting an audience with you."

"Can't you see I'm busy here?"

"Sir, I told him your schedule was full, but he insisted on seeing you. He said it was extremely urgent."

Varus heaved an exasperated sigh. "I will see him, but this better be important."

The German leader was ushered into Varus's chambers. Segestes was in his mid to late forties. He walked proudly. He had adopted the Roman form of dress, wearing a tunic that was cream colored, appearing to be of a fine weave. He had a short cloak of scarlet around his shoulders and leather sandals on his feet. He wore his hair short and had a small, pointed beard on his chin. Segestes had been a loyal ally of Rome for many years. He was no stranger to Varus. They had met and discussed German affairs on other occasions. The man had even been a guest several times at Varus's legendary banquets.

Segestes stood before Varus, then bowed. "A pleasure to see you once again, General. I hope you're in good health?"

"Segestes, it's always a pleasure to see one who's loyal to Rome. What brings you here unannounced today?" Varus emphasized the word *unannounced*, hoping Segestes would get the hint that an appointment might be in order for any future meetings.

Segestes looked at the tribune and various servants who were present.

Varus nodded to his servants. "Bring us some wine, then leave us." He signaled with a wave of his hand for the tribune to leave his presence. "You'll join me in a cup, won't you, Segestes?"

"By all means, General. How could I refuse your hospitality?"

The two men sat at the camp table with their cups of wine, drinking deeply in polite silence. The room was now empty. Varus gazed at Segestes. "So tell me, my friend, why the need for this clandestine stuff?"

"General, is it true you'll depart for Vetera within the week?"

"Yes, it's that time of year when the legions break for winter quarters."

"I've also heard you'll divert from your normal route to fight an alleged rebellion."

Varus was taken aback at those remarks.

"Word spreads quickly, doesn't it, Segestes? I informed my officers but the night before last, yet all of Germania knows my plans already. But to answer your question, yes, the Chatti have revolted. I intend to teach them a lesson they won't soon forget. Now, Segestes, don't take offense, but some of you Germans never learn. It doesn't profit you to fight Rome. You lose every time. But I'm curious as to your choice of words. You said *alleged* rebellion."

Segestes gulped some of his wine. He wiped his mouth with his sleeve and paused before speaking in a low tone, even though just the two of them were present. "Sir, I have information that this is but a trick to lure you into the forest, where you'll be ambushed by a sizable collection of German tribes."

"Ambush my army?" he replied incredulously. "Who's behind such a plot?"

"None other than Arminius," said Segestes.

Varus laughed loudly. "Arminius. You must be joking. That's preposterous." Varus looked at Segestes with a bemused smile.

Segestes mustered his courage to continue the discussion. "He plots treachery. He plans to organize an ambush in the land of the Chatti."

Varus wagged his finger at Segestes as he replied. "You would have me believe that this man who has distinguished himself in battle for Rome and was knighted by Tiberius, the emperor's adopted son, is a traitor? He's like my right hand. Arminius has been an invaluable aid to me in dealing with some of your fellow chieftains who, I might remind you, have been real pains in the ass. They I would suspect of treachery, not Arminius."

"General Varus, I'm telling you what I've heard from reliable sources."

"Look here, Segestes. Arminius was the one who brought me the head of this Jurus fellow, the one who ambushed one of my cohorts several weeks ago. No, Segestes, I can't buy into this plot business."

"General, you know me as a friend of Rome. I have no reason to lie."

There was a brief silence. Varus pondered the remarks of Segestes. The general looked into Segestes's eyes, then smiled triumphantly.

"But is it not true that Arminius is your unwelcome son-in-law? Did he not elope with your daughter when you denied him permission to marry? I remember her. Lovely-looking woman." He paused a moment in thought. "Thusnelda! Am I correct?"

"Yes, that's her name, and it's true about my displeasure with their union," he said bitterly. "I don't like the arrogant rogue. My feelings are known, but that has nothing to do with this."

Varus interrupted. "You know how we feel about certain people sometimes colors our thinking about their behavior. Are you sure your personal feelings aren't getting in the way here? I know Arminius, and I've feasted with him and his father. I'm proud to have them as an ally of Rome."

"General, I beg you reconsider my remarks. My sources for this treason are highly credible."

Varus appeared to pause in thought.

"I'll tell you what. Let me think about it, make some inquiries, and I'll get back to you. You know I value your friendship. I'll talk to some of my staff and see what they think. What do you say?"

Varus rose, indicating the meeting was over. Segestes stood, knowing he'd lost. The general had no intention of pursuing the matter any further. To Hades with him. It was his ass that would be skewered. He had never liked him much anyway.

"Yes, of course, General. I am always at your service," he replied deferentially. Segestes turned and hurriedly departed.

Valerius leaned back from the makeshift table in contentment and let the warm sun caress his face. The day was indeed a gift from the gods not to be wasted, but savored. From his location on a small knoll on the outskirts of the camp, he shifted his gaze to the fortress below. He returned his attention to those others gathered around him. Today was something special. Valerius had been invited to a small repast hosted by Julia. Others in attendance included Julia's father,

Petrocolus; Lucius and his two friends, Cassius and Domitius; and, rounding out the group, Marcus Vitellius, the physician.

The table was festooned with the remnants of the small feast, including fresh-baked bread, an assortment of cheeses, roast wild boar, and large clay containers of wine, now almost empty. The conversation, which at first was muted, had become more animated with the consumption of copious quantities of wine.

Valerius smiled in satisfaction. Outside of Marcellus, he hadn't the pleasure of polite conversation with others since his arrival. The lives of those seated with him were so much different from his own, yet he enjoyed hearing about their daily struggles. Perhaps others of his social standing would be aloof and sneer at the common people around him, but that was not his way. Besides, one of those common people had saved his life in the skirmish several weeks ago.

He sipped his wine again, gazing at the wooded hills beyond the camp. What kind of wilderness would the army march into next week? His recalled the near panic on Marcellus's face when he had described the Teutoburg. Valerius had a healthy respect for the centurion's military intuition and savvy. He'd almost predicted the ambush when he went out on patrol with the legions. Valerius, absorbed in his thoughts, realized his name was being called.

Julia smiled at him. "So, Tribune, do you have a special someone waiting for you upon your return to Rome?"

All were staring at him, waiting for his response.

"As a matter of fact, I do. Coincidentally, I was thinking of her right this moment," he lied artfully. "Her name is Calpurnia. She's an exquisite beauty. I'm saddened to be away from her."

"Are you betrothed to her?" asked Petrocolus.

Valerius grimaced. "Actually, no. You see, my parents don't approve of her because her family is not..." He paused, somewhat perplexed as to how he could explain this to his audience, who probably had little idea about the politics and social structure in the heart of the empire.

Everyone looked at him expectantly.

"You see, in Rome, marrying is all about your family's status and wealth. My parents have great ambitions for me, which means I must marry into a family with good political connections. I hope to convince my parents that my life will be complete and fruitful with Calpurnia. I'm making headway with my mother, but my father is a challenge."

Julia jumped into the conversation. "How sad for you, Tribune. If they really care about your future, surely your parents will let you marry the one you love. I know you'll eventually convince both your parents."

Valerius smiled at her. "Thank you. I sure hope so. Julia, you'd really like Calpurnia. She's such an easy person to talk to. I'm sure she could advise you all about the latest fashions in Rome."

"Oh, I'd love to speak to her sometime."

Their conversation was interrupted as a bevy of cavalry thundered past them toward the outskirts of the camp.

Cassius, never one to be outside of a conversation for so long, spoke, slurring his words. "So, Tribune, we've all heard rumors of a detoured march to teach some rebellious Germans a lesson. Can you confirm that for us?"

Valerius paused to gather his words carefully. No need to sow anxiety among the soldiers and Julia.

"Yes, Cassius, you're quite correct. It's nice to know that the grapevine in the legions is alive and intact."

Everyone chuckled.

"Are you permitted to share with us where we'll be going?"

"Sure. I don't suppose it's any secret, and if it was, it certainly is not anymore. You probably know more than I do."

Everyone laughed again.

"Based upon the briefing by General Varus that I attended a few days ago, the legions will be moving north, then west to take care of a minor rebellion from a local tribe. I don't believe there'll be any great danger, but it'll definitely be a longer march. I think all the more reason to celebrate when we reach Vetera," he said in a light one.

Valerius rose from the table, nodding at the group.

"My apologies. I'm sorry, but I'll need to be going now. I have duties that must be attended to back at the camp related to the coming march out. Thank you, Julia, for the wonderful feast. It was magnificent. I meant what I said about meeting Calpurnia someday. You never know where goddess Fortuna will take us."

Julia replied, "I'll not hold you to any promise, Tribune, but I definitely would like to meet her."

Lucius stared after the departing figure of Valerius. Something had not been quite right with his response about the upcoming march. His tone was too flippant, his facial expression forced. What was the tribune hiding? Lucius looked over at Julia to see if she had picked up on anything. She usually had good intuition on these things. Not today, he thought. She'd been totally disarmed with the talk of Rome and Calpurnia. He glanced at Cassius and Domitius. He frowned in dismay. Forget them; they had had too much wine. He stared again at the now-distant figure. He was tempted to go after him and ask a few pointed questions, but that would be rude and impertinent. What was the tribune not saying?

Today was the day. The legions were striking camp and moving against the Chatti. Valerius sat on his horse, perched on a small hill outside the encampment. The animal was a large roan that stood apart from the other horses because of its deep-red hue. Valerius had been assigned his mount some ten days ago. He wasn't exactly thrilled with the choice. If there ever was an attack, he was going to stand out from every other soldier on the battlefield. Why would he want to be on this horse?

Nevertheless, man and beast had quickly bonded over the intervening days, so there was no thought to changing his assigned horse. If he was to be conspicuous, so be it. Valerius had no idea what he was supposed to bring with him, so his saddlebags were crammed with all kinds of gear. He had extra rations and more than a few personal items, including a washbowl, extra tunics, and scrolls for reading. He even had materials for writing and record keeping.

Most important, his satchel containing the war bow given to him by Marcellus was attached to the rear left side of the horse along with a large cache of arrows. He guessed that he probably had too much stowed on his horse and that he looked more like an itinerant merchant than a Roman officer of the legions. But his horse was big and sturdy, so the extra weight shouldn't be too much of a burden. If it came down to it and his mount struggled under the burden, he could discard some of the nonessentials.

He shaded his eyes from the morning glare. The lead elements of the legions began marching out of the fort. In the distance, the Weser River sparkled in the early-morning sunlight. He unsuccessfully attempted to shake off the effects of his wine consumption from last night. He could feel bile rising in his throat. He spit the disgusting contents on the ground, silently cursing Marcellus for making him overindulge in the drinking. It had been quite a night of coarse jokes, plus some of Marcellus's famed poetry. He was paying the price for last night's revelry.

The first infantry units of the legions exited the encampment. It was an impressive display, worthy of a triumph down the Appian Way in Rome. Even from a distance, perched upon the hilltop, Valerius could make out the *aqilifer*, or eagle bearer, holding the silver bird high so the morning sun glinted off the symbol of the legion. Several officers on horseback trotted behind the eagle standard, then the horn players. The trumpeters brought the curved instruments to their lips and let out three long blasts. The sounds echoed down the valley.

The first ranks of soldiers filed by his perch in silence. Every man wore his helmet and chain mail. The shield was fastened high on the left shoulder. Each legionnaire carried his gear on a pole over his left shoulder while his right hand carried the pilum. The sun reflected off the helmets and armor of the troops. The red shields, replete with gold thunderbolts, provided a colorful display. The soldiers marched in step. The iron-studded bottoms of the caliga made a distinctive thump. It was a natural rhythm that was music to any soldier's ear.

Valerius compared the legionnaires streaming by below him to the German warriors who had attacked them weeks ago. It was no contest. The armor and the weapons of the Romans were far superior to the crude fighting tools of their foe. It was little wonder the legions had kicked their asses in almost every engagement over the past fifty years. Marcellus had warned him of possible danger ahead, but Valerius took comfort in the awesome exhibition of military might that marched by him. Century followed century as the massive force exited the summer encampment.

At the house of Maximus over nine hundred miles away in Rome, Valerius's parents were hosting a small dinner party. A total of three couples were in the formal dining room, the *triclinium*. It was a magnificent late-autumn afternoon, replete with brilliant sunlight. There remained a pleasant summerlike warmth in the air as the six people gathered in the elegant setting, chatting idly about their day in Rome. The group consisted of the parents of Valerius, Sentius Maximus and his wife, Vispania; Sentius's brother, Jallius, and his wife, Cornelia; and the guests of honor, the venerable Senator Graccus and his wife, Claudia.

The men and women were reclining on the three couches surrounding the polished and gleaming wooden serving tables. One side of the dining table remained open for the servers to present the food. The men were resplendent in their finest white togas, and the wives were tastefully dressed in the most fashionable stolas and adorned with glimmering gold jewelry inset with precious stones.

Sentius had selected a choice Falernian as the wine to be served, not so much to impress anyone but because he enjoyed the delicate, fruity flavor of the grape. The wine was hideously expensive. These special grapes grew only on the slopes of Mount Vesuvius, limiting the vintage to a small quantity, thus escalating the price so just the wealthy could enjoy it. He reminded himself not to drink too much of the stuff, which he was inclined to do from time to time. He knew his wife would be watching him like a hawk. She'd chastised him to no end about an episode three weeks ago at a dinner party when he'd admittedly had too much wine. Sentius had to be helped into the carriage by his host's servants to get home, much to the mortification of his wife. That was all he'd heard from his wife over the next week. So he had had too much to drink. Everyone in Rome got drunk once in a while. It wasn't as if it were a crime, except maybe in his wife's eyes.

Above the murmured conversations of the diners, Sentius caught the eye of his head steward and nodded in silent affirmation to begin the first course. With a clap of the hands from the steward, a parade of servers streamed from the kitchen carrying all sorts of delicacies, including grilled mushrooms, mussels, crabs, egg dishes, and small meat and fish pastries. The steaming silver platters were placed gently on the table in reach of all. The reclining men and women served themselves from the table. The diners sighed with contentment as they popped the tasty morsels into their mouths.

Senator Graccus, between mouthfuls, spoke. "Forgive me for not inquiring sooner, but have you heard from your son? He's with Governor Varus in Germania, is he not?"

Claudia, the senator's wife, spoke. "How thoughtless of us not to ask. I hope he is in fine spirits."

Sentius responded, "Thank you for inquiring. As a matter of fact, we've recently received a letter by military dispatch from Valerius. He made it to Germania safely. He was most impressed with the captain of his transport ship, who taught him how to navigate by the stars. His military encampment is on the Weser River. He apparently has made friends with a veteran centurion named Marcellus, who's taught him how to shoot a giant war bow. He raves about the man."

Graccus stroked his chin in thought. "If I recall my geography correctly, isn't the Weser the northernmost boundary of the empire?"

"I believe it is," said Sentius. "It's a long way from Rome."

"So everything is going as expected for the young tribune," said Claudia, the senator's wife.

Sentius paused in thought for a moment.

"I guess so. His letter is somewhat...oh, what's the word I'm looking for?" He hesitated in thought for a moment. "Aloof. Yes, that's how I would describe it. Outside of this Marcellus fellow, he doesn't say too much about his experiences as a tribune in the army. He hardly notes anything about the legions, his fellow tribunes, or his duties. It's so unlike him. Valerius is usually not reserved in his expression. I don't know. Maybe I'm expecting too much of him to tell us about the ways of his daily life in a letter. I saw Cato, his former tutor, the other day. I asked if he'd received a letter. He said that yes, he had. I inquired if Valerius had told him how he was doing. Cato was kind of vague other than that he said that he believed Valerius was fine. Something bothered me about his reply. His response seemed guarded."

Graccus spoke. "I am sure life is probably a bit overwhelming for Valerius. After all, he's been thrust from a life of culture and sophistication in Rome into the role of a soldier in the land of barbarians."

Jallius, Valerius's uncle, entered the discussion. "Maybe Calpurnia has heard from him. Have you asked her?"

There was a stunned silence at the table. Valerius's parents glared at Jallius. His wife, Cornelia, gave him a scathing look. Senator Graccus and his wife looked quizzically at everyone, not quite sure what was going on and unaware that Jallius had committed a horrible social blunder in mentioning Calpurnia's name. Knowing he had erred, Jallius, somewhat flustered, attempted to salvage the situation. He quickly resumed the conversation.

"It's a hard transition for a young man from civilian to military. I know when I did my service in the legions, it was difficult at first."

Jallius's wife, Cornelia, interrupted sharply. "Jallius, you were stationed with the *virgiles* in Rome. How could you possibly compare yourself?"

The men and women laughed at the humor of it.

"I know, I know," he said defensively. He held up his hands in a placating gesture. "But the comparison I was making was on the transition to the military. I found it to be difficult. It must be terribly hard on Valerius, entering the legions and being in a strange land so far away."

The senator, aware of the awkwardness of the situation, although not exactly sure of the cause, smoothly decided to offer a toast as a means of restoring the previous level of conversation. "Here's to young Tribune Valerius on the northern frontier. May the gods protect him."

Everyone raised their goblets in a toast.

The servants cleared the trays and platters for the next course. Hand towels were passed to all to wipe their hands. A large fish platter and a roast of pork were brought out by the servants for the main course.

Vispania inquired of Graccus, "Tell us what's new in the Senate. What's the latest order of business?"

The senator paused from his eating and delicately wiped his mouth.

"Oh, you know, the usual—new building projects, appointments to various posts throughout the empire, and where they should raise levies to finance all of this. Of course, the Senate and the whole of Rome are buzzing about all of these omens that have been appearing lately."

"What sort of omens?" said Vispania.

"You don't know? The entire city has been talking about them. First, the last several nights have been blazing with comets and meteors shooting across the night sky. They're all heading north. Yesterday, on the Campus Martius, the Temple of Mars was struck by a thunderbolt. In the mountains to the east and north, there have been rumblings. Reports state that entire peaks of some of these hills have fallen."

"So what?" said Sentius. "There have always been earthquakes, shooting stars, and lightning storms."

"Many say they're portents of doom. Rome is about to experience a disaster of great magnitude," replied the senator.

"Graccus," said Sentius, "surely you don't believe this rubbish? I mean, if the gods really wanted to talk to us, they would just do it and not through these so-called omens."

Graccus replied, "I'm not by nature a superstitious person. I don't necessarily believe that these signs are omens of doom, but on the other hand, I don't dismiss them. There have been too many coincidences in the past to ignore such warnings."

There was an awkward silence. Sentius needed to do something quickly to change the mood at the table and salvage the dinner. He had had no idea that Graccus believed in these portents. Sentius's belittling of these omens was probably insulting to the senator, who, after all, was the guest of honor and a powerful person. Sentius spoke. "Let's give a toast to life and to Rome. Enough of this gloom-and-doom talk." He laughed lightly, raising his goblet high into the air.

"To the future."

Everyone echoed, "To the future."

Graccus in turn raised his goblet. "To Rome. Long may she prosper."

Everyone smiled politely and echoed his toast. Vispania jumped right in and immediately engaged the two women on the latest colors and styles of women's stolas. The dinner lasted into the night. The conversations of doom and disaster were forgotten for now.

The army had stopped for the day. Their progress had been excellent and without difficulty. They had journeyed perhaps fifteen miles, maybe a little more. Spirits were high, almost festive. The legions, per standard operating procedure, had fashioned their fortified marching camp in a field along the banks of the river. The ramparts and palisades had been constructed. It was a legionnaire's dream. The land was mostly clear of obstacles and the earth easy to excavate.

To a man, the soldiers weren't thrilled about the detour from their normal route. It would be a longer journey and more tiresome, but that was all quickly forgotten. Besides, the soldiers had received their stipendium, and the rumor was that they'd be entitled to booty when they engaged the Chatti. Most didn't believe they were in any imminent danger. Instead, they were thinking of their winter quarters with floors and roofs; a real Roman bath, not one carved out of a section of the riverbed; and how they would spend their money. Besides, there was little the men could do to change their plight, so they accepted it and looked forward to their more permanent quarters.

Within the fortified encampment, great fires were lit, and torches burned everywhere. All of the tents were pitched in the prescribed order. Everything was in place by century, cohort, and legion. The watches were set for the night and the password issued. The men had been given an extra ration of sour wine to fortify themselves for the next day.

In the center of the encampment, Arminius approached the general, who was seated in a chair enjoying a rather large goblet of wine. He reclined in his chair. He was pleased with the progress of the army on the first day, his spirits ebullient. Several of the most senior staff surrounded the general.

He looked up, wiping his hand across his mouth. "Arminius, what brings you here at this late hour? Care to join us?"

"No, thank you, General. Sorry to bother you after the long day, but I'd like to request permission for some of my auxiliary forces and me to depart early in the morning. I want to advance ahead of the main column and reconnoiter the territory ahead. I will engage any enemy forces of lesser strength than my own. I'll leave some of my best men behind to guide you toward the Chatti lands. My plan is to soften them up for you."

Varus replied, "Certainly. By all means you may proceed, but I want you to be tough on them. No mercy. Understand, Arminius?"

"Of course, sir, no mercy. My plan is to place my cavalry ahead and raid any villages I see. If I come across a large force, I'll withdraw back to the safety of the main body of the army."

"Excellent, Arminius. Good hunting. Don't take any unnecessary chances. You are too valuable to me. Leave some of the fighting to us. After all, my soldiers are anxious for plunder."

"Then I'll see you ahead tomorrow, General Varus. I look forward to some good fighting." Arminius turned to go.

Varus stopped him with an outstretched hand. "Remember, no mercy, Arminius."

The German paused briefly and smiled wolfishly. "No mercy," he repeated.

Marcellus and Valerius found themselves walking aimlessly through the camp for lack of anything better to do.

"Marcellus, you have to admit that today was fairly easy as far as marches go." Valerius paused for a moment before continuing. "I was expecting much worse, especially with that hangover you compelled upon me last night."

"Tribune, I didn't exactly force that wine down your throat now, did I? And as I recall, you were the one who insisted on one more round before retiring."

"Maybe so," said Valerius, "but I wouldn't even have started drinking except for you."

Marcellus offered a mocking smile. "You high-ranking officers always blame us lowly centurions." In a more serious tone, he continued, "Back to your original statement, Tribune; yes, it was easy traveling today, but I expected no less. Remember, we were on a Roman-constructed road, although a crude one. That'll change in a hurry once the army pivots away from the river and heads west into the interior. I told you before, I don't like it at all that Varus is leading us into this wilderness."

The two men continued to walk on in silence. Valerius attempted to ward off the trepidation. He would have liked to believe Marcellus was exaggerating the potential problems they would encounter in the terrain ahead, but the centurion wasn't one to overstate the seriousness of anything, based upon the limited time he had known him.

"A *denarius* for your thoughts, Tribune."

Valerius frowned in thought. "I'm concerned about this expedition we're on. That ambush I went into was bad enough out on the patrol. I can't imagine our entire army attacked by a large force of Germans."

"Tribune, odds are nothing will occur out here. It's just that the legions will be so vulnerable in that sort of terrain. Know what I mean?"

"Yes, I guess so. The legions are a superior fighting force, and we will just need to maintain our vigilance."

"Spot on, Tribune. We'll need to keep our eyes and ears open."

Lucius, Cassius, and Domitius, free of their duties, went in search of Julia. They trekked among the baggage wagons and found her sitting alone by a fire.

"Would a pretty lady mind some company?"

"There you are. I've been waiting all evening for the three of you," she said in mock petulance.

"We've come to lift your spirits, lady," said Cassius.

"How was your day, Julia?" said Lucius.

"Tiring. I rode most of the time in the wagon. It was boring. Occasionally, I could see your cohort ahead when the road was straight. Of course, the dust was everywhere. We were in a cloud of the stuff all day."

Lucius spoke. "I reminded Cassius and Domitius about your promise to host a feast when we arrive on the Rhine. You mentioned that all kinds of delicacies are available from the markets. They even bring wine from the vineyards north of Rome."

With his mouth half full, Cassius looked up from the piece of bread he was munching on. "Count me in. I'm not fussy. After these army rations, I'll be in the mood for anything. What kind of food do you have in mind, Julia?"

"It'll be a surprise, Cassius."

Julia's father ventured into the firelight. His hair was disheveled, and his cloak was spattered and smeared with mud. "Lucius, Cassius, Domitius, how are you holding up?"

"Fine, sir," Lucius replied. "If you don't mind my saying, you look a little ragged."

"I know, and I look like I feel. This is just the start. These marches are days of pure Hades for me. It never stops. There are always animals that break down. You have to make sure you have fresh replacements—plus unhitching the beasts without holding up the entire army. I've been up and down this column all day. Enough of my troubles. Let us all relax."

At that moment, Valerius and Marcellus entered the area of the campfire.

Lucius looked up at the two men. "Tribune Valerius, how are you?"

"Hello, everyone. How are you all this fine evening? I hope you made it through the day without too much inconvenience. May I present Centurion Marcellus, my colleague and right-hand man, and perhaps the finest centurion in the Army of the Northern Rhine."

Greetings and pleasantries were exchanged all around. Valerius continued. "Marcellus, Lucius is the legionnaire I spoke of who saved my life back at the ambush."

The centurion nodded. "So you're the brave young man the tribune told me about. Thank goodness, or I'd have to do the pay records by myself once again."

"Why don't you two sit and join us? It's a beautiful evening, and we could use the company," said Julia.

"We'd love to, Julia, but the two of us have one more meeting of the headquarters staff tonight. I'm not sure about what, but our presence is requested. Perhaps when we reach Vetera?"

Julia spoke. "Then I can count on the two of you joining us for dinner once we arrive there."

"How could we refuse such an offer? Many thanks. Maybe we'll see you on the march tomorrow." The two men departed the glow of the campfire and walked off into the night.

Valerius and Marcellus glided into the darkness.

Valerius spoke. "I've promised myself to kind of keep an eye out for that young legionnaire who saved my butt in the ambush. I believe I'm indebted to that soldier. Maybe I can repay the favor one day."

Marcellus laughed. "An admirable sentiment, Tribune. It's not a bad thing to watch over the needs of the common soldier. Think of it. He saved you that day. You, in turn, saved Centurion Clodius and the entire cohort."

Valerius grinned back. "But I'm serious. I'd like to help that young man someday if I have the opportunity."

"Who knows, Tribune? You may indeed get a chance."

The two men ambled on into the darkness, talking about the upcoming march in the morning.

Lucius, Cassius, Domitius, Julia, and her father continued their discussion around fire, enjoying the fall evening. They were all munching on bread and goat cheese that Julia had saved for the occasion. It was a welcome supplement to their standard fare of hard biscuits and porridge. The small fire flickered, illuminating their faces in the twilight and providing a bit of warmth against the evening chill.

Lucius addressed Julia's father. "Sir, do you and Julia ever get a break from the legions? I mean, do you stay with them all the time?"

"We've taken some journeys now and then. Several years ago, Julia and I went to Rome to visit friends."

Lucius looked at Julia. "You never told me that."

Julia just shrugged. "I didn't think it was that important. Beside, you never asked."

Lucius was incredulous. "You didn't think it was important? Maybe to you it wasn't, but to me, one who's never been there, it's extremely important."

Lucius turned toward Petrocolus. "Tell us what it was like."

Cassius and Domitius leaned forward, eager to hear what her father had to say. Like Lucius, they'd never been to the big city. "Yes, tell us," they echoed.

Petrocolus thought for a moment.

"The city has many magnificent buildings and temples made of polished stones. They're huge. To put it in perspective, bigger than hundreds of your tents combined. There are many people, perhaps five hundred times the number of soldiers in this army, maybe more."

They all gawked in amazement. The men hung on every word. "Sir, you're mocking us, of course," said Cassius. "These things could not be true."

Julia laughed. "But they are, Cassius. Everything my father has said is factual."

"I must see this someday," replied Cassius enviously. "Lucius, we need to be in the Praetorian. I told you that."

"What else is there?" inquired Domitius.

"Let me think. The Circus Maximus, where they have the games and the chariot races, seats about three hundred thousand."

"I definitely must go there," said Cassius.

Petrocolus, delighted to have such a captive audience, proceeded to tell them about the public baths, the large supplies of running water from the aqueducts, the fountains, the temples, the Forum, the imperial palace, and many other sites. Each description fostered incredulous looks from the soldiers. He spoke of the Senate house, the Vestal Virgins, and the incredible wealth, with some of the richest men owning hundreds of slaves.

"We had better get back to our tent. It's going to be another long day tomorrow," said Lucius. The three soldiers stood and prepared to leave.

"Many thanks for your hospitality and accounts of Rome, sir," said Cassius.

Julia laughed. "My father loves an audience. He'd stay up all night with you and tell stories."

Her father grinned back, knowing the statement was probably true. Lucius and Julia looked at each other longingly, knowing that they'd not have any time alone. With a casual wave, Lucius and his two friends departed from the fire.

Lucius, Cassius, and Domitius wandered through the darkness toward their tent area. It was but a short distance, perhaps a hundred yards. By chance, Lucius happened to catch a furtive movement in the darkness in front of them on the right. He immediately put his arm out to stop their forward progress. Cassius and Domitius looked expectantly at Lucius. He signaled them to be silent and pointed ahead. Both men stared into the blackness to see what was there, then looked back at Lucius quizzically. Lucius pointed to his sword, and the three men drew their weapons in one motion. They edged steadily forward, swords extended in front.

After about twenty paces, Decius and his followers emerged into their path. They stopped in their tracks when they viewed the sheen of the blades in the moonlight.

Lucius coolly eyed the group of thugs, now clearly unsettled by the drawn weapons.

"Looking for someone? Or maybe you found who you're searching for?" Lucius waved the sword for effect. "What are you waiting for?"

The followers looked to Decius for a response. Two of the men with him had been there when he'd attacked Julia. Decius looked uncertain as to what to say. Finally he spoke. "This is not over. When you least expect it, we'll strike. You'll beg for us to stop. We'll make a mess out of you."

In response, the three men advanced silently, with swords at belly level. "Why not now, Decius? There are five of you and three of us. Certainly the odds favor you."

"We don't have our swords with us," replied Decius.

"A pity, and we do." For emphasis Lucius carefully examined his blade. "And the reason we all have our swords is because of you. So I would suggest you leave our presence at once before we make a mess out of you and your cronies."

Decius and his companions backed away into the night, followed by the mocking laughter of Lucius and friends.

"Whew, good eyes, Lucius. Those guys weren't out for an evening stroll. They knew we might be coming back this way."

"Most likely, Cassius. I don't think they would try anything in the encampment here, but you don't know with that bunch."

"Let's get some sleep. I'm bushed," said Domitius.

Lucius undressed, hung his armor and weapons on the pegged pole, and crawled under his blanket. Everyone else was settled in for the night. He was totally exhausted from his tiring day carrying his heavy load, yet he couldn't sleep. Lucius stared at the roof of his tent, willing himself to get some needed rest, but something was pulling at his consciousness. He couldn't identify it. Perhaps it was the most recent confrontation with Decius. He dismissed that. He wasn't even disturbed by the events just moments ago. No, this was something different, but he couldn't place it.

Sleep wouldn't come. He continued to toss and turn. "Damn," he muttered. The others were already sleeping, snoring softly. Lucius pictured the walled fort they were going to and what life would be like with Julia there. Yes, he thought, this was something to look forward to. He finally drifted off into the arms of Morpheus.

Lucius marched under the heavy burden of equipment and weapons with the men of his century through a wide forest. There was heavy fog everywhere. He could see nothing to the sides of the marching column. Heavy clouds of impenetrable white blanketed the soldiers. The dark shape of trees would occasionally emerge from the ethereal world they had entered. Lucius thought he saw something move fleetingly to his left. Must be my imagination, he thought. Soon another shape flitted past his vision. He nudged Cassius.

"Did you see that?"

"What?"

"Something is out there."

Cassius shrugged. "There is nothing out there, Lucius. You must be imagining it." He continued staring straight ahead, not even looking.

Lucius saw another shadow, then another.

"Cassius, you must have seen that."

He didn't answer.

Lucius gave up on Cassius and nudged the man in front of him. "Did you see that?"

The man kept marching without turning around. Lucius tapped the man again on the shoulder. He didn't respond. Lucius broke formation, pointed at the mists, and shouted to the entire century. "Surely you see. By the gods, can't you see them?"

No one answered. Centurion Frontinus yelled for him to get back in the ranks or he'd be severely punished.

Lucius shouted, "There are men out there. Look at all of them."

Germans armed to the teeth, brandishing swords and spears, materialized out of the mist. With a mighty cry, the enemy warriors fell swiftly upon the unsuspecting Romans. Lucius cringed as he watched Centurion Frontinus die as several spears struck him. Men fell everywhere. His entire century was being butchered before his eyes. As Lucius turned to his left, he saw Cassius on the ground, stabbed repeatedly by a host of German warriors. He yelled above the din.

"Not you, Cassius." Before Lucius could rush to his aid, a German warrior jumped in front him. Lucius drew back. He couldn't believe what he saw. Before him was the same German from the ambush who had wounded him with the spear and in turn was gutted by Lucius with a deep sword thrust. How could the man have survived? The warrior wore a malevolent grin. The front of his tunic was covered in gore. Lucius stabbed him again. In response, the man laughed maniacally. Four other Germans joined the blood-soaked figure, jabbing at Lucius with their spears. Lucius leaped back like an agile cat from the menacing spearpoints. He heard a haunting female voice he couldn't place. "Lucius, Run! Run for your life."

Lucius warily retreated as the warriors relentlessly advanced. He looked to his century for help. All he saw were dead men with bleached skulls for faces. Lucius tripped backward and landed with a thud. He was helpless. The Germans all stabbed him simultaneously. He shuddered as the sharp points entered his flesh and sank deeply. Lucius screamed.

He found himself sitting up in his tent in a cold sweat. Everyone in the tent was awakened by his scream.

"You all right, Lucius?" said Cassius.

"Yeah, I guess so. Sorry, guys. Bad dream."

"Asshole," muttered an unidentified voice from his squad.

He was still shaking but relieved it was only a dream. His heart was pounding. He quickly patted his torso for any bloody holes. It had seemed so real. He attempted to go back to sleep, fading in and out of consciousness. A strange odor permeated the tent. He couldn't place it. It was an uncommon smell but one he'd experienced before. Then he remembered. No, this was not real. It was the scent of the incense burning when he had visited the sibyl so long ago. It had been her haunting voice telling him to run from the ambush.

The camp was beginning to stir in the semidarkness of early morning. Lucius was up before the others, standing alone on the earthen ramparts, chewing a piece of bread. He stared absently toward the towering trees on the edge of the field beyond the encampment. Cassius sauntered up to Lucius and gazed at his haggard countenance. Lucius returned the look in silence and continued munching on his bread.

"Lucius, if you don't mind my saying, you look like shit."

"Thanks. Good morning to you, too."

"What was that about last night in the tent? Are you having difficulties?"

"I'm ready for another day of busting my hump through that friggin' forest." He motioned with his arm in the direction of the towering trees.

Cassius replied, "Yeah, me too. I'm not looking forward to another day of this. By the way, what in the Hades was that smell last night in the tent? It was like something sweet was burning. I never smelled a perfumed fart before."

Lucius blanched. He stopped chewing on the bread.

"Lucius, you sure you're all right?"

Lucius attempted to recover.

"I'm just fine, Cassius. I just didn't sleep too good." Lucius brushed imaginary crumbs from his tunic, then walked away. Cassius stared after him.

XVIII

*T*he German auxiliary scout, Thulus, put his knees into the flanks of his horse, urging his mount forward. The winding dirt path was bordered on either side by massive oak and larch trees. His commanding Roman officer had ordered that he and his small retinue reconnoiter ahead of the Roman army. His scouts were allegedly familiar with the terrain to their immediate front. They were to report back immediately if they saw any hostile threats. Heedless of the low-hanging branches, horse and rider thundered down the path, flinging huge clots of earth behind them.

All was set. The trap was about to be sprung. Thulus was of the Cherusci tribe, the same as Arminius. Like the other scouts, he was employed as an auxiliary of the legions. The pay as an auxiliary was much less than that of a Roman legionnaire, but it sure as Hades beat farming and herding cattle for a living. The German cavalry, under the direction of Thulus, had the responsibility of forward security for the ponderous Roman column that now extended for miles down the narrow trail. Thulus and his band were all loyal to Arminius. They would aid in the treacherous attack that was about to unfold. Those Germans who had been opposed to the plot had met an unfortunate end or just disappeared.

Thulus slowed his horse to a trot. On his left side was a wide marsh, and to his right was a steep hill with dense woods. He gazed intently at the higher ground and through the foliage to his right. At last he saw them. Perhaps twenty-five yards from the trail was a wooden ambuscade of logs and sticks, behind which stood hordes of German warriors. The intervening foliage of over-grown brush and massive trees obscured the rampart except to the keenest of eyes.

The German fighters silently waved to him with bundles of throwing spears in their hands. He acknowledged them by thrusting his arm into the air. For this many Germans to be so quiet was truly extraordinary. Urging his horse onward, he galloped ahead toward the lead elements of the Roman column to make his report to his superior. No doubt the legions were where he'd last seen them. They were waiting for his return and the all-clear sign ahead. The ambush would unfurl just as Arminius had planned. The Romans were totally unsuspecting of the punishment about to befall them.

Thulus rode ahead, rounding a slight curve in the trail. He spotted a bevy of pioneers whose purpose was to clear the track for the advancing army. They were furiously hacking at overhanging branches and clearing debris from the makeshift road. Under normal circumstances, the Roman cavalry would be ahead of the column, but just as Arminius had planned, the Roman commander had pulled the cavalry out of the line of march because of the treacherous terrain and the lack of knowledge of the territory in front of them.

Beyond the pioneers, Thulus saw the lead soldiers at the head of the Roman file with their precious eagle in front. The Roman legionnaires were standing, many wearily resting on their upright shields. Other soldiers mingled in small groups, their coarse laughter echoing down the trail. They were waiting for orders to proceed forward, which was contingent upon Thulus giving the go-ahead to his commanding centurion. To think that the entire Roman army was waiting on him, just a lowly German auxiliary scout. What fools! If only they knew what was intended for them.

Thulus gazed forward, seeking his Roman master, Centurion Sutonius, the senior centurion of the First Cohort of the Seventeenth Legion. He was the officer responsible for the lead element of the legions. Sutonius was busy conferring with several other centurions, their arms moving in animation. Thulus dismounted, grabbed the reins of his horse, tied them to a nearby tree, and approached the group. He stood respectfully, waiting to be recognized. Centurion Sutonius broke off the discussion with the other centurions and looked impatiently at the German.

"Thulus, damn your craven heart to Hades. Where have you been? I need you to tell me where this column is supposed to go. The entire army is halted, waiting for your sorry ass to get back here to me. Now, what's going on ahead?"

"Sorry for the delay, sir. We encountered a bit of a problem forward with a low-lying swamp, but we've found a way through it. After that, all is clear, and it should be easy going once we get through it. I've sent my men farther up the road to scout for a night encampment."

"Thulus, no signs of any villages or bands of warriors?"

"No, Centurion, not yet. Nothing but forests."

Sutonius frowned at the report. Were they ever going to find these elusive insurgents in this primitive land? These woods appeared to go on forever. The centurion stared at a map he held in his right hand.

Thulus waited for the centurion to say something more, but Sutonius remained silent. Thulus grew uncomfortable, feeling that perhaps somehow the legions had gotten wind of the ambush. He finally broke the silence. "Sir, permission to join my men?"

Sutonius dismissed him with a gesture of his arm. Thulus trotted toward his waiting horse, anxious to leave the presence of the Romans. The centurion shouted after Thulus's retreating form. "But I want to know immediately if you see anything suspicious."

Thulus waved back in acknowledgement. The scout vaulted onto his horse and headed back toward the hidden positions of the waiting Germans.

In the distance, echoes of thunder reverberated through the forest from an approaching storm. Centurion Sutonius looked at Thulus's retreating figure, then toward the sky. He could see a boiling mass of clouds through small gaps in the overhead branches. The centurion muttered an oath in frustration. The soldiers of his lead century looked at him expectantly, waiting for their orders. Wearily, Sutonius signaled with his arm for the legionnaires at the head of the column to begin moving again.

The soldiers recognized the centurion's foul mood. They quickly gathered their shields and equipment without a word of complaint. They plodded forward on the trail, which now sloped down, with a steep embankment on the left. The first cohort of the Seventeenth Legion, the lead unit of the Roman column, advanced perhaps five hundred yards before reaching the morass. They stepped gingerly through the muck of the trail, which was more like a quagmire.

Suddenly, hard-driving rain, the kind that took one's breath away, pounded the forest. Men were bunched up, trying their best not to fall on their faces in the mud. Centurion Sutonius grimaced at the sight of his men wallowing through the swampy mess. He swore softly. If he could grab that fool Thulus now, he'd surely strangle him. What kind of trail was this? There was a huge marsh to one side and a steep, forested hill to the left. The winding path transversed portions of the bog, making footing near impossible.

Some of the men had sunk up to their knees in the muck. How would the baggage trains ever get through this mess? His deliberations were abruptly ended. All at once, a multitude of spears descended in waves upon the unfortunate legionnaires of the Seventeenth Legion, killing and wounding many. Centurion Sutonius lay on the ground with a spear through his groin. He watched in horror as his life's blood squirted out through the gaps in his fingers. Cursing Thulus with his dying breath, he realized that he had been betrayed.

Centurions shouted orders to form ranks. A shower of spears rained down from the ambuscade at side of the hill. The Roman column was at a standstill. To their credit, the Roman centuries quickly formed up and brought their shields into a defensive posture, but there were just too many spears. The unprotected legs and heads of the men were struck by the javelins. Men fell left and right, transfixed by the razor-sharp points. The Battle of the Teutoburg Forest had begun.

Meanwhile, at the rear of the Roman column, the German chieftain, Gorgas, crouched amid the thick bushes within javelin-throwing range of the narrow trail. He had watched patiently as the legions, with all of their soldiers, animals, and wagons, had passed by him. The moment was almost at hand to assault the Romans. Just about now, he thought, the ambush at the front of the Roman column was taking place. Once the head of the snake was pinned at the front of the column, he and his men were to attack the back end.

His clan would be the first to assail the Romans from their rear. Others up the length of the trail would take their cue from him. It was an honor for him to be selected as the one to spring the ambush, and he was proud of it. Of all the chieftains, Gorgas was entrusted with this responsibility. The war council had discussed the planning of the battle long into the night. There had been much shouting and thumping of chests. Several of the tribal leaders had almost come to blows over the best way to attack the Romans.

Gorgas pondered the events from the night before. He understood why they always lost to the legions. The bickering and petty feuds were impeding his fellow Germans. They were their own worst enemies. If they devoted as much time and effort to defeating the Romans as they did to fighting among themselves, perhaps they would have been more successful in the past. Arminius had stepped in to mediate and soothe injured feelings. He had pleaded and cajoled to get a consensus.

The chiefs had finally concurred with Arminius's plan. The best tactical results would be achieved by ambushing the Romans at the front of the column where the swamp bisected the trail, thus pinning down the entire army. The main German force would assault the Roman column beginning from the rear, then the flanks. Like a ripple in the water, the attack would make its way up the length of the army column. The terrain in which the Roman army would be positioned when ambushed was a natural valley with sloping hills on both sides of the trail. The valley extended from the swamp location at the head of the Roman column all the way back toward where Gorgas and his men waited. He and his men would strike the blow to send these Romans to the underworld. Their gods could deal with them there.

Gorgas's name had been put forth as the one most worthy to lead the assault. He was a wise choice. He was a great warrior and controlled his men absolutely. He was the chief of a small clan, or *pagus*, of the Angrivarii tribe. Although a noble by birth, this alone didn't assure his place. He was an imposing figure who towered above the others and had attained many individual victories in combat against neighboring tribes and Roman soldiers. No one would dare challenge him. His reputation as a fearless combatant and leader of men was unsurpassed.

Gorgas despised these Romans and their new arrogant leader. This new military governor, Varus, had inflamed the tribes even more with his disdain for them, treating the Germans like conquered people, demanding more taxes from them. It was high time these Romans suffered. It was time for revenge. Varus and all his soldiers must die.

Some weeks ago, in the sacred grotto when Arminius had spoken to the gathering of nobles and chiefs from different tribes of his plan, Gorgas had been appalled, even angered, that some were hesitant to take part in the ambush. He had silently rejoiced when Arminius executed that fool, Jurus. He was the typical German hothead who never got it right. His fate was deserved, in the opinion of Gorgas, and if he had his way, a few others would have shared a similar ending that night.

He knew some of the chieftains were extremely jealous of Arminius. There was bad blood between the tribe of Arminius, the Cherusci, and others. Perhaps worst of all, more than just a few of the nobles were enjoying the fruits of Roman occupation. They were granted generous favors and wealth. Gorgas could understand the animosity among the tribes, for there were some serious blood feuds. He had a few that he intended to settle after they punished these Romans. But to even consider befriending these Romans was unthinkable. He knew which of the tribes hadn't committed their forces, rekindling a cold anger in Gorgas.

Gorgas dispelled these angry thoughts. He must focus on the task at hand. He checked again to his right, left, and behind him to ensure everyone was hidden. His retinue, or *comitatus,* numbered over 250 warriors. He knew them all. To a man, they were without fear and ready for battle. His primary concern was that they might get impatient and attack too soon. His men were brave, but they lacked the discipline of the Roman legionnaires. Gorgas had instructed them repeatedly that they must wait for his signal. Only then could they attack. He'd promised to do some unpleasant things to anyone who disobeyed his orders.

Gorgas glanced at his weapons to ensure all was ready. He had an axe hung on his belt and a small oval shield made of cattle hide painted bright blue. He wore cloth trousers. He'd decided to discard his cloak because it might inhibit his arms. Leaning against a nearby tree, he had a half dozen throwing spears, or *frameae.* In his right hand was his favorite weapon, a long iron sword he had captured from a Gaelic chieftain on one of the raids across the Rhine into the Roman province of Gaul. He gripped the wooden handle of the sword tighter in anticipation. In the distance, he could hear the ominous rumbles of thunder echo through the forest. A storm would be perfect, he thought. It would hide their movements until the final instant, and then they would strike hard. They were ready.

Marcus Caelius was the centurion of the Sixth Century of the Tenth Cohort of the Nineteenth Legion. Centurion Caelius and the sixty-five men of his century were all veterans, skilled in the art of war. His unit, like some others, was understrength from the normal complement of eighty men. He'd badgered the senior centurion as much as he dared for replacements to his unit, but his pleas had been politely rebuffed. Refusing to accept no for an answer, he'd continued his entreaties until he'd been told rather bluntly by the senior centurion to stick his request up his ass. That had finally stopped him.

Caelius had continued to hold out hope for more men, but there were no replacements, at least for his century. As for the present, he and his men were the last heavy infantry unit in the lengthy Roman column, plodding through the thick German forest along the serpentine trail.

Centurion Caelius considered himself a capable leader. He was a seasoned legionnaire who had risen through the ranks to achieve his officer status. He'd been in his current position as centurion of the Sixth Century for almost ten years. It was most unusual for a centurion to be in the same command over such a long period of time. Standard doctrine of the legions dictated transfer of centurions out of their commands after five years or so. The Roman army believed that a centurion might become too familiar with his men and not exercise the proper discipline required in the legion.

Perhaps the legions were correct on this account, he mused. He had developed a certain bond with his men. He understood them all, their strengths, their weaknesses, and how far he could push them. He watched over them, making sure they were fit for duty, obeying orders. In a sense, the men had become his family. But he had never slacked off on proper discipline. He considered himself tough but fair and knew his men respected him.

Centurion Caelius was extremely pissed at his current situation. He and his under-strength century were given the responsibility of the rear guard for the entire column of the Roman army. As he performed the mathematical calculations in his head, the entire column encompassed 180 centuries plus the baggage trains and auxiliaries. All of these forces, which stretched over four miles, perhaps longer, were ahead of his unit. The worst part was that he was marching behind all of the pack and draught animals for the three legions.

There was 1 mule per contubernium, 10 mules per century, 60 mules per cohort, and 600 mules per legion. If one multiplied this by a factor of three for the number of legions, that totaled 1,800 mules just for the common soldiers. It didn't include the pack animals needed for the officer corps, which included the centurions, tribunes, optios, *aquilfers*, prefects, and legates. Including support staffs and auxiliaries, one would expect over 2,300 mules and two hundred wagons pulled by two oxen each. For security, the baggage trains were located behind the Seventeenth and Eighteenth Legions and in front of the Nineteenth Legion. Normally they would be located in the rear, but given the tactical situation, the baggage trains were placed in the middle.

It was bad enough that the ground was rutted and pitted by the marching of some fifteen thousand soldiers, plus auxiliaries, servants, and camp followers, but to be wading through the ubiquitous piles of mule and ox dung was, in a word, disgusting. The foul excrement now coated him and his century from head to toe. Their feet and legs were totally covered in a veneer of filth. The men were slogging through heaps of the stuff. There was no way to avoid it.

The road, if you could call it that, had deteriorated into a narrow dirt trail. They were now marching in a column of fours. What was worse, the weather, which had been delightful under hazy sunshine for the first two days of their march, appeared to be taking a turn for the worse. The sky, what little of it they could see through the canopy of the dense forest, was darkening to a deep, boiling purple. Rumbles of thunder from the approaching storm could be heard in the distance. The tops of the towering evergreens were swaying to and fro as they were buffeted by the ever-increasing winds.

The centurion knew why he'd been designated for this assignment as rear guard for the legions. Not four nights ago, he'd beaten the *pilus prior*, the senior centurion of his cohort, the same one who had denied his request for replacements, at dice. Thanks to a run of good fortune, he'd practically cleaned the poor fellow out. It served the bastard right, he thought, for not getting me my proper quota of soldiers.

Since the pilus prior was essentially the commander of the cohort, it was he who determined the marching order of the cohort. Centurion Caelius flushed with anger as he remembered the smug smile of the senior centurion as he informed him of his assignment of rear security. Caelius rationalized that it was but a small price to pay, given the tidy fortune he'd won from the centurion.

He frowned as a blast of thunder echoed through the forest. He knew from his years of experience that this was going to be a bad storm that would make their lives even more miserable. He knew his men would overcome this hardship. He could recall times of bitter cold, scorching heat, and long, bone-wearying forced marches that just sucked the life out of a soldier. Yet his men had always prevailed against the elements, returning intact and fit for duty the next day. Even now, above the ominous rumblings of the approaching storm, the centurion could hear his men joking about their current predicament. They were laughing at their own discomfort. The soldiers knew complaining did no good, so they made light of the situation. By the gods, he was proud of these legionnaires.

The approaching tempest wasn't what truly concerned Centurion Caelius. The responsibility of his century was to provide rear security. This was a task he shared with the German auxiliary cavalry, of which he'd not seen man nor beast for quite some time. He peered anxiously once more for some sign of the German scouts, but all that met his gaze was the shadowy ranks of massed tree trunks. The thickening gloom appeared menacing, almost suffocating in its density.

He fought the mounting apprehension and the queasiness in his belly that something was wrong. His years of experience in the legion had given him a sixth sense. He made sure to mask his trepidation from his men. The centurion muttered a curse at General Varus for putting himself and his men in this predicament. He didn't know how Varus had gotten his position, but he wasn't impressed. Caelius attempted to put that thought aside. Who was he to question the wisdom of Augustus Caesar, the imperator who had appointed Varus? He was just a centurion, a lowly one at that.

But it didn't make sense; it just didn't. The three legions were basically conducting a movement to contact in deteriorating terrain and bad weather with full baggage trains. The accepted tactical doctrine was to leave the baggage trains behind with plenty of security, then seek and destroy the enemy. This tactical march through the woods with the baggage trains had a bad feel to it. He'd heard that this commander, Varus, had previously been governor of Syria. He'd better learn quickly that this wasn't Syria. This was Germania, and these people loved to fight.

The column stopped moving for what seemed like the hundredth time that day. Caelius gave permission for the men to break out their rations of bucellatum, the hard wheat biscuits usually consumed on the march, and to partake of their acetum, the sour wine. They should eat now before the heavens opened and drenched them head to toe. The food and drink would raise their spirits. As a precaution, he required that all must face outward from their positions on the trail with their shields and weapons at the ready. There was to be no lying down or quick games of dice.

The men removed their rations from their kit bags. The veteran centurion again scanned the surrounding forest for any possible sign of danger. Some were leaning upright against their grounded shields, a sure sign of weariness. It had been a long day already, with the promise of more difficulty ahead. There was a startling crack, then a large peel of thunder burst from the heavens, followed almost instantaneously by a bolt of lightning. The white flash illuminated the surrounding forest, casting the Roman soldiers in an eerie glow. The bolt stuck a large evergreen some one hundred meters from their position, toppling the upper half of the tree onto the forest floor. The stench of burned wood filled the forest air. With a rushing sound, the rain began to fall in torrents. Great blasts of thunder echoed throughout the forest. The wind whipped the treetops wildly about in a frenzy.

The soldiers huddled closer together in a tight perimeter, as if the close proximity to one another would somehow ward off the torrent of rain. The men were dutifully facing outward, their lines tied in to the next century ahead of them in the column. They all had the rain goathide covers over their shields to prevent them from becoming waterlogged and thus too heavy to use. Some of the men angled their shields to protect them from the pounding rain, not that it did much good.

The centurion gazed once more into the depths of the forest, but with the driving rain and dark skies, visibility was almost impossible. Another bolt of lightning shot from the sky, accompanied by a blast of thunder. The flash illuminated the forest. There was movement from beyond their perimeter toward the drenched legionnaires. Caelius looked again in disbelief. It took the startled centurion an instant to comprehend that there was indeed a large body of Germans rushing his position.

Gorgas leaped from his concealed position in the thick bushes and ran at the cluster of Roman soldiers. He knew his warriors were watching, waiting for him to begin the charge. Once they saw his hurtling form, they knew the moment had arrived. For a big man, he surged forward with remarkable agility. He covered the ground between his hiding place and the Roman soldiers quickly. He didn't need to look behind him. He knew his men were with him. The pounding of the rain masked the sounds of the rushing warriors.

Gorgas had discarded his shield and left it behind with his inventory of throwing spears. He was racing forward with his right arm cocked, his hand holding just a single javelin. His left hand held his prized sword, which he would quickly change to his right after releasing the spear. Gorgas was pleased that they had yet to be discovered. They rapidly approached the Roman soldiers. He was almost on top of them before the cry of alarm was sounded. He and the rest of his warriors threw their assorted projectiles at the Romans. He grinned in satisfaction as he heard the cries of pain from the stricken soldiers. Now his men could yell. With a shout, he was among the Romans, swinging his sword. He nearly decapitated the first soldier he hit. He leaped over the twitching body to the next legionnaire in front of him.

Centurion Caelius bellowed with all of his power, "SHIELDS, ATTACK."

He hoped to alert the men to raise their shields immediately. Remarkably, most of his men heard the warning above the driving rain, but it did them little good. The hapless contingent of soldiers was showered with spears.

One of the spears struck the centurion in his left leg. He collapsed to his knees. The incredible pain made him gasp. Falling, he was struck a glancing blow on the head by an ax. In a daze, he could barely sense the presence of two large figures with long, flowing hair above him. He screamed in terrible pain as his lower body was pierced through and through by two spears, pinning him to the earth.

The rest of his men fared little better; many were struck by assorted missiles and quickly overrun by a superior number of the foe from all directions. Given the short range, many of the legionnaires were hit directly in the unprotected face or throat with spears or axes, causing grievous wounds. Centurion Caelius was unable to move. He didn't even feel the driving rain on his face as a heavy darkness descended upon him. The last sounds the centurion heard were the screams of the wounded and dying. The overwhelming force of German tribesmen annihilated to a man Centurion Caelius and his century. The rear of the Roman column was now being rolled up in a most savage manner.

Lucius stood with the other men of his century, halted on the trail, waiting for the column to begin moving again. Like the others, he rested wearily upon his shield, which was in an upright position. His haggard appearance attested to his sleepless night and his haunted dreams. He shuddered slightly in remembrance of the nightmare that buzzed in his brain. He shook his head slightly, hoping that might cleanse his senses. He inhaled deeply, taking in the scent of the forest. The sweet smell of evergreens and the pungent aroma of rotting wood filled his nostrils. That made him feel a bit better. Still, he had a sense of uneasiness, of foreboding, that he could not shake.

He glanced about at the towering hemlocks and oaks. By Jupiter's balls, he had never seen anything like this. The size and density of the trees blocked almost all light, casting the rutted trail in semidarkness. It was so eerily similar. His century was stationary but remained in formation, four abreast on the winding forest road. Cassius stood next to him, swearing. Moments ago, he'd firmly planted his foot in a fresh, giant mule turd. Lucius ignored Cassius's diatribe, staring out at the forest around him. He'd lost count of how many times the entire column had just stopped and waited. This already was a long day, with much more to go.

At every standstill, Lucius glanced behind to see if he could spot the baggage trains where Julia was traveling. The baggage carts were to the rear of the Eighteenth Legion, to which Lucius's century belonged, and to the front of the Nineteenth Legion. Lucius was in the last cohort, the tenth, of the Eighteenth Legion. His century was third out of the six centuries in the cohort in the order of march. That made two centuries in front with three others behind him. On occasion, when the road was fairly straight, which wasn't that often, he caught sight of the wagons.

Now, the winding forest road blocked any chance of view. Further restricting his vision was the darkness of an approaching storm. Ominous thunder boomed through the wooded setting. Lucius's frequent rearward stares weren't lost on his fellow legionnaires. Cassius had made sure his fellow soldiers knew of Lucius's relationship with Julia. He had embellished the story of Julia's bullying of the orderly at the hospital tent. She was sort of a hero to the soldiers. The men admired her pluck for putting the authority of the legions in its place, and, of course, the matter of uncovering Lucius's naked form under the blanket with the able assistance of Cassius.

One man quipped, "Should we ask the centurion's permission for you to ride with the baggage trains? You know what a kindhearted man he is. I'm sure he'd be happy to grant a new legionnaire this special favor." Lucius didn't mind the ribbing. He just grinned back somewhat sheepishly. If truth be told, he would love to be sitting next to Julia in the wagon.

Tribune Valerius sat on his horse, anxious to get moving again. It was slow going this day. Each passing mile pushed them deeper into more rugged terrain. The trail became less defined. The army had forded several clear rushing streams, crossed ravines, and ascended hilltops. He tilted his head as far back as possible to see the tops of the towering trees. They were immense, as thick around as three men joining arms in a circle. He turned in his saddle as a rider approached from his left. It was Tribune Calvus. He grinned at Valerius and motioned to his surroundings.

"What do you think? Nothing like Rome, is it?"

"I never would have imagined a world such as this existed. It's magnificent in a strange sort of way."

Calvus laughed. "I've seen parts of Germania like this before. It's beautiful. Not that I like marching through it with an army, but it's definitely not Rome."

Valerius was silent. He sensed this was more than a social visit from the senior tribune. He waited to hear what Calvus had to say. When it became apparent that Valerius wasn't going to speak, Calvus continued.

"Now then, listen, Maximus. I'm sorry about the way the general has treated you. It was a rotten deal. But when you returned triumphant from the ambush, that was priceless. You really put Castor in his place. For that matter, you brought the general down a notch or two. I shall remember that scene for a long time. For what it's worth, that Castor is an officious prick."

Valerius smiled at his new ally.

"Thanks to you, Tribune Calvus. You made it possible by giving me permission to go out with the patrol. I hope I didn't land you on the wrong side of our esteemed general."

"No, not really. He inquired of me about it, but I explained that it was but a simple request from you to join one of the cohorts out on patrol. I can handle myself with the general. He relies on me heavily for a lot of things, so Varus didn't push it any further. He seemed to accept my explanation without any further ire."

Calvus leaned closer to Valerius so as to not be heard by others. "I'm behind you all the way, but there's not a lot I can do to protect you. Those two are powerful in this camp, so to the greatest extent possible, steer clear of them. Don't let your guard down. Give them no opportunity. I've overheard the two of them talking. Castor still means you harm. I believe Varus has concerns right now other than a petty feud between tribunes. If I were you, though, I'd be wary of both of them."

"Your warning is noted, Calvus, and thanks for the advice. I appreciate what you did for me. If I can repay the favor someday, let me know."

Calvus nodded in reply, then turned his horse back to the rear.

Tribune Valerius sat astride his horse, as the roan fidgeted, snorted, and stomped the ground. He reached down and stroked the animal's neck. The horse continued pawing at the earth and turning its head side to side. He considered dismounting to feed his horse some oats that he kept in his saddlebag. He decided to forego that action until the next stoppage. It was too early in the afternoon to feed the animal. Something was spooking his horse.

He shifted his gaze to the sides of trail. He'd heard that the forests were inhabited by ferocious bears, wild boars, and wolves. He peered into the shadows of the giant trees but could see little in the darkened recesses. Out of the corner of his vision, he spotted a stealthy movement to his right. He turned in the saddle to see what had caught his attention, but just then, a rumble of thunder resounded down the trail. The sky darkened. He looked back to the location where he thought he'd spied something, but all was hidden in the deepening shadows. *It was probably nothing, just my imagination.*

Julia was holding the reigns of the four oxen. The day had been worse than anticipated. Between the frequent stops and the billowing clouds of dust raised by the other wagons, it had been a miserable morning. They had been moving since daybreak. She wiped her arm across her face to clean the grime off, knowing it was a futile gesture. No amount of rubbing was going to clean the caked dirt off of her person. She jiggled the reigns, urging the oxen forward. "Hah," she said. The huge animals slowly advanced.

Her father had dismounted a few minutes earlier to check on some of the animals toward the rear of the column. He'd been informed that several mules were hobbling and needed his attention.

He'd handed the reins to Julia, then wandered off without as much as a mumbled farewell. Julia hadn't paid any attention to where he went, for he'd done this same task many times today. She was looking forward to the encampment this evening, when she could rest and be with Lucius again. Like everyone else, she was exhausted.

With a blast of thunder, rain began to roar through the towering forest. The driving rain created a mighty din that reverberated throughout wooded area. Bright flashes of lightning spawned a momentary brilliance that illuminated the men and surrounding trees. Now we're in some pretty shit, thought Lucius. Other sentiments expressed by his fellow soldiers were equally as vulgar. At least they were ahead of most of the mules and oxen. That was something to be thankful for. The legionnaires of Lucius's century instinctively hunched their shoulders, waiting for the driving rain to hit them.

Amid the claps of thunder and the roaring deluge, the strident sound of the trumpets carried above the pounding rain. Three quick blasts in succession signaled the order to establish a tactical formation for immediate enemy contact. They all perked up and looked about as the cornicens blared. There was hesitation. They looked at one another with puzzled expressions. Surely this must be a mistake. How could there possibly be enemy contact in this forest? There was nothing here but towering trees and ravines.

Centurion Frontinus wasn't one of those perplexed by the horn signals. He ran back and forth in front of the century, urging the soldiers to drop their gear and get their shields up and ready.

"Let's go. What are you waiting for? DRAW SWORDS. DRAW SWORDS."

The men stared at him for a moment, dumbfounded at their new orders, then their training took over. In a matter of moments, the century linked to the one in front and the one behind it. The centuries adjacent to Lucius's unit had become, in the blink of an eye, a solid wall of shields bristling with swords.

Lucius glanced toward his rear. Perhaps a hundred yards from where he stood, a wedge-shaped cluster of men emerged from the shelter of the trees. They smashed into the rear centuries of the cohort, including the attached contingent of archers and slingers. The unfortunate legionnaires hadn't yet formed lines and weren't prepared when the Germans hit them. The attackers charged into them with speed and force, then pierced the lines and breached the formation. The Germans fell upon the soldiers quickly. The two sides grappled with each other in a frenzy, stabbing at one another amid the fury of the storm. The archers and slingers had no protective shields or swords. They were easy prey for the Germans, who dispatched them quickly. Lucius stared in disbelief at the scene unfolding before him. The nightmare of last evening had become reality.

Centurion Frontinus bellowed above the cacophony of noise from the rain, thunder, trumpets, braying mules, and screaming Germans. "MAKE SURE YOUR SHIELDS ARE UP AND GET READY. FORM SHIELD WALL."

Bellowing commands, he pantomimed with his arms, demonstrating the raising of a shield. Lucius heard several objects whistle by his head. Something hard, perhaps an axe, struck his shield with a solid thump. Cries of pain echoed among the ranks. He didn't dare look around, but he kept his eyes focused to the front.

"STEADY," roared the centurion.

After a barrage of spears and axes came the charge of the barbarians. Germans assaulted out of the woods on both sides of the trail, attacking Lucius's unit. The legionnaires stood with swords at belly level. They were ready. Lucius braced himself against the onslaught. A bearded figure jabbed a short spear at his head. Lucius swiftly raised his shield, blunting the blow. He immediately brought his right foot forward, jabbing hard with his gladius. The blade penetrated at least a half foot into the lower side of the German tribesman. The man screamed in pain and wobbled away, holding his side, with bright crimson flowing from the mortal wound.

Lucius didn't bother to give the man a second glance. He immediately smashed his shield forward into a thin, wiry man wielding an axe. Before he could follow up with a sword thrust, Cassius, to the right of Lucius, delivered a slashing blow. It laid open the man's arm to the bone. The man crumpled backward, dropping his weapon.

Through the driving rain, two more Germans, screaming guttural curses, charged at Cassius and Lucius. Both were armed with their wickedly sharp, short stabbing spears. The broad Roman shields deflected the initial spear thrusts. With a howl, the German warrior facing Lucius lunged at his exposed neck with the spear. The maneuver was so quick that Lucius barely had time to parry it with his shield. Better watch out for this one. This guy knew what he was doing. Lucius focused his attention on the center of the man's chest. No matter what his head or feet did, the man's arm with the spear was attached to his chest. He stayed purely on the defensive. He didn't want to take any offensive action and risk being gutted like a fish with the tip of the javelin.

Barely aware of the great clamor occurring on all sides of him, he focused on this dangerous warrior facing him. The man tried another lightning thrust, this time at his leg. Lucius shifted the shield down quickly to block the thrust. The spearpoint broke off on impact with the shield. Before Lucius could take advantage of the situation, the man threw the useless spear shaft down and retreated.

With no one pressing him, Lucius came to the aid of Cassius. He appeared to be barely holding his own with a hulking figure. The man roared and jabbed at Cassius with his spear. That opened the German's left flank. Lucius made a rapid thrust at the man's vulnerable side, stabbing him in the leg. The man howled in pain from the wound and attempted to turn on Lucius. The combination of the mud and the wound caused the man's leg to buckle. He went down in a heap. Cassius leaped forward and nearly severed the German's head with a mighty stroke from his gladius. The blood fountained in the air, splashing over Cassius. The German died quickly, trying to hold his throat closed while blood gushed from the wound to mix with the rain and mud on the ground. Cassius nodded his thanks to Lucius as they stood shoulder to shoulder awaiting the next onslaught.

There was a temporary respite from the attacking waves of men upon Lucius and his century. The Germans were spent from their furious charges into the Roman lines. They retreated back a short way into the forest to regroup before the next wave. Centurion Frontinus quickly took advantage of this opportunity to change lines.

The front lines smoothly flowed to the rear as the second rank advanced. The dead and wounded of his century were hurriedly pulled into the middle of their formation, along with the rest of their gear. Lucius grabbed a man under the arms and dragged the unfortunate soldier over the uneven ground. The man left a blood trail on the forest floor. As Lucius dropped him to the ground, the soldier, between grimaces of pain, nodded his thanks to Lucius.

Centurion Frontinus issued new orders. "Gentlemen, let's give them a little taste of your javelins. Hurry now and pick them up."

The soldiers scurried to grab their spears and quickly formed up, javelins cocked and ready for release. The Germans were massed and in the process of regrouping, perhaps as close as thirty yards away from the Roman column.

"OPEN RANKS."

"PILA READY. RELEASE."

The Germans paid dearly for the pullback. The front-loaded spears found their marks and tore through the lightly armored and thickly massed Germans. The pyramid-shaped heads of iron penetrated legs, arms, torsos, and even heads up to a depth of half a foot. At least twenty Germans were prostrate on the ground. Others were on their knees, feebly attempting to extract the deadly weapons from their bodies. The century cheered their small victory and waved their swords, daring the Germans to approach once more.

Lucius, now in the second rank, peered anxiously over the shoulder of the man in front of him. In retaliation for the Roman volley, a hail of missiles flew out of the woods. It had little impact. The Romans had their shields up and ready. The enemy charged once again. Lucius felt an object glance off the back of his helmet, knocking it askew. His ears ringing from the blow, he calmly adjusted his helmet back into position, thankful for its protection. The outside ranks of the century absorbed the initial impact of the charge with their shields, then counterthrust with their gladii.

Lucius, with Cassius beside him, stood ready in the second rank, prepared to fill in if someone in the front line went down. The rain was falling harder. The wind ripped through the forest, breaking branches and in some cases felling trees. The clamor of clashing arms, blaring trumpets, shouts, and screams of the wounded were deafening. The ground was quickly becoming a morass of mud mixed with blood. The Germans again hurled themselves in reckless abandon at the Roman lines and were repulsed once more.

Valerius had become separated from the headquarters element, lagging behind the main body. He decided to proceed up the trail to catch up. He kicked the horse's flank. The mount balked, not moving. He nudged the horse again. The animal reluctantly trotted up the trail. The approaching storm sent shivers down Valerius's spine. The clouds darkened, and the thunder rumbled. It began to rain, accompanied by brilliant lightning. Distant shouts and screams echoed through the forest, then trumpets. What was that all about? He heard two distinct thuds. He looked to his front and was startled to see two lances protruding from Tribune Valtrunus Altus, one of the officers with whom Valerius shared his quarters. With a horrified expression, the man toppled from his saddle and fell directly onto one of the protruding javelins, driving it entirely through his body. The man grunted, then was still.

Valerius heard several objects go whistling by his head. Shockingly, ahead he witnessed the Roman infantry formations under assault by a mass of German warriors. Several more objects went whizzing by in a blur. Valerius turned his head to the left and right, attempting to control his panicky horse. He was unsure of what he was supposed to do. He stayed mounted, turning his head in all directions.

One of the centurions on the legate's staff ran up to him. "Tribune, get the Hades off the horse. You're making yourself a perfect target." The man never finished his next words. An axe hurled by one of the Germans struck him squarely in the face, splashing the tribune in a shower of blood and gore.

Valerius quickly dismounted, then tethered the animal to a nearby bush. Drawing his sword, he rushed to the nearest cluster of legionnaires, about twenty-five paces away. He was about halfway there when in front of him, a German warrior leaped onto the back of one of the mounted Roman cavalry, then stabbed him in the throat. The two toppled from the horse to the ground. Valerius rushed forward, then slashed down hard on the German's sword arm, forcing him to drop his weapon. Before the enemy could recover, Valerius viciously stabbed the man completely through the body, pinning him to the ground.

The tribune tugged to get the sword loose, but it was stuck in the mortally wounded foe. He pulled even harder, with no results. The man screamed as Valerius savagely yanked on his sword again, unable to get it free. In a panic, he put his foot on the man's chest and heaved with all his strength. The German shrieked as finally the blade came free. Both the German and the Roman cavalryman twitched about in their death throes on the wet earth, now stained with gouts of bright-red blood.

Valerius rushed forward to the massed century of soldiers who were now engaged in hand-to-hand combat against the screaming horde that had materialized out of the forest. He stumbled over the uneven ground and around several bodies of legionnaires. He picked up a shield from a dead Roman soldier, then dashed toward a centurion who appeared to be in charge.

"What would you like me to do, Centurion?"

The centurion stared at the tribune for a moment before responding.

"Stay by me, Tribune. They'll be after you. Your uniform stands out from the rest. It would be considered a great honor for one of them to take your head."

A javelin struck Valerius's shield.

"See what I mean, Tribune?"

Valerius silently congratulated himself on his wise decision to retrieve the fallen shield. There was a brief respite from the hail of flying javelins. He looked up and down the Roman column. As far as he could see, all of the centuries were under attack. Bodies of the dead and wounded were scattered over the trail. It appeared that the first thrust had been costly to the legions. Valerius glanced in the direction of the legate and his staff, noting a heavy concentration of friendly forces, perhaps several massed centuries. They were repelling the Germans in good order. He thought about attempting to make his way toward the staff of General Varus, which was really where he was supposed to be. He would feel more secure fighting alongside Marcellus. He quickly discarded that idea. The distance was at least a hundred yards. He wasn't sure which side controlled that real estate. Better to stay put with the centurion and the troops in this vicinity, at least for now.

A charging wedge of German warriors renewed its assault on the century that Valerius had adopted as his temporary refuge. Several of the foe managed to break through the ranks by sheer force. One of the two managed a stab at Valerius with his short spear. The tribune nimbly shifted his scutum to deflect the thrust. The century closed its ranks, and the two Germans were struck down by several swords and finished off quickly. Valerius said a silent prayer to his instructor back in Rome, Centurion Mauritinius. The endless sword-and-shield drill had saved his life. The regrouped century, now a bristling mass of steel, was ready to take on any who might be so foolish. Valerius stood with his adopted comrades-in-arms, waiting for the next assault.

Lucius and Cassius stood side by side in the second rank. They swiveled their heads back and forth, looking for any potential threat. The number of spears and other objects aimed at their century had diminished to the point of sporadic projectiles. The ferocity of the German assaults had ebbed with each successive attempt. The soldiers maintained tight and disciplined formations. To a man, Lucius and his fellow legionnaires knew they couldn't let the enemy split their tactical formation and lines. If they succeeded, the Romans were lost. The compact tactical units of the centuries were tied into one another, as were the cohorts.

Lucius turned his thoughts to Julia. He visualized the Germans leaping onto the wagons, then slaughtering the defenseless drivers. How could Julia possibly escape the carnage? He looked back in her direction, trying to think of what he could do.

Cassius turned toward Lucius, keeping a wary glance to his front. "I wonder how the other guys are doing—Antonius, Severius, Julius."

Lucius, preoccupied, didn't say anything, then absently shook his head. "Don't know. Looks like a lot of dead and wounded. I hope they're all right."

"Here they come again," shouted a legionnaire. Another wedge of Germans charged from the surrounding forest. They attacked, screaming, followed by loud grunts. They crashed into the shields of the front lines. The Germans withdrew, leaving more of their fallen brothers on the forest floor. All was quiet once again. Seeing no immediate threat, Lucius again cast glances rearward, wondering if the enemy was assaulting the wagons with the same ferocity.

"Don't even think about it," said Cassius. "I know exactly what you're contemplating, so don't try to deny it."

Lucius turned to Cassius. "Deny what?"

"Oh, come on, Lucius. How many times have you looked back at the baggage carts? What do take me for, a fool?"

"So what about it?"

"At least you're admitting it. You're not leaving this unit. Understand?"

"Why not?"

"Because your duty is here."

"I don't owe the legions anything." But his voice lacked conviction.

"Yes you do, Lucius. You're part of this century, like it or not. You must stay here. Besides, you'd never make it if you tried. Think about it. A lone Roman running beyond the lines? The Germans would pick you off before you got twenty yards from here. Hah! If they didn't get you, I'm sure some ill-tempered centurion would. Then what good would you be?"

Lucius didn't respond but continued staring rearward, feeling helpless.

"Look," said Cassius, "the baggage trains are heavily guarded by the legions. She'll be protected."

Reluctantly, Lucius realized the folly of even attempting to dash off to the rear toward the carts and wagons. Cassius was correct. He'd never make it that far with the entire column under assault. He'd have to stand fast with his unit for the present. Besides, his duty was here. He recognized that he'd better get his head together and concentrate on the enemy to his front, or he wouldn't be around to see Julia again.

"I suppose you're right."

Upon hearing this, Cassius said a little prayer to the gods. He wasn't sure he'd persuaded Lucius to stay. In truth, if Lucius did run off, Cassius would probably follow him.

Julia began to shiver as the air chilled, and the wind began to blow harder through the trees. She placed a cape over her head to ward off the heavy rain that was starting to fall. She heard terrible screams. There were shouts, then the sounds of trumpets. Julia looked about in bewilderment, then froze in horror as a horde of Germans materialized out of the forest. They began killing with abandon the soldier escorts. Not twenty feet in front of her, a German rushed onto the road and slashed a legionnaire in the neck, nearly decapitating him. Everywhere she turned, she could see Germans grappling in close combat with legionnaires. The Germans leaped onto the wagons, killing the defenseless men driving the carts and baggage trains.

She nimbly jumped off the wagon and slipped among the four oxen, drawing her dagger from the sheath at her side. Her position among the animals gave her some protection—at least it was better than being out in the open. Holding the knife in front of her with trembling hands, she shook in terror at the sights around her She knew she would stand little chance with her slight weapon against these imposing killers. She crouched among the animals, looking about through the legs of the oxen for her father.

With a shout of triumph, a German ran toward her, waving his sword in the air. About forty legionnaires sallied forth into the clearing and dispatched him with several sword thrusts, leaving him a bleeding heap on the road. Other marauding Germans in the vicinity were ruthlessly cut down by the legionnaires. The reinforcements quickly secured the immediate area. The centurion leading the men cupped his hands to his mouth to be heard above the driving rain and shouted at her, "Stay here, lady, and don't leave this spot." He pointed to the cart for emphasis, then yelled again, "Don't go away; it'll be safer. We're forming a perimeter around the wagons."

The centurion turned away from her and coolly directed his men where he wanted them. The legionnaires quickly trotted to their assigned locations and established a circle around the wagons.

Julia frantically searched again for her father. There was no sense yelling. She wouldn't be heard above the din of the battle and the drumming sounds of the heavy rain. She realized she had no choice but to stay put and hope that her father was safe.

She thought of Lucius and said a prayer to Vesta, the goddess who protected her, that Lucius would survive this battle. She wondered if she'd ever see him again. Julia gripped the dagger tighter and waited. More time passed. The screams and shouts diminished. Perhaps it was safe now, she thought. Caution be damned; she decided to venture forth from her sanctuary among the oxen. She emerged hesitantly, still not sure what she was going to do.

Bodies were sprawled everywhere in expanding pools of blood. Some of the Roman wounded were being attended to on the ground. She wandered around the wagons searching aimlessly. Where was her father?

As she glanced to her left, in the distance she spied a crumbled heap with blotches of crimson staining the familiar tan tunic her father wore. With a cry, Julia rushed to the figure. She turned the person over on his back. She stared into the lifeless eyes of Petrocolus. Her father was dead.

XIX

*T*ribune Calvus remained composed despite the events unfolding around him. He could hear the clamor of battle rising above the wind and the rain. It was not his personal safety that concerned him. He was well protected. He stood next to General Varus and Caecina. They were surrounded by a cordon of Varus's personal bodyguards. These beefy men, selected for their prowess at armed combat, stood silently by with swords and shields at the ready. Circling them was a second ring of legionnaires from the First Century of the First Cohort of the Nineteenth Legion. He was safe, but it was the conduct of his immediate superior, General Varus, that had him unnerved.

Moments ago, a messenger from General Flavius, legate of the Nineteenth Legion, had staggered into the command center. The news he had conveyed was not good. The rear cohorts of the Nineteenth Legion had been devastated by the German ambush. Casualties had been especially heavy in the Ninth and Tenth Cohorts. Many of those centuries had been totally annihilated by the attack.

Varus was paralyzed by the news and appeared incapable of making any command decisions. He paced back and forth, wringing his hands. He gasped. "How could this happen? How dare these Germans attack us! Bring me Arminius. His reinforcements will lead us out of this."

Calvus attempted to hide his dismay. He was just a tribune, but even he knew they had to take decisive action to stabilize their position and develop a plan for extricating the army from this mess. By the gods, they needed to do something besides stand there. He was tempted to go over to Varus and suggest a course of action to consolidate their forces, but he decided against that. Although the general relied on him for many administrative matters, he was just a young tribune and his suggestions, no matter how subtle, would be judged impertinent. He muttered a brief entreaty to Mars for assistance.

The gods must have been listening, or perhaps it was just blind luck, but at that moment a messenger appeared. Gasping for air, he burst through to Varus's position. His uniform was stained with blood, and he sported a long gash on his right cheek. Tribune Calvus grabbed the man and held him upright.

"Sir," he gasped, "I need to see General Varus urgently. Message from General Licinus."

Calvus quietly guided the man over to Varus. The messenger stood as erect as possible, still breathless.

"Sir, General Licinus has come upon open ground up ahead. He is establishing a defensive perimeter for the army. He requests your permission to begin building fortifications. He urges that you advance the army forward."

Varus appeared relieved. Gaining some semblance of control, he replied in his command voice, "Yes, a reasonable course of action. How far up the trail is this perimeter?"

"Sir, about three miles from here, as best I can tell."

Varus frowned at the news of the distance. "Three miles? Our column is stretched that far?"

The messenger gulped. "That is my best estimate, sir."

"Tell General Licinus the army will proceed forward to his perimeter."

"Yes, sir."

The man turned to leave.

"Wait," said Tribune Calvus, grabbing the messenger's arm.

Calvus turned toward a group of soldiers who were part of Varus's personal bodyguard.

"Brutus, Colus, go with this man." The two legionnaires looked at each other in dread. Calvus didn't have to explain why. These two were for insurance in case the man never made it to Licinus's forward position. The three soldiers obediently departed out of the perimeter.

The goddess Fortuna smiled on Varus and his army this day. The Seventeenth Legion, the lead heavy infantry at the head of the long column under the command of General Vitruvius Licinus, had broken through the initial ambush position of the Germans at the head of the Roman column. He'd skillfully massed his forces and punched through the German ambush position, which was strangely not reinforced—a poor strategic decision on the part of Arminius and his associates. Otherwise, they would have had the legions hopelessly trapped.

Licinus had rightly concluded that it would be a huge tactical mistake to remain stationary. He had forged ahead with vigor. The German scout Thulus and his brothers-in-arms, who had occupied such a pivotal role in the German ploy, lay dead along the trail. Licinus had ordered the Roman cavalry forward and to attack. He had then personally directed the assault by two full infantry cohorts on the German ambush positions while the enemy was engaged with the cavalry.

The Roman soldiers had charged the flimsy ambuscades erected by the Germans and broke through the enemy lines. Surprisingly, there was little opposition once the Roman soldiers had stormed past the German ranks. The cavalry of the Seventeenth Legion had forged ahead. They encountered a wide meadow on higher ground not too far from the initial German ambush site at the swamp. Once informed of the terrain ahead, Licinus had quickly assimilated the tactical situation, then determined that their best course of action was to immediately begin construction of a fortified camp in the pasture ahead.

Lucius and Cassius stood side by side, shields up and swords in their right hands, waiting for the next threat. They'd been at their present location on the narrow forest trail since the ambush had been sprung. The rain continued unabated amid peals of thunder. They were soaked, and their shields weighed heavily on their tired left arms. The ground was a now a mixture of mud and blood. Dead soldiers, both German and Roman, covered the immediate vicinity to their front, some intertwined like macabre lovers and others in various contorted poses. There was a lull as the Germans ceased their attacks.

Their entire century, less those unfortunates incapacitated or killed, stood resolute and unbowed. They were ready to take on whatever the Germans could throw at them. The Germans would need to do much more if they were going to overcome this defiant bunch on this day. A similar picture arose for many of the other centuries. The Romans' superiority in weapons and armor, plus the discipline of the legions, had staved off defeat, at least temporarily. Lucius turned to his left and saw Centurion Frontinus conferring with several other centurions of his cohort. As the officers talked, they glanced toward the front and rear of the column, then huddled again in deep conversation.

Lucius could only guess what they were discussing. He sensed he would find out soon enough. The group broke up. Centurion Frontinus moved down the middle of the century, shouting encouragement. Like a true leader, he set an example for the men. He was without fear and was a steady influence.

"Get ready to proceed forward. We're forming a perimeter ahead. Leave the dead. Help the wounded. Maintain your interval. No gaps."

The centurion stopped, then turned back to Lucius, Cassius, and Domitius. "How are you three holding up?"

Cassius answered for the group. "We're fine, Centurion."

Lucius and Domitius nodded in acquiesce.

"Good. Don't worry; we'll get out of this mess. I promise you."

Lucius understood the centurion was checking up on the "new guys." But as far as he was concerned, one didn't have to be a veteran to know things were in the shitter now. The centurion trotted to the rear of the century to ensure they were tied into the next unit. The men continued to stand ready, waiting for some time until they saw movement to their front.

"What are we waiting for? Let's get moving," shouted Frontinus. The men faced outward as they advanced cautiously. Lucius kept one eye outward and one toward the ground. Debris and dead bodies were everywhere. Shields, splintered javelins, swords, helmets, packs, and other equipment were strewn about the landscape. Lucius had never seen such carnage. Even his first taste of combat in the ambush some five weeks ago couldn't prepare him for the grisly sights along the trail. In some places, there were piles of Germans and Roman soldiers. Body parts were scattered about randomly, with lances stuck obscenely out of bodies from all angles.

They continued to shuffle up the trail at an awkward pace, shields at the ready. Lucius concentrated on moving one foot in front of the other in slippery mud. He tripped on an object, then watched in disgust as a legionnaire's head with helmet still attached roll away from his foot. Where was Julia? A bloody heap on the side of the path like so many others? These ghastly images continued to gnaw at him as he hurried forward down the trail of death. For now, all he could do was stay focused and survive.

They continued on this way for some time, clumsily sidestepping their way along the path with shields facing outward. The advancement to the perimeter up ahead seemed to take forever. There were numerous stoppages as a result of German harassing tactics. The occasional spear or arrow flew out of the woods but did little damage. In the clearing ahead, Lucius could see the brown earthworks of the defensive perimeter. The century ventured closer to safety, then the pace picked up, almost to a run. They burst into the laager almost at a sprint. Centurion Frontinus was singled out by Centurion Clodius. He shouted instructions, then waved his arm to the left and pointed. Frontinus nodded in acquiescence. He in turn waved for the men in the century to gather round him.

"Let's get going now. There's no time to rest. We've been assigned a sector to complete the earthworks for the laager." He pointed with his sword. "I want the ramparts to begin here and to extend to where you see those legionnaires digging."

They rushed to a position near the left rear of the encampment. Centurion Frontinus immediately organized them. About three quarters of the men began digging the ditch and building the rampart. Those not engaged in digging were on guard for any possible attack by the Germans. Lucius was one of those initially assigned guard duty as his comrades feverishly excavated the earthworks. Dirt flew through the air as men dug with their pickaxes.

Earthen walls and ditches quickly took shape. Lucius anxiously glanced back toward the entrance to the encampment, about one hundred yards from where he stood, to see if the wagons had come in yet. They shouldn't be far behind. Lucius continued to stare at the entrance, willing the wheeled vehicles to appear.

At length, he could see the first wagons entering the laager. Centurion Frontinus had heard of Lucius's concern for the girl. While a stickler for discipline, he could be a compassionate man on occasion. Besides, the new legionnaire had performed better than expected under adverse circumstances, perhaps better than some of his veterans. The centurion needed someone to check on rations for the men, so it might as well be Lucius.

"Palonius."

Lucius rushed over. "Yes, Centurion."

"I want you to go toward the entrance to the laager, find the quartermaster's staff, and ask for Centurion Ruggerius. I want to know when we can draw more rations. Do you think you can do that for me?"

"Yes, Centurion. I'm on my way." Lucius began to run.

"Wait, Palonius."

Lucius stopped, turned around, and looked back toward the centurion.

"Bring back as much food as you can. This may be our last opportunity to replenish our supply."

"Yes, Centurion."

He sprinted toward the entrance his century had passed through not long ago. More troops and carts were streaming into the safety of the perimeter. Lucius reached the area and turned his head in every direction, hoping to spot Julia. He would seek the quartermaster out later. He needed to know the fate of Julia. He ran among the wagons, looking about for her. He dodged around a pack of mules, then side-stepped a cart drawn by oxen. The driver of the cart wrestled with the reins, cursing Lucius for spooking the animals. Lucius paid him no mind.

Frantically he began calling her name amid the shouts of commands and the curses of the drivers. More wagons, mules, servants, and support staff entered the area. People looked at him with blank stares, most in total shock at what had taken place during this fateful day. His heart raced. Off in the distance, about fifty yards away, he spotted a figure that looked like Julia being held in the arms of an older woman. Yes, that was her. He raced over. She looked up as he shouted her name. Her face was one of pure anguish. Lucius raced over, and she collapsed into his arms sobbing.

"Oh, thank the gods you're alive," said Julia. "My father. They killed my father. Oh, Lucius, help me," she cried. Lucius held her as she grabbed his head tightly with her arms. They stayed that way for a long time as Lucius held her and attempted to comfort her, oblivious of the remainder of the legions that funneled into the Roman perimeter.

Along the hastily constructed ramparts of the camp, watch fires cast their eerie glow. There was no sign of the Germans. The pounding downpours had mercifully ceased a little while ago. The officers and tribunes were meeting in an area close to the center of the camp. Torches were placed in the ground to provide illumination as twilight slowly settled. Various staff were making their reports in front of the assembly of the senior officers. The staff adjutant was addressing the gathering.

"Sir, as a result of the attacks by the German tribes, we've suffered significant casualties. As of the latest count, the legions have incurred over 2,500 dead and 2,000 wounded. These losses exclude servants, attached staff, and auxiliary forces. Many of the wounded aren't expected to survive. By far, the greatest losses were incurred by the Nineteenth Legion. Several of their units were completely annihilated. Commanders are currently engaged in consolidating their forces. In addition, almost the entire contingent of archers and slingers was annihilated without so much as one arrow or stone fired in retaliation."

Varus numbly stared at the adjutant in disbelief. "Are you telling me that we've experienced over 4,500 casualties among our fighting force?"

"Yes, sir," the adjutant replied dutifully.

"Any word on the four cohorts of German auxiliaries?"

The adjutant nervously cleared his throat. He was unsure how to phrase an answer. No one else came forward to assist him on this matter. He looked about for support, but all avoided his gaze.

"Uh, sir, it appears the auxiliary troops have joined the attackers. There were several confirmed sightings of the supposedly friendly auxiliaries, and they were part of the attacking hordes. There was a report that Arminius was among them."

The haggard Varus remained silent. His one eye twitched in nervousness. He wrung his hands together, unsure as to what to do next.

General Licinus approached Varus. "Sir, we need to face these Germans tomorrow with a plan that will enable us to escape."

Varus looked up in relief that someone had salvaged the quandary for him. "Yes, you're quite right."

"Sir, this is where we think we are." He pointed at a large map that had been placed upon the ground. Several staff held torches for illumination. "We can't be certain, of course, but we believe we're in this general vicinity. The army has marched approximately thirty-five miles from our departure point on the Weser. As I see it, we have two choices. The army can turn around and go back to our summer base, or we can continue upon our original course. This would take us due west another ten miles, maybe less. We would then turn and pivot to the south for about thirty-five miles to the established route along the river. Our intermediate objective will be to reach the supply base at Alisio on the Lippe. Its defenses are barely adequate, but it'll have to do. From Alisio, it's another thirty or so miles to Vetera on the Rhine."

Varus spoke. "It appears the obvious choice is to turn around and retrace our steps. We will have sanctuary on the Weser encampment."

General Antonius Flavius, commander of the Nineteenth Legion, cleared his throat. "Sir, I'm not sure the option is available to us."

"And why not?" Varus demanded. He'd regained some of his command arrogance.

"Sir, there are two reasons. First, my men at the rear of the column reported seeing the Germans felling large trees across the path over which we had journeyed. That road may now be impassable. The second reason is that going back will place us even farther from the relative safety of the Rhine forces. I believe we need to reach our intermediate objective of Alisio as quickly as possible, then call for reinforcements from the Rhine bases. Also, going back to our point of origin would place us farther away from any supplies. Our rations will last another two or three days."

Varus didn't say a word but stared out into the darkness.

General Licinus coaxed Varus into a decision. "Sir, I believe General Flavius is correct in his assessment. We have no choice but to continue upon our original course. The chances of a successful outcome appear much greater."

"Yes, yes. We'll continue on our current direction," he acquiesced.

"Sir," continued Licinus, "the army will need to proceed as quickly as possible. We must abandon all the baggage trains and carts. That includes the mules."

Varus looked up in horror. "Abandon the baggage trains, you say? What of all of our possessions? Are you mad?"

"General, our possessions will do us little good if we're all dead. We need to progress with as much speed as possible to get out of these forests and marshes. Our situation remains perilous as long as we're in this terrain. The sooner we extricate ourselves from this forest and get onto open ground, the better our chances."

Varus reluctantly came to the conclusion that there was no other choice.

"If that's what we must do, we'll abandon the carts and wagons. But I want them burned. I don't want those barbarians getting their hands on any of our goods. The very idea is humiliating. I want all of the valuables, including the silver bullion, buried deep in the ground."

"Sir, we'll torch them as we depart the laager in the morning."

Lucius and Julia sat huddled at the base of the earthen ramparts, wrapped in his heavy cloak to ward off the chill of the evening. Julia was wracked with grief at the loss of her father. A small fire burned close to them. The air was permeated with the smell of wood smoke and the scent of freshly turned earth. Cassius and Domitius were next to them, trying to add some words of comfort to Julia.

Julia looked up at Lucius and friends and spoke in a choked voice. "This was a horrible day. How can we possibly escape these woods? They'll kill us all."

Lucius spoke with as much conviction as he could. "We'll survive. These Germans won't beat us. We owe it to your father to endure this ordeal. The Germans can't overcome the legions. They've attempted many times in the past and failed. You'll see. We'll prevail."

Cassius added his encouragement. "Lucius is right. We mustn't get dispirited. I'm sure the legions have been in tighter spots before and managed to carry the day. I say that when we get to the Rhine, we have a funerary toast to your father. We'll all live to do that."

"We'll have a proper ceremony to honor your father once we reach safety," said Domitius.

It didn't help. Julia sobbed uncontrollably. After a while, she stopped.

"Lucius, I'm so scared about tomorrow," said Julia.

"We all are. Every soldier here is scared. We must overcome our fear and beat these barbarians back. What do you say, Cassius and Domitius?"

"Right, Lucius," they replied.

"For now, I think we all need to get some sleep. The three of us have the third watch."

Lucius curled up with Julia on their makeshift bed, which consisted of his waterproof shield cover and some pine boughs. He reflected on his words of encouragement but wasn't sure he believed any of the things that he'd just said. What he'd told Julia might have sounded heartening, but beneath it all, he had his doubts about the ultimate outcome. He guessed his fate would reveal itself over the next several days. Holding the sobbing Julia tighter to him, he once again recalled the sibyl. So this was what that bitch had seen. He certainly could understand her look of horror. The carnage he'd witnessed today would make most men ill. The day had been terrible, but he needed to prove the sibyl wrong. He muttered an oath and silently vowed to survive this horror to defy her unspoken prophecy.

"Did you say something, Lucius?"

"No, Julia, go to sleep. I was just talking to myself."

Julia snuggled closer and was silent.

Marcellus stared glumly out at the imposing tall trees beyond the ramparts. He sat alone by a smoldering fire; the wood was so wet that it barely blazed. It cast a pitiful light and even less warmth. So, Centurion Marcellus Veronus, is this where it all ends? Out here in the forested wilderness without a proper funeral and nothing to mark your passing? You should have known the risks by now after all these years. Remember fighting those bandits in the hot desert night far away in the eastern part of the empire? You could have bought it then had you not glanced to your left and seen the descending sword strike. You just barely raised your shield up in time to block that sword that would have cleaved your head like a ripe melon.

The cries and screams that terrible evening, with the cold steel flashing under the desert moonlight, had been harrowing indeed. There was much spilled blood as the desert sand became wet with crimson gore. Many perished around you in the darkness, friend and foe alike, but you prevailed. What about that day you singlehandedly charged the German stronghold and caught the legate's eye, earning those decorations? What made you do it? Everyone was scared that day, afraid to die, but you charged like some crazed animal. Over the years, how many spears and arrows have you felt the whisper of their passing, death but a small distance away? How will you die here, centurion? A sword thrust, or perhaps a javelin thrown from close range? Will you see it coming or just find yourself lying on the ground with your life's blood pouring out of you?

Marcellus savagely kicked at the wet earth and raised a clog of mud for his efforts. No, he thought, there's still a chance. I'll not give up hope. The centurion spat, angry at himself for his defeatist thoughts. These Germans aren't that smart. If they had any sense, they would have continued to press the attack upon the fortifications that the legions now stood behind. I'm not finished yet, he thought grimly. If I perish, I will take more than a few German souls to the underworld with me. He'd not seen combat for some time now. He offered a tight smile in anticipation of tomorrow morning. He looked up from his musings to see the tribune stumbling toward him in the dark. He heard him mutter a curse as he tripped over something in the dark.

Valerius fumbled in the shadows, stepping over scattered supplies and other equipment. There wasn't a lot for him to do now. The officers and centurions of the line units would be busy planning the breakout in the morning. He had little in the way of responsibilities. His precious pay records would be left behind. How ironic, after all his work and slaving over the records, that they would be abandoned. As he thought about it more, he didn't give a shit. He looked ahead to where he'd last seen Marcellus before the officers' meeting.

"Over here, Tribune."

"Oh, there you are. Is that the best you could do for a fire? It's not exactly a beacon, you know." Valerius smirked.

"Best I could do with everything soaked by the rain. What's the good word, Tribune?"

"We lost a lot of men, about 2,500 dead and another 2,000 or so wounded."

"What about tomorrow, Tribune? I know we can't stay here."

Valerius repeated what had been spoken at the officers' meeting. "The army will continue on its present course. No other option. It's far too late to turn back."

Valerius was silent. He gathered his thoughts before asking his next question, hoping his trembling voice wouldn't reveal his fear. "Marcellus, what do you think of our situation?"

"I can't say for sure. I don't know the enemy's strength. If it were me out there, I would have continued attacking all day and into the night and not let us build a fortified camp. If the Germans reinforce their ranks with more men than they showed today, things could get nasty indeed. These forests and bogs aren't the terrain we can maneuver in against the enemy. This setting weighs heavily in their favor. As they say, we're *inter canis et lupus*."

Valerius looked at Marcellus quizzically. "Between a wolf and dog?"

"Exactly, Tribune. You know, between a rock and a hard place."

"Marcellus, I should have known. More Livy, correct?"

"Actually, it was a former centurion of mine."

Valerius laughed briefly, then became more somber. "What are our chances, Marcellus?"

The centurion paused in thought. "Don't know, Tribune. The legions have been in tighter spots before and won the day. The crux of the matter is that the legions had commanders like Drusus or Julius Caesar. Look who we have."

There was a silence between the two men. The watch fire crackled and hissed in the darkness.

"I'm a bit unnerved, if you know what I mean," said Valerius. As much as he tried, he could not stop his voice from quavering.

"We all are, Tribune. We all are. No shame in admitting that. Don't let any man tell you different. Every swinging dick in this army is scared. Tomorrow, you stick with me. Between the two of us, I think we can offer some discouragement to these Germans with our bows. It's about time the two of us unleashed a little Hades on the Germans. What do you say, Tribune?"

Valerius brightened at the thought and smiled back in the gloom. "Hey, I'm up for it."

Marcellus replied, "That's the spirit. By the way, Tribune, you have any more biscuits? I'm starved."

"As a matter of fact, I do. I knew you'd be famished, so I purloined an extra stash of these bricks that they call biscuits." Valerius reached into the satchel he was carrying around his neck and tossed several Marcellus's way.

"Bless your soul, Tribune. You know how to take care of your centurion."

The two men sat munching on the hard biscuits, staring morosely into the small campfire and wondering how tomorrow would end.

Arminius stood in the clearing with his hands folded across his chest. He attempted to compose himself and not exhibit the anxiety that had gripped him. Events had met his expectations today to a point. The surprise ambush had been a smashing success. They had inflicted significant casualties upon the Roman army. He should be exuberant, but the Germans had become overzealous and eager to exhibit their bravery against the legions. They had hurled themselves recklessly at the shield wall of the Romans, only to be thrown back with huge losses. Tonight, there would be many new widows among the German tribes.

As in past encounters with these Romans, the heavy infantry tactics, armor, and weaponry of the legions had carried the day. He frowned, disappointed his forces hadn't inflicted greater punishment on the legions. Despite the element of surprise and the Germans' huge numerical superiority, the Romans had survived the onslaught. He had to give the legions their just due. They had managed to endure. His loose coalition of German tribes was still in an excellent position, but they would have to alter their tactics slightly. The last thing Arminius needed was for some of the leaders of the clans to become discouraged and leave the field because of their losses.

In hindsight, he realized he should have ensured the ambush position at the front of the column was better fortified. He'd intended for a number of different tribes to be at the site where the trail entered the marsh, but somehow, the word hadn't gotten to the right people, or, most likely, his instructions were ignored. The Romans, once they had recovered from the initial assault, had punched through the ambuscade at the head of the column rather easily. Arminius seethed, knowing that some of his fellow Germans had wandered off to attack along the length of the Roman column rather than stay as a reserve force to fortify the front ambush position. He should have guessed that some of his newfound allies wouldn't listen to what he'd requested them to do. If they had, odds were that the Romans would be trapped on the trail at the site of the initial attack. But the damage was done, and there was nothing he could do about it now.

He surveyed the collection of chieftains assembled before him in the wooded glade. They were waiting for him to address them and tell them the plan for the next day. In the distance, he could make out the flickering watch fires from the Roman laager. They had the legions ensnared. The German tribes could achieve a great victory if they played it smart. He must exude confidence. He needed to convey to them that their victory was almost at hand. He boldly strode to the center of the gathering, holding up his arms for silence.

"Listen to me, great warriors. We enjoyed a tremendous triumph today, but we have much more to do. We killed many of their soldiers. There will be no escape for them. I know some of your clans suffered heavy losses. I grieve for your kinsmen, but in the end, it will be worth the price. Tomorrow, we'll let the Romans march out. When they enter the heavy forest again, we'll strike. We don't have to overwhelm them right away. We need to whittle their forces to a level where we can overpower them. You'll know when this time comes. We'll concentrate our forces to attack their command element. We know precisely where Varus will be located."

One of the minor leaders—which tribe the man was from Arminius did not remember—stood and addressed everyone.

"I lost many men today in the assault. I didn't think this would be an easy task, but my men were slaughtered by the Romans. They didn't break as we had expected, and they fought back ferociously. I can't afford many more dead and wounded. This is a steep price we're paying."

There was a murmur of approval from others.

Arminius quickly responded before others whined. "I'm saddened by your losses, but now is not the time to grieve. Did any of you think these Romans would give up?"

His remarks were greeted with silence.

"No, of course not. We can't afford headlong assaults against the Roman lines unless we're certain we can break them. We need to bleed them piece by piece, and then the moment will come when we can overrun them and kill them all. We have them surrounded. They can't flee. Victory may not be tomorrow, the next day, or the day after, but we will eventually have our way."

His remarks were greeted with silence, surely not a good sign. His mind raced. He needed to come up with the right words, and quickly.

The gathering of clan leaders suddenly parted, making way for new arrivals. Three individuals entered the clearing, beaming at Arminius. They were chieftains from the Frisii, Usipetes, and Batavi tribes. They had not previously committed their forces to the rebellion.

"Do you think you could use some more help to kill these Romans?" shouted one of the three.

Arminius was elated. This was just what he needed at just the right time. He walked over to the leading man and clasped the chieftain on the shoulder.

"Ah, Juthung, you've decided to join us. You know your assistance is always welcome. I was hoping you'd come over. In fact, I was counting on it. How many warriors did you bring?" he asked eagerly.

"The Frisii bring you four thousand."

"Another three thousand for the Usipetes," said another of the chiefs.

"The Batavi offer you four thousand warriors eager for Roman blood."

There was a roar of approval from the others. All were on their feet cheering. Arminius let the throng revel for a time, then held up his arms for silence and spoke.

"Your reinforcements are just what we needed, and at the right moment, too. With your help, we'll crush this army of Varus in this forest. He'll never escape. Come with me. I'll speak to you about what we must do in the morning."

With the addition of another eleven thousand warriors, they now enjoyed a vast numerical superiority, perhaps as much as four to one. There were now over forty thousand warriors pitted against the Romans—and who knows, maybe more were on the way.

XX

*B*efore there was a glimmer of daylight, the entire contingent of soldiers, support staff, servants, and other noncombatants was up and about within the laager. Grim determination was etched upon their faces. Legionnaires stared at the makeshift gate from which they would soon exit. The cavalry, acting as the advance guard for the entire army, and immediately behind them the first elements of the Seventeenth Legion, formed. These men would be the vanguard of the army—and most likely the first to be attacked and to die.

Men silently moved into their positions. A heavy, almost suffocating, mist hung low in the air. Everything was gray like smoke. Moisture beaded on the soldiers' shields, helmets, and body armor. The ground was saturated. The earthy smell of damp humus filled the air. Men appeared like apparitions through the early-morning vapor. Absent was the usual joking and grumbling, replaced by an air of urgency. The methodical and plodding way of the legion had been transposed to one of desperation. The men realized their actions over the next several hours would determine their ultimate fate.

The wagons and carts were bunched together to facilitate their burning in the center of the encampment, Varus had gone into a tirade about the baggage trains and their destruction. The general took it as a personal insult that his belongings were to be abandoned. His personal treasures were secretly buried in the dead of night by a few trustworthy staff. He'd ranted at length about the need to ensure that nothing—and he'd emphasized the word *nothing*—remained for the Germans to loot. The thought of the uncouth barbarians in possession of his personal property had driven him into a frenzy. The legion commanders didn't care. They were far more concerned with their own plight and the need to escape the German entrapment.

The mules and oxen had been freed of their tethers. They wouldn't be joining the marching legions and were to be abandoned. A tense silence pervaded. The lead centurion of the cavalry turned slightly in his saddle and signaled his men forward. He cursed himself as a bloody fool, realizing that few, if any, could possibly see his gesture. He circled back to his men and informed them in a hushed tone that it was time. The mounted legionnaires slowly departed through the gap in the earthworks into the ominous forest. They warily turned their heads from side to side, expecting a horde of German warriors to descend upon them at any moment, but nothing happened.

Lucius stood alone in his century's assembly area, apart from the other soldiers. He looked back through the impenetrable mist toward where he had last seen Julia. Lucius thought back to their final moments. They had embraced without saying much, then broke apart, their hands lingering in a soft touch. The two continued to stare at each other as they slowly backed away in opposite directions before both were engulfed in the mist.

Lucius rested his shield against his side while he nervously gripped the hilt of his sword, sheathed in its scabbard. His right hand wandered to his neck, absently checking the chin strap of his helmet for the umpteenth time that early morning. He again peered through the gloom to where he believed Julia would be. She would be with the rest of the civilians and servants, protected by the forward elements of the Nineteenth Legion. He guessed the distance to her would be no more than several hundred yards to his rear once the column had fully exited the encampment. The need for a tighter secure column had reduced the distance from Lucius's location to Julia. But it might as well be miles, for he couldn't provide her any protection. It wouldn't be long now before his century exited the safety of the night laager to venture forth into the forest once again. He turned about, then dutifully headed to his assigned spot.

Centurion Frontinus calmly stood in front of his men. In little more than a whisper, he spoke.

"Century, stand ready." He watched patiently as the unit in front of their century slowly filed past, toward the exit point of the night laager. When the last soldier of the preceding century was about even with the centurion, he calmly issued the command.

"Draw swords." The air was filled with the deadly rasping sound of cold steel being withdrawn from the scabbards. The men stood ready, swords in their right hands.

"Move out."

Lucius and his comrades silently cleared the perimeter walls and entered the danger zone. Like all of the other soldiers in the three legions, they wore their armor and helmets. Shields were in the left hand and gladii in the right. The other items they carried included their belted daggers, water skins, some rations, and assorted digging tools that hung from their belts. Personal objects and packs had been discarded. His century cleared the gate, then the surrounding meadow without incident. They ventured into the murky darkness of the foreboding woods. There was nothing but eerie stillness. Even the birds were silent on this early morning. All eyes were directed to the sides of the trail. This was where the attack would surely come.

The lead elements of the Roman column were now about a half mile ahead of Lucius's unit. The serpentine thread of soldiers treaded slowly in ghostly silence through the dense forest. Up and down the length of the forest trail, the legionnaires fervently hoped that perhaps the Germans had spent themselves yesterday and retired from the field. That sort of behavior had occurred in previous engagements with the barbarians. These people were as unpredictable as they were wild, notoriously undisciplined, and frequently feuding among themselves. Why not now?

Lucius and Cassius walked side by side, staring into the misty gloom for signs of the Germans. The ground oozed with moisture as their heavy sandals churned up the earth. Lucius's feet were already soaked and cold. Mud covered his marching boots and bare calves, but he paid the discomfort no mind. He had far greater concerns today than cold feet. They plodded steadily onward. Suddenly, the brush to the right some fifty paces away rustled, as if many men were crashing through it. The entire century froze in their tracks. All eyes in Lucius's unit turned toward the noise.

Shields formed quickly into position with a noticeable crack as each legionnaire's shield interlocked with the man next to him. The squared-off century presented an impenetrable wall of shields bristling with swords. The legionnaires strained to see through the swirling mists, gripping their swords even tighter. The units to their immediate front and rear readied themselves in a similar fashion for the imminent attack. Centurion Frontinus went to their front. "STEADY MEN. STAND READY."

Like the ripples of water from a stone hurled into a still pond, up and down the Roman column the centuries halted one after another, shifting their shields to the ready position. In anticipation of the attack that was sure to follow, Lucius dug his feet into the soggy ground to ensure he was firmly planted. He flexed his fingers to ensure a tight grip on his sword. But nothing happened. Where were they? Surely they must be visible by now.

A great snorting sound erupted from the heavy brush. A huge wild boar of enormous girth materialized out of the mist, bounding out into the clearing. Twin razor-sharp tusks that could gut a man or horse protruded from the giant head of the beast. Its tiny black eyes gleamed malevolently. The boar stopped, then stared at the soldiers. Grunting in derision at the armed legionnaires, it charged across the trail into the woods and out of sight. All was still again. The men snickered at the false danger. The soldiers lowered their shields, smiling in grim humor. Everyone heaved a huge sigh of relief; so far, so good. The legionnaires advanced down the trail.

Back at the laager, the rear elements of the legions departed, leaving behind the burning wagons. The vehicles and their contents were soaked with pitch to facilitate their destruction. They had been set ablaze as the final units departed. The badly wounded who weren't ambulatory remained in the laager to fend for themselves. Most wouldn't give a tiny copper *as* for their chance of survival. Some had already requested that their comrades finish them off before the Germans got to them. A quick sword thrust into the neck and down to the heart made the death relatively painless. While this practice was frowned upon by the legions, the commanding officers, given the alternatives for the wounded, looked the other way.

The Roman column advanced forward at a cautious pace, waiting for the attacks to commence once again. The mist dissipated slowly; the day began to brighten. Shafts of sunlight now penetrated the woods, providing some illumination amid the dimness of the primeval forest.

Abruptly, the attack began. Up and down the Roman column, wedges of men charged out of the forest, hurling javelins. The legionnaires braced themselves for the onslaught. They were hardly surprised, except perhaps by the overwhelming numbers that charged at their formed lines. Despite the readiness of the Roman formations, German missiles found their marks. Legionnaires went down in heaps with wounds to their unprotected heads and legs. With a mighty roar, the massed Germans hit the Roman lines. Many refused to embrace the hit-and-run tactics Arminius had preached to the chieftains the previous night. It wasn't in their nature, and they weren't about to change. They recklessly hurled themselves at the wall of shields and swords of the heavy Roman infantry. They attacked straight on in waves. Countless died upon the short stabbing swords of the Roman soldiers.

Lucius was on the outside rank. He could see the Germans off to the side of his unit marshaling their forces at the edge of the tree line. With a giant shout, the barbarians thundered into the column of soldiers. The legionnaires met the Germans with an impenetrable wall of shields. The number of attackers in his immediate area wasn't as concentrated as some other sectors. Nevertheless, the line buckled in places from the impact. Lucius stood firm. Men yelled and groaned in the fierce combat that swirled around him. Lucius stabbed with his sword in short thrusts. Suddenly, another wedge of perhaps twenty Germans charged toward Lucius's side of the century at an oblique angle. They hit the vulnerable flank of the legionnaires, who were engaged with the initial attackers.

Decius was on the inside ranks of the century. He'd neatly positioned himself so that his followers were on the outside ranks protecting him. He raged at his current predicament, cursing the stupidity of the legions for putting him in such grave danger. He had been looking forward to winter quarters, where he could visit the whores regularly. He would finally settle the score with this Lucius. Now here they were, fighting for their lives. His thoughts were interrupted when his right-hand man, Brutus, gurgled a strangled cry and pitched forward with a spear through his throat.

Decius attempted to withdraw back toward the center of the century and out of harm's way. The outside wall of legionnaires in front of him collapsed. Decius savagely cursed as one of his own men was knocked into him. His sword went flying from his grasp. He fell helpless on his back. He shifted his shield to cover as much of his torso as possible. He turned his head to the left seeking help from one of his fellow-legionnaires. About six paces away stood Lucius. Decius made eye contact with him., pleading for assistance.

Lucius saw Decius's plight. There was a German converging upon Decius. Lucius's duty was to protect the area to his immediate front, not the space to his left and right. This had been drilled into all of the legionnaires. The shield wall must not be breached to their front. Lucius considered rushing to rescue Decius, but realized this was not the correct course of action. He had made his decision. Lucius's features were devoid of pity. He broke eye contact with Decius and stared straight ahead. Perhaps if it was someone else, he might have acted differently.

A barbarian hovered over Decius, then kicked the shield aside. He savagely thrust downward. Decius screamed like a woman as a lance entered his groin. As he frantically struggled to free the offending spear, the German withdrew the lance, lifted it high, and plunged it through Decius's eye, silencing him permanently. The barbarian grinned at his handiwork, but he had little time to savor his personal victory. He was killed an instant later by an unseen legionnaire who stabbed him through his back, slicing open his kidney and severing his spine.

The rear rank of the century stepped up and handed out some punishment, slaying most of the Germans who had penetrated the front line. The breach was sealed. Lucius glanced to his left to see how Cassius was faring. He appeared to be holding his own, but there was blood trickling down the side of his face. Lucius could feel the air as a javelin whistled by his head. It struck a legionnaire in the second rank in the side of the neck. He went down, gurgling in his own blood.

The Germans withdrew with heavy losses from their initial assault, but then a second wave attacked the century.

Lucius battled a warrior to his immediate front. Both men thrust and parried with their swords. During an exchange of blows, Lucius's gladius went flying out of his hand. There was no way he could retrieve the weapon without exposing himself to sword and spear. He immediately drew his dagger and stabbed with it as he would his sword, then blocked blows with his shield. His opponent, a tall, gangly warrior, grinned triumphantly. He had this legionnaire as good as dead. The man lunged at Lucius several times, but the large Roman shield deflected his blows. Lucius managed to hold the assailant off with a series of forward thrusts of his shield and dagger. A legionnaire from the second rank saw his plight. He stepped forward and stabbed the surprised German. The man crumpled to the ground. Lucius nodded his thanks to his fellow legionnaire and quickly retrieved his gladius.

On some type of signal, most of the Germans assaulting Lucius's century retreated into the forest. Lucius heard the ever-vigilant centurion Frontinus shouting his commands. The man was a lion, fearless with a commanding presence.

"NO GAPS. FACE OUTWARD. SHIELDS UP."

Lucius turned his head in both directions, surveying the scene around him. He was dismayed to see their numbers had been whittled down even further. Combined with the losses of yesterday, he guessed the total strength of the century at less than forty men, below fifty percent. There were piles of bodies, especially to his right where the second wave had hit them.

"You all right, Cassius?"

Cassius replied without turning his head, keeping it focused to his immediate front. "Yeah, but my friggin' arms feel like lead. How about you?"

"I'm alive, but that was close. They almost broke us."

"Lucius, I must have stabbed six of the bastards."

Lucius turned toward Cassius. The apparition he saw was appalling. His entire arm holding his sword was bright crimson. Likewise, his shield, helmet, and legs were coated with thick blood. Lucius swallowed hard, returning his gaze to the forest. This was worse than yesterday, and it was still early.

"Don't feel bad, Cassius, but our good buddy got skewered but good." Lucius pointed with his sword at the bloody heap that was Decius.

"So he got his. You know, Lucius, we need every man, but we're better off without him. Worthless fuck."

Lucius turned to Cassius. "How's Domitius?"

Cassius glanced to his left. He peered intently but couldn't see much through the shields. He hailed his comrade. "Domitius, are you still with us?"

"Yeah, I'm here. They came close to getting me that time. You and Lucius are all right?"

"We are."

All three turned and grinned at one another, thankful for their good fortune.

Marcellus and Valerius plodded along the trail on foot. The path was now muddied by the passage of the Seventeenth and Eighteenth Legions. The two officers marched with the headquarters element of the legion.

"Marcellus, do you think they've retired from the field?"

"Not bloody likely, Tribune. They have us right where they want us. It's their element, not ours."

"But they haven't attacked yet."

"No, but they will. They want us back in the heavy timber and away from the camp, where we could take refuge. They'll have more cover, and we'll have more difficulty maintaining our formations."

"I haven't seen a one of them since we departed the perimeter."

"No, I haven't either, but they're out there. I can sense them."

Valerius peered into the forest once again but could see nothing.

"Are you sure, Marcellus? Are they really out there?"

"Trust me on this, Tribune. They're watching us as we speak. I wish I were wrong on this, but the bloody barbarians are out there lurking."

Both men carried their swords in their right hands and shields on their left. Their satchels for their bows were strapped to their backs, along with bulging quivers of arrows. They hurried along once more in silence. The pair had advanced another two hundred yards when the first sounds of battle reached them. Centurions up and down the Roman column shouted for the men to stand ready. A heavy concentration of forces hit the headquarters element. The German strategy was simple: cut the head off the snake, and the rest of the body will die.

Waves of Germans attacked out of the forest, intent on breaching the Roman column and destroying the higher command. Marcellus and Valerius stood sword in hand, waiting for the attack to commence in their sector. There were legionnaires on all sides of them, shields up and swords ready. The first wave emerged from the forest and charged. The two forces collided with a tremendous crash. The initial attack was met and repulsed.

A second surge of Germans recklessly attacked. It was equally ineffectual against the Roman formation. The enemy appeared to bounce off the wall of shields, then crumble in piles of bodies. The legionnaires thrust relentlessly with their swords into German flesh. More of the enemy, roaring fierce battle cries, emerged out of the forest. Another wave came forward, then another. The area was a swirling mass of humanity as the two forces hurled themselves at each other in savage combat.

The units closest to Marcellus and Valerius held firm against the onslaught. A bit farther to their rear, where General Varus and his staff were located, perhaps fifty yards, the Germans mounted a massive thrust and broke through the ranks onto the ground held by the senior officers and their bodyguards.

Marcellus turned and shouted to the centurion in charge of the reserve force. "We need to bring your century over there. They're overrunning the command staff." He pointed his sword at the German concentration of forces.

Without waiting for a reply, Marcellus and Valerius turned and dashed to the defense of the headquarters. The centurion in command of the reserve force understood immediately what was expected of him. Waving his sword, the centurion rushed forward, leading his men in pursuit of Marcellus and Valerius.

The two men, trailed by the massed century, ran up through the swirling host of combatants. The Roman reinforcements struck hard, killing a slew of Germans. They surged toward the center of the fracas. Tribune Calvus went down with a spear to his torso. In quick order, the deputy commander, General Caecina, was slain with a sword to the throat and the staff adjutant with a sword thrust to the chest. The Roman reinforcements led by Marcellus and Valerius ran onward, killing more Germans. The influx of legionnaires slowly forced the Germans to break off their attack on the command element. They made the enemy pay a steep price for their attack. The penetration of the headquarters had been stopped, but the damage had been done. Many of the headquarters senior staff had been wounded or killed. General Varus was on the ground. He attempted to support himself on one elbow before collapsing once more. Blood cascaded over his breastplate and down his arm.

One of Varus's aides bent over his prone form. "Get the physicians over here right away. It's General Varus. He needs urgent attention."

Two corpsmen who were tending to a wounded soldier a short distance away abandoned him. They quickly came running with their medical bags to attend to the wounded general. The ranks of the legionnaires formed a solid wall around the huddled figures. As Valerius rushed past the fallen general, he noted a gaping wound just under the breastplate of Varus. Blood stained the ground and armor of the commander. The man grimaced in pain and gasped for air.

At the head of the Roman column, perhaps a mile ahead of the head-quarters element, Vala Numinius, commander of the cavalry, sat astride his mount, cursing the scene before him. He and the several hundred horsemen under his command had been forced to halt their advance. A heap of fallen trees and a large force of German warriors blocked their path. Numinius saw an incredible concentration of men ahead. There was no way he could advance up the trail, yet his men couldn't stay stationary. They were easy targets for the Germans with their javelins. A number of his men had already succumbed to the German missiles. He noted their bodies lying in contorted positions with lances protruding from their flesh. Numinius ordered the men to move off the trail. He waved his sword over his head, pointing in the direction he wanted his men to go.

"Decurion Sabinus, have the men direct their mounts this way. Do it quickly. We can't stay here, or we'll be cut to pieces."

The decurion waved in acknowledgement to his commander. He prodded his horse forward to relay the orders.

The decision to go around the obstacles was a fatal mistake, one that the Germans had anticipated. Once off the trail, the men and horses had precious little room to maneuver through the dense trees and thickets. The mounted legionnaires slowed their horses in an at-tempt to maneuver through the maze. They were attacked by hordes of men on foot. Some Germans leaped from trees on the unsuspecting riders. They wrestled the Romans from their saddles and easily dispatched them with daggers and swords.

Numinius, appalled at the slaughter of his men, urged his horse to a gallop through a gap in the trees. He turned to look to his right at an approaching foe but failed to see a stout tree limb at the level of his head. He was knocked from his saddle and landed hard. The blow caused his helmet to slam forward, breaking his nose. Blood poured from his shattered face. Amid incredible pain, he groggily stood and attempted to lift his helmet from his head. As he did, he faced his executioners. Several Germans rushed forward and stabbed him with their spears. He screamed as the iron spearheads slammed into his torso. Numinius died withering on the end of several lances. His entire cavalry was wiped out shortly after entering the forest.

Julia huddled with the other civilians and noncombatants. She held her small dagger in her right hand. It would be of little use against these warriors, but it gave her some comfort to hold it in front of her. Julia and her group of stable hands were protected by the centuries of the Nineteenth Legion. She watched in horror as the attack began. Like everyone else, her hopes plummeted as she realized the Germans hadn't gone away. She saw several of the animal handlers, people she'd worked with so closely over the summer, fall as they were struck by a hail of missiles.

The assaulting forces against the civilians were smaller in number. The Roman troops protecting her held off the foe, at least temporarily. Julia glanced to the front of her and saw a huge number of warriors streaming out of the forest. Their attack was focused on the command elements of the legion. More men charged out of their hidden positions to engulf the Roman lines. The Germans were in among the staff officers, stabbing with their spears and creating havoc almost immediately. Now she understood why they weren't threatened. They were unimportant. In the end, they would all be killed, but for now, the energies of the Germans were focused on the officers of the legions.

Julia instinctively withdrew from the fighting. There was a sound like a rotten fruit being dropped. A man she knew from her father's staff was pierced in the neck with a thrown spear. She was splattered with his blood. She knelt to comfort him, but he died quickly. Julia turned in a panic. She realized there was nowhere to go. She was trapped with the others. She felt hopeless. There was no way any of them would ever get out of this nightmare of a forest.

The century began to edge slowly forward on the trail. Lucius experienced the satisfying thump and the shock running down his left arm from the object that struck his shield. He swiveled his head back and forth, searching for possible danger. There were shouts as another wave of attackers charged at Lucius and his century.

"Here they come again," roared Frontinus.

The legionnaires answered with a roar as the two sides clashed. Men grunted and screamed as they battled one another in the deadly game of individual combat. Lucius thrust his shield at a man of unusual girth. His shield bounced off the man as if he were a tree trunk. Using his gladius more like an ax, Lucius chopped swiftly downward on the man's right arm, opening a huge gash that sent him retreating to the safety of the forest. Another foe jumped into the fray to challenge Lucius. He was young, probably not more than sixteen; his beard wasn't fully grown. He jabbed ineffectively with his spear several times. Realizing he was clearly overmatched against Lucius, he fled. As quickly as the attack had come, it dissipated. The men melted back into the forest, but not before doing more damage. More legionnaires from his century were down.

Valerius and Marcellus stood among the remnants of the headquarters staff. Many of the tribunes and staff officers were lying dead. Their wounds were gruesome; some were missing their heads. Several physicians hunched over the prostrate form of Varus. The tactical situation had been stabilized for the moment. The ranks had reestablished a cordon around the command staff. The Germans had withdrawn, at least temporarily, to the protection of the forest. The legionnaires could see the Germans circling among the trees. Occasionally, some would leap out and throw their lances.

Marcellus turned to Valerius. "I for one have had enough of their insolence. I think it's time we provided some discouragement to these sniping Germans. What do you say we string these bows and send them a message?"

"Let's do it, Centurion."

Both men calmly prepared their bows and made ready. Marcellus pointed to a clump of men off to their right about fifty yards distant. The Germans believed they were safe, knowing that the legions had expended their supply of javelins the previous day. They shouted taunts at the legionnaires, knowing the Romans wouldn't break ranks and charge out from the trail. The Germans were barely concealed behind some bushes.

"I say we rapid-fire a volley of three arrows each into that mass of men, just like on the archery range. Ready, tribune?"

"Say when."

Valerius pulled the string back to his right ear and aimed toward the center of the men.

"Now."

Valerius released the bowstring slightly before Marcellus. The projectile flew with enormous velocity. The feathered shaft streaked in a blur toward the bunched-up Germans. His first shot was slightly off target. It struck a German along the side of his face, etching a bloody groove that took the man's ear off. The man screamed, holding his face. Marcellus's arrow was true and struck the man square in the chest, sending him crashing down to the forest floor.

Without even looking at his shot, Valerius notched and fired at the same target area. He then fired a third. Both struck home. The Germans in the low brush ran in panic from the devastating barrage, leaving four men pierced with the feathered shafts in their wake. Marcellus and Valerius surveyed their damage with satisfied grins.

The two men directed their attention to another target area forward of their position so that they were firing at an oblique angle.

Their new marks were a greater distance away, but that mattered little given the power of the bows. They unleashed a stream of arrows in that direction, with similar results. More men went down, writhing with the feathered shafts deeply embedded in their flesh. The air assault forced the Germans to retreat deeper into the forest. Several of the enemy yelled, pointing at Marcellus and Valerius. A few attempted to retaliate and threw their javelins at the two archers, but they fell short of their mark.

A lone German boldly ran forward, heaving his javelin. It fell just short at Valerius's feet. The tribune looked down at the offending spear, then in reprisal calmly notched an arrow and sent it streaking toward the warrior who had thrown his spear. The feathered shaft struck him squarely in the torso. The force of the arrow smashed him to the forest floor. Another man crept forward, holding his cowhide shield in front of him and a javelin in the other hand.

"This one is mine," shouted Marcellus.

He smoothly retrieved an arrow from his quiver and sent it flashing toward the approaching German. The arrow penetrated the man's shield, pinning it solidly to him. He collapsed to the ground, groaning. The remaining Germans in the vicinity scattered and melted back into the forest, seeking cover.

Marcellus and Valerius hurried to the opposite side of the trail. It was time the enemy in this vicinity experienced some of their thunder. The enemy on this flank was unaware of the carnage brought upon their brethren opposite them. Both men effortlessly drew their bows back and let their arrows fly. Their volleys were devastating. More were struck down. The others looked about wildly for the cause of this unexpected assault. The Germans screamed, then retreated deeper into the forest. The ranks of legionnaires in the vicinity cheered the small victory. Marcellus clapped his hand on Valerius's shoulder.

"Tribune, I do believe you're getting good with that bow."

Valerius grinned back at the centurion. "I had a good teacher."

General Licinus, who was now with the command element, walked over to them, followed by several of his aides.

"By Jove, that was an amazing demonstration of archery. If I had another five hundred men like you, we wouldn't be in this mess. Those bows are awesome weapons. My thanks to both of you. I don't believe I know either of you, although, Centurion, you look familiar."

Valerius, the senior of the two men, responded to Licinus, as protocol demanded.

"Sir, I'm Tribune Valerius Maximus, somewhat new to the legions. The man next to me is Centurion Marcellus Veronus. He has been with the Army of Rhine for a good number of years. He's also the man who instructed me in the use of this weapon. We're both assigned to headquarters in charge of the payroll. We both thank you for the complement."

Licinus had a brief flash of recognition across his face. "Tribune, you're the one who went out with Centurion Clodius and saved the cohort in the ambush. So it appears your reputation is deserved. I don't understand why two men such as you are stuck with the payroll. What in the Hades is this army coming to?" Licinus pondered his comment and then nodded to them both. "My thanks again for putting those Germans in their place. Keep at it. That'll put some fear into their bellies."

A messenger ran up to Licinus. "Sir, your presence is needed ahead with Centurion Palus."

The general smiled at both, then walked away.

XXI

*I*t was near twilight. Surveying the forbidding picture around him, Valerius stood alone near the center of the encampment. He slowly scanned the laager, noting the hastily formed earthworks that encircled and protected the remnants of the three legions. Weary legionnaires were draped over the earthen battlements or simply lay at the base of the wet earth, too tired to find any drier ground. To his right, he could hear the moans of the wounded coming from the hospital area. There were no tents, pack animals, wagons, or any other manifestation of the Roman army that had departed but a few days ago. Improvised torches cast eerie shadows on the mud-spattered faces of the legionnaires. Their expressions reflected grim despair. Most were thankful that they were still alive, but for how much longer?

Earlier that afternoon, General Licinus made the decision to form a defensive perimeter. There was no other alternative. They were trapped and couldn't move in any direction. The Germans were content to let this happen. The noose was tightening. Even more Germans had joined in the rebellion. The numbers of the men in the legions dwindled.

Totally exhausted from the day's battle, Valerius leaned wearily against a tree. So this was what it had come down to. He cursed Varus for bringing the Roman army to its current state. If the man had listened to what others had attempted to tell him, he and everyone else would be close to Vetera by now. The fool. The pigheaded, arrogant fool. How could Augustus have appointed such an arrogant twit? What a piss-poor excuse for a Roman legate.

The cold reality that he would never see Rome again, hold Calpurnia in his arms, or return home to his parents hung over him. Valerius kicked the wet earth in disgust, then rose. He'd been informed a short while ago that his presence was requested. A meeting was planned to discuss alternative strategies for the next day. He wearily picked up his sword, buckled it in place, and hastened up the slight rise that marked the location of the senior staff.

He mingled within a loose semicircle of the other surviving officer corps. Looking about, he realized how serious the losses were among the centurions, tribunes, and senior officers. The usual complement of staff who attended officers' call had shrunk by at least half, if not more. Some of those present bore blood-soaked bandages. General Licinus, the most experienced field commander, had taken control for the incapacitated Varus, and he stood before them in the flickering torchlight, his dark eyes burning with intensity.

He nodded to one of the headquarters staff tribunes who had assumed the duties for the unfortunate adjutant, slain earlier in the day. "Please report the army's status."

The nervous tribune stepped forward and cleared his throat. He began reading from a piece of parchment, reciting the numbers in a loud, clear voice.

"Overall strength of the three legions is below fifty percent. Casualties among the centurions of the line are between sixty percent and seventy percent. Seven of the ten cohorts from the Nineteenth Legion no longer exist. The survivors of these units are now combined to form a single cohort. Four cohorts of the Seventeenth Legion and three from the Eighteenth are no longer combat effective. Our cavalry and all of their officers are believed dead."

The tribune reporting the numbers began to trail off, choking on his words.

"Please continue your report, Tribune," commanded Licinus.

The officer looked from the scroll, then back down again before continuing. "Many of the senior headquarters staff are dead, including General Caecina and Tribune Calvus. General Varus is badly wounded. In short, the remaining ranks of the army are marginally effective as a fighting force."

There was silence among the assembled officers. One could hear the torches crackle and fizzle in the stillness of the night. Licinus stared at the officers for a moment before speaking.

"It's not a pretty situation, is it, gentlemen?" He paused and looked at each of the men present as if measuring them.

"We have several options open to us. First, we can stay here and reinforce the defensive perimeter. Unfortunately, assuming we can hold off the Germans from breaking through our defenses—and that's a big if, given our losses—we would soon run out of food and water. Furthermore, there are no relief forces to aid us. No one knows our whereabouts, and if they did, I'm not sure they would arrive here in time or in one piece. There are a lot of Germans out there.

"Second, we could surrender to the Germans. They would like nothing better so they could sacrifice us like animals before their bloody shrines. Frankly, neither of those first two options is appealing to me—or, I would guess, to any of you."

There was some nervous laughter among the assembled men. Licinus continued.

"So this is what we're going to do. Before first light, we're going to depart here as a compact fighting force heading rapidly southwest. My intent is to punch through the German lines before they know what hit them using tactical surprise under the cover of darkness. Once through their lines, we'll advance with all possible speed in the direction of Alisio. We must get out of this forest and onto the plain as rapidly as possible. I mean we will be running. Questions, anyone?"

A centurion from the Seventeenth Legion stepped forward. "Sir, what about the wounded?"

Licinus responded without hesitation. "If the wounded can keep up with the main body, they can join us. If not, they're on their own."

The officers looked at one another in grim realization of the probable outcome for those unfortunates.

Licinus continued. "I want you to go back to your units and consolidate forces. I want a column of six men for each century. We're going to shorten our formation and be linked closely with each other. Understood?"

The officers replied in unison. "Yes, sir."

"Good. I'll have orders dispatched to you as to the order of march. You're all dismissed. Let's make ready."

Valerius wandered back toward his previous location, looking for Marcellus. He wasn't around anywhere that he could see. He slumped wearily against the base of a birch tree. A small fire cast a feeble glow. He stared into the night. Torches burned on the improvised palisade. He could hear distant guttural shouts from the Germans beyond the perimeter. Valerius couldn't comprehend what they were saying, but he could certainly guess.

The tribune tilted his head back against the rough bark of the tree and closed his eyes. He analyzed their tactical situation. He couldn't understand why the Germans didn't press their advantage and attack the Roman encampment. The makeshift walls and ditches that protected the remnants of the three legions were hardly insurmountable. The defenses had been hastily prepared in desperation and were certainly not up to their normal standard palisade that characterized a legion's marching camp. Yes, if he were the Germans, he would make an all-out push and attack while the army was on its heels.

His thoughts turned black once again. Tomorrow would most likely be the end. He thought briefly of Calpurnia. How would she react to the news of his demise? His parents wouldn't even have a body for a proper funeral. His corpse would be rotting here in the German forest, subject to the pickings of the animal scavengers. He flashed back to the German priestess with her long dagger, remembering the chilling words of the interpreter about how these women sacrificed their human captives. They will not catch me alive, he thought.

He pictured himself falling on his sword. Would it be painful? How would it feel to have the cold steel slicing through his entrails? He shuddered involuntarily.

Marcellus ventured into the flickering light.

"By the gods, you look glum."

"They're not taking me alive," Valerius blurted.

Marcellus frowned. "Best put a stop to those kind of thoughts, Tribune. We're not dead yet. Besides, I have every intention of surviving this debacle so I can tell my grandchildren."

"Marcellus, you don't even have any children."

"Exactly, Tribune."

Valerius laughed at the idea of it. "It's a pleasant thought, anyway."

"Tribune, be prepared. Tomorrow we'll fight our way out of this mess. If the gods decide otherwise—and I don't see how they could— then I'll take as many of these German barbarians to the underworld with me as I possibly can. But listen to me, Tribune. By Jupiter's holy ass, I'll find a way to survive this mess."

Valerius chuckled. "Jupiter's holy ass? Isn't that blasphemy?"

Marcellus grinned back. "Tribune, maybe to some. But the gods and I have an understanding of sorts about these things. I'm still here after all of these years, aren't I?"

"True, you're still here."

"There you have it, Tribune."

Valerius stared back at the centurion, his morale somewhat boosted. He would be with the centurion the next day. If he perished, it would be alongside Marcellus with a sword in his hand.

"You stick with me tomorrow, Tribune. We'll protect each other's back."

"I can't say I'm looking forward to it, but yes, I promise to be right by your side."

Lucius and Julia huddled at the base of the earth wall. Cassius and Domitius sat nearby.

"Julia, tomorrow, if things start to fall apart, look for Cassius, Domitius, and me. We'll come and get you."

"Lucius, how will you be able to leave your unit? I know the ways of the legions. That's not possible."

"Listen to me. We'll not be far from you, probably less than a hundred yards. The word is that the column will be shortened. Frontinus told us not too long ago. Look for us if things are going badly."

"Lucius, I'm scared."

"You think I'm not? But I vow I'll not let my life nor yours end in this forest. Julia, look for us to come to you. Until then, stay with the headquarters. They'll have the best and strongest units protecting you."

Lucius didn't add that the Germans would probably concentrate their attack there. No need to worry Julia further. The two of them huddled together to get what rest they could. They would be moving out in the middle of the night.

Arminius sat in front of a small fire along with other chiefs. The men were in a small clearing surrounded by towering trees, plotting their strategy for the next day, assigning sectors for the various tribes along the expected route of the Romans. He was pleased with the progress of the battle. They had weakened the Romans even more this past day. His confederation of tribes had lost more men than he would have liked, but it was worth the price. Better yet, he had not heard any of the chiefs complain about their losses.

The legions were hopelessly trapped in the forest. He had them pinned down. Even the most skeptical and undecided of the tribes were now committed. Hordes of additional men were funneling into the German encampment. They grew stronger by the hour and the Romans weaker. Perhaps tomorrow he'd finish them off. Up ahead, the trail funneled to a spot where there was a low-lying swamp on one side and a hill on the other. They would never get through that bottleneck. His warriors had constructed ambuscades above the trail on the sloping ground, ensuring the Romans' destruction. It would end there.

A large body of warriors was now on its way toward the fortress of Alisio, the only Roman stronghold of any size on this side of the

Rhine. The Germans enjoyed such a large numerical superiority here that Arminius could afford the luxury of diverting some of his army toward the Roman outposts.

They would be truly free of these would-be conquerors. He had toyed briefly with the idea of attacking the forts along the Rhine, which included the large bases of Vetera and Moguntiacum, but he discarded that plan. Those fortresses were too large and heavily defended. His warriors would be at a significant disadvantage attacking them. They would be far from their home bases. It would be a logistical nightmare to feed the coalition of tribes he called an army. Furthermore, he had no siege equipment. No, he wouldn't proceed to the Rhine. Besides, he'd accomplished his objective of destroying the legions and anything Roman east of the Rhine. He smiled in anticipation of tomorrow. He would have their precious eagles in his possession. It would be a glorious day for Germania, not soon forgotten.

It was dark, almost black. Faint slivers of moonlight managed to peek through the heavy cloud cover—perfect conditions for what General Licinus had planned. Lucius was running with his fellow soldiers. His breath came in gulps. He stumbled several times in the darkness on exposed roots and rocks but ignored the pain and kept on moving. The units had raced out of the laager.

The quick exit of the Romans achieved tactical surprise, spawning confusion among the German ranks. They hadn't believed the legions would attempt a breakout at night. Lucius could hear the shouts of alarm from the Germans throughout the forest as they attempted to intercept the fleeing Romans. If the goddess Fortuna smiled on them, they might possibly escape, surviving to fight another day. The question was how far she would take them before the Germans organized and attacked.

The tramp of their heavy footsteps on the earthen floor of the forest and the jingling of their chain mail echoed along the trail. The desperate men gulped for air, racing in the darkness. Lucius swung his shield forward in his left hand and his sword in the right, pumping his arms in rhythm with the other legionnaires of his century. He was tired. He guessed they had progressed some distance from the laager but wasn't sure how far. It was all a blur. He noticed the pace was slowing as fatigue began to set in. Perhaps more concerning was the light of dawn, now beginning to permeate the forest floor.

Lucius heard with dismay the now-familiar cries. The attacks had begun again. The shouts and the clamor of swords striking shields echoed throughout the forest. Their speed slowed even more, almost to a stop. Lucius peered ahead over his shield toward both sides of the trail. To his left, he saw that walls had been constructed along the side of the trail. Javelins flew out from behind the wall, striking the Roman column. Suddenly, great masses of warriors materialized. A multitude of German warriors charged out of the barricades, pressing the tightly massed units of the legions. The front ranks met the first charge head-on and held. Piles of dead Germans formed. The enemy wildly hurled themselves at the wall of Roman shields and swords. A second wave, then a third, struck Lucius's beleaguered century. Lucius stepped forward into the breach as the legionnaire in front of him went down, stabbed simultaneously by two Germans.

More Germans swarmed upon the outnumbered legionnaires. The area was a surging mass of men locked in mortal combat. Off to his right side, Centurion Frontinus was overrun and slain. The attacking German wedges split Lucius's besieged century into three pieces. Lucius and Cassius, plus a small number of other men, found themselves toward the rear of the splintered formation. They shifted to the left instinctively to have their backs protected by several large oak trees, forming a tight circle to ward off the attacks. Through a gap in the mass of men, Lucius saw Domitius lying on the ground unmoving, covered in blood. Another friend was gone.

Unheard by most above the clamor of arms and screams of the wounded and dying was the ominous rumble of rolling thunder. More men fell as the Germans swarmed over the positions. The lines were breached everywhere. Lucius's century ceased to exist. It was every man for himself. Lucius and Cassius were side by side, now separated from the other survivors. Somehow they were also free of any attackers. Lucius knew that the time had arrived if he was going to make a break for Julia.

"Cassius," he screamed above the din, "let's go."

"I'm ready. What about Domitius?"

"He's gone. Start running."

The two men bolted back toward the rear, where the lead elements of the Nineteenth Legion were located. They ran through gaps in the struggling men. Two Germans obstructed their path. Lucius and Cassius lowered their shields, then charged. The two Germans were bowled over, flying ass over heels. The two legionnaires dodged blows, evading several more foes. They heedlessly surged ahead through the maelstrom. Lucius dashed through a bush, ignoring the tearing thorns. A large German noticed them fleeing down the trail. He sent a spear whistling at the retreating figures, barely missing Lucius.

Lucius leaped over a pile of tangled bodies, then dodged to his left around a mass of men grappling with one another in the throes of combat. He charged straight ahead through a narrow gap in the melee. He hurdled two men rolling on the ground, hurrying ever closer to Julia, hoping he wasn't too late.

Miraculously, a space opened up before Cassius and Lucius that offered them an unobstructed path toward Julia's location ahead. But just as quickly, the breach closed. A large bearded man leaped out at Lucius. With a mighty cry, he aimed a thrust with a long sword. Lucius nimbly sidestepped the jab and ran on. The man howled in fury, pursuing him. Lucius heard the man's guttural curses behind him. Another German stepped into their path. Cassius rammed his shield into the man's face, sending him to the ground senseless. The two continued running in tandem around and through the German forces as their shields served as battering rams.

Lucius tripped over a heap of discarded equipment and landed in a waterlogged depression. Lying flat on his belly, Lucius struggled to rise, but he could get no traction in the mud. He glanced over his left shoulder. The large bearded German was closing on him. Lucius desperately dug his caliga into the earth, but his feet slipped out again.

The German shouted a cry of triumph, raising his sword to finish him. Lucius rolled over on his back, lifting his shield in defense.

Before the man could strike, Cassius rushed over and stabbed him through the midsection. The man screamed in a pitched voice, then fell across Lucius, pinning him to the earth. Cassius leaned over and savagely heaved the man off Lucius. Cassius extended his hand, then pulled him erect.

The two sprinted forward. Ahead, he could see the group of civilians and noncombatants. That had to be the support staff, where Julia would be. They were almost there, perhaps fifty paces away. Lucius's glance forward almost cost him his life. An enemy warrior emerged from his right, lunging at him with a sword. Lucius took a direct hit to the torso. Fortunately, it deflected off his chain mail. He felt as if he'd been hit with a club. He grimaced in pain, slowing almost to a halt, doubled over. Lucius glanced down quickly to see if the sword cut had breached his armor. He noted with some relief that there was no blood.

Cassius raced on, unaware of Lucius's plight. The German charged again at Lucius, screaming at the top of his lungs, then directed his sword downward in a mighty arc for the finishing stroke. Lucius raised his shield. The blow thumped harmlessly against it. With a grunt, Lucius put all his force behind a thrust, savagely stabbing the man through his chest. His gladius penetrated to the spine. The man collapsed and withered on the ground. Lucius shakily struggled to his feet, holding his side as he limped onward. Cassius had stopped some distance ahead and was about to return to aid Lucius. When he saw that Lucius had taken care of business, he waited for him.

Lucius ran hard to catch Cassius. He was gasping for air, his legs wobbly. United again, the pair rushed forward. The two burst into the perimeter of the legate's staff. They passed through the command elements of the headquarters. Nobody questioned what Lucius and Cassius were doing in that area. Everyone was too preoccupied with his own problems. The cordon around the civilians was holding. Lucius and Cassius found Julia almost immediately. She saw them and came running over.

"Sweet Minerva, you made it."

"I told you we would."

They grabbed her by the arms and headed toward some sheltering trees. As they did, they witnessed stronger attacks on the lead elements of the Nineteenth Legion. The mighty First Cohort of the legion crumbled. Large numbers of German warriors were caving in the ranks. Things were rapidly going to Hades. More of the enemy, with blood lust in their eyes, rushed out of the forest. The Roman lines collapsed as the masses of Germans overran them. The three looked about in confusion, unsure of what course of action to take.

Valerius and Marcellus were standing near the command element, swords in hand. So far, they hadn't had any significant penetrations of the lines. Just then, masses of warriors swarmed from behind the ambuscades. The lines buckled in several places. The two found themselves about twenty yards from the location of Varus. Even from a distance, he looked ghastly. The general, with great effort, rose to a standing position and then drew his sword. The legate pointed the blade at his midsection, then fell on it. The point jutted out his back. Varus screamed, blood streaming from his mouth. He twitched and lay still. His staff looked confused and shaken. Germans swarmed into the area, finding easy pickings. The warriors were shouting with great lust as they speared the panicked staff of the headquarters.

While the battle swirled around them, Marcellus and Valerius found themselves in a dense thicket with several other legionnaires. They were surrounded by a number of Germans. The clang of metal against metal and the grunts of the combatants sounded above the pounding rain. Suddenly, to their left side, the ranks of the Germans collapsed. Two legionnaires materialized out of the rain, stabbing the unsuspecting enemy. Valerius looked up in astonishment.

"Lucius, Cassius, Julia; what are you doing here?"

"We figured you could use the reinforcements. Right, Cassius?"

"What of your century?"

"We're all that's remaining."

Valerius grimaced at the news.

The Germans regrouped from their sudden loss and charged again at the small group. The legionnaires beat the Germans back temporarily, then the heavens opened. Rain came down in torrents. It blinded everyone, it was so thick. Everything just stopped as the huge drops pounded down amid peals of thunder.

Marcellus couldn't see much through the driving sheets of water, but he instinctively knew all was lost with the army. It was hopeless. One didn't have to be an experienced centurion to recognize this. He also recognized that if they were going to get out, now was the time. If he were in command of a unit of soldiers, he would stay, but he was not. His small staff of clerks had been wiped out the previous day when the Germans overran the headquarters. But above all, the centurion understood that the legions on the Rhine must be warned of this disaster lest they suffer a similar fate. Someone needed to get through the Germans and alert the Roman forces. The rain was their ally. It was just possible that with the limited visibility and the confusion spawned by the storm, they might slip out. It had to be now.

Their force consisted of one tribune, one centurion, five legionnaires, and one young woman. It would have to do. He made the decision to flee. He knew the tribune wouldn't mind if he temporarily usurped command of the small group. Protocol be damned; their survival was at stake. This was their opportunity. They had to act quickly.

Marcellus waved his sword, yelling for them to follow him through a gap in the trees. They didn't hesitate. The group charged blindly through the forest, Marcellus leading them. The tribune brought up the rear. He gripped his sword tightly, holding it in front of him, ready to thrust it into the midsection of the first German he encountered. Surprisingly, there was no one there. Marcellus hesitated briefly, waiting for the others to catch up to him lest they be separated.

Not quite believing the absence of any foe, he pointed with his sword to the right. "This way," he shouted above the din of the pounding rain.

They dashed into the thick woods.

Lucius discarded his waterlogged shield, which was now useless, then grabbed Julia's hand. They charged through the heavy brush. He'd never run so hard in his life. Julia was keeping right up with him. Their survival depended upon putting distance between themselves and the battlefield. They rushed through the thick vegetation in the driving rain, heedless of thorns and other brush. A branch savagely lashed Lucius in the face. He did not flinch. They came to an area where the ground sloped down and away. The two, hand in hand, soared through the air and landed halfway down the slope. The pair stumbled but maintained their balance. Their lungs ached from the strain as they ran for their lives.

The heavy downpour limited visibility and masked the sounds of their passage. They thundered through the brush and around the trees, ever deeper into the forest. They continued fleeing, almost at a full sprint.

Marcellus held up his hand, signaling for them to halt. They gathered in a small circle and knelt behind a huge evergreen. Everyone was bent over at the waist, desperately sucking in air. The centurion looked warily about. Valerius quickly ran up beside Marcellus. In a hushed tone, Marcellus pointed to their front.

"There's a wide trail about twenty yards ahead. My guess is that they might have men watching this area. At least that's what I'd do if I were them."

Valerius scanned the area. "I can't see a thing. Do you think they're there?"

"These men are hunters. You'll not see them. They've spent their entire lives tracking game. Now we're their prey. I suggest we cross this trail as quickly as possible. I see no other choice. We can't stay here or look for a way around this thing. There's no time."

Valerius nodded and replied, "Let me explain the situation to the others."

"Do it quickly, Tribune. I do not like our position here. We need to get out of here."

Valerius signaled for the others to come up and join him. Lucius, Cassius, Julia, and the three other legionnaires huddled around him in a dense thicket. He spoke in a hushed tone. "There's a trail immediately to our front." He pointed in that direction. "The centurion believes there is a good chance it's being watched. Be ready to sprint across it. Understood?"

They all nodded in agreement. Marcellus looked back to make sure everyone was ready. All eyes were on him. He turned forward and began running at full speed. The others followed him, one after another. Shouts of alarm echoed from the woods. Once again, they were sprinting for their lives.

Lucius grabbed Julia's hand and dashed ahead. He could hear sounds of pursuit above the drumming of the rain. He dared not look back, for that would slow them down. There were more guttural cries, then crashing noises of large men moving through the brush. Another band of warriors, alerted by the cries of those in pursuit, materialized to their left. Marcellus veered to their right, away from the threat, charging onward. A third group of the enemy came out of nowhere to their immediate front, effectively sealing the Romans in, ending any hope of escape. It was time to fight.

"Swords," yelled Marcellus.

Lucius felt awkward without his shield. In its place, he drew his dagger and held that in his left hand. He'd never fought like this before, so he'd better be a quick learner. A youthful German warrior charged at him. Lucius could tell right away that the man had never experienced hand-to-hand fighting. His eyes gave him away. He appeared bewildered, almost panicked, not sure what to do.

The adolescent German saw the others engage the legionnaires, so he hesitantly followed their lead. The man thrust hard toward Lucius's midsection with an ugly-looking spear. Lucius easily parried the blow with his sword, then sidestepped the jab and lunged forward with his left arm, which held the dagger. He raked the man's face with the short blade. Blood exploded over Lucius's left hand. The figure retreated screaming, holding his head. Without hesitating, Lucius slashed down hard to his right with his sword where Cassius was locked with another German. The blow sliced open the warrior's arm. The man dropped his spear and ran. These were obviously not experienced warriors, thought Lucius. Thank the gods for that. Maybe they did have a chance even though highly outnumbered. Two more barbarians, unsure of what to do, stood before them, They advanced hesitantly toward Lucius and Cassius. After a brief exchange of blows and the parrying of thrusts, the two Romans sent them fleeing.

XXII

The German warrior, Ardvas, seethed, his anger growing as the weather turned uglier. Rain cascaded upon his unprotected head, further aggravating his foul mood. Because of the downpour, he and his band of men could no longer hear the clash of arms and the shouts of men in battle. They were all itching to leave their isolated positions away from the main battle and join the fray against the Romans. But they dared not.

Ardvas was the brother-in-law of Gorgas, his chieftain. Gorgas was the warrior selected by Arminius to initiate the attack on the rear of the Roman column. Gorgas and Ardvas had quarreled days ago over what Ardvas had considered a petty matter. He'd gotten drunk and led his men on a wild hunting expedition into the forest. They were supposed to be in their assembly areas ready to attack Varus and his Roman legions.

When he'd returned from his hunt—an unsuccessful one at that—Gorgas had been waiting for him, his face contorted with unbridled fury. The exchange between the two men had become so heated that his fellow warriors, knowing better than to attempt to intervene, had moved away from the two, leaving them alone in the middle of the camp. Gorgas had gotten right up to Ardvas's face, telling him that if he'd been captured by the Roman scouting party, he could have blown the entire ambush. Ardvas had casually retorted that he'd not been caught, so what difference did it make? His last insolent refrain had infuriated Gorgas even more. Ardvas knew he'd pushed Gorgas too far with his impertinent response. He became silent, his defiance gone. He recognized he was as close to death as he'd ever been.

Ardvas didn't fear many things in this life, but he'd witnessed Gorgas's fury in battle. He understood that this was a man one didn't want to be at cross-purposes with when he was angry. Gorgas effortlessly picked him up by his neck, then heaved him through the air. Ardvas didn't rise from his fallen position, remaining prone, rubbing his injured throat. Humiliated though he was, he knew better than to attempt to get up or, even worse, draw his weapon. That would signal that he was challenging Gorgas. After staring at Ardvas in silence for some time, Gorgas had stalked away without another glance at his fallen brother-in-law.

As punishment for his transgression, Ardvas and his men were relegated to the third echelon of troops, away from the main battlefield. The deployment of the German warriors in the forest surrounding the Romans was quite simple. The main body of combatants, the most experienced warriors and the privileged Germans, would conduct the actual attack. The less experienced men and those considered too old or too young would be assigned the second and third echelons. The mission of these second- and third-echelon warriors was to seal any breakout by the Romans from the main battle area and to hunt down any stragglers who attempted to escape.

Ardvas was disgraced in front of his peers. He was a warrior of some repute and skill, yet here he was waiting in the forest away from the main battle, consigned to be with the boys, who had yet to grow beards, and old men. This was the greatest battle of his life with the Romans, but he and his men weren't part of it. He could do nothing to change his plight. As much as he desired to leave his present position to join the battle, if he disobeyed the command from Gorgas, his status as brother-in-law wouldn't save him. Gorgas would kill him; of that he was sure. So Ardvas fumed as his men crouched beside him. They were watching a wide trail to their immediate front in the event that it might be used as an escape route by fleeing Romans. Other pickets of third-echelon men were scattered throughout the landscape.

Ardvas's ears perked up. He heard shouts of alarm to his left. Some Romans must have escaped the trap. Maybe he would share some of the glory today after all. He quickly shouted to his men, "Get off your asses. It's time to fight."

Ardvas and his men pounded through the forest in the direction of the clash of arms. The distinctive reverberation of steel meeting steel rose above the drumming of the rain.

Cassius and Lucius, now unengaged by any Germans, pivoted toward their left, where the other legionnaires were occupied. The two attacked the exposed flank of the assaulting warriors. The Germans were now under attack from two directions by the Roman soldiers. The remainder of the force disengaged from the small band of Romans, and began a ragged retreat, but then the group of eight warriors led by Ardvas appeared.

The fleeing Germans stopped when they saw Ardvas's men. Bolstered by their unexpected reinforcements, they reversed course and advanced upon the Romans. The two opposing forces clashed again. Lucius gave ground, as he was engaged with two of Ardvas's men. He recognized immediately that these new combatants knew their craft. They handled their spears with uncanny grace. All he could do to stay unscathed was to retreat against their onslaught. One of them jabbed his spear, nicking Lucius in the arm, drawing blood. Lucius grunted in pain. The other man feinted at Lucius's head with his spear, then slashed at his exposed legs. Lucius nimbly jumped back. He wasn't sure what he could possibly do in this situation, but he realized he'd better think of something quickly, or this would have a bad ending.

He decided to be aggressive; it was his only chance. Lucius hurled his dagger with his left hand at the man's head to his left. Instinctively, the German raised his arms to protect his face, exposing his entire midsection. Lucius swiftly pivoted away from the man to his right and jabbed a lightning thrust with his gladius into the man's midsection. The German screamed, going to his knees. Lucius yanked his sword out so he could engage the other assailant. In doing so, he lost his balance on the muddy slope and slipped down a small embankment on his back. With a triumphant shout, the surviving German hurried down after him for the kill.

He wasn't quick enough. Out of nowhere, Julia leaped on the man's back. She stabbed him in the face with her dagger with one hand while holding him around the neck with the other. With a bellow, the man threw her off, sending Julia flying into a nearby bush. The warrior's face was bleeding freely where she had sliced him open. In a fury, he forgot about Lucius, going instead after Julia. She was groggily attempting to untangle herself from the large thicket into which she had been catapulted. Lucius regained his feet and attacked. He swung his sword as hard as he could against the man's neck, severing tendons and muscles before severing his spine. The foe went down gurgling in his own blood, choking from the massive wound in his throat.

Lucius heard his name screamed, then another gurgled cry. He stumbled back up out of the slight depression he'd tumbled into. In horror, he saw two men jabbing Cassius with their spears. He withered in the mud. Lucius rushed over the open ground with his sword extended in front of him. He struck the man from behind on the top of the head. His head split open, and he collapsed. The other turned toward Lucius, but too late. In a rage, Lucius slashed the man across the face with all his strength. The man screamed and went to his knees. Lucius chopped him in the throat, and he collapsed.

Cassius was barely moving. He was covered in blood from a half dozen deep wounds. Blood trickled from his mouth. In a violent spasm, he vomited a gout of blood. His eyes met Lucius's, beseeching him for help, then glazed over. He was gone. Julia hurried up to Lucius and saw Cassius.

"No," she wailed. She knelt and cradled his head in her lap.

"Not you, Cassius." Julia wept.

Lucius was numb and couldn't absorb the death of Cassius now. He silently looked on as Julia held Cassius, his blood staining her sodden garments.

The Romans were for the moment unengaged by the temporarily leaderless foe. Ardvas had received a blow to the head courtesy of Marcellus's sword pommel. The strike had had sent him reeling to the earth. Before Marcellus could finish him, some of his followers had come to his assistance. Ardvas crawled to his hands and knees, shaking his head to clear it.

Marcellus shouted, "Let's get out of here."

Lucius tugged Julia to her feet. They ran for their lives again. Julia looked back at Cassius, but Lucius pulled her away. On the way, he snatched his dagger off the ground by the body of the recently slain German. Two other legionnaires were on the ground, unmoving.

Lucius was running with Julia in tow. He looked back over his shoulder, perhaps fifty yards away. The Germans wavered, unsure of what to do. Their leader rose from the ground. He began waving his sword, shouting for the men to follow him, urging them forward. The surviving Germans, realizing they still outnumbered the Romans, charged at them once again.

"Marcellus," shouted Valerius, "they're pursuing. Bows?"

The centurion looked back and saw the Germans chasing them. He nodded at the tribune.

"Let's give them some discouragement." The two quickly unlimbered their bows across their backs and strung them in an instant. The Germans proceeded closer, now emboldened at seeing that the group had stopped.

Valerius quickly notched an arrow. "That one out front is mine."

He drew the arrow back and let it fly. It struck the lead man squarely in the chest, knocking him backward. Marcellus's arrow narrowly missed another figure. The pursuing Germans stopped at the new threat, unsure of what to do. This was a bad decision on their part. Now two more arrows were in flight. Both reached their intended targets. Two more men went down hard. Another volley of arrows followed. Germans tumbled to the earth with the projectiles embedded in them. The few surviving Germans fled.

Marcellus turned to Valerius. "Nicely done, Tribune."

Valerius grinned. "Let's beat tracks out of here."

Ardvas lay in the mud on his back, unable to move. The rain pounded his unprotected face. He was attempting to understand what had happened to him. They had attacked the small Roman force, killing several of them, but they had allowed them to flee. The Romans had run away again. In a fury he'd exhorted the surviving warriors to pursue after them. He'd led the way, howling in fury. He'd seen the Romans suddenly stop. His men advanced on them. A tremendous blow had struck him, knocking him violently to the ground. He cast his eyes downward and looked at the bloody mess that was his chest. He could see the shaft of the arrow deeply buried in him. His last thought was that he guessed the arrow had penetrated through his back, and then he died.

The group of Roman survivors, now down to five—Valerius, Marcellus, Lucius, Julia, and another legionnaire named Martius—slowed to a walk. They'd been running for some time. The drumming rain continued unabated. They finally stopped at a small clear steam and drank greedily. After they had finished, Valerius spied a clump of bushes for the group to hide in. He waved his arms and motioned for everyone to hurry in the direction of the thicket. They huddled together in the dense brush, hidden from view.

Valerius spoke. "It would be an understatement to say we're in extreme danger. I'll defer to Centurion Marcellus, as he has many years of experience in this territory. He also knows something about this forest, which I do not."

Marcellus slowly scanned those before him. He hastily cleared the ground of debris in front of them to create a place to map their position. He paused to look around to be certain that there were no more Germans about, then began drawing a diagram in the dirt.

"Here was our base camp on the Weser." He marked the spot with a small stone. "I'm guessing we're about here."

He scratched an X in the dirt. He then marked a line to the right of his marker. "This represents the Lippe River, about thirty to forty miles or so from here. This is our sanctuary, Alisio." He marked it with a twig. "Somehow we must evade the Germans and get to this base. There are several cohorts stationed at Alisio. Between is some of the most rugged terrain in Germania—ravines, swamps, and forests. As I said before, the distance is about thirty to forty miles, southwest of here. The problem I see is that Alisio might not be standing. There aren't enough men within the fortifications to hold off a large force. This uprising is no small matter. They may be attacking it at this very moment. If Alisio has fallen, we'll go farther west to Vetera, the original destination of the army, where the Rhine and Lippe meet. There are reinforced troops there. An entire legion, the Second Augusta, is stationed there."

"What are the chances Alisio is standing?" said Valerius.

"Unless I've totally misjudged this uprising, I believe Alisio will be taken or has already fallen."

"We'll need food," said Lucius.

"Whatever we can find. We'll have to live off the land."

Everyone looked at one another. Their expressions were grim.

Marcellus continued. "I suggest we discard all of our armor and helmets. We need to move fast and quiet. The lighter the better. Any questions?"

There was silence. The men began hurriedly stripping off their armor and helmets.

"Time is wasting. Let's go."

Gorgas and his men rested on the wooded knoll, some leaning on their spears to support their weary bodies. Many were bloodied from wounds. In the center of the group was deposited their pile of booty. There were Roman shields, swords, spears, armor, standards, and other treasures. Gorgas smiled in triumph, although he was disappointed that his men wouldn't take part in the final assault of the remaining forces of the legions. A short while ago, he'd been taken aside by Arminius and told that his clan had done enough. They had suffered more than their share of losses. He'd let Gorgas know that it was important that some of the tribes that had joined just the last day or two be allowed to participate in the destruction of the Roman army. Arminius didn't want them to feel slighted. He needed unity among all of the tribes. Gorgas had nodded sagely in understanding.

He stated that his men stood willing and able in case those other tribes faltered. Arminius had clasped Gorgas on the shoulder, then departed without saying anything else.

So Gorgas and his band of warriors watched in grim fascination as the German forces, including most of the unbloodied tribes whom Arminius had spoken of, assaulted the remnants of the Roman army.

Gorgas frowned at the sight of a lone figure staggering toward his position. One of Ardvas's men stumbled into their midst, gasping for air and bleeding from several places. He looked about, spied Gorgas, and stumbled toward him.

Gorgas stood, alarmed at the man's presence, wondering what was going on.

"Iazyges, what are you doing here? Where's Ardvas? Where's my brother-in-law?"

The man gasped for air, still winded. "Dead. Almost all are dead. Ardvas was killed by the escaping Romans."

"How many of them?" Gorgas was alarmed. It was Arminius's plan that none of the Roman soldiers escape to warn the others at their forts along the rivers. This was the main reason for the various echelons of warriors from the main battle area. It was critical to his overall plan that the river forts some forty miles away receive no warning. "A large force?" Gorgas queried.

Iazyges, now fearful of Gorgas's anger, stuttered. "I would guess six or seven."

"Six or seven? How many men were guarding the trail I assigned to you?"

"There were over thirty of us, including the other groups, but they used these terrible bows and slaughtered us."

Gorgas, his ire rising, spat back a reply. "There were thirty of you, and you couldn't stop a few Roman soldiers?"

The man cowered and replied defensively. "We killed a few of them, but they escaped, including a woman." As soon as he spoke of the woman as part of the force, he knew it was a mistake.

Gorgas became even angrier. "And how many of you did the woman kill?"

He hung his head in silence. Gorgas stared back at the man in fury. "What happened to Ardvas?"

"He was killed by an arrow."

"That worthless prick. I assign him one simple job, and look what happens. Now I'm going to have to tell my wife, who's his sister, about this. Let's go; get yourself together. We're going after these Romans. Can you show me where all of this occurred and in which direction they fled?"

The man nodded silently. Gorgas shouted out the names of his lieutenants. "Ampsiva, Traiecta, I need fifteen men to come with me after some Romans who escaped. We need to hurry before they get too far ahead of us."

There were shouted orders as men began to assemble and gather up their belongings. A few scurried in search of their weapons and packs, which they had thought would not be needed until tomorrow. Gorgas waited until all the tribesmen who were coming with him had formed up behind him. He nodded in approval at the choice of men, all experienced and tested warriors. His gaze stopped, focusing on one man. He watched the warrior grimace in pain. Rawhide strips were wrapped tightly on a large bandage around his right leg. Blotches of blood dotted the cloth dressing where it had seeped through. He attempted to stand upright, averting his gaze.

Gorgas walked over and gently placed his hand on the warrior's shoulders. "Not today, Trestus. You'll slow us down. We'll need to move fast."

The man looked up in dejection, unwilling to argue the point.

Gorgas stepped back and shouted, "Come on; let's get moving here."

Gorgas smiled. After all, this might be good sport, to chase after these Romans. The men trotted after him through the forest.

XXIII

*M*ost of the Roman cohorts were destroyed. Century by century, the lines were breached and the men annihilated. The remnants of Varus's headquarters were overrun. The few surviving officers were hunted down and ruthlessly butchered. Some attempted to flee, but there was nowhere to hide. They were cut off from escape, then brutally dispatched.

Castor somehow had managed to survive the carnage. He'd lost his sword, not that it would have done him much good. He fled as fast as his ample body could carry him, which wasn't far. He blindly crawled into a clump of bushes, but not unnoticed. There were shouts of discovery. Several German warriors pursued. Castor rose to run but tripped over an exposed tree root. He lay on the ground panting, unable to rise. Several German warriors surrounded him, their eyes devoid of any pity. They studied him silently. The leader rushed forward, leveling his spear at Castor's chest.

"What have we here? A Roman tribune. He obviously eats well."

The others laughed, mocking the fat Roman officer.

"What shall we do with this quivering mass?"

Castor was terrified. He had no idea what were they saying in their harsh language. He wet himself in his fright. He managed to squeak out in reply in a falsetto tone, "Please don't kill me. My family has money. They will pay a high ransom for me."

The Germans didn't understand a word. They laughed in disdain at his terror.

"Shall we kill this bag of shit and be on our way?"

The speaker readied his spear for a downward thrust. Castor screamed and put his hands in front of his body. Another man held his arms out, temporarily sparing Castor.

"I have a better idea. Let's turn him over to the priestesses. I'm sure they can find an interesting use for him."

They all shouted their accord in unison.

"Yes, the priestesses can have him. That should be fun to watch."

The leader motioned with his spear tip for Castor to rise. He was stripped of his armor and all clothing. They surrounded him menacingly, prodding him forward with their spears, poking him in the ass just enough to draw blood. Castor whimpered, scampering along as fast as he could.

The surviving units of the Seventeenth Legion had banded together. Under the leadership of General Licinus, perhaps nine hundred men formed a tight perimeter. Thousands upon thousands of Germans besieged the ragged remains of the once-proud army. The besieged Romans were exhausted and bloodied, but they held firm. They had repelled waves of assaults by the Germans.

The piles of German bodies in front of the Roman lines attested to their fighting prowess. General Licinus stood in the middle of the perimeter, exhorting his troops. He wouldn't consider the possibility of defeat. He was making the Germans pay a steep price for their attacks. Like many of the soldiers, he was wounded in several places, but he refused to let that bother him.

Arminius's scheme had worked as planned. Although the Romans had gained some tactical superiority as a result of their predawn exit, in the end they had fallen into the ploy. The bottleneck formed from the sloping hill on the left side and the morass on the right had trapped the Roman army. In the end, the Romans had just hastened their demise by running ahead.

Arminius and several of his top lieutenants boldly strode from their perch upon a small knoll toward the last bit of Roman resistance. He watched in grim fascination as the Romans repulsed yet another attack, leaving heaps of German dead, like so much cordwood stacked for the winter in front of the Romans' fighting positions. It was time to end this. He signaled for the tribal chieftains to come over to him. He consulted with them briefly.

"We must attack as one force, not in pieces. Our numbers are overwhelming. Let's end this now," he shouted. The leaders nodded in acquiescence.

There was a brief lull as the Germans organized their warriors around the Romans. Thousands of them began to shout and chant their war cries. The noise reached a fevered crescendo. The Romans held their wall of shields in place, ready for the onslaught. On Arminius's signal, the Germans charged, hurling their spears at the Roman perimeter.

A shower of missiles descended on the legionnaires. Men fell everywhere, among them General Licinus. He knelt on the ground with a spear embedded in his leg. With a groan he pulled it out. A torrent of blood rushed out of the gaping wound. Within seconds, the weakened general collapsed. The loss of Licinus plus the gaps created in the Roman perimeter was enough to tip the balance. The Germans overran the last Roman position, slaughtering the remaining soldiers.

Severus Septimus was the eagle bearer, or *aquilifer*, of the Eighteenth Legion. He'd held this post for some five years. He would rather die than give up the sacred eagle standard, the *aquila*. His normal place was at the head of the Eighteenth Legion, but there was no longer an Eighteenth Legion, only the battered fragments of the once-proud unit. They were the last piece of organized Roman resistance. He was being pushed rearward by the relentless German pressure. He'd no choice. If he attempted to make a stand, he'd be dead. Worse, the eagle of the Eighteenth Legion would be in enemy hands.

The Germans had almost captured the standard moments ago. Septimus had been knocked over in a tangle of struggling bodies. A German had stood over him, stabbing at him with a long spear. His Roman armor saved him from death, but not before a huge gash had been opened on his thigh. Luckily for him, one his comrades had slain the German warrior just as he was about finish off Septimus.

He approached a swollen stream, its current swift and muddy. He tried to wade across, but he fell so that he was almost completely submerged. He desperately maintained his iron grip on the standard. There was nothing more important to him. He crawled his way up the embankment. Drawing upon his last reserves, he stood upright so that the surviving legionnaires could see the eagle was still in his hands.

Septimus staggered onward, looking about for a place to make a stand and rally the troops. He was with a group of about fifty. They formed a makeshift perimeter in a small hollow. There was no high ground, so it would have to do. He understood that their situation was hopeless. Large numbers of the enemy surrounded them. There was no way they could possibly escape this trap.

Suddenly, blinding sheets of water struck, with peals of thunder and lightning. The Germans rushed the Roman position. The outline of men fighting became a blur as the deluge hit them. Waves of rain pounded the combatants as the wind howled throughout the forest, bending the treetops. Branches whipped wildly about as leaves and other debris flew in the air. Septimus stumbled as his wounded leg gave way. With a cry, he collapsed near a large bush. From his spot on the ground, he saw an animal burrow. His face pressed in the dirt, Severus numbly eyed the hole in the earth. In a moment of clarity among the escalating madness of the battle, he knew exactly what he was going to do.

Severus shoved the precious silver eagle deep into the hole, then savagely broke off the standard from the wooden pole to which it was affixed. Using his booted feet, he caved in the surrounding earth until the eagle was totally buried. He looked about to see if anyone had witnessed his deception. He was pleased that no one could observe him in the driving rainstorm. Those bloody barbarians won't get my eagle. With renewed energy, he raised himself, casting away the wooden standard pole, then picked up a discarded gladius from a dead Roman legionnaire. He charged into the fray, screaming an oath. He was slain moments later as the German warriors stormed over the circle of legionnaires, killing every last man. His secret of the buried eagle died with him.

Later that day, Arminius sat in a nearby sheltered grove with the other chieftains. He smiled as the German warriors paraded before him, carrying the prizes of their victory. First to be displayed were the armor and helmets of the top officers, including that of Varus. This was followed by the unit standards. The men paraded by with each of the cohort standards.

Arminius shouted to his chiefs, "The mighty symbols of the Roman army are nothing. We own them now. They have no power. These will never appear marching through our lands again."

The assembled throng cheered his speech. As a final touch, Arminius reached down to his side and brought up the bloody head of Varus. He held the grisly object before him and spoke to it.

"Look at what has become of your army, great general. You were the one who taxed us, asking for tribute to line your pockets. Behold your mighty standards. I shall send your head to the mighty Caesar in Rome. He'll know not to come here again."

Arminius tossed the head aside, then shouted to his assembled throng. "Bring me the eagles."

He leaned forward in anticipation of the ultimate prizes. Groups of men paraded forward bearing two of the silver eagle standards. The Seventeenth and Nineteenth eagles were proudly brought to the feet of Arminius.

Arminius leaped down from his elevated position, ignoring the two prized standards. "Where's the third eagle? There were three eagles, one for each of their legions. Where is the Eighteenth?"

Arminius turned to his assembled throng of leaders, his face contorted in rage. "If any man is hiding the third eagle, I'll personally disembowel him. I want that eagle. It can't have disappeared. It belongs to all of us." He turned back to the chieftains. "Find that eagle. I must have all their eagles."

There was a stunned silence among the celebrating Germans. The chieftains all looked at one another suspiciously. Some surreptitiously exited the gathering to make inquiries among their men. No one seemed to know anything about it. Furious, Arminius stalked off, trailed by his top lieutenants.

The brief lull in the festivities caused by Arminius's tirade was soon forgotten and the revelry continued, but without, it should be noted, the third eagle. It had mysteriously not been captured.

The celebration lasted long into the night. The men drank and boasted of their prowess in battle. To amuse themselves, they began killing the remaining captives in an orgy of violence. Their end wasn't pleasant. Some were crucified to trees, while others were burned alive. To mark the site of their great victory, many of the Roman dead were beheaded. The grisly objects were nailed to trees or placed on posts throughout the forest to glorify the battlefield for years to come.

Several men with spears prodded the naked form of Castor forward. He would squeal each time he was jabbed by the spearpoint, drawing blood on his huge bare buttocks. He was led into a grove with a makeshift stone altar. The entire area was illuminated with hundreds of torches. There were thousands of men cheering and shouting. He was roughly pulled onto the stone block so that he was lying on his back. His hands and feet were securely tied down.

In front of him materialized a large woman with flowing blond hair. She wore a white robe spotted with blood. She smiled at him. He stared into the woman's eyes, then started to scream. His shrieks reached a crescendo as the woman began sawing open his belly with a long-bladed knife. After a while, there were no more sounds. The woman held a pile of entrails in her hands and raised them for all to see. The throng cheered at her presentation.

XXIV

*T*he surviving band of five trotted south through the forest, determined to put as much distance as possible from the main battlefield. The rain continued unabated throughout the remainder of the day, masking their movements. If anything, it was raining harder. Gusts of wind blew through the trees, bending even the thickest of branches.

Marcellus was in the lead, pushing through the dripping foliage. Valerius noticed the centurion's pace was slowing. He continually rubbed his old leg wound as if that would put spring to his step. But it wasn't only the centurion wearing down; everyone was getting wobbly. They had been at it since before dawn. For the good, they hadn't seen nor heard any Germans since they had dispatched the last group with the arrows. They were in rugged terrain, and they were cold, wet, hungry, wounded in numerous places, and generally miserable. But they were alive.

Marcellus stopped, and everyone huddled together.

"We need to stop and find some shelter. The sooner, the better. I think we're all reached our limit. At least I have."

"You won't get an argument from me," said Valerius. "I'm whipped also. Do you think we're being pursued?"

"Don't know, Tribune. We may be. There were a number of them who escaped our wrath back there when we fought them off. The Germans might not want anyone alerting the garrisons along the Lippe and Rhine, which means they'll be after us. But from what I've seen of them in the past, they're most likely too busy celebrating, getting drunk. I could be wrong. If they are stalking us, I would hope our trail has been wiped clean by the rain."

"So you believe it's prudent to stop now?"

The centurion paused in thought.

"I'm not so sure we can go much farther, given our condition. If the Germans are in pursuit, they'll also have to stop in the dark. You want to continue on, Tribune?"

Valerius just shook his head wearily in response. "I think we need to rest."

Lucius leaned against a tree and gingerly lifted his tunic to examine his side where he'd been struck with the sword when he and Cassius were running up the column to find Julia. He winced at the sight of the dark purple patch on his ribs. He decided there was nothing he could do for his ribs except bear the pain. Besides, he was fortunate it wasn't bleeding.

Julia sat at the base of a tree with her knees bunched up to her chest, her eyes closed. She appeared as if she'd been in a fight with a large animal, losing badly. Deep scratches covered her cheeks and forehead from when she'd been flung into the bushes courtesy of the German she had attacked with her dagger. She began to shiver uncontrollably. Lucius hobbled over and hugged her, hoping his body warmth might help. She was one tough lady. She had not complained once of the hardship.

His thoughts were interrupted as Marcellus signaled for them to rise. He waved his arm forward, indicating for them to follow him down a narrow game trail. They journeyed on it for a short distance before coming to a clear stream. It was running high, deep and swollen with rain. Marcellus looked around to make sure all were present.

"We dare not set up camp near the path we have been trekking. That's why we've moved. We'll set up our camp somewhere around here, but far enough away from this stream so we can hear anyone approaching. We can rig some sort of shelter to keep out of the rain."

"What about a fire?" said Julia. She looked at the two officers expectantly.

"Not a chance," said Marcellus. "I don't mean to be gruff about it, but it would signal our presence." He peered about, then pointed. "Let's go over that way."

The group walked ahead toward a pine grove about twenty-five yards from the stream. At Marcellus's direction, they silently cut some branches off some small evergreens with their swords, fashioning the roof and walls of a crude shelter using two side-by-side pine trees as a base. The construction of the shelter was simple yet effective. A long, thick branch was lashed with leather straps horizontally between the two pine trees at a height of about five feet. Against this support, wooden poles, which they had fashioned by hacking the smaller limbs from large branches, were laid diagonally to the ground. These were in turn lashed to the horizontal support with more leather straps. The source of these straps was the shoulder supports for their scabbards. Thick pine boughs were interwoven among the sloping roof poles to create a lean-to shelter that shed most of the rain.

They added more pine branches to the top of the crude structure. Marcellus crawled into the enclosure and looked about. "By the gods, it's dry. Everyone get in here." All five managed to fit into their temporary quarters. Lucius and Julia curled up together on their cozy nest of pine needles. They could hear the rain drumming on the surrounding trees.

"What about watches tonight?" said Valerius.

Marcellus paused in thought. "I think not, Tribune. There's no way anyone could possibly find us here. We're not near any trails, there's complete darkness, and it's raining hard. I think we all need the rest."

They collapsed into an exhausted sleep.

Gorgas cursed loudly. Since midafternoon, his men had been chasing the Romans who had killed Ardvas. But now his chief scout and tracker had lost the trail in the darkness. They would need to stop for the night. The Romans were moving surprisingly fast. Gorgas guessed his men had gained some ground on them, but he was still not close. One good thing: the Romans were making no attempt to cover their trail, which made tracking them somewhat easy even in the driving rain. The signs were all there for anyone to see: a broken branch, a deep footprint in the mud, dislodged stones on the trail, moss scraped off rocks by a careless step. They probably had no idea they were being followed.

Gorgas's men looked at him expectantly for instructions. Although exhausted by the rapid pace he'd set for them, they would do anything he asked, even if it meant moving all night.

In response, Gorgas motioned for his head tracker, Vilix, to come over. "Well?"

The man shook his head in response. "I know what direction they're moving, but I've lost the trail. I can't locate any signs of their passage. I could continue to travel in the general direction that I think they're headed. We might intercept them later tomorrow if they've stopped for the night. The risk is we could lose them altogether."

Gorgas silently weighed the words of Vilix. The man was good. If he lost the trail, then nobody could find it. He needed to catch these Romans. He must not let them alert the Roman garrisons. They were headed in the direction of the Roman fort at Alisio. He had little doubt about that. There was the chance that the forces that Arminius had dispatched toward Alisio might intercept them, but that would not do. No, he needed to be the one to catch these soldiers and kill them. He didn't want to be nagged by his wife, Ardvas's sister, that he was unable to avenge his death. He knew word would eventually get back to her if he let the Romans who killed her brother escape. He pictured many a cold night without her plump form next to him. He frowned at the thought. He was tempted to continue on even in the dark but decided not to. He still had time. The fleeing Romans would be worn out. Also, he knew something the Romans didn't. The terrain got worse ahead—in fact, much worse. He was confident that he would eventually catch up with them, and then he would wreak his vengeance upon them.

"We stop here for the night," he pronounced. "Tomorrow we will overtake them."

The next morning dawned cold and chilly. The rain had stopped sometime during the night. The Romans emerged from their shelter. The mist rose from the forest floor, and strange bird cries echoed eerily throughout the forest. Everyone rose stiffly, then ventured outside. They all attempted to shake the stiffness from their bodies.

Valerius began to speak. "Which direction—"

Marcellus motioned with his arm for silence. Everyone stopped what they were doing and gathered around the centurion.

He spoke in a hushed tone. "There's no more rain to muffle our sounds. We must observe strict silence. We have no idea if there are any Germans around. They might be tracking us, so let's keep it quiet. Communicate by hand signals. Speak softly, only when necessary."

They walked out in single file. Marcellus led, traveling by instinct, heading south toward the safety of the river fortress of Alisio. The small band walked rapidly for most of the morning and into the early afternoon without incident. They continued trekking at a furious pace, almost at a run. As the day wore on, the wobblier became their steps. Julia was reeling. Lucius had to support her on several occasions, yet they continued without letup through the rugged terrain.

Valerius, who occupied the rear in the file, noted that all of them were close to their breaking point. Julia was about to collapse. Marcellus was visibly limping. The centurion was pushing them hard. Valerius hastened to the front beside the centurion, then spoke quietly.

"Centurion, are you able to maintain the pace? You appear to be heavily favoring that leg something terrible."

Marcellus gave him an icy stare and spoke in a clipped tone. "Tribune, I'll outfight and outrun any man here. Why don't you mind your own capabilities?"

"Centurion, if the Germans don't kill us, your pace certainly will."

"Tribune, just so that you understand, our lives depend on the speed and the distance we can cover over the next several days. Our duty is to alert the garrison of Alisio. If it's fallen, then we must go to the forts on the Rhine."

Valerius was somewhat taken aback by the response. "If you say so, Centurion."

"I say so."

"By all means, lead on."

Fixing Marcellus with a hard gaze, he returned to the rear. Valerius decided the best thing to do was to ignore the diatribe and drive on. Blame it on fatigue, he thought. None of us are at our best. His message must have gotten through, for their progress was at a slower pace. One stretch of ground featured a forest of massive trees, mostly oaks, beeches, and alders, with a few towering evergreens. They were dwarfed by the massive trunks growing straight and tall. The walking was relatively unimpeded; the forest floor was clear of heavy brush and rocks.

Toward the middle of the afternoon, the landscape changed for the worse. The heavy timber gradually gave way to more tangled masses of shrubbery and dense undergrowth. The ground sloped downward. They exited the relative comfort of forested plateau to a place not as inviting. The group found themselves confronted by a bog of unknown dimensions. Lucius and Martius, the other surviving legionnaire, separated, scouting to the left and right. Both men returned from their reconnaissance shaking their heads. Marcellus stared grimly straight ahead at the mess to their front.

"We'll have to take our chances and go through this. I don't like it, but we have no choice. These bogs can extend for miles in all directions. We could spend all day trying to find a way around this thing. We have no time for that. Let's go."

Already dull with exhaustion, the group waded into the morass, mostly ankle deep. Marcellus led the way. He had not gone far when suddenly he sank to his waist in the stinking ooze. "Go back. We can't travel in this direction."

Valerius, at the rear of the formation, shifted to his left, diagonally from their original direction of march.

"I believe the ground is firmer this way."

The others followed close to him. He slogged another twenty yards, then almost disappeared.

"Stercus," he cried. He was almost up to his chin in foul-smelling water. In desperation, he grabbed at a branch of a nearby bush, unfortunately for him, covered in thorns. His hand was pierced in numerous places by the villainous spikes. Valerius held his hand in anguish, choking on the brackish water that he'd inhaled. Despite their fatigue, a refrain of muffled laughter was directed at the tribune. Valerius dragged himself out of the mire. He paused to wipe sweat trickling down his face with his arm. All he succeeded in doing was smearing the goo on the one part of his body not already covered in the ooze. He spat some of the offending material that had reached his lips.

Marcellus smirked. "Pardon me for saying so, sir, but you don't look very tribunish."

Valerius stared back at the centurion, spitting more of the foul liquid from his mouth. "Very funny, Centurion. You'll have to excuse me if I can't think of a proper retort."

Marcellus pointed to his right. "This way, Tribune. At least we won't have to worry about the Germans. Surely no one would follow us in this quagmire."

Valerius continued in the lead. He probed ahead with a long stick that he'd found floating in the morass. Their progress was slow and measured. They bypassed those areas that appeared too deep to transverse. Their plight remained unchanged for the remainder of the afternoon. He looked back to ensure the remainder of the group was with him and then scanned the horizon. Now where? Slightly to his right, he saw a healthy-looking stand of trees in the distance. Now, that looked promising. He pointed ahead at the trees, waving the group forward. Hopefully, it wasn't an island in this swamp but the end of it.

With renewed determination, the tribune headed toward the copse of trees in the distance. The ground became firmer, with patches of solid footing. They were finally out of it. They continued to journey on while there was daylight remaining, progressing several more miles through wooded terrain before dusk was upon them. It was time to stop and establish another night camp.

They started constructing the shelter.

Lucius stopped. "If you don't mind, I'm going to forage for some food. I'm starved, and I know everyone else is also."

They nodded in numb silence. Lucius walked over to Julia, who had collapsed at the base of a small tree. She absently twisted the hem of her cloak with her eyes cast downward. As Lucius approached, her eyes met his. Lucius noted a sparkle of defiance in them.

"Julia, I'm going in search of some food. Will you be all right?"

"Yes, Lucius. If you come across some goat cheese, would you bring me back some?" She grinned back at him at her own dry wit.

"Goat cheese it is, Miss Julia."

Lucius hurried off as dusk was approaching. He knew exactly where he was going. When the group had crossed the stream several hundred yards back, Lucius had spotted some deep pools that might hold fish. He ventured off, taking note of his bearings lest he become lost in the approaching darkness. He crept up to the first pool in as stealthy a manner as possible. His clumsiness got the better of him. He dislodged a rock with his foot, sending it tumbling into the dark waters, but he had his answer. Several forms flashed and darted about in the water. There were fish here, by Jove, and he was going to get them. Lucius studied the pockets of water upstream, determined to bring back dinner tonight.

Lucius scanned the trees lining the banks of the stream and spotted what he wanted. He selected a stout branch from a young tree, straight and true, that would suit his needs. He hacked it off with his sword and trimmed off the growth. He withdrew his dagger and fastened it to the branch with a part of his leather belt. He held his spear aloft to examine his handiwork, then stopped in disgust when he realized the dagger was covered in blood. He quickly washed it in the stream. Not exactly the equivalent of a Roman javelin, but it would do.

Ignoring the chilly waters, he waded slowly into the stream from below the next pool, careful not to disturb the fish. He waited patiently with poised spear, and then his arm flashed downward. It reappeared with a thrashing trout on the end of his dagger. It was as big as his foot, fat in the belly with flesh. He grinned to himself in triumph. Yes, that would do quite nicely. He tossed it up on the bank. Now for some more, he thought. His next several attempts resulted in misses. He wasn't even close. The fish were too disturbed in this pool for any more fishing, as they were darting crazily in panic. After stowing his trophy fish behind him on a supple branch threaded through the gills, he waded stealthily upstream. He found another promising pool about ten yards farther up. He was once again victorious on his first attempt. Lucius hastened upstream in search of the next spot. He was rewarded with two more fish. He stooped by the streamside and quickly gutted and cleaned the fish. He headed back to the camp in almost total darkness with four fat trout. He held up the fish triumphantly as he entered their night position.

Marcellus was impressed.

"By Jove, Lucius, they look delicious. You're quite the fisherman."

"A skill I acquired from my former life," he replied.

Lucius laid the fish out on a flat rock and cut filets into even portions with his dagger. They wolfed down the fish raw. Nobody complained.

Darkness was closing in fast. The German tracker Vilix returned from the front of the pack of German pursuers to face Gorgas, then gestured with his arms in the air. He'd lost the Romans' trail. Gorgas spat an oath in frustration. He'd hoped to be almost on top of them by now. Just as he'd anticipated earlier in the day, the Romans had ventured into the great swamp. It was his plan that they intercept the Romans as they exited the mire. Gorgas and his men knew a way around it. It was a longer journey, but in the end a much quicker route. To attempt to transverse the mire was to invite misfortune. Some who entered these swamps never did come out. Now that he and his band had circumvented the quagmire, they hadn't picked up the trail of the Romans. Perhaps they were hopelessly stuck in the mess. No, he could almost sense them. They had gotten out. He was sure of it. They were out there. These few Romans had powerful gods to have survived this long. The question was, where were they?

Gorgas fretted, although he gave no outward appearance of worry to his men. He knew he'd made up valuable time by avoiding that slimy piece of ground and that the Romans had wasted many hours crossing it. They couldn't be too far away from this very location. It was a matter of honor to catch these legionnaires, then dispose of them. But it would certainly not be this day. He also knew that if they continued on at his present course, they might eventually run into the warriors dispatched by Arminius to take down the Roman supply points and the garrison of Alisio on the Lippe. He glanced up from his deliberations, noting his men looking at him expectantly.

"We'll sleep here for tonight, then resume again tomorrow."

The warriors went about setting up their camp. They knew that they'd be off at dawn once again to find these Romans.

The next day, Marcellus, leading the way, pushed through the heavily forested terrain. The sun was bright, although the air was cool. The wind filled the tops of the trees, swaying them ever so slightly. The dark green of the hemlock, pine, and fir contrasted against a backdrop of the browns, yellows, and reds of the fall colors. By midmorning, they came across indications of large groups of men passing through the area. Marcellus held his arm up, signaling them to halt, then silently pointed out the telltale signs to the group: a recently severed limb from a sapling, trampled and bruised moss, and large footprints in the damp earthen floor.

Marcellus spoke in a hushed tone. "There are signs all over the place. For damn sure, they aren't the legions."

No sooner had he said these words than they heard the sound of coarse laughter and shouts in the distance. The five all turned in unison at the direction of the noise. Marcellus gestured with his hand for them to drop down.

Valerius spoke in a hushed tone. "Marcellus, I say we hole up here and wait. If we're discovered, I don't like our chances. We should travel strictly under the cover of darkness."

The centurion nodded in agreement. He looked about, then quickly directed them to a particularly large clump of dense bushes to their right. They silently made their way over to the dense foliage and collapsed in a heap in the thicket. It was a good place, concealed from any casual observation. Unless someone stumbled right upon them, they couldn't be spotted, and they weren't near any foot trails. There was no reason anyone would venture into the thick cover of their hideout. The four men and one woman hunkered down to wait for darkness.

Valerius had first watch. The dense brush provided overhead cover from the sunlight. The solitude gave him a chance to reflect on the events of the last several days. When he became a tribune, he knew that there was an element of danger, much more so than if he served his tour of duty in Rome. Soldiering had an element of risk, but what he'd witnessed in the Teutoburg was beyond belief. Indeed, he reflected upon some of the dire warnings he'd been given prior to his departure. He recalled the words of caution by the centurion at the wharf in Ostia. The man had been spot on about the impending doom of the place.

The times the Roman legions had been hacked to pieces in the last hundred years or so were few and far between. Just his bad fortune, he guessed. He thought of his family, his mother, father, sisters, and most of all, Calpurnia. Would he ever see her again? He'd gotten this far, which was better than most. The entire army was now a bunch of moldering corpses strewn about the German forest. Thank the gods for Marcellus. If it weren't for the savvy centurion, he'd be lying back there with the rest of the army.

His thoughts turned to Calpurnia and his illicit romance. He longed to hold her once again. His mind lingered for a moment on her delicious curves, the way she swayed so gracefully. He had written her several times, thinking of her often. He'd read her return letters to him many times. Unfortunately, those very letters were in the saddlebags of his horse, which he had been forced to abandon. If he made it out of this debacle, he'd marry Calpurnia despite his parents' objections. Life was what was important and not status in Rome's finer circles.

He chastised himself for letting his mind wander. He had best pay attention to his present circumstances, or none of them would ever make it to safety. He continued to scan the surrounding area. He was awakened twice as his head hit his chest. It dawned on him that he had almost gone off to arms of Morpheus. This wouldn't do. He shook Marcellus awake. He whispered, "I'm fading rapidly. Do you mind?"

Marcellus shook his head back and forth and stretched his neck. "No, go ahead. I'll keep the watch."

Before Valerius closed his eyes, Marcellus spoke to him softly. "Tribune, sorry about my outburst the other day. There was no excuse for that."

"Marcellus, no offense taken. I should have been a little more discreet in my remarks. Forget it."

He squeezed Marcellus's shoulder to assure him there were no hard feelings. The centurion nodded in agreement. "Tribune, I'm honored to have served with you. You're a fine soldier and officer of the legions."

Valerius smiled in the darkness, then turned toward his resting spot. He fell into an exhausted sleep.

They ventured forth when it was fully dark, heading south. Marcellus cautioned them all again, no noise. Sounds carry much farther at night, he told them, so absolute silence was imperative. They walked in single file, close together so they wouldn't get separated. They could hear strange chants and singing echoing through the darkness, plus occasional wild howls that sent chills down their backs. Campfires pulsed in the night.

"Marcellus," whispered Valerius, "what in the Hades are they making all that noise about?"

"Don't ask me, and I have no intention of finding out. Now let's get out of here."

Under Marcellus's direction, the group ventured cautiously onward, avoiding the German night encampments. The group veered away from any fires, sometimes even reversing the direction they'd been moving. They pressed onward, silent and watchful. Close to dawn, they arrived at a dirt road suggestive of Roman construction. It was wide enough to accommodate two carts. They followed it for a brief distance, and then, ahead, a ghostly silhouette materialized before them in the mist. It was difficult to make out the true shape in the dim light, but it was evident that this was a man-made structure. They approached, their weapons held at the ready. The hard angles of intersecting walls and a sloping roof materialized.

Wisps of dirty gray smoke drifted out from the windows and gaps in the roof. Valerius quickly recognized the sickly sweet odor of burning flesh. Once experienced, the smell was never forgotten. He spat on the ground to rid himself of the foul taste that had quickly permeated his nose and mouth. He looked toward Marcellus for guidance. The centurion held up his hand to halt the group. They stood still and listened. Above the silence, there was the slight crackle and pop of burning embers, but nothing else.

Marcellus motioned for them to progress into the clearing. Valerius gripped his long sword tightly, walking in front of the others, his head on a swivel. They crept silently forward. Several creatures went scurrying into the woods. As they ventured cautiously forward, the sights that greeted them were revolting. There were bodies in all forms of contorted positions around the structure. One man was nailed to the door. Another hung upside down from a tree, his entrails dangling from his body like a gutted fish. A man's head was spiked to a tree trunk. Other mutilated corpses and body parts were strewn around the area. Splintered javelins and assorted pieces of uniforms were scattered about the ground. Marcellus grimly surveyed the carnage, motioning everyone to the dark shadows of the walls. He spoke in a whisper.

"This must be a way station above Alisio. At least it looks as if they went down fighting. Probably took a few Germans with them."

He pointed to several thick blood trails along the ground.

"This road must lead directly to the fortress. The Lippe River can't be far from here. I don't believe it would be prudent to maintain our present course. We need to get back in the bush and off this path now."

Valerius spoke. "Marcellus, how far west do you reckon we have to go before we hit Alisio?"

"My guess is fifteen miles, but I can't be sure."

Valerius continued. "From the tone in your voice, you don't believe that will be our sanctuary."

Marcellus paused a moment, grim faced, before speaking. "All of these Germans heading this way must have a purpose. My guess is that it's to take down Alisio. You just saw some of their handiwork. Let's get out of sight where we can discuss some more. I don't like being exposed out here in the open."

The group walked for a distance to get away from the site of the slaughter, then proceeded into a dense clump of bushes. Valerius went to his knees and cleared the ground of debris to make a crude map in the dirt in the early morning light.

"If you're correct, Marcellus, we're about here." He marked the spot with a twig. "Alisio is here to our front." He drew a squiggly line to indicate the Lippe River next to Alisio. "As you said, there are probably not enough men holding that stronghold to withstand a siege by this many Germans. There are what...two understrength cohorts, maybe three, at the Alisio garrison? Certainly not good odds with the number of Germans on the loose. If the fort is under assault as you suggest, then we have one course of action open to us. We must bypass the garrison and proceed west to the original destination of the legions, Vetera. It's imperative we reach the fortress as soon as possible to alert high command. They need to prepare their defenses. The legions in Gaul and Spain will be recalled."

Lucius spoke. "Sir, how far do you reckon it is to Vetera?"

Valerius shrugged and looked to Marcellus for an answer.

The centurion thought for a minute. "As I said earlier, we're fifteen miles from Alisio. If I recall the map correctly, we're another thirty to forty miles from Vetera. We'll not be able to use the road along the Lippe River. As you've just witnessed, the supply posts along the river are now history."

No one said anything. Valerius thought a minute and spoke.

"It's a lot farther away, but it'll offer safety once we arrive. There are ample troops—at least a full-strength legion, maybe more—in garrison at Vetera on the Rhine. It's my sense that the Germans would be hesitant to attack it. It's a permanent fortress with massive fortifications and defended with many ballistae. That'll be our destination."

Marcellus spoke. "You heard the tribune. Let's get going."

They traveled but a short distance, for it was now almost full daylight. They needed to go into hiding once again. The haggard group shuffled into a dense clump of shrubs. Lucius volunteered for the first watch. He settled himself into a comfortable position, keeping vigilance while the others slept. Julia was curled up next to him in her ragged cloak. The odds of anyone stumbling upon them in this remote setting of the forest were unlikely, but stranger things had happened, so Lucius maintained his watch.

They journeyed forth at dusk, continuing to head south. They would then pivot west toward the Rhine. It was imperative to provide warning to Vetera of the Germanic uprising. It was just possible that the fates of the provinces of Gaul and Hispania were contingent upon their alerting the Roman forces of the impending danger. With an army as massive as the one assembled in the Teutoburg, who knew what they were capable of doing?

The going was slow. Prudence was essential, outweighing their need for speed. If the Roman survivors selected a pace that was too hasty, throwing caution to the wind, they would never have the opportunity to alert the garrison at Vetera at all.

They staggered on throughout the night, drunk with fatigue, groping their way along the rugged forest trail. They halted several times, the rest periods becoming longer and longer with each stop. It was torturous to get up each time. They could smell smoldering campfires and occasionally the aroma of cooking food; they were that close to the Germans. As the first signs of dawn appeared, they looked again for another location to hide. Valerius motioned toward a spot in a heavy thicket that wasn't endowed with thorns. To ensure no one continued forward in the semidarkness, he grabbed each person and pointed to their place of concealment.

The four men and one woman quickly entered into a copse, and it was a good thing they did. Sounds of men moving about were everywhere. Faint voices echoed in the early dawn. Branches and twigs snapped and rustled on the forest floor. As it grew lighter, the noise and movement increased. A German warrior wandered over toward the thicket in which they were hiding and stood almost on top of them. As more daylight filtered through the trees, their dilemma became apparent. They were in bushes and hidden, but just a few paces from a major trail. The track hadn't been visible in the darkness when Valerius had selected their hideaway. Bad luck!

Nobody moved. Lucius held Julia tightly as they warily eyed the danger around them. Another figure approached the thicket and began to lower his trousers, his intentions obvious. Valerius gripped his sword in readiness. Marcellus was also poised. But there was no way they could possibly kill the man without someone hearing or seeing the act. Another man called out in guttural German to the squatting figure. He stopped and answered in a laughing manner. The other warrior, most likely his chief, wasn't amused. He addressed him in a harsher tone. The man grumbled, then pulled up his trousers. He wandered back toward the other Germans.

Sounds of many footsteps reverberated past their location. The Germans were advancing toward Alisio. Judging from the activity around the hidden Romans, there were lots of them. They were loud and boisterous. When there was a break in the flow of men passing by, Marcellus stealthily crawled over to each person and assisted in their concealment. By means of hand signals and the mouthing of words, he instructed them in the art of camouflage.

Marcellus helped them slowly smear mud and dirt over all of their exposed flesh and piled whatever debris he could find in the thicket on top of them. It was all deliberate, no sudden movement and no noise. When he had finished, they were totally obscured. They could only be discovered if someone stepped on them.

The number of men passing by slowly dissipated as the afternoon dragged on. There must have been thousands who traveled through this particular area. They waited until there was no more activity. The four men and one woman slowly rose from their hiding place in the encroaching darkness.

They embarked once again, heading due west, paralleling the road along the Lippe River. The mud-covered group walked in single file, Lucius in the lead as point man, with Marcellus providing the direction of march. Forward of their position, perhaps twenty feet, the moonlight glowed upon a wide trail worn smooth by men passing. Lucius halted and turned back to consult with Marcellus. Both men slowly edged forward to scout the trail. There was no one in sight, just the worn, muddy path. Marcellus motioned for Lucius to cross the track. Lucius had just stepped out onto the path when, from his right, a sole German walking down the trail collided with him.

The man barked a question at him. Lucius was paralyzed. He didn't know what to do. The others hadn't yet broken cover onto the path. The man repeated his question much louder. Lucius looked toward the group for assistance. The German followed his gaze and saw the others. He began to yell in alarm.

Lucius drew his gladius and thrust into the man's midsection. The man's shout was cut off in midsentence. Blood shot out onto Lucius's sword arm and face. Marcellus leaped out of the woods with sword raised high and hacked the man in the throat, finishing him. Valerius rushed to the scene and helped drag the man into the brush. There were shouts of inquiry from within the woods. The alarm was sounded as many men merged into the vicinity. The band of Romans ran with abandon through the forest, oblivious of thorns, embankments, and pits. They were dashing for their lives once again. There was no direction to their flight; they were just putting as much distance between themselves and the Germans as they could.

Marcellus steered the way, rushing headlong through briars and shrubs. Lucius held Julia's hand tightly, almost dragging her along. Occasionally, Marcellus would look back over his shoulder to make sure they were all accounted for, then continue his desperate charge into the darkness. After a time, they halted. Everyone doubled over, gasping for breath. Far off in the distance, they could hear the shouts of their pursuers. It appeared they had shaken off the Germans once again.

Valerius, between gulps of air, spoke. "I suggest we continue on, but that we walk in silent fashion. No sense in crashing through this brush like a wild boar."

Marcellus gasped, clearly winded, then rested his hands on his knees for a moment. He spoke in a half whisper. "Right you are, Tribune. The bloody buggers have lost our trail. There's no way they can pick it up unless we alert them. We slow it down and pick up our bearings, heading west once more. Everyone ready to resume?"

There was no response as everyone stared silently at the ground in exhaustion. Marcellus paused for a moment.

"You know, there's an old saying in the legions for times like these. It goes like this. If you feel like you're going through Hades, you'd best keep going."

Valerius muffled a laugh. "That's a new one for me, but actually it makes perfect sense."

The others looked up and grinned at the humor of the centurion. With renewed determination, they arose as one. They traveled throughout the night, although at a much slower pace, until early the next morning. They halted. Once again they took refuge in heavy cover. Valerius asked the question on everyone else's mind. "Marcellus, how much farther to Vetera?"

"If we're where I believe us to be, my guess is about twenty-five miles."

Valerius made a quick decision. "I say we risk traveling at all possible speed even in daylight. We're past Alisio and heading west. I don't believe the Germans are coming to Vetera, at least not for the moment. Have you noticed that there have been no signs of Germans for some time now? I think that we're now ahead of them, and they're preoccupied with Alisio. What say you, Marcellus?"

The centurion nodded. "A bold plan. I agree. Another day, and maybe we'll be there. We should rest awhile, then depart. Is everyone up to it?"

He received weary nods in reply.

Gorgas's scouting party that had been sent ahead of the main body spotted the Romans from about one hundred yards. Instead of waiting for Gorgas and the remaining men to catch up, they attacked. The tracker, Vilix, yelled to his comrades, pointing at the Romans with his sword. With a mighty shout, the force of eight charged.

Valerius and Marcellus had their bows ready in an instant. Calmly, they both unleashed a torrent of arrows directly into the mass of rushing men. It was hard to miss with them all bunched together on the trail and at such close range. By the time the advancing group was within twenty-five yards, they had lost of half their force. The remaining men hesitated, which made matters worse. Marcellus and Valerius were able to get off another volley, both of which struck their intended targets. The four Roman soldiers charged with their swords, finishing off all but one of the Germans. The lone figure fled weaponless toward the safety of the woods. Marcellus sent an arrow streaking at the retreating figure. The flight was true, directed at the center mass of the target, but the trajectory was thwarted by a tree branch. The man escaped.

The Romans quickly checked the dead for any food. There was a moan, then a brief scuffle. One of the Germans was still alive. Martius was about to finish him off with a sword thrust to the throat. Marcellus rushed over and put his arms in front of the fallen warrior.

"Hold that thrust, Legionnaire. We need to find out what this bunch was up to."

Marcellus knelt next to the wounded German. The unfortunate man had two arrows protruding from his chest, either one of which was a mortal wound. He was surprised the man was alive. Marcellus glared at the prone figure, drawing his dagger. The German looked back at him in hatred.

"Were you hunting us?"

The warrior stared back defiantly He coughed a bright spot of blood, which ran down his chin. Marcellus drew the dagger closer so it was at the man's eyeball.

"Tell me or I'll cut you to pieces, slowly."

In response, the man glanced again in the direction he'd come from. Marcellus had his answer.

"Tribune, I think these men were stalking us, and the rest are not far behind. This was no chance encounter. We need to get the Hades out of here, and I mean now. Let's go."

Marcellus mercifully cut the wounded man's throat with a quick slash of his dagger. The five quickly ran from the scene into the forest.

XXV

Valerius glanced toward the rear once again for any signs of pursuit. He winced as his left foot struck a rock. Glancing down, he noticed blood welling from somewhere above his tattered marching sandal. He stared numbly at the ruin of his foot. The hard, iron-studded sole was nearly detached from the leather bottom. Surveying the others of the group, he realized that they were in no better shape, perhaps worse. The centurion was barely walking. He appeared to be dragging his bad leg.

Lucius was supporting Julia, almost carrying her. Valerius had to admire her spunk. Few women could have survived the last harrowing week. Valerius realized that if the Germans attacked them now, they would be unable to mount much of a resistance. This last day had been particularly hard, depleting whatever reserves they had remaining.

"Marcellus," Valerius asked wearily, "how much farther do you think we must travel?"

The centurion was about to speak when his eyes lit up. He held up his hand for silence. Lucius propelled Julia to the side and behind him for protection, whipping out his sword, then looked in all directions for a possible threat. The others quickly drew their weapons and held them out menacingly in front of them. In response, Marcellus smiled.

"Listen. Don't you hear it? It's the most wonderful sound I've ever heard." He cackled like an old woman and started dancing about as if he'd been drinking in a tavern all night. The other four looked at one another, wondering if Marcellus had finally broken. The emotional strain and physical demands must have finally put the poor centurion over the edge.

Julia stepped forward. A broad grin creased her lips. "Oh, yes, I hear it. By the gods, it's sweet music to my ears." She laughed, hobbled over, and hugged Marcellus. He then pumped his fist into the air over and over.

Martius, Lucius, and Valerius looked at one another with puzzled expressions. Marcellus could contain himself no longer. He bellowed a laugh.

"Don't you hear it? It's the sound of water rushing, and it can mean one thing. We've reached the Rhine."

The three soldiers smiled in response. Valerius yelled, "What are we waiting for? Let's go."

The five figures broke into a shuffled run down the trail, where another surprise awaited them. They entered a small clearing where the dirt trail turned into a real Roman road constructed of wooden planks. The sound of the rushing water became even stronger. They hurried down the thoroughfare, crazed to gain sight of the river. The group rounded a slight bend. Before them stood a huge pontoon bridge stretching across the Rhine. On the other side stood the mighty fortress of Vetera, its giant walls looming above the river's edge. They stopped and gaped at the citadel, its walls of solid timber over fifteen feet high. Julia turned and hugged Lucius, then sobbed. The men exchanged glances in relief. They were safe.

Farther back down the track, Gorgas watched in grim resignation the fleeing backs of the Romans. He saw them begin to cross the bridge toward their sanctuary. He muttered an oath, knowing he had let them escape.

One of his men standing to his right addressed his chieftain. "We can still take them. Look at that pathetic group. We'll make short work of them. Let's go after them."

Gorgas held up his hand for silence. "You think we can take them, do you? Ardvas, my now-deceased brother-in-law, and Vilix, my chief tracker, thought so too. Look what happened to them. No, I believe we'll give these Romans a wide berth. They must have powerful gods to have survived the main battle in the forest and then taken down my men."

Gorgas's subordinate wasn't finished. "But Gorgas, there are just four of them plus a woman. Surely we'll prevail against them."

"I think not. Even from here, I can see those large bows strapped to their backs. You want one of those feathered shafts sticking out of you?"

The man was silent.

Gorgas continued. "I don't want any part of them. Besides, we're too near their fort. I don't want the garrison alerted and coming down on our head. Let's get out of here now."

They turned about and departed.

With Marcellus in the lead, they crossed the bridge and rushed hastily toward the gates of the fort. Sentries stood on duty in the twin towers on either side of the huge gates, which were closed tightly. The looming guard towers were over twenty-five feet high and constructed of massive wooden beams. The sentries stared down at the pitiful-looking group, wondering where these tattered figures had materialized from. The men's uniforms were in rags. Julia was no prize either, with her twisted and tangled hair. All were filthy and covered with cuts and abrasions. The only things military about them were their weapons and marching sandals. Valerius and Marcellus carried their bows with the quivers of arrows clearly visible on their backs. Valerius hobbled forward toward the gate.

One of the sentries called down, "State your business, if you please."

Valerius replied, "Call the officer of the guard. I'm Tribune Valerius Maximus of the Army of the Northern Rhine. I need to see the commander of the garrison immediately."

The sentry answered, "You don't look like any tribune I've ever seen." He then laughed at his own sarcastic attempt at humor. He looked about at the other sentries to see if they shared in his wit.

Valerius fumed. After all he'd been through, he didn't need this shit.

"Soldier, I will make this request once more. You will get me the officer of the guard now, or I will personally see to it that you have latrine duty for the next year. Furthermore, you will observe military courtesy and address me as sir. Is that understood?"

The sentry looked again at the group, then for the first time noticed the array of weapons and the steely glares directed upon him. The unfortunate man glanced about for support from his fellow sentries. The other soldiers averted his gaze and remained silent. His fatuous grin disappeared in a hurry. "Of course. Right away, sir."

Marcellus smirked from behind.

Valerius turned to Marcellus. "What?"

"Oh nothing, Tribune, but I do believe you've the makings of a good officer. You've picked up some of the finer points."

Valerius beamed back at Marcellus, pleased with the compliment.

After a brief wait, the gates opened. A centurion flanked by eight guards walked out calmly and deliberately to meet them. They all had their hands near the hilts of their swords. The centurion eyed them warily.

Valerius wasted no time. "Centurion, thank you for coming so quickly. I'm Valerius Maximus, a tribune with the army of General Varus. This is Centurion Marcellus. We need to see the garrison commander immediately. We have urgent news."

The centurion frowned. He didn't introduce himself. He stared at them suspiciously. "If you don't mind my asking, how do I know if you are speaking the truth?"

"For the gods' sake, man, who else would come out of the woods carrying Roman weapons, wearing Roman boots, and speaking Latin? You think we're a bunch of bloody Germans?"

The man hesitated, not sure what to do. The five survivors stared at him in silence. The ambivalent centurion finally made up his mind. He turned toward the gates. "Follow me."

The group passed through the fortress gates.

The five figures, accompanied by the centurion and his guard contingent, strode down the main road of the encampment, passing a succession of buildings. The air was thick with the odor of fresh-cut wood. Soldiers passed by, glancing at them in idle curiosity. As they proceeded farther into the complex, a new smell hit them—the sweet scent of fresh-baked bread from the legion's commissary. Their mouths watered, as they had been without real food for over a week, except for the raw fish.

The road ended in front of another gate. This was the main intersection of the fortress, where the two main thoroughfares came to a T. They were now in front of the administrative headquarters. It was an impressive structure of two stories with a colonnade. Unlike the other buildings they had passed, this one was anything but crude. It even had a red tile roof like most houses in Roman cities and towns.

The centurion advanced quickly to the entrance and hollered at the men manning the inner gates to open them. The gates swung dutifully wide. The centurion waved for them to enter. They came into a large courtyard flanked on all sides by extensions of the buildings and passed into the main building. The group was guided to a waiting area that was sparsely furnished. Valerius motioned for the others to sit on the wooden benches. He remained standing. This was his show now.

The centurion of the guard turned toward Valerius. "Wait here." He disappeared into another a room. They could hear muffled voices from where the centurion had disappeared. The person to whom the centurion was speaking was clearly annoyed at the intrusion. There was another angry retort. The centurion reappeared, followed by a tribune, who stared at them, visibly sneering at their appearance.

"What's this about wanting to see the garrison commander, General Saturnius? He's a busy man. Who are you, anyway?" To emphasize his point, he wrinkled his nose in disgust at the odor emanating from the group.

Valerius was not to be denied. "I'm Valerius Maximus, tribune with the Army of the Northern Rhine. I know my appearance and that of my colleagues is a bit out of the ordinary, but that's unimportant for the moment. Do you see this group here?" For emphasis, he gestured to the survivors.

The tribune from the office replied, "Yes, they all look a bit ragged."

"This *ragged*-looking bunch, as you call them, may be all that's remaining of the army of General Varus."

The centurion and tribune blanched at this comment. The tribune did an about-face and hurried back through the offices. There were shouted instructions and the sounds of hurried footsteps. After a brief period, he returned.

"Follow me," he said. The man turned and went quickly through the doorway. Valerius hurried to catch up with the urgent strides of the tribune from the fort.

Valerius was led through a series of offices until he reached another doorway. The tribune who guided him knocked once and entered. A senior officer whom Valerius assumed to be General Saturnius was standing waiting for him. Saturnius eyed him coolly, taking in his appearance but saying nothing. The man was tall with an aristocratic face, handsome yet with a trace of haughtiness. His countenance was angular, with square cheekbones and a somewhat narrow nose. His brown hair was cut short, almost to the skin. His eyes were dark, boring into him. Valerius understood right away that he was dealing with a true no-nonsense soldier and not some political appointee. He also knew he'd best be careful in what he said and how he presented himself.

Valerius didn't wait until he was addressed. He reported. "Sir, my name is Tribune Valerius Maximus. I have urgent news. I was with the army of General Varus. The three legions were trapped and massacred in the Teutoburg Forest by a massive force of Germans. There may be more stragglers, but the army was for the most part annihilated. I've been on the run for four days. We attempted to get to the garrison at Alisio, but that was under siege. My guess is that anything Roman east of the Rhine is probably overrun and destroyed.

The German forces may be on the way here, although I have no true knowledge of their intentions."

The general grimaced at the news. He stared coldly at the tribune. Valerius returned the stare but didn't elaborate on his statements. After a few more moments of silence, Saturnius turned to his staff tribune. "Find the other senior officers and get them here now. We have work to do."

"Yes, sir."

"Oh, and also, Tribune, I want the guard doubled and on full alert. All men outside the fort are to be recalled immediately. Is that clear?"

"Yes, sir." The tribune almost ran out of the office.

Turning back to Valerius, he spoke. "I want you to tell my staff and me the entire sequence of events. Don't leave out any details. I'll be the judge of what is or is not essential. Is that clear, Tribune?"

"Yes, sir. Would you mind, sir, if I requested that the survivors who were with me be given care? They're in dire need of food and medical attention. They've endured severe hardship over the last week. They're in the outer office," he said, pointing in the general direction.

"Of course," replied the general. Saturnius turned toward the open doorway. "Centurion Glaxus. I need you here for a moment."

A centurion immediately appeared in the opening. Valerius guessed the man had probably been listening to every word. "Yes, sir."

"Centurion, there are a number of soldiers requiring food and medical attention in the outer waiting area." Saturnius turned toward Valerius. "How many did you say?"

"Four, sir. A centurion, two legionnaires, and a woman."

Saturnius addressed the centurion. "See that they get proper care and some food."

"Yes, sir. I'll take care of it right away."

By now, the officers of the general's staff were entering the room. They stared in curiosity at Valerius, unsure of what to make of him.

Saturnius spoke. "This is Tribune..." He paused. "What did you say your name was?"

"Valerius Maximus, sir."

"Ah, yes, Maximus. He was with General Varus. He has delivered some unfortunate news. He's informed me that the Army of the Northern Rhine has been defeated and massacred by a massive force of Germans."

There was an audible gasp around the room. The general held up his hand for silence. "He will tell us what he's witnessed. From the top, Tribune, if you please."

"Yes, sir. As you know, the legions were to march from the summer encampment on the Weser to this fortress for winter quarters. Just before we were to march, there was a report of a rebellion of one of the native tribes to the north of the encampment. I believe it was the Chatti. Apparently they killed several of the tax collectors and wiped out some outposts. General Varus was infuriated at the insolence of this tribe. He decided that he'd take care of this business even though it was a considerable departure from the normal route of march."

"Hold on there for a moment, Tribune." Saturnius turned to one of his aides. "Go get the large maps that we've stored in the outer room next to the records area."

There was an uncomfortable silence as they all waited for the aide to return. After a brief period, the man returned, and the map was spread out on a wooden table.

"Please continue, Tribune, and show us on the map if you can."

"Yes, sir." Valerius studied the map for a moment. "The legions were here, of course, on the Weser." He traced on the map with his finger. "We traveled in this direction. The army proceeded in good order on a northwesterly course along the Weser, then pivoted west into the Teutoburg Forest. That's where things went to Hades in a hurry."

One of the senior officers interrupted. "Are you telling us he went into the Teutoburg with his full army and supply trains? Are you shitting me?"

"Ah, yes, sir, that he did."

The general spoke sternly to the gathered officers. "Let the tribune tell his story. Please continue."

Valerius paused to gather his thoughts. "Several of the senior commanders attempted to dissuade General Varus from his plan of operations, including General Licinus. Varus wouldn't listen. There were also rumors that one of the German chiefs attempted to warn him that he was being lured into a trap by the supposedly loyal Germans on his staff."

Saturnius asked the main question. "Who was responsible for this subterfuge? What was the leader's name?"

"Arminius, sir. He was the liaison officer. He was highly trusted by Varus. He even feasted with the man and his father."

"Bastard," voiced one of the officers.

"As I was saying, we marched maybe thirty miles from the camp and made good progress for the first few days. The roads were passable and the weather good. Then things started to deteriorate. We found ourselves in a towering forest with poor roads. Our progress was extremely slow with the baggage carts and wagons. The Germans struck us from all sides in a driving rainstorm."

The men nodded in remembrance of the weather last week.

"How many Germans?"

"Difficult to say, sir. There were large numbers in the initial ambush. Perhaps we were outnumbered three to one at the beginning. My centurion, Marcellus, believes they were reinforced over the next several days."

An officer Valerius guessed to be the deputy commander of the garrison interrupted. "Tribune, would you be referring to Centurion Marcellus Veronus, stationed with the Army of the Rhine?"

"One and the same, sir. He led us out."

"I know the man. He's an outstanding soldier. By Jove, I'm glad to hear he's alive. I'll need to talk with him later."

"Please continue, Tribune," said the general icily, clearly annoyed by the interruption.

"The legions sustained heavy losses. The rear was chewed up pretty bad, but the army regrouped. We punished the Germans for their attacks. They hurled themselves at our shield wall. We made them pay. Slaughtered quite a few of them. General Licinus found open ground in front of the column. The three legions went into a defensive laager, then the army dug in for the night. The camp was heavily fortified, and the Germans didn't attack us."

A servant appeared, bearing a large tray with goblets of wine. Valerius eagerly accepted the offering. Without a glance at the other officers, he chugged the entire contents. He sighed in contentment and wiped his chin with his forearm. He looked up to see the others staring at him.

"Uh, sorry. I forgot my manners. It's been many days without any proper food or drink."

The general sipped his wine and calmly put the goblet down. "Continue, Tribune."

"The next day dawned with no rain. We abandoned the carts and animals in the laager. They would be a hindrance to us. We also left the wounded who couldn't travel. I can only guess what happened to those poor souls. The wagons were torched as we departed. Our goal was to journey south toward the established route of the Lippe. We couldn't turn back at this point.

"The army marched out in good order. We made some progress before they were on us again. There was actually some optimism that the Germans had retreated, but it was false hope. They lured us deeper into the forest, in the terrain of their choosing. I concur with my centurion's belief that they were probably reinforced over the night, with more of the tribes joining the rebellion."

"How did you come to that conclusion, Tribune?" Saturnius had an edge to his voice.

"Sir, not to overstate the obvious, but there just seemed to be more of them. They hit us from all directions along the length of the column. It wasn't just my belief. Several of the senior officers opined that the Germans had reinforcements."

"I see. So it's the day after the initial contact with the enemy, the army is attempting a breakout, and it's about midmorning. Correct?"

"Yes, sir. As I said, we made some progress, but the army's advance came to a halt. Trees were felled in our path to halt our progress and break up our formations. They wiped out the cavalry under

Vala Numinius. The Germans attacked us, then backed off before we could engage them. They came at us in successive waves. It seems they always had fresh bands of warriors to launch at us."

"The Germans have never fought like that," said the camp adjutant. "This Arminius must know his stuff."

"Yes, sir. I was told that he served for over three years in the Pannonian revolt. He knows the tactics and capabilities of the legions."

"Go on, Tribune," said Saturnius.

"We suffered more losses. The combat was ferocious. The men fought hard, sir. There was no panic, but our tactical situation was untenable. We were hemmed in on all sides by towering trees and thick brush against overwhelming numbers. The army formed another night perimeter. The men were exhausted. The cries of the wounded and dying were everywhere."

"Shit," swore one of the senior officers. "Those treacherous swine are going to pay for this."

Valerius went on. "That night, most of us didn't sleep. General Varus was incapacitated by his wounds, so Licinus took over the command. It was his idea to attempt to flee while it was still dark. Before dawn, we bolted out of the encampment, hoping to catch the Germans by surprise. We all knew it was a desperate maneuver at best, but it was probably the only option open to us. All equipment was abandoned with the exception of armor and weapons. We rushed out quickly and actually made surprising progress. The Germans were caught a bit off guard, but not enough. We were trapped between sloping high ground to our left and a swamp to our right. They eventually surrounded us and moved in for the kill. By that time, the surviving units were down to less than fifty percent strength. They attacked in waves. One by one, the lines between centuries, cohorts, and legions were breached. Units were cut off. The Germans besieged the surviving soldiers, overwhelming the last remnants of the army. I witnessed Varus taking his own life. Everyone knows what these Germans do to their captives. The First Cohort of the Nineteenth Legion, perhaps the finest fighting unit, was overrun and destroyed before my eyes."

Valerius's voice was getting husky with emotion.

"Your escape, Tribune," said the general quietly.

"Yes, sir. I was in a small pocket of resistance at the edge of a large copse of trees with the remnants of the main headquarters and command element. Centurion Marcellus and I were fighting side by side. We were isolated from the main body of troops, or at least what remained of them. A tremendous rainstorm enveloped the battlefield. Centurion Marcellus, some other soldiers, a woman, and I fled into the forest. Otherwise, we would have been slaughtered. Our corpses would be moldering back with the rest of the army.

"We fought our way out of the woods and encountered resistance from roving bands of warriors. Some of our force were slain, but we managed to kill most of them who attacked us despite being heavily outnumbered. Since then, we've been on the go over the last four days. Our original plan was to get to Alisio, but that was under siege."

One of the staff officers quizzically eyed the enormous bow strapped across Valerius's chest. "What's with the bow, Tribune? An unusual weapon for an officer."

Valerius reached and briefly caressed the weapon. "Centurion Marcellus introduced me to this Egyptian war bow. It's a good thing, too. These bows saved our asses. We left a fair number of them rotting in the woods with feathered shafts sticking out of them."

There was a brief silence. "Any more questions for the tribune?" The general looked around the room, waiting. "Tribune, you're dismissed. I'll conduct a formal board of inquiry, as is required under these circumstances, and interrogate all of the survivors. I'll see to it that you and your men are properly cared for."

The general turned his back on the tribune and began addressing his staff. "Gentlemen, we have much work to accomplish. Let's begin."

Valerius, realizing his presence was no longer needed and knowing he had been snubbed by the general, departed the room.

Lucius, Martius, and Marcellus were alone in a large bathhouse. Earlier that day, Julia had seen a familiar face from her previous stay at this post. Having heard what she had been through, the family had taken her in, fussing over her. She'd assured Lucius she was fine and would see him tomorrow. They were getting ready to exit the bath when Marcellus held them back with his extended arm, gazing about in the wisps of steam for anyone who might possibly overhear their conversation. It was late, and with the exception of few stragglers, the bathhouse was almost empty.

Marcellus spoke to them in a quiet tone. "They'll have an inquiry into this Varus mess. Each of us will be questioned at length. You all know that the penalty for deserting the battlefield and one's unit is severe. There are many instances where the legions have exercised harsh measures, if you get my drift. Tell the truth. Be honest. Don't embellish. If they think you're lying about any of this, we're all going to be in some thick stew. Report exactly what you saw and experienced in your unit and how we managed to escape. Above all, remember, it was the tribune and I who led you out. Understood?"

Lucius and Martius nodded in agreement.

"Let's call it a day, but remember what I just explained to you."

That night, Lucius sat on the edge of his cot. He thought about the centurion's words. He'd do exactly what the man had said, up to a point. He'd best leave out the part when Cassius and he ran the gauntlet up the length of the Roman column to the rescue of Julia. The story would be that the two had been separated from their century when the Germans overwhelmed the Roman lines. Somehow Cassius and he had been forced into a small copse of trees with Marcellus and the tribune. He wouldn't reveal his relationship with Julia. He mentally began to compose his story, but he didn't get far. He was asleep instantly.

"Palonius, Lucius Palonius, where are you?"

Who in the Hades was calling his name? Lucius groggily raised his head from his cot.

"Palonius, identify yourself. You are wanted at headquarters immediately for questioning."

"Over here," Lucius croaked.

He rose to a sitting position, shaking the sleep from his head. He looked about, noting just a few occupants of the barracks. In fact, it was almost empty.

"What do you want from me?"

The messenger, an optio, stared hard at him. "You're wanted at headquarters immediately to answer questions about your escape. You are to proceed there, as in right now, without delay. Do you understand?"

Lucius was still half asleep, drunk with fatigue from his ordeal. The fact that Lucius was tired and looked as if he'd been beaten repeatedly with cudgels studded with thorns wasn't considered important.

Lucius blearily slipped on his new clothing, which had been issued the previous evening to replace the bunch of torn and bloodstained rags that he had been wearing upon his arrival at the fort. He'd eaten until his belly was full last night, but now he was ravenous again. His hunger would have to wait. Lucius quickly splashed some water on his face to freshen himself.

The optio looked on in displeasure. "Hurry it up there, Legionnaire. You are keeping important people waiting."

"I'm coming. Just give me a moment, will you?"

The optio said nothing, staring icily at Lucius. Now feeling somewhat presentable, he followed the optio. Suddenly, the figure of Marcellus filled the doorway. The centurion knew immediately what was up but didn't let on. "Lucius, off early this morning, I see."

Lucius gestured with his hand toward the waiting soldier. "They want to ask me some questions at the headquarters."

Marcellus examined the optio briefly before dismissing him as nothing important. He turned back to Lucius. "I won't keep you waiting. We can continue our discussion from yesterday when you get back. You remember what we talked about, right?"

"Sure, I remember, Centurion. This shouldn't take long, I hope." Lucius stared at the optio for confirmation, but the man said nothing.

"I'll look you up as soon as I get back. Maybe we can get some food then." Lucius turned and exited the doorway.

The optio and he walked down a broad avenue lined with workshops and storage sheds before arriving at a series of wooden buildings. Lucius was ushered into a small room. He stood at attention before a centurion and a rather haughty-looking tribune.

Both of the officers were seated at a table along with a clerk taking notes. Lucius's first impression was that the centurion was most likely a good soldier who understood men in the ranks. He had that air of competency about him and the weathered look of a man who had served in the field for a good many years. The tribune was a different story. He had a rather pointed nose and an arrogance about him that spelled trouble. His armor was shiny, as if it had never been in use, which it probably had not. Lucius quickly recognized where the peril lurked and put on a blank expression.

The tribune started right in on the questioning without explanation. "My name is Tribune Sevillus, and the man next to me is Centurion Crispus. Let's get right to it, shall we? Your name and service with the legions."

"I'm Lucius Palonius. I've been with the legions a little over six months. I'm from Gaul."

"I didn't ask where you were from, nor do I care. Just answer the questions you're asked. Understood?"

Lucius nodded. He saw the centurion lower his face at the laconic tone of the questioning. I have an ally. He also knew that his impression of the tribune was correct. He was a dangerous man. Lucius needed to be cautious in his remarks.

"I didn't hear a reply, soldier. It's customary in the legions to reply to an officer using military courtesy. I asked if you understood my instructions."

"Yes, sir. My apologies." Lucius stood a little taller and stared straight ahead.

"Very good. What unit were you posted to?"

"Sir, I was assigned to the Eighteenth Legion, Tenth Cohort, Third Century."

"Now, Palonius, let's get right to it. Please tell us how you managed to escape the battlefield while most of your comrades did not." The tribune emphasized the word *escape*, as if to imply that it was more likely a desertion from the battlefront.

Lucius could feel his anger mounting but remembered whom he was addressing and why. He composed himself. His life could be at stake, depending on how he answered.

"By the morning of the third day, we were totally exhausted. The army broke out of our night laager while it was still dark so that the legions could escape the Germans. We ran as an army in a tight formation, a column of six men abreast for...I don't know, several miles before the Germans descended upon us. They came at us in huge waves of flying wedges. My century was already less than half strength. I would say closer to forty percent. We held off the first charge, then a second charge, but then, more waves of men came rushing out of the forest. They had erected some kind of barricades on the hill next to the trail. The Germans threw their spears and then charged out to engage us. There were Germans everywhere. We killed so many of them with our swords, but they just kept coming out of the woods, more and more of them. They broke through our ranks. I saw my centurion slaughtered, then witnessed the killing of almost all of my friends and the men in my century. The Germans were chopping off heads and stabbing the dead over and over until there was nothing remaining but a bloody mess. It was beyond horrible."

Lucius stopped for a moment. His thoughts of Cassius had turned his voice thick. He shifted his position to get more comfortable. There was silence in the room. The centurion intervened and took over the questioning from the tribune.

"Please continue," he said softly.

"Yes, Centurion." Lucius needed these officers to believe the next part. He put a mask on his face and stared straight ahead. He cleared his throat, then spoke in a low tone.

"My friend Cassius and I were fighting back to back with some big trees protecting our rear. We were about the only ones left from my unit, at least as far as I could see. We were holding off a handful of Germans between the two of us. Then this huge storm pounded us. The water came down in torrents. The wind was knocking off branches from the trees. I don't know who joined who, but the next thing I know, Cassius and I were fighting alongside Tribune Maximus, Centurion Marcellus, and a bunch of other legionnaires."

All was quiet in the room. The tribune had stopped asking questions. Lucius's graphic account of the battle appeared to have muted his convictions. He almost looked sympathetic. He nodded in deference for the centurion to continue with the inquiry.

The centurion spoke to Lucius. "Had you ever met Centurion Marcellus or Tribune Valerius before?"

"The tribune and I became acquainted earlier in the summer. Our cohort was out on patrol. We were ambushed by the Germans. The two of us were fighting next to each other on that day."

The tribune nodded as if he was in satisfied with that answer. "Tell us what happened after you joined Tribune Maximus and Centurion Marcellus."

Lucius stared right at the two officers. He hadn't mentioned Julia at all. She wasn't a soldier and need not be part of this, nor did he want to make them aware of his relationship with her. It would just invite more questions, some of which he might not have a good answer to.

Lucius continued. "The storm got even stronger. The wind howled, and the rain battered us. Everything seemed to stop on the battlefield. We couldn't see anything. Centurion Marcellus and Tribune Maximus ordered us to follow them off the main trail and into the woods."

"And you followed him?"

"Yes, Centurion, of course I did. They were officers."

"You mentioned this Cassius fellow. I don't see his name on the list of survivors. What happened to him?"

Lucius swallowed hard and paused. His voice was now low, barely to be heard. "After we left the main trail, we were trapped by a band of about thirty Germans. We killed almost all of them between our small group of six soldiers. The Germans killed my best friend, Cassius, and two other legionnaires. I never knew their names."

Tribune Sevillus interrupted, his tone haughty and demanding. "Oh, come on now, Palonius. It was what...six of you against thirty, and you prevailed? Are you not exaggerating the numbers a bit, soldier?"

"Tribune—I mean sir—you've never seen anyone bring as much Hades as Tribune Maximus and Centurion Marcellus with those bows of theirs. In fact, the number of Germans might have been more than thirty. I didn't have the time to count them all." Lucius grinned in remembrance.

The centurion and the tribune exchanged puzzled looks.

The clerk had stopped writing, and the room was quiet again. Outside the room, one could hear the sounds of nails being hammered somewhere in the fort. The centurion and the tribune exchanged glances.

The tribune spoke. "I think we're done here. You're dismissed, Palonius."

Later in the day, Lucius and Julia were strolling around the compound.

"Julia, Lucius."

Both looked up as Tribune Valerius approached them.

"There you two are. I've been searching for you. I've wanted to speak to both of you."

"Yes sir," replied Lucius.

"No need for formality, Lucius. Listen, I haven't had the opportunity to talk to you since our arrival."

Julia interrupted. "Would you like me to excuse myself?"

"No need for that. What I have to say, I'll say to both of you. First, I'm sorry about your friend Cassius. If it's any consolation, he died honorably, a soldier's death. I know how close you both were to him. And of course, Julia, I'm sorry about your father. He was a brave man who did a great service for the legions."

Julia eyes started to fill up. She grabbed Lucius's hand tightly.

"Also, I want you to know that it was an honor to serve with both of you. I owe my life to you. You're a real soldier, Lucius. That goes for you, too, Julia. You're as tough as any legionnaire I've ever met. Not many people could have endured what we went through together."

Julia smiled at the compliment. "Thank you for those words, Tribune. I shall always remember how you and Centurion Marcellus led us out of that nightmare. We owe you our lives."

Valerius grabbed Lucius's shoulder. "Listen to me, Lucius. Don't worry about this board of inquiry mess. Marcellus spoke to me about it this morning. I believe I can handle this matter. I do have some other resources available to me if necessary. If there's ever anything I can ever do for either of you, let me know. I am indebted to you both. If you're ever in Rome, look me up. The house of Maximus on the Aventine Hill."

"Thank you, sir. I hope one day to visit the great city. Maybe I'll take you up on that offer."

"Good. I'm counting on it. Once this inquiry mess is completed, we'll see what the legion has to say about your future plans. You're from Gaul, correct?"

"Yes sir. A small town called Belilarcum."

"Perhaps we can arrange for you to be assigned somewhere in Gaul. It's the least the army can do after what you have been through. We will talk some more afterward. For now, just relax, stay low, and don't worry about this hearing. Understand?"

"Yes, sir. Thank you once again for your offer of assistance."

Two days later, the four soldiers—Martius, Lucius, Marcellus, and Valerius—stood at attention in front of a military tribunal consisting of General Saturnius; his deputy commander, Marcus Favonius; and Tribune Sevillus, the one who had questioned Lucius. The three were seated behind a wooden table on a raised dais facing the four legionnaires. A clerk sat in the background taking notes. All four had been interviewed at length concerning their conduct and behavior over the last ten days.

Valerius stepped forward. "Sir, for the record, I'd like to make a final statement concerning the conduct of these fine soldiers with me."

"Tribune Maximus, I believe we've already heard all of the testimony concerning this affair."

"Nevertheless, sir, I feel compelled to make a final statement for the record on their behalf. Permission to proceed, sir?"

The general looked up from his scroll and sighed. "You may, Tribune. Please be brief."

"Thank you, sir." Valerius cleared his throat.

"I know that the legions frown upon men fleeing the battlefield. The punishment for such behavior is severe. A soldier is expected to follow orders. He's expected to stand with his unit and fight for his comrades and the emperor. There's no disputing this. I would make two points. First, it's implied that when a man flees the battle, he's a coward. Nothing could be further from the truth with these men standing before you. These soldiers have killed more Germans over the last week than perhaps the entire complement of soldiers in this garrison. These few survivors were covered in blood and gore, mostly German, but also some of their own, as they fought their way out of the forest.

"They're brave men. They're warriors. I would gladly serve with them anywhere.

"Second, as to deserting their units, I would say, what units? All semblance of an organized fighting century was obliterated in those final terrible hours in the Teutoburg Forest. They witnessed the deaths of their friends and fellow soldiers. Their officers were dead. There was chaos at the end. It was I who led them out of the death trap. They followed my orders."

Valerius stepped back.

"Anything else you wish to add, Tribune?"

"No, sir."

"I've considered your testimony. I came to the same conclusions myself about this debacle. Nevertheless, a tribunal is necessary when unfortunate events such as this occur. I'll now pass judgment.

"Legionnaires Martius Calerus and Lucius Palonius, step forward, please."

Lucius and Martius dutifully strode forward.

"Fleeing the battlefield in the face of the enemy is a serious offense in the legions. But given the circumstances and the accounts of your bravery, the punishment for this offense will be commuted. But unfortunately, you would always be known for your association with the defeated legions in this battle. You would be considered unlucky by your fellow legionnaires, and you did flee the battlefield.

Therefore, I'm expelling you both from the legions for the good of the army. Do you understand what I've just told you?"

Lucius was stunned. He felt betrayed and confused. He'd done nothing wrong. He opened his mouth to speak. Looking back over his shoulder toward the centurion for guidance, he saw Marcellus give him warning glance and a shake of the head.

The general waited. "I asked, do you understand?"

Both men mumbled, "Yes sir."

"Your expulsion will take effect immediately. You'll be given your final pay and travel monies. Dismissed."

The two performed an about-face and exited the room. The general stared at Marcellus. "Centurion Marcellus Veronus, step forward, please."

Marcellus advanced one pace, staring straight ahead.

"Centurion, I'm told you've served the legions with distinction for many years. Also that you've earned many awards and decorations in your years of service, including the Corona Muralis for actions against the Germans. I applaud your valor. I wish you could have served with me at some point. My deputy commander"—he nodded toward the seated Favonius—"does nothing but rave about you. Given the stigma associated with the Teutoburg battle, I have no choice but to retire you from active service with full pension. I have one more assignment for you that I'll explain shortly. Understood?"

"Yes, sir," said Marcellus. He stepped back, awaiting the order to be dismissed. It wasn't proper for a centurion to witness the judgment of a higher-ranking officer, but no order was forthcoming. He remained standing at attention.

"Tribune Valerius Maximus."

Valerius stepped forward. "Yes, sir."

"I'll not pass judgment on you. I'll let Rome deal with that. I have an important assignment for you. You're to proceed with all possible speed to Rome. There, you'll personally inform the emperor of the defeat in the Teutoburg Forest. Centurion Marcellus and another soldier who is retiring, Centurion Albinus, will accompany you as escorts. It's imperative that the emperor be informed of this event as soon as possible. Do you understand your assignment?"

Valerius responded, "Yes, sir." He paused for a moment.

Saturnius looked on impatiently. "Yes, Tribune? You were about to say something."

"Sir, I'm not sure I know how to tell the emperor of this news."

The general laughed harshly. "You'll have to find a way, Tribune. You were there. You'd better be prepared to tell him exactly what happened and why. If I were you, I'd make ready for this meeting. The emperor isn't going to be pleased with this news. I hear Augustus, or Rome's first citizen, as he likes to be called, has a temper like you wouldn't believe."

Valerius swallowed the lump in his throat.

"Again, do you fully understand your orders, Tribune?"

"Yes, sir, I believe so."

"Good. I will provide you with passes and letters of requisition for horses and supplies on your journey. I expect you to leave immediately. This board of inquiry is concluded." General Saturnius stood, then exited without further comment.

Marcellus and Valerius hurried out of the room. When they were out of company of the other soldiers, Marcellus addressed Valerius. "Tribune, we escaped with our asses intact. That's a minor miracle considering what's occurred. I'll assist you with your preparations. Let me find this Albinus fellow, and we can get moving."

"But I promised to see Julia and Lucius again after the tribunal."

"We have no time, Tribune. We need to leave as soon as possible. I'll leave word with Lucius. They'll understand. I believe Lucius can handle these matters."

"I still feel bad about it. I promised them."

"Trust me on this, Tribune. We need to leave this place within the hour. I'm sure Lucius and Julia will forgive you. Now we need to get moving. The emperor awaits us."

XXVI

*V*alerius perched wearily upon his horse. What he wouldn't give right now for a chilled goblet of wine. He surveyed the winding road ahead. His leather saddle creaked as he leaned forward to view the seemingly endless avenue. He rubbed his stubbled jaw in thought. Nothing in sight yet, but soon. Glancing down at the paved road, he noted with grim satisfaction the worn polygonal paving stones. They were getting damn close to Rome. The quicker they arrived there, the better. He and his two companions had been riding nonstop for ten days, traveling over eight hundred miles from Vetera on the Rhine toward Rome. His ass was flatter than a crushed biscuit.

The trio had changed horses several times, spending eighteen to twenty hours a day in the saddle. Glancing to either side, Valerius could see the avenue was shaded by tall, narrow cypress trees. He gazed ahead, attempting to concentrate on the task ahead of him. This was becoming increasingly difficult, given his fatigue. He had never fully recovered from his flight out of the Teutoburg, yet here he was on an extended passage that was taxing his last reserves.

Their journey had been somewhat circuitous from the fort on the Rhine. All roads may lead to Rome, but they don't do so in a straight line. He and his companions had traveled southeast from Vetera to the fortress of Moguntiacum on the Rhine, then southwest for about fifty miles, then due south through Gaul to the Mara Nostra. From there, they proceeded to travel east along the coast before reaching Italia and then headed southeast toward Rome.

His orders from General Septimus Saturnius had been quite explicit. He was to ride with all possible speed to Rome and personally convey to the emperor, Augustus Caesar, the news of the defeat of Varus in the Teutoburg Forest. It normally took a marching army eight or nine weeks to get from Rome to the Rhine. Valerius and his escorts were doing it in a little over a week.

The two centurions hadn't complained once about the pace he had set. They understood the importance of the tribune's orders and the urgency of arriving in Rome as soon as possible. The two junior officers were in complete contrast to each other. Marcellus was glum about his forced retirement. It was a shattering blow to him. He had devoted his entire life to military service. It was all he knew.

Albinus, who seemed to be a decent enough fellow, couldn't wait for his soldiering days to be over. He had put in twenty-five hard years with the legions. He'd proclaimed that once this final assignment was finished, he intended to look up some old friends, then do some serious drinking and wenching. After that, he'd declared, he would decide what to do with the rest of his life.

Valerius had thought a lot about Marcellus on the journey. He owed the man a great deal, including his life. Without him, he would be another rotting corpse on the forest floor of the Teutoburg. He knew Marcellus didn't have the foggiest notion of what to do with himself. It was simply a question the centurion had never pondered— or wanted to, for that matter. He'd always been a soldier, nothing more, nothing less. Life beyond the legions had never been contemplated.

Valerius hadn't told Marcellus yet, but he intended to use his family's considerable influence to find him a civilian position suitable for his talents. The man had too much pride to accept anything from him, so he planned do it in a subtle manner. He wasn't sure how, but he and his father could conjure up something. That was assuming Valerius survived his encounter with the emperor.

His fogged mind realized that his exhausted horse had almost stopped completely. He would never get there at this pace. Valerius kicked the flanks of his mount, urging his horse to a trot. He could think much better with his mount moving at a brisk tempo. Over the entire journey, he'd grappled with how to break the bad news to Caesar Augustus. He'd yet to arrive at a satisfactory approach. Back at Vetera when he had been informed of his assignment, he'd asked General Saturnius what he was to say to the emperor. The general had laughed at him in scorn. There had been no help from that quarter.

How was he going to get an audience with him? He was just a sorry-ass tribune. He would need to communicate the urgency of his dispatch to whatever imperial staff he might encounter. One didn't just stroll to the emperor's home and request to chat with the most powerful person in the Roman world. Valerius couldn't use his father's name. He wasn't that important a man in Rome. He would need to be resourceful and employ guile. Valerius knew that the Praetorian Guard was extremely selective of who entered the palace. He would appeal to their sense of duty. Yes, that would be the answer. He would portray himself as a fellow soldier performing his duties as ordered by his superiors. That at least might gain him some sympathy with the Praetorians.

What was he going to tell the most powerful individual in the Roman world about his destroyed legions? He urged his horse into a full gallop, leaving the two centurions far behind. Killing Germans was one thing; delivering bad news to the most powerful man in the world was another. He'd heard about Augustus's temper. His harsh treatment of those who displeased him was common knowledge. Many had been banished to faraway places, including his only daughter, Julia. Valerius pictured himself on some rock in the middle of an unknown sea. Would that be his future?

Marcellus viewed the rapidly disappearing form of Valerius.

"Now what in the Hades has gotten into the tribune?"

Motioning Albinus to stay behind and with a quick kick to the side of his mount, Marcellus urged his horse forward to a gallop. He eventually caught up to Valerius. He signaled the tribune to slow the pace.

"Something bothering you, Tribune, or are you just angry with your horse?"

"Yes, something is bothering me. Is it that obvious?"

"Written all over your face."

"Marcellus, how in Hades am I going to tell the emperor what happened? What can I possibly say to ease the terrible news? I just can't find the correct words."

Marcellus rode on in silence for a while, pondering the question. At length, he spoke.

"Tribune, there's no way to pour honey over shit and make it smell good, so don't try. Report the facts as you know them like the military officer you are. This is not your fault, so don't try to mince words. Above all, don't apologize. My guess is he'll call for his military advisors, so be ready to explain in detail as bluntly as possible. That includes the blunders our now-deceased and former esteemed general committed. Don't try to defend him."

"But Varus was a relative of the imperial family."

"He was, but not blood related. So give it to him straight; no nonsense."

"Do you think that's how I should go about it?"

"I do. Of course, I've never addressed an emperor, but that's the way I would do it."

"Marcellus, I think there'll be great anger directed at me."

"Tribune, you can bet your ass on it. Three of Rome's finest legions are now a bunch of moldering corpses. Try not to be intimidated. They'll grill you and want to know how you escaped while the others perished. Don't be defensive. Tell them the facts."

"Thanks, Marcellus. I'll try to keep that in mind."

The pace slowed, and the two continued riding in silence for a while. This allowed Albinus to catch up, and the three rode abreast gazing ahead down the open road. Marcellus began chanting in his booming voice:

There was a legionnaire meek
Who invented a lingual technique.
It drove the women frantic
And made them romantic.
And wore off the hair on his cheek.

Albinus and Valerius burst out laughing. Valerius turned to Marcellus. "I know; Livy, right?"

"Tribune, don't you know your classics? That was Homer."

"I'll remember that. I'll be sure and look up my former tutor when I get back and mention that to him."

The last milestone Valerius checked noted five miles to the city walls. Carts and wagons traveling in the opposite direction increased in number. It was now close to dusk. The sides of the road were now bereft of trees; instead, they were populated by numerous funeral monuments competing with one another in terms of grandeur. They were traveling on the Via Flamenia, which entered the city from the northwest. The road would take them on a straight shot to the Palatine and the home of the emperor.

The three rounded a bend to the crest of a small hill. They slowly made their way amid the road traffic to the summit. There, before them in the distance, stood the magnificent city. Massive stone walls surrounded the metropolis. Even at this late hour, the buildings of white marble perched upon the hills of the city were resplendent in their glory. The faint, slanted rays of the evening sun sparkled off the distant monuments and buildings. The brown haze of countless cooking fires within the city cast a slight pall over the otherwise magnificent display of buildings. Marcellus, who in all of his years of service had never been to this center of power and glory, simply stopped and stared. Nothing could have prepared him for the sight in front of him. His jaw dropped open. He was speechless, which was truly remarkable for the centurion. The three mounted men remained motionless.

At last he spoke. "I'll be dyed seven shades of shit."

"That certainly sounds attractive," remarked Valerius.

Without turning his head from the view in front of him, Marcellus spoke softly. "It was what my first centurion used to say when he was bewildered." The three continued to stare at the city in the distance.

To Valerius, after living these past months in the forests and plains of Germania, the sight was breathtaking. Even from this distance, he could make out some of the individual buildings on the Palatine and the Capitoline hills. Valerius edged his horse next to Marcellus and pointed.

"That building on your left with the large dome and the massive white pillars is the Temple of Jupiter. Over there is the Temple of Saturn, and that's the Forum, and the group of buildings up on the Palatine hill is where we'll be traveling. That's where the palace of Augustus is located."

It was quickly getting dark. He realized they should hurry. At dusk, the gates of the city were closed. He had two options. He could travel straight to the residence of the emperor now or wait until morning. If he reported now, he'd be following his orders fully. The problem was that he looked like Hades. His uniform was covered with mud from the road, he hadn't shaved in almost a week, his face bore a number of scabs from various cuts and abrasions, and he smelled bad. He hadn't bathed since leaving Germania.

Valerius decided he was going to report immediately. This wasn't a spurious decision. He reasoned that, given his current appearance, he looked like a soldier who was delivering an urgent dispatch. This would provide him a better chance to gain access to the emperor. His harrowed look might give him greater credibility. On the contrary, if he chose the spit-and-polish image the next day, it would hardly fit the look of a survivor of a disastrous battle. Yes, he thought, he wouldn't delay; he would go to the emperor tonight.

He led his horse into a gallop. He shouted over his shoulder at the two centurions. "We need to hurry before they shut the gates for the night."

The three mounted soldiers galloped down the road, heedless of the obstacles. People and carts dodged out of the way, uttering curses as the men thundered past. In places where there were traffic jams, the men rode around the obstructions, moving in and out of tight places, then charging off into the open space. Their horses were lathered by the time they reached the massive walls surrounding the city. Their hurried approach was to no avail. Night had fallen. The imposing gates were firmly shut. They were too late. The trio was at the foot of the massive gate, its stone arch rising twenty-five feet and fitted with an immense wooden door strengthened with iron bands. Torches along the wall illuminated the area around the gate. Valerius could see the silhouettes of the sentries on guard duty. He wearily dismounted.

In a fit of impatience, Valerius cupped his hands around his mouth and yelled up at the soldiers. "Open the gates. Urgent dispatch."

"Sorry, sir, the gates are shut for the night. No admittance. Besides, no horses are permitted on the street after dark."

Before Valerius could explode, Marcellus intervened. "Soldier, do me a favor and get your centurion here now."

The man looked down at Marcellus and stared. He hesitated, then peered back down and noted the tribune and two centurions. They far outranked him, so he quickly complied with the request. He would let his superior deal with this.

"I'll be back shortly with the centurion."

The three men waited impatiently below. It seemed to take forever until the centurion of the guard appeared. When he finally did show up, the officer was grumpy, annoyed at being disturbed so early in his watch. The centurion cupped his hands and shouted from the wall. "What's going on?"

Marcellus calmly explained the situation. "Centurion, we need to enter the city now. We have urgent dispatches for the emperor. I know you have standing orders about entrance after dark, but it's critical that we be permitted admittance now."

The man hesitated. Marcellus saw his indecision.

"Centurion, take a close look at us. We've been riding for over a bloody week without letup."

Valerius waved his written orders from General Saturnius in the air. It was a bluff, of course. Those papers authorized him access to horses and supplies on the journey to Rome, nothing more.

The centurion shouted down at them, "Come a little closer into the light so I can have a better look at you."

The three men nudged their mounts forward. Valerius tightened his grip on his reigns. The duty centurion, wary as he was, appeared to be leaning toward letting them gain admittance. Valerius knew now was the time to seize the opportunity.

"We don't have time for you to fetch the commander of the guard. This is a matter of state and an extreme emergency. If you obstruct us any more, there'll be Hades to pay. It'll be your ass. Now please open the gates."

The centurion bought it. He yelled at the sentries, "Open the gates."

The massive doors slowly creaked open. A small gap appeared between the wall and the door. The three shot through the partially opened gate and past the astonished soldiers. They bolted down the city avenue and rode like the wind. They stormed past a city patrol, who shouted angrily after them about riding in the streets. The two centurions and the tribune paid them little heed, advancing down the narrow avenue. Valerius listened closely but could hear no sound of pursuit. They rode with all possible speed through the twisting thoroughfares as Valerius guided them ever closer to the Palatine Hill. The horses' hooves made a terrible clatter as they sped down the paved street. They drove the mounts onward, maneuvering around a sharp corner, their cloaks trailing them in the wind. A group of night revelers scattered, taking shelter in the safety of a shop alcove. Valerius, in the lead, pointed up a hill dotted with grand domiciles.

Above the clatter of the hooves, Valerius shouted, "We're almost there. This way." He pointed to his right emphatically.

Valerius rode up the hill and urged his horse up the stone steps as far as he dared. He dismounted and handed the reins to Marcellus. "Hold my horse for me. I'll take it from here. Wish me luck."

"Good luck, Tribune. We'll be here waiting for you."

Valerius paused briefly to ready himself, then, despite his weariness, bounded up the stone steps two at a time to the entrance of the marble palace. He was intercepted by several of the Praetorian

Guard, Germans no less. The last time he'd seen any of these bastards, they were attempting to skewer him.

"Get me the officer of the watch, and make it fast."

The soldier looked back with a blank stare.

"Go now!"

The man hurried off to find the night commander.

Valerius paced back and forth, now alarmed more than ever at the growing lateness of the hour. The officer of the guard finally materialized out of the darkness. His appearance was impeccable. His armor gleamed in the torchlight. Valerius could make out the figure of the scorpion, the symbol of the Praetorian Guard, on the man's breastplate. The officer looked at Valerius, taking in the tattered state of his uniform and general appearance. He sneered in derision. Valerius held his temper in check. He was almost there. He must be forceful but polite. It didn't pay to fuck with these Praetorians. They were an arrogant bunch, but they had absolute power, and they knew it. He decided to wait for the commander to speak.

"What do you want, Tribune?"

"I need to see the emperor right away."

"You want to see the emperor at this hour with your appearance? You look a bit shabby, if you know what I mean."

Valerius needed to gain the man's sympathy.

"I look this way because I've been riding almost nonstop for over a week from Germania. I have urgent dispatches for only the emperor's eyes. Do you really think I'd report to the emperor looking like this if it weren't important?" Valerius flashed the papers again.

"This can't wait until morning, Tribune?"

"I was ordered to proceed by General Saturnius, commander of the garrison at Vetera on the Rhine, at all possible speed to Rome and to convey personally to the emperor these communications."

The commander of the guard was still not satisfied. He eyed the papers Valerius held tightly. "Do you know what this is about, Tribune?"

"I do. It's imperative that I see the emperor now. I'm to report only to Caesar."

He added this tidbit so the officer of the guard would realize the importance of the message. He hoped it would stop him from fishing for information.

The Praetorian looked toward Valerius hoping for an explanation, but there was none coming. Valerius stared straight ahead, his face an immobile mask. The officer frowned in disappointment.

"All right. I will get the imperial chamberlain and let him deal with you."

Valerius cooled his heels awhile, waiting for his next human obstacle, hopefully the last one. After a short while, the chamberlain appeared. He was a tall, elderly-looking man wearing a white toga. He was bald with a gray fringe of hair around his crown. He looked annoyed.

"What's this about wanting to see the emperor at this hour? Are you crazy? Besides that, you smell like a horse."

Valerius was resolute. "I need to see the emperor now. It's a matter of extreme urgency."

"I'll be the judge of that. What's this about?"

"My orders are directly from General Saturnius, commander on the Rhine, and are quite explicit. I'm to report only to Caesar. I can't tell you the nature of this business. If you don't let me report, it'll be your ass that's hung out." Valerius said this somewhat vehemently, hoping this would crumble the man's defenses.

The chamberlain sighed. "Tribune, this better be important, or you'll be a tribune no longer. It'll be your young ass that's hanging out."

Valerius grinned inwardly, proud of his deception. It had worked again. Valerius, accompanied by the chamberlain, walked down a narrow corridor. At various intervals, small torches provided illumination. There were Praetorian guards, big beefy men in full armor, strategically stationed down the length of the hall. Valerius's metal studs on his leather sandals tapped a resonating cadence on the tiled floor. They moved ever nearer to the emperor's inner sanctum. Now that he was in an enclosed space, Valerius realized how bad he smelled. How in the Hades had he gotten into this situation?

He tried to remember what Marcellus had said. He was a military officer in the Imperial Roman Army reporting as ordered. He tried repeating this mantra to himself. "I'm just reporting as a proper tribune should."

He smiled to himself, thinking that his father had hoped one day that Valerius might be appointed a senator. Hah! After this debacle, he had about as much chance of making senator as finding a virgin in a whorehouse.

They arrived at a pair of massive doors over twelve feet high flanked by two more burly guards. The chamberlain turned to Valerius and spoke tersely. "Wait here." The chamberlain entered through the doors, closing them behind him.

Valerius, in an attempt to be presentable, tried to wipe some of the grime and splattered mud from his face. He gave up. It was useless.

Torches illuminated the dining hall where the imperial family lounged. They were fueled by a sumptuous banquet followed by ample quantities of wine. The walls were replete with beautiful frescoes, and the marble floor gleamed in the torchlight. At the head couch was the aging Caesar Augustus, accompanied by his wife, Livia. There had been rumors about her that would curl one's toes. Possible murders and poisonings within the imperial family were linked to her.

At the couch to the right was Tiberius, stepson to Augustus, now his adopted son and next in line for the throne. Adjacent to them was Germanicus, son of the mighty Drusus. Germanicus, although only twenty-one, had already established himself as a great military leader and was a favorite of the people. Completing the circle of diners were Claudius, brother of Germanicus, and finally the Lady Antonia, mother to Germanicus and Claudius.

The chamberlain edged closer, but he still kept a respectable distance from the emperor and waited to be recognized. There was great laughter emanating from the group, and the conversation was boisterous.

Augustus looked up in irritation at being disturbed. "Yes, what is it?"

"I'm sorry to interrupt, sir, but there's a tribune who insists he see you now with an urgent dispatch from Germania."

"Do you realize what time it is? Can't it wait until morning?"

"He's quite insistent, Caesar. I attempted to discourage him, but he says it's imperative that he report to you and no one else."

"Bring him in now, but this better be important." The emperor didn't attempt to conceal his anger.

The chamberlain hurried out to retrieve Valerius. Augustus rose from his dining couch, facing the entrance to the room, and waited for the tribune to appear.

The chamberlain came back through the double doors and stood directly in front of the waiting Valerius.

"Tribune, you have your wish. The emperor will see you now, but I'll tell you, he's most displeased at the interruption at this late hour. I hope you know what you're doing."

Valerius stared back at the chamberlain, not saying a word. The man turned his back abruptly, then led Valerius into the private quarters of the imperial family.

Valerius, carrying his helmet in the crook of his left arm, was guided by the chamberlain to a short connecting hallway, then into the dining room. He noted a number of servants standing back toward the shadows. He came to the position of attention just inside the doorway. All eyes of the imperial family focused on him. Valerius swallowed hard and made ready. It was time.

Augustus walked in front of him. Valerius had never seen the emperor except from afar. He had no idea he was this old. In the torchlight, he could see the age spots on the man's face. He could feel the piercing eyes of the emperor examining him. As protocol demanded, Valerius stared straight ahead, not moving, waiting to be addressed.

"This is the way a tribune in the Roman army presents himself to Rome's first citizen? You're filthy. You smell dreadful."

Valerius was ready for that one. "Sir, I've been riding almost constantly for over a week from Vetera on the Rhine."

"Yes, I know where Vetera is," Augustus said sarcastically.

Valerius maintained his composure despite the stinging rebuke from the emperor.

Germanicus and Tiberius, both soldiers, now joined Augustus, surrounding Valerius.

Tiberius spoke sternly. "What's your name? What unit are you with, Tribune?"

"Sir, I'm Tribune Valerius Maximus, son of Sentius Maximus. I was of the Northern Army of the Rhine under General Varus."

"Was?"

"Yes, sir. The three legions of the Northern Rhine Army were ambushed and massacred in the Teutoburg Forest. They no longer exist."

Augustus dropped his silver wine goblet. It clattered across the marble floor. There were gasps of shock in the room, followed by a stunned silence.

Tiberius asked sharply, "And Varus?"

"Dead by his own hand, sir. He was wounded badly and took his own life."

Germanicus stood before him. He said accusingly, "How did you escape?"

"We fought continuously for two days. By the third day, the army's strength was less than fifty percent. The Germans assaulted early that morning. They outnumbered us by perhaps as much as six to one. All units were overrun. There was no cohesion in the ranks. We were surrounded. A small band of us managed to fight our way out of the area. We fled toward Alisio, but that was under siege. From there we escaped to Vetera."

Tiberius was quick to grasp the strategic situation. "So, Tribune, with the exception of the few legions in the garrisons on the Rhine, there's nothing to protect the provinces of Spain and Gaul from the Germans?"

Valerius was silent for a moment, then murmured, "Yes, sir, that would be correct."

Tiberius shouted for the house slaves to get the maps out, then turned back to Valerius. "Tribune, you'll show us where this happened and how."

"Yes, sir."

By now, Augustus had recovered his composure but was still visibly upset. "I never liked that Varus. He was a damn fool."

Livia, the emperor's wife, looked up coldly from her couch. "I didn't appoint him. You did."

"I know, I know. Don't remind me," he said testily.

Yes, he was the biggest ass I've ever met, thought Valerius. The tribune glanced slightly off to his left, noting the cold, piercing eyes of Livia fixed upon him. She stared at him briefly before turning away, dismissing him as a man of little importance.

A servant hurried in with a large rolled-up map while others brought forth additional oil lamps for lighting.

Tiberius spread the map out on the dining table, flinging dishes and goblets to the floor.

"All right, Tribune, show us."

"Just before the departure to winter quarters, there was a report of a rebellion by the Chatti in this vicinity."

Valerius pointed at the map. "The Teutoburgiensis Saltus?"

"Yes, sir. Varus decided to march the entire legion plus baggage trains almost due west into the area and then head south to the normal route after he took care of business."

"He dragged the baggage trains into that area, into the Teutoburg?" said Germanicus incredulously.

"Yes, sir. He wanted to teach the Germans a lesson they wouldn't soon forget. General Licinus, commander of the Seventeenth Legion, attempted to dissuade him, but his suggestion was ignored. In fact, Varus reprimanded him in front of the entire officer corps."

"That damn fool," blurted Augustus.

"Go on," said Tiberius.

"Sir, it was rumored that a German chieftain friendly to Rome tried to warn him of treachery. He told him that his German deputy liaison, Arminius, plotted treason. He was the leader of the rebellion."

"So, Arminius was behind this," said Tiberius. "I know that man. I'll see him in Hades for this."

Germanicus urged Valerius on. "Please continue, Tribune."

"When we had marched maybe thirty miles, we found ourselves in a dense forest along a narrow road. There was no place for us to maneuver. A heavy rainstorm struck. They came out of the forest from all sides and hit us. We beat them off but suffered heavy losses and formed a night laager. The next day we went out, marching west again. The wagons were left in the laager to burn. They attacked again in even greater numbers. We constructed again a defensive perimeter and spent the night." Valerius stabbed the map with his finger. "About here, I believe. The next day, it rained hard again. The Germans attacked in force and overran our remaining units as we moved out. They overwhelmed us by sheer numbers. I saw them capture at least one of the eagles."

Augustus erupted in rage.

"QUINCTILIUS VARUS, GIVE ME BACK MY LEGIONS!"

Everyone turned and looked at the emperor.

Livia began to guide Augustus away. "Come with me and retire now. Tiberius and Germanicus will begin plotting the military strategy. Won't you?"

"We'll develop a plan for you to review in the morning," said Tiberius.

Augustus broke away from Livia, stopped, and slammed his fist on the tabletop with a resounding crash. His face was livid with rage. "I WANT MY EAGLES BACK."

Livia sauntered over toward Augustus's side and gently guided him toward the doorway.

Germanicus steered Valerius over to the side, out of earshot, while Augustus exited with Livia.

"By Jove, you've got a pair of stones. I can't believe you came in here looking like you did, presenting yourself to the emperor. And you rode from Germania to Rome in what...a little over a week? Impressive, Tribune. I like your style. See me after this mess has settled down. I may have a place for you." Germanicus grinned knowingly at Valerius.

Tiberius came across the room to join them. "Stay with us, Tribune. We are not through with you yet. We have more questions."

"Of course, sir."

Valerius spent the next several hours explaining in detail the preparations for the march, the ambush, the tactics, the number of Germans, the weather, his escape, and the actions of General Saturnius for fortifying the Rhine bases and calling up the legions from Gaul and Spain. Both Tiberius and Germanicus were relieved to hear that additional legions were being recalled by Saturnius from the southern provinces to bolster the remaining two legions on the Rhine. Valerius was at last dismissed, with the provision that he might be recalled to explain the battle to others the next day.

XXVII

Now past midnight, Valerius bounded down the steps from the emperor's palace, taking three at a time. He burst unexpectedly upon both Marcellus and Albinus, startling them.

"Centurions, what are we waiting for? Let's get going. I can taste that wine already."

The three mounted their horses to begin the short journey through the city streets to the home of the tribune. Valerius felt ebullient. A tremendous burden had been lifted from his shoulders. He led the way through the narrow avenues. Flickering torchlight illuminated their passage through the deserted streets. Above the clatter of the horses' hoofs, Marcellus impatiently urged Valerius to recount what happened.

"Are you going to tell us, or do we have to beat it out of you? We're waiting, Tribune."

Valerius flashed a mocking grin at him in the darkness. He paused, collecting his thoughts before speaking. Marcellus became more vexed by the absence of a reply. Valerius shouted back above the noise of the horses, "Don't get your pee hot. I'll give you the short version now and explain the rest when we arrive at my parents' house."

"Spill it, Tribune. Who was there?"

"First of all, I interrupted a little social gathering of the emperor's family. They weren't at all pleased to see me. I'll explain later how I bluffed my way in. The little gathering included the great Augustus; his wife, Livia; Tiberius; Claudius; Lady Antonia; and Germanicus."

"You actually saw the emperor?" asked Marcellus incredulously. "I never thought you'd get that far."

Valerius smirked. "I did indeed. When I entered, everyone was annoyed. Apparently I disrupted their revelry. They took great offense about my appearance. As you suggested, Marcellus, I reported the news of the disaster in as direct a manner as possible. The emperor didn't take the news well. He called for Varus to give him back his legions. Tiberius and Germanicus grilled me about the battle in detail. I believe they are at this hour making plans for military operations against the Germans. In the end, I think my ragged and filthy appearance worked to my advantage."

Marcellus questioned Valerius. "Are you on safe ground, Tribune? What did they say?"

"I believe my ass is safe, at least for the present. Germanicus took me aside and told me he admired my mettle for reporting in the manner I did. He said to come and see him about a place on his staff after the dust had settled on this affair. Perhaps he might have a place for a certain centurion I know."

Marcellus grinned back at him in the moonlight.

The trio turned to the left on a street that ascended a hill dotted with villas and homes of considerable wealth. At last they stopped in front of Valerius's house, with the prominent white marble columns. Valerius's spirits were soaring. He was actually home, a place that he thought he'd never see again. The tribune jumped off his horse and handed the reins to Marcellus. Despite his weariness, the tribune ran up the stone steps to the massive wooden double doors of his residence. Mounted on each of the doors was a large bronze wolf head with a large ring in its mouth. He grabbed one of the rings and slammed it against the door several times. The booming sound reverberated in the stillness of night along the empty street. That should get someone's attention. There was a muffled query from the other side of the door, asking who was there. Valerius recognized the voice of Horace, the household butler.

"Horace, you old goat, open the door. It's me, Valerius."

A single wooden door swung slowly open. Horace was holding an oil lamp up. He peered into the dark. "Master Valerius, it's you. Please enter."

"Horace, wake my mother and father. Fetch them here if you would, please. We'll be in the study." Another servant appeared in the doorway. Valerius instructed him to take the horses. He beckoned the two centurions on the street below to enter the house.

Valerius led the way and entered a small room off the atrium, the *tablinium*, which was used to entertain guests and business associates. Marcellus gaped in fascination at the residence. He'd never seen anything like it in his life. His quarters had always been a crude wooden barracks or a goatskin tent.

The tribune lit several oil lamps. He indicated seats for the two centurions. Horace reappeared with a jug of wine in a bowl surrounded by ice.

"Ah, Horace, my good man, you knew exactly what I was thinking."

The servant grinned a knowing smile. The men greedily drank the wine. Following Valerius's action, they wiped their mouths on the sleeves of their dust-covered tunics. They all held their cups for refills.

Valerius's mother, Vispania, and father, Sentius, entered. Both appeared somewhat disheveled in their bedclothes. They were taken aback at the sight of the two huge centurions replete with armor, weapons, and their son. All three of the soldiers were filthy. The gamy odor assailed their nostrils as soon as they entered the room.

His parents had to squint in the dim lamplight to make sure that it was indeed their son.

"Valerius," said his father.

"Yes, it is I."

His mother gasped, ran to her son, and hugged him. After a time, Valerius gently disengaged her.

"Let me mind my manners. Centurions Albinus and Marcellus, these are my parents, Sentius and Vispania Maximus. Mother and Father, may I present Centurions Albinus and Marcellus."

Both parties nodded politely to each other.

Sentius spoke. "Marcellus, you must be the centurion my son wrote so much about in his letters."

Marcellus politely replied, "The tribune and I have spent much time together in the service of the legions."

"You're probably wondering what I'm doing in Rome," said Valerius.

"We're glad to see you so unexpectedly," said his father. "We didn't anticipate seeing you for several more years."

Valerius interrupted his father before he could continue. "Let me get right to it, Father. There's been a terrible disaster in Germania. The legions of General Varus, in which I served, have been massacred in the German forest. Marcellus and I are two of a handful of survivors. I've just been to the imperial palace to personally inform the emperor of the catastrophe. It wasn't a pleasant duty."

His father stared at him in disbelief. "Varus, I believe, had three legions under him. They're all gone?"

"Yes, Father, they are no more."

His father, squinting in the darkness, looked at his son more closely. "You went to see the emperor dressed like that?"

"Yes, Father, it was necessary."

Sentius recovered quickly. "Enough of this unfortunate business. We can talk more in the morning. I'll have the servants prepare the guest rooms."

Sentius turned to the two centurions. "You must be famished. The kitchen fires are out, but I'll have fruit, cheese, and bread brought to you. I'll also get some more wine. I believe I need a cup after what I've just heard."

Valerius grinned back at his father. "That would be splendid, Father. Please join us."

With tears streaking down her face, his mother again embraced Valerius.

The tribune reflected on the last time he'd been here. It had not been so long ago, but so much had happened since then. The person who had departed this house six months ago was not the same man now. The young tribune so concerned about performing his duty for Rome in the service of the emperor was no more. He had served with distinction and done his duty, and let no man say different. He would think of his future later. He gazed briefly at Marcellus. How lucky he was to have met the man. Fortune had indeed smiled upon them. He retrieved the wine pitcher and refilled everyone's cups. They all raised their flagons and drank deeply.

Epilogue

*A*fter what seemed like an endless number of days, Lucius was finally given his official release from the legions. Marcellus and Valerius had departed weeks ago, yet here he was, still within the fortress walls. The general had stated his dismissal from the legions was effective immediately, yet he had to wait. He probably should have known that when the legions had said that his dismissal was effective immediately, they had their own definition of that time.

But Lucius was finally going home. He clutched in his right hand the small piece of parchment noting his discharge. On his belt dangled his scant pouch of coins. He hurried to Julia's quarters on the main thoroughfare, then knocked politely at the wooden entrance. Julia answered. Lucius waved the discharge paper in front of her.

"We're getting out of here." He opened his pouch and poured some money into her hand. "Get what you think we'll need at one of those civilian stores. I'll be back for you as soon as I can find out about any transportation."

Lucius turned to leave, but Julia stopped him. "But what should I buy for us?" She looked at him quizzically.

Lucius shrugged. "I don't know. I guess food, clothes, and some blankets for starters. I got to go." He turned and departed.

Now that the moment was at hand, Lucius needed some direction on to how to get home. With Marcellus gone, he didn't know whom to ask. He was not acquainted with anyone at the fort. He wandered over to the transport area, where the wagons were parked. He figured this might be a good a spot to find someone who might be a reliable source of information. He saw a centurion supervising several soldiers loading a cart. Lucius surmised that this centurion looked like a soldier who understood the way the military worked and somebody who would know how to get from point A to B in the quickest time.

Lucius caught the centurion's eye, then walked up to him. "Centurion, I sure could use your advice on something."

The officer eyed him warily. "Go ahead."

"I need to travel to Gaul. I know I have to go through lower Germania, then the province of Belgica, and finally into southern Lugdunensis. The problem is, I have no idea how to go about getting there. Can you give me some pointers?"

The centurion viewed him suspiciously. "I know you're a legionnaire. You have the look about you, and you wear the caliga. How is it you're going into Gaul when all leaves are canceled because of the disaster in Teutoburg? You a deserter?"

"No, Centurion. I'm not a deserter. If you want to know the truth, I'm being discharged for the good of the service." Lucius was about to explain the circumstances surrounding his separation.

The centurion interrupted. "What did you do to deserve that? You a troublemaker or something?"

"After what I've been through, they decided it best to have me leave the service of the legions. I was in the Teutoburg."

"So you are one of them? I heard a few made it out. Tell me, was it as bad as everyone says?"

"Worse, much worse, Centurion. I don't know what you've heard, but it was an absolute goat fuck. We were trapped for three days in that bloody forest in the rain, with Germans coming at us from all over the place. The last day, they just overran everything and everybody. I don't know how any of us managed to get out. I witnessed the killing of all of my friends and soldiers in my unit."

The centurion nodded in sympathy.

"I guess after what you've been through, maybe you should get out. Let me give you some advice on travel. Now, you were talking about going to Gaul. If it were me, I'd hitch a ride with one of the wagon convoys leaving here for Gaul. Stay with the convoys. They're a safe haven. These roads can be dangerous places, with bandits and thieves. I believe one is going out tomorrow. Take that as far as you can. Get directions from that point and hook up with anyone you can find. It'll take you at least a couple of weeks, maybe longer. With the German problem, we got lots of troops coming up this way on the roads. They'll be jammed. I heard they got legions coming from as far away as Spain."

"Thanks, Centurion. Any idea where I might find that convoy?"

"Sure do. Be right here early in the morning."

Lucius and Julia climbed aboard the ox-drawn cart early the next day with their few meager possessions. They sat in the half-empty cart matted with straw. They slowly departed down the road, away from the fort. The autumnal weather had turned cold. They wrapped themselves in their recently purchased cloaks. Lucius put his arm around Julia. They snuggled together to keep warm. The pair stayed that way for the entire morning and part of the afternoon. For several days, they plodded along in a westerly direction.

The centurion's prediction rang true. The roads were clogged with large formations of troops marching in the opposite direction, going toward the Rhine. The sight sent chills up Lucius's spine. The wagon he and Julia occupied was forced to the side of the road many times as endless numbers of centuries marched by, the ranks filled with grim-faced soldiers carrying the tools of their trade—shields, swords, and javelins. Their hobnailed sandals rang on the hard road as they marched, their backs and arms burdened with equipment.

On the fifth day, they stopped for a midday meal at a small village on the border of Gaul in the province of Belgica. They were seated at an outside table of a dining establishment. About half of the other tables were occupied. The two shared a simple meal of bread and cheese with some wine. A harried figure rushed about, then stopped in front of Lucius and Julia.

"Did you hear about the disaster in Germany? They wiped out three legions. I heard the Germans are going to invade Gaul next."

Lucius just stared in silence at the man. When the man received no reply from the stranger, he moved on. Lucius stood abruptly. He realized that by now, word had reached his hometown. His family knew he was stationed with the Army of the Northern Rhine and probably thought him dead. Julia stared back, unsure of what was wrong.

"My parents," he said. "They think I have perished with the army back in Germania. You heard the man. The word is spreading everywhere. We must reach them as soon as possible."

Julia gasped. "But what can we do get there sooner?"

Lucius paced about, then stopped and shrugged. "I don't know. We will just have to continue as best we can. It's going to be at least another week."

Lucius couldn't finish his meal, his anxiety getting the best of him. Julia nibbled at her food, but she left most of it scattered about her plate. The pair went for a walk after lunch, hand in hand. The two of them were enjoying the afternoon sunshine when Julia let go of his hand and bolted to the side of the road. She retched repeatedly, emptying her meal to the ground.

Lucius hurried over when she was finished.

"Julia, are you ill?"

"No, not exactly."

"It sure looks like it. What does *not exactly* mean?"

"It means I think I'm with child."

Lucius was stunned. He'd never even contemplated that possibility. "How did this happen?"

Julia looked at him as if he were stupid.

"Sorry; dumb question."

"Lucius, how do you feel about it?"

"I'm a little shocked, but I kind of like the idea."

"So do I." Her voice started to break. "We'll have a son and name him Cassius Petronius."

Lucius winced, remembering the death of his friend. He truly missed him. Cassius of the quick wit and ready smile, always with a story to tell. Cassius, the one who had dreams of Lucius and he serving in the Praetorian Guard together. It would be fitting to name their son after him. The two embraced for a long time, then walked back to the wagon.

Lucius's mother, Aquilonia, sat in front of the stone house in which her family resided. She was so proud of their dwelling. It was a solid structure, built to last. With its sloping tiled roof, it offered protection for her family from the elements. Off to the left was her garden, where she grew her herbs, vegetables, and flowers. There had been many happy moments in this house, but those days were in the past. She absently washed and cut vegetables for the evening meal in a wooden bowl. The sun was setting in the western sky. The heavens were colored with bright magenta hues of an autumn sunset. She ordinarily took much pleasure in this simple beauty, but not so anymore.

Her anguished thoughts were solely for her lost son. She had had such high hopes for him. He was her eldest child, her firstborn, occupying a special place in her heart. She smiled briefly, remembering his birth. What a beautiful baby she had brought into this world. For what? she thought. To have an ending like this? The recent news spreading throughout the province had robbed her of any peace of mind. The word of the defeat in Germania had sent panic through the land. She had understood immediately the impact of the disaster. Her son was with the Army of the Northern Rhine. His letter had even noted the upcoming march to winter quarters.

She frantically inquired everywhere about the extent of the defeat and even attempted to gain an audience with Piso, the magistrate, but he had refused to see her. At first, Aquilonia had held out hope that her son might somehow have escaped the carnage, but the story was the same. The entire Roman army had been massacred in the Teutoburg Forest, no survivors. How could such a thing happen? she asked herself. Her son hadn't belonged in the army in the first place. He should have been here with his family.

All she could think about was her son's body rotting away in some distant forest. She glanced up from her labors, looking westward toward the setting sun. She saw two figures in the distance dismount from a cart along the road and walk toward her. She had to squint because of the glare. She guessed they were probably two travelers on their way into the town to spend the night. This was the main road into the center of town. Many passed this way. It appeared to be a man and a woman.

Something looked familiar about the walk of the man. His tall figure was erect, and the gait was rapid. The two began to hurry in her direction. Aquilonia stood. Her heart was in her throat. She dared to hope for the impossible. The two figures drew closer, but she still couldn't see them distinctly. Aquilonia shaded her eyes with her right hand. The couple became more visible. Might it possibly be?

The strangers started running toward her. The man cried out, "Mother."

She screamed, dropping the vegetables onto the ground. "Lucius, by the gods, Lucius. Lucius, you're alive."

The two ran at each other and embraced. She kept repeating his name over and over as tears streamed down her face. The other family members, alarmed at the screams, rushed outside. Drusilla, Lucius's younger sister, bolted from the entrance of the house, running toward her brother. She leaped through the air and embraced her mother and Lucius. The father and brother, still unsure of what was happening, came running. Tears streamed down the faces of the family members. Julia, who was standing to the side, wiped her face at the poignancy of the moment.

Lucius at last broke apart for a moment and held up his hands. "I want you to meet someone special." He grabbed Julia's hand and smiled at her. "This is my wife, Julia."

That was the first time he'd used that expression. A small smile crept onto Julia's lips.

"Julia, this is my mother, Aquilonia; my father; my sister, Drusilla; and my brother, Paetus."

"How do you do. Lucius mentioned you in his letters." Drusilla shyly went over and held Julia's hand.

Aquilonia spoke. "Lucius, we thought you were stationed with the army that was killed in the Teutoburg Forest."

Lucius paused for a moment with a pained expression. "Julia and I were there. It was a horrible. Julia lost her father there. Few of us survived."

There was an awkward silence.

Aquilonia went over and put her arm around Julia. "You poor woman. Let's all go inside. You must be exhausted. We'll talk there."

The reunited family began to walk toward the house. Lucius stopped and turned to look back toward the setting sun. The events of the last several months flashed through his mind—his basic training, meeting Julia, the ambush of his cohort, the Teutoburg, the death of Cassius, the days in privation in the forest, and his release from the legions.

All of this had occurred in a period of just seven months. He hadn't asked for this life. It had been thrust upon him. It was time to heal now and forget the horror of the Teutoburg Forest. He was sick of the killing and slaughter. Lucius grimaced in remembrance. It had been a hard journey, but at least he'd beaten the sibyl's prophecy—or had he? Maybe this had been in the stars for him from the beginning. No matter; he'd survived. It was now time to live. He owed it to Cassius and all of the others.

His family called back to him to come into the house. He stared a moment longer. A dark, foreboding cloud momentarily obscured the sun, and a chill breeze blew unexpectedly in his face. He quickly turned away, then hurried after them.

END

Author's Note

*T*he Battle of the Teutoburg Forest did indeed occur in the autumn of 9 AD. It was one of the most decisive military conflicts and forever altered the history of Western civilization. The devastating defeat of the Roman forces resulted in the destruction of three entire legions, over 10 percent of the Roman army. These legions were never replaced. It marked the end of the Roman expansion. The border of the Roman Empire became the Rhine River. It also established Germany as a future nation-state.

The location of the battlefield was an enduring mystery until the last twenty-five years, when startling artifacts were uncovered by a British army major near Kalkriese. No one is sure exactly what transpired over the course of the Varussschlacht (Varus Battle), as there are various conflicting accounts. Some historians say it lasted three days; others believe it was only one day. One thing is certain. A shattering ambush occurred, and it ended badly for the Romans. I have provided an interpretation based upon historical sources including Vellius Paterculus, Tacitus, Florus, and Cassius Dio.

The main characters are fictitious, but others were real historical figures, including Caesar Augustus, Tiberius, Germanicus, Arminius (whose German name remains unknown), Quinctilius Varus, Vala Numinius, Segestes, Sigimer, and Thusnelda. Augustus died a few years after the news of the defeat in the Teutoburg Forest. Tiberius succeeded him as emperor. Germanicus, on Tiberius's orders, invaded Germania on a punitive expedition six years after the battle and recovered two of the eagles. He marched his troops to the final battle scene in the Teutoburg Forest and buried the dead, who had been left where they had fallen. The legions of Germanicus never completed their conquest and were pulled back to the safety of the Rhine. Arminius continued to battle the Romans, including Germanicus. He was later poisoned to death by his own tribesmen. His pregnant wife, Thusnelda, was seized by the Romans. She and her son died in captivity in Rome.

Caesar Augustus did utter the immortal words *Quinctilius Varus—give me back my legions.* It is unknown how he received the terrible news. I borrowed the scene in which Tribune Valerius informs the emperor of the Teutoburg disaster from the BBC production of Robert Graves's *I Claudius.*

The weapons, armor, and tactics of the Roman legions noted in *Legions of the Forest* resulted in the creation of arguably the greatest army in history. The gladius, scutum, pilum, and *pugio* were employed with devastating effectiveness. Some have described the Roman infantry as a walking wall of iron. I embellished the giant war bows used by Marcellus and Valerius. The Roman army was not known for its archers, the *sagittarii*, and, in fact, most of the bowmen employed by the legions were auxiliaries from various client states.

The Roman forts of Vetera and Moguntiacum on the Rhine and Alisio on the Lippe were actual fortresses in antiquity. I chose to call the rivers of the Rhine and Lippe by their modern names rather than the Latin versions of Rhenus and Lupia.

In Chapters Two and Three, I describe the basic training of the legionnaire. There is little in the way of historical sources that describes the indoctrination of the recruits. There may not have even been training bases. In the final chapter, I note that the gates of Rome are locked for the night. This was not the case. They were kept open to facilitate the flow of traffic throughout the city. I chose to have them locked to develop the culminating scene in the book.

In the fall of 2013, I visited the Teutoburg battlefield and museum in Kalkriese. The landscape has changed over two millennia. The ancient battleground is now rolling farmland, quite a bucolic setting and certainly not redolent of the savage conflict that occurred there so many years ago. On that crisp autumn day, I approached the actual trail the ill-fated Roman legionnaires had traveled upon, then stepped onto the marked path, the actual killing zone. A cold shock went down my spine, and the hair stood up on the back of my neck. It was eerie.

Finally, the Roman historian Lucius Anneus Florus recorded that two of the imperial eagles of the legions lost in the Teutoburg forest were recovered in subsequent Roman punitive engagements against the Germans. He noted that it was believed the third eagle was secreted in a marsh by the standard bearer during the battle. The whereabouts of the third eagle has remained a mystery. Perhaps it is buried in an ancient animal burrow as described in this book, waiting to be discovered.

Mark Richards (legions9ad@aol.com)

Coming Soon in 2016: Return of the Eagles

The year is 14 AD, five years after the disaster in the Teutoburg Forest. Augustus Caesar has died leaving his step son, Tiberius, as the new emperor. Rome has not forgotten the humiliation of the crushing defeat of the Varus legions by Arminius and his confederation of German tribes. Tiberius appoints Germanicus, the son of his late brother to command the invasion of Germania. With him on his staff are Tribune Valerius and Centurion Marcellus. The legions of Rome make war on the German tribes, seeking retribution for the disaster in the Teutoburg Forest and recovery of the precious eagle standards. Will the Roman legions succeed or will they fall into the same trap as Varus?

Made in the USA
Middletown, DE
18 January 2015